# The Whiskey Run Chronicles

## Volume 1

## (Episodes 1-7)

# B.R. Snow

Copyright © 2017 B.R. Snow

ISBN: 978-1-942691-24-2

Website: www.brsnow.net/

Twitter: @BernSnow

Facebook: facebook.com/bernsnow

Cover Design: Reggie Cullen

Cover Photo: James R. Miller

# Other Books by B.R. Snow

### *The Thousand Islands Doggy Inn Mysteries*

- The Case of the Abandoned Aussie
- The Case of the Brokenhearted Bulldog
- The Case of the Caged Cockers
- The Case of the Dapper Dandie Dinmont
- The Case of the Eccentric Elkhound
- The Case of the Faithful Frenchie
- The Case of the Graceful Goldens

### *The Whiskey Run Chronicles*

- Episode 1 – The Dry Season Approaches
- Episode 2 – Friends and Enemies
- Episode 3 – Let the Games Begin
- Episode 4 – Enter the Revenuer
- Episode 5 – A Changing Landscape
- Episode 6 – Entrepreneurial Spirits
- Episode 7 – All Hands On Deck

### *The Damaged Posse*

- American Midnight
- Larrikin Gene
- Sneaker World
- Summerman
- The Duplicates

### *Other Books*
- Divorce Hotel
- Either Ore
-

To everyone who doesn't mind the occasional cold one on a hot day.

# Episode 1

*The Dry Season Approaches*

"The government just shut down one of the country's biggest industries, lost a huge chunk of its tax revenue, passed a law that is impossible to enforce, and pissed off most of the people in the process. It's nice to know that we can always count on them to go really big and really stupid when the chips are down."

Milo Razner

# Three Shots to the Wind

**Milo nodded to the well-dressed man** in black he passed on his way to the bar. He wasn't a huge fan of fedoras as a rule, but they had their time and place. Just like the one on Milo's head here and now. And Milo had to give the man credit for the way he wore his. Like he was confident about how good he looked; proud of the hat, and not apologizing at all for looking like a bit of a dandy.

Hats were tricky to pull off as far as Milo was concerned. A lot of folks pulled them down way too far, then made it worse by keeping their heads down when they walked past you. Like they were hiding something or weren't quite as confident as they were trying to appear. When that happened, Milo always got the impression that the hat was wearing the person, not the other way around.

Yeah, hats were tricky.

But if you got the angle of the hat cocked *just right*, held your head high, and looked people in the eye when you passed them on the street, you'd always get a nod out of Milo.

Even if you did look like a bit of a dandy.

Milo tipped his hat to a group of three women standing in the hotel lobby near the entrance to the bar. Working girls, he decided when he caught their taunting smiles and eyes that lingered just a touch too long.

"Ladies, I hope you're all doing well this beautiful evening," Milo said, continuing past them toward the bar.

"We could all be doing a lot better," one of the women said.

The other two women laughed, and the one who'd spoken to Milo met his eyes when he stopped and turned around. She cocked her head and stared at him, oozing confidence. No hat needed on this pretty young thing, Milo decided.

"I guess everyone could always be doing better, right?" Milo said.

"Indeed. I like your hat," the woman said, studying his fedora. "I never wear them myself."

"Because it would be redundant, right?"

"I beg your pardon?"

"Nothing. Merely a passing thought on my part. I'm Milo."

"Daisy," she said, glancing over her shoulder at her two companions before locking eyes with him again. "That's Maxine. This is Betsy."

"It's very nice to meet you ladies," Milo said, bowing slightly. "I hope you all have a wonderful evening."

"If you're looking for some company, feel free to stop by Fannie's later," Daisy said. "I'm sure I could make your stay here much more pleasant. Or, if your tastes run in that direction, all three of us."

Milo smiled and continued to match her stare.

"That's very thoughtful of you. Unfortunately, I have some business to attend to at the moment. But I must say, if I were ever honored to be in your company, Miss Daisy, including anyone else would be a pointless gesture. An exercise in futility if you will. For I would hate to ruin my reputation as a gentleman since I would undoubtedly be completely ignoring everyone else who happened to be present at the time."

Her two colleagues tittered and Daisy flushed bright red, but before she had a chance to recover and respond, Milo tipped his hat again, then turned and entered the bar. He glanced around and decided to sit at the bar. The bartender, a tall man who barely looked old enough to drink, approached and nodded his head at the three women who were still hovering near the entrance.

"Not many men can say no to Daisy," the bartender said, wiping down the mahogany in front of Milo.

"I didn't say no," Milo said. "I just said not now."

"Well, Daisy is a right now kind of girl and not used to men having to think about it," he said, laughing. "But judging by the way she's hanging in the doorway, I think you got her attention. What can I get you?"

"I think I'll have a beer with a back."

"Whiskey?"

"Actually, I heard a rumor that if I ask you real nice, you'll bring me a taste of some local refreshment."

"Who told you that?" the bartender said, now on alert.

"Just a guy who likes to spread rumors."

"I hate guys like that."

"Me too. But sometimes the rumormongers can be useful."

"Useful as in finding out where to get the best local shine?"

"Yes, among other things," Milo said, smiling. "Don't worry, your secret is safe with me."

"The hotel doesn't know I bring it in. Or if they do know, they haven't said anything about it yet. It's only for special customers," the bartender said, wiping his hands with a fresh towel. "But when you're working for tips, you do what you can, right?"

"Yeah, I get that. By the way, I'm Milo Razner."

"Nice to meet you, Milo. My name's Tom. Tom Collins."

"Tom Collins. After the cocktail? That's a good name for a bartender I would imagine," Milo said, nodding.

"Actually, my name is Jerry Collins. But a buddy gave me the nickname when I was working in a joint that only sold moonshine. Most women can't stand the taste of it, so I started messing around with different juices and fruits you could use to make the shine go down easier. I got kind of a reputation for my concoctions."

"And the nickname stuck?"

"Yeah. And the name's a real conversation starter," Tom said.

"And good for tips, right?"

"You're a quick study, Milo."

"You have no idea, Tom Collins."

Tom reached below the bar and poured clear liquid into a shot glass.

"You want to join me?" Milo said. "I'm buying."

"Thanks, but I'm working," Tom said, shaking his head. "This stuff will set your brain on fire. Two of those and I wouldn't be able to make change."

"What is it?" Milo said, holding up the shot glass and staring at it up against the light.

"Billy calls it his Midnight Miracle," Tom said. "It's around a hundred and fifty proof but smoother than Daisy's skin right after she gets out of the bath."

"Should I ask how you know that?" Milo said, still staring into the shot glass.

"It's no secret how Daisy makes her living," Tom said, shrugging. "I learned about her soft skin a long time ago. But that was back in the days when I could still afford her."

"I see," Milo said, holding the shot glass to his nose. "I'm getting the scent of something sweet."

"Billy won't tell me what that is," Tom said. "But I think he uses a touch of maple syrup."

"Interesting," Milo said. "Well, here goes nothing."

Milo tossed the shot back and felt the warmth surge through him, then it subsided and left him at a loss for words.

"Good, huh?" Tom said, nodding.

"Remarkable. Who's Billy?"

"Billy Crankovitch. He's a local. We go way back. And when it comes to making shine, I think he's a genius."

"And he makes moonshine for a living?"

"Nah. It's only a way for him to make a few extra bucks on the side. I do my best to help him out by selling some of it here."

"What does he do for a living?" Milo said, gesturing for another shot.

"Well, he's a farmer. But as his wife keeps reminding him, he's just not a very good one."

"Ah, farmers. Salt of the earth. I'd like to meet this Mr. Crankovitch," Milo said, holding up the fresh shot to the light again. "It's crystal clear."

"I'm sure that can be arranged," Tom said. "He'll start cooking this year's batch as soon as he gets his corn harvested. But if he's got any left from last year, you can buy a quart for three bucks."

"Twelve dollars a gallon?"

"What?"

"Nothing. Just doing some math in my head."

Milo and Tom both looked toward the lobby when they heard the noise of a crowd that was punctuated with shouts and protests and getting louder by the second.

"Somebody's not happy," Milo said, glancing around at the crowd.

"Beulah must be here," Tom said. "She's speaking tonight in the ballroom."

Milo looked at Tom and waited for more.

"Beulah Peppin. She's the head of the local temperance movement."

"Ah, yes," Milo said. "The Women's Christian Temperance Union. The WCTU seems to be everywhere these days. Which one is Mrs. Peppin?"

"Miss Peppin," Tom said. "And she's the one in the white dress."

Milo studied the young woman who continued to casually give instructions to several people who were surrounding her even as the shouts of protests continued to swell.

"I take it she has her detractors," Milo said.

"Yeah, and I'm one of them. What is it with some people? They're always on a mission to ruin everybody else's fun. The way the winters are around here, if you take away people's right to drink, they'll be nothing to do six months out of the year."

"Yes, I'm afraid the Dries have gotten a lot of traction," Milo said, downing the second shot and again having the same reaction. "This is truly a remarkable concoction."

"Lucky for us, the President vetoed that stupid law, huh?" Tom said.

"Congress is getting ready to override his veto," Milo said, taking a sip of beer.

"But they won't be able to pass it, right?"

"Oh, I'm certain the veto is going to be overridden."

"How do you know that?"

"I've been told that by some people I know in Washington," Milo said.

"You have friends in Washington?"

"Oh, my, no," Milo said, laughing. "I would never call the people I know in Washington friends. They're just lawyers who managed to convince enough voters they're worthy of making decisions on their behalf."

"I take it you're not much of a fan of politicians," Tom said.

"I dislike politicians," Milo said. "But I detest lawyers. Combine the two, and you usually get a very nasty product."

"Like bad moonshine," Tom said.

"Yes. If it doesn't kill you, the odds are it will leave you blind," Milo said, gesturing for a third shot.

"You want another?"

"One more."

"Be careful. This stuff sneaks up on you in a hurry."

"Let's call the third one additional field study. Sort of a personal research project."

"It's your funeral," Tom said, pouring the shot. "By the way, what are you doing in town?"

"Actually, I have just relocated to your wonderful town. This is my first day here."

"Really? What do you do for work?"

"I'm currently in transition, and I'm looking for a change. Something in my head is telling me that it's time to do something different."

"Like what?"

"I thought I might give dairy farming a shot," Milo said, tossing back his third shot. "Whew. I see what you mean about it sneaking up on you."

"Uh, no offense, Milo," Tom said. "You could have given me a hundred guesses, and I wouldn't have come up with dairy farmer. You know much about cows?"

"Other than they have four legs and produce milk, not a single thing."

"Okay. I guess you gotta start somewhere, right? Look, Milo, dairy farming is no picnic. And there aren't any days off. You do know that cows have to be milked twice a day every day, don't you?"

"I did not know that," Milo said, shaking his head. "I'm glad I stopped by, Tom Collins. Not only have you provided me with some of the best alcohol I've ever tasted, but you've also taught me something."

"Why on earth would you want to be a dairy farmer?"

"Well, there's just something calling me to it. When booze is outlawed, I have a gut feeling that my milk is going to be in very high demand. And I always try to go with my gut instincts."

Milo shook his head to clear it and glanced back at Beulah Peppin who was still chatting with several people milling around her.

"She is a very striking woman," Milo said.

"She is. Too bad she never seems to put her looks on better display. It's like she does everything she can to hide them," Tom said. "But I do like her hat."

"Yes, I agree. And she wears it well."

# The Dries Are on the Move

**Beulah Peppin had only been speaking** for ten minutes when Milo became convinced that the leading proponent of Prohibition within a hundred-mile radius was a force to be reckoned with and someone he definitely wanted to keep a very close eye on. Perhaps it was the third shot of Midnight Miracle, but Milo also found himself having less than gentlemanly thoughts about what was hidden underneath the several layers of wool she was wearing.

He didn't worry about paying too much attention to what she was saying. Milo had heard similar speeches and several of the same exact phrases all too often as he traveled the country the past few years. But her passion and delivery kept him on the edge of his seat as she worked herself into a frenzy honing her message about the evils of the dreaded barleycorn until it was razor-sharp and captivated half the audience.

At first, the other half of the audience, mostly all men who worked for a living and relied upon a dose of Mr. Barleycorn just to get through the night and out of bed the next morning, listened patiently to what Beulah Peppin had to say. But like Milo, they were studying her, not necessarily hearing the words coming out of her mouth. Instead, they were watching her mouth, watching the way her pouty lips moved and the way her tongue would appear for a moment then disappear behind her pearly whites.

But now, that half of the audience was interrupting her speech and being downright rude. Milo shook his head at their behavior. Just because you disagreed with another person didn't give you license to stop being a gentleman. But Beulah Peppin, a veteran of events like this one, plowed ahead undeterred, finished her speech, then asked for questions.

From his front row seat, Milo turned and noticed several hands in the air. To her credit, Beulah took a question from a man whose face and hands were caked with grease. She put her hands on her hips and listened to the man who sounded like he was making a speech of his own before a question finally appeared.

"I understand, sir," Beulah said, nodding. "And perhaps I might even agree that alcohol seems to offer a bit of respite from some of life's challenges. But the destruction that your *hooch*, as you so eloquently refer to it, brings to individuals and their families, for me, far outweigh that minor benefit."

"A lot of us need a little help to get through the day," the man who'd asked the question said. "And that includes my wife."

"Yes, I think I understand why your wife might feel the need for some assistance," Beulah said with a straight face.

The crowd on both sides of the debate roared with laughter. Beulah Peppin continued her stare down with the man until he sat down red-faced. She was about to move to the next question when the man recovered.

"I guess it's easy for you to come here and tell us how to live our life. Then you get to go home to your fancy house and things," the man said. "We don't all live a life of privilege like you, Miss Peppin."

A round of applause was punctuated with several shouts from both sides of the debate.

"With all due respect, Mr. Calhoun, you have no idea about the life I live," Beulah said, not backing down an inch. "But I will say it most certainly isn't privileged."

Milo slowly raised his hand. Eventually, Beulah's eyes landed on him. Milo thought he saw her flinch a bit when their eyes met, but it could have just been the Midnight Miracle.

"Yes, sir," Beulah said. "What's your question?"

"Thank you, Miss Peppin," Milo said, rising and turning to face the audience. "You'll have to excuse me if I sound ignorant about some of the issues and problems you're having with the question of Prohibition. You see, I've just moved to your lovely town today and am woefully short on local history. For that, I apologize. But I have heard many of the same conversations and witnessed firsthand the destruction this *debate* is having in communities like this one around the country. And while I'll be the first to admit that I have been known to sip a cold beer on a hot day and enjoy a dram of whiskey when it's cold, I do understand the argument Dries, like Miss Peppin, are making. When consumed in large quantities, alcohol can certainly be a destructive force."

Milo waited for the murmurs and whispers to stop before continuing.

"But cannot the same be said for food? Or leisure time? Even sexual congress between consenting adults? Or, at the risk of sound sacrilegious, even religion? Can't too much of anything, in the end, become destructive?"

"An old argument, sir," Beulah said. "And it has its merits, but we're talking about the evils of alcohol at the moment."

"I understand, Miss Peppin. But surely you can agree that a town torn apart by any issue is not a community."

"People disagree, sir. In fact, it's an essential part of the social fabric."

"You will get no argument from me on that, Miss Peppin," Milo said.

"Is there a question coming, or should I move on?" she said, hands on hips.

"I apologize for meandering, Miss Peppin," Milo said, turning back to the crowd. "My question is to all of you. When Prohibition is finally passed, what is each and every one of you willing to do to make sure that the social fabric of this community doesn't unravel like a two-dollar suit?"

"What do you mean when Prohibition is finally passed?" the man sitting next to Milo said. "The President just vetoed the law."

Milo glanced at the man, and then at Beulah, who was staring intensely at Milo, before addressing the crowd.

"The President's veto will be overridden when Congress votes on it. And when the veto is overruled, it is my belief that Prohibition will become the law of the land early next year," Milo said.

A long round of whispered murmurs filled the room. Milo patiently waited it out.

"How do you know this, sir?" Beulah said.

"Let's call it an educated guess," Milo said. "But congratulations appear to be in order. It looks like you and your Dry brethren have won, Miss Peppin. Well done. For the sake of the country, I hope you and your colleagues know what you're doing."

The room fell silent as people considered what Milo had told them and the questions dried up. People began to leave, and Milo heard some of the Dry supporters laughing as they slapped each other on the back on their way out. But most people shuffled out quietly seemingly alone with their thoughts. Eventually, Milo was left alone in the large room with Beulah and the man who'd been sitting next to him. She began packing up her papers and stuffing them into a leather satchel.

"You seem to be an educated man, sir," Beulah said, pausing to look up at Milo and nodding hello to the other man.

"At least as far as my guesses are concerned, right?" Milo said, smiling.

"Yes, of course," she said, giving him a quick flash of a smile.

"My name is Milo. Milo Razner," he said, bowing slightly.

"It's nice to meet you, Mr. Razner. You're certain that the President's veto will be overturned?"

"I am."

"I take it that decision won't please you," she said, draping the satchel over her shoulder.

"I'll be fine with it, Miss Peppin," Milo said. "I try not to let the decisions of politicians affect me too much one way or the other. Over the years, I've learned that when one thing is taken away, usually something else quickly fills the space that's left behind."

"So, you're a philosopher," she said, brushing the hair back from her face.

"No," Milo said, laughing. "Like you, Miss Peppin, I'm just someone with a lot of opinions. Where we differ is that I tend to keep mine to myself. But I do have to say that I would love the opportunity to sit down with you at some point and share some of them."

"Over a dram of whiskey, I assume," she said, staring blankly at him.

"Weather permitting."

"Of course," she said, nodding. "It was nice meeting you, Mr. Razner. But if you'll excuse me I have another meeting to get to."

Milo extended his hand, and she returned the handshake.

"It was a pleasure to meet you, Miss Peppin. I hope our paths cross again soon."

"I'd be surprised if they didn't, Mr. Razner. Good evening, sir."

Milo watched her until she disappeared from sight, then shook his head and grinned.

"Now there's a woman," Milo said to the empty room.

"I liked the way you handled her."

Milo turned around and studied the man who'd been sitting next to him during Beulah's speech. Milo did a quick assessment but didn't get past well-dressed and probably a successful businessman, or doing everything he could to convince others he was.

"I'm not sure I really handled her," Milo said.

"You did better than most of us have the past several months," the man said. "I tell you, she's a real beauty but the sort of woman who could drive a man to drink. That's pretty funny when you think about it."

"You mean ironic, don't you?" Milo said.

"Yeah, ironic. That's the word I was looking for," the man said, extending his hand. "I'm Melvin English."

"Milo Razner. A pleasure to meet you, Mr. English."

"Call me Melvin. Or Mel is fine if you like nicknames. I'm named after my grandfather. He was quite the character. Rabble-rouser is the term most people used to describe him. He was a lawyer who made most of his money as a land swindler. A bit of a drinker, but folks around here liked him. Well, maybe tolerated is the better way to put it. Yeah, people tolerated Grandpa Melvin. But most people call me Melvin."

"Okay, Melvin," Milo said, still studying the man who talked way too much and way too fast. "What sort of work do you do?"

"I'm a lawyer, but I spend most of my time selling real estate," Melvin said, shuffling back and forth. "Now I know what you're thinking."

"I doubt that, Melvin."

Melvin laughed.

"Following in my granddaddy's footsteps and all that, right? But I do a lot of good around here, and you can check that out. Ask around, and folks will tell you that they-"

"Tolerate you?"

Melvin laughed again. To Milo, the laugh sounded thin and tinny like a cheap honky-tonk piano.

"I guess it's my lucky day," Milo said, placing a hand on the man's shoulder.

"How's that?"

"I'm actually in need of a good real estate person."

"Are you looking for a house?"

"Not at the moment. I'll be staying here at the hotel until I can figure out my needs in that area. But I am in the market for a farm. A dairy farm in particular."

"A dairy farm? You?"

"Yeah, I guess I don't look the part, huh?"

"Actually, no," Melvin said, scrunching his face into an odd scowl.

"It's a new passion I've discovered," Milo said. "And I'm learning a lot already. Did you know that cows have to be milked twice a day?"

"Yeah, I've heard that," Melvin said, his scowl deepening.

"Do you happen to have anything like that available at the moment?" Milo said.

"As a matter of fact, I do," Melvin said. "It just came on the market. The widow Wilson has decided to sell the place and move on. Her husband, the previous owner, had a tragic accident just the other day."

"You don't say?" Milo said, sitting back down in his chair. "I'm sorry to hear that. What happened to the poor fellow?"

"He fell off the roof of his barn onto a pile of rocks. Simply dreadful," Melvin said, shaking his head at the prospect, then quickly recovering. "But the farm is up and running. It comes complete with a house, the barn, all the equipment, and fifty cows. And the acreage, of course. A hundred acres, including a beautiful stretch of River shoreline you can get a boat in and out of easily."

"It sounds very nice," Milo said, nodding casually. "I'd like to see it as soon as possible."

"Of course. I'll get something set up for tomorrow if your schedule permits."

"It does," Milo said. "You wouldn't happen to also handle some of the island properties in the area, would you?"

"Yes, I do," Melvin said. "Would you be looking for an island near town? During the summer, most of the people who own islands like to be near town so they can pop over anytime they like in their boat."

"Actually, I'd probably be going the other way," Milo said. "You know, someplace more remote. I've spent so much time in cities, I find myself craving solitude these days."

"Sure, I get that. I've got a couple of islands downriver you might be interested in. There's nothing on them, but they have some good acreage, and you'd be able to build whatever you want."

"That sounds perfect, Melvin. Just give me a call in the morning here at the hotel."

"I'll do that, Milo," Melvin said. "This has certainly turned out to be a most productive evening. Who knew that coming to a Prohibition meeting would turn out so well?"

"Indeed," Milo said, talking to Melvin English but thinking about Beulah Peppin.

# The Gentleman Farmer

**Milo stood on the town dock** and looked out at the mighty St. Lawrence that stretched for miles in all directions. The area certainly lived up to the hype, and Milo was further convinced that this was the place to be. But he reminded himself the sun was still warm, and the breezes brought comfort this time of year. Keep telling yourself this is the place to be in January Milo said to himself then nodded in agreement. He watched several boats go past and smiled at a group of kids swimming and splashing each other in the shallow water off one side of the dock.

When he saw Melvin English piloting his boat slowly toward the end of the dock, Milo headed that way to greet him. The lacquered wooden vessel, about twenty-foot long, seemed to purr when Melvin idled the engine. Milo greeted him as he tentatively climbed aboard and sat down. Melvin reversed the boat away from the dock, pointed the boat downriver, and gunned the engine.

"What's the deal with that castle?" Milo said, staring at the massive structure that dominated a small island near town.

"Some hotel guy named Boldt was building it for his wife," Melvin said. "But she died, and he stopped working on it."

"He built it for his wife?"

"That's how the story goes," Melvin said, not even bothering to look at the structure. "Romantic, huh?"

"I guess. But maybe flowers and whiskey just didn't do the job."

Milo continued to look back at the castle until it hurt his neck, then focused on the constantly changing view in front of them.

"I thought we'd take a look at the farm first," Melvin said above the roar of the engine. "It's just as easy to get there by boat and only a couple of miles from town. After that, we'll keep heading downriver. There's an island about twenty minutes away I think you might like."

"Okay," Milo said, glancing around at the impressive collection of islands that came in all shapes and sizes. "Is that Canada over there?"

Melvin glanced at the island Milo was pointing at and shook his head.

"No, the Canadian mainland is behind a couple more islands in that direction, but it's not far," Melvin said. "Rockport is the closest Canadian town to Alexandria Bay. It's about three miles by boat."

"Three miles?" Milo said. "That's all?"

"That's all," Melvin said, shrugging. "What can I say? We're right on the border."

Milo smiled and leaned back in his seat as the boat cut through the water and sprayed mist against his face. In the hot sun, the mist felt refreshing, and Milo decided to move getting a boat up on his list of things to do.

"How fast does this thing go?" Milo said.

"Oh, it'll get you where you're going," Melvin said, opening the throttle a bit more. "But this boat was built more for comfort. Do you like to go fast, Milo?"

"I've never really given it much thought. This is the first time I've ever been on a boat."

Melvin glanced over at Milo and studied him.

"You don't know anything about cows, but you're thinking about buying a dairy farm. And you've just moved here, a place surrounded on three sides by water, but have never been on a boat. No offense, Milo, but one could say you're an odd man."

"I suppose they could," Milo said, nodding as he continued to stare out at the changing landscape. "But I probably wouldn't recommend it."

"I'll take that under advisement. But if you're in the market for a boat, you need to go see Frank Slack. Be sure to tell him I sent you."

"Frank Slack," Milo said, committing then name to memory. "He sells boats?"

"Sells them, services them, he even builds them. As a matter of fact, he built this one."

"It looks very nice. But I'm obviously not much of an expert," Milo said, glancing around at the polished wood and plush leather seats. "He's a local?"

"Oh, yes. You can't miss Frank's place," Melvin said, slowing the boat and heading toward shore. "We're here."

"That was quick," Milo said, studying the gentle slope of the land near the water's edge.

"It's a bit further by car, but not bad," Melvin said, glancing over the side of the idling boat. "If I remember, there's a small shoal around here. Oh, there it is." Melvin steered around the pile of rock just below the surface.

"Shoal?" Milo said, staring down into the shallow water.

"Submerged rocks," Melvin said, bringing the boat to a stop in a small cove that was tucked away out of the wind. "They're something you definitely want to avoid. They don't move. No matter how fast you're going." Melvin found that comment funny, and he laughed as he hopped out of the boat onto a large rock. "There's no dock or boathouse, and they're probably something you'll want to consider adding. But I think the boat will be fine here for now. There's not much wind and the water's calm."

"If you say so," Milo said, climbing onto the rock to stand next to Melvin.

Melvin tied the bowline to a tree and nodded for Milo to follow him. They made their way to shore and up a grassy incline until they reached the fence line of the dairy farm.

"Let's walk around the outside of the fence," Melvin said. "I think they have a bull. Another thing you'll definitely want to avoid."

"Bulls are one thing I do understand," Milo said.

Milo took the property in as he followed Melvin toward the main house. As they walked, Melvin continued to prattle on about acreage, the current price of improved farmland, and milk yields. When they reached the house, they were greeted by the grieving widow who looked fifty but couldn't have been more than twenty-five. She gave them a tour of the house, then showed them the barn that sat on the edge of the acreage that extended off the back of the property.

"If you decide to buy the place, you're going to have to make a few decisions in a hurry," the widow said. "I've kept the two summer farm hands on to handle the milking, but the rest of the corn and hay needs to get cut and into the barn soon."

"How much of each crop are you planting, Mrs. Wilson?" Milo said as he stared out at the tall rows of corn gently swaying the breeze.

"We did eighty acres of hay this year and around ten of corn," the widow Wilson said. "We would have liked to do a bit more corn, but the cows eat the hay faster than we can grow it, so that was the priority."

"And you mix some of the corn in with the hay when you feed them?" Milo said.

The widow gave Milo an odd look, then glanced at Melvin who shrugged back at her.

"Well, you don't really mix the corn in with the hay," she said. "But, yeah, Shorty liked to give them some of the ground corn from time to time. He said it produced a sweeter milk. But Shorty rarely knew what the hell he was talking about so take that with a grain of salt."

"What are your plans after the farm is sold, Mrs. Wilson?" Milo said.

"I'm heading back home."

"Where's home?" Milo said.

"Philadelphia."

"Nice town. I actually lived there for a while," Milo said. "It's one of my favorites, in fact."

"If you love a city like Philadelphia, what on earth are you doing here?" she said. "This place may not be the end of the earth, but I'm pretty sure you can see it from here."

"I take it this isn't your favorite spot," Milo said.

"I agreed to come here because my husband sold me on the beauty of the River and the islands," she said, her voice rising and her gestures becoming animated. "The playground of the rich. Spend your days exploring the River and your nights enjoying a fine meal as you watch a glorious sunset."

"That does sound nice," Milo said.

"Sure, in the tourist brochure," she said, her eyes turning dark. "I've been here five years, and I've been on the River exactly one time. And that was on a tour boat. The only thing that tour showed me was all the things other people had that I didn't. And the only fine meals I enjoyed were the ones I cooked. But we did usually eat watching a *glorious* sunset. That was because I worked the farm every day from sunup until it, mercifully, went down."

"Yes, well," Melvin said, seeing his sale about to vanish into thin air. "As I was saying to Mr. Reznak, dairy farming can be a challenge and isn't for everyone. But you were able to make a living, right, Mrs. Wilson?"

"You can scrape by," she said, nodding. "If you're willing to work yourself down to the bone."

"Yes, I can see that," Milo said, giving the widow a small smile. "And I think I've seen enough. Thank you for your time. And I'm so sorry for your loss, Mrs. Wilson. I'm sure your husband was a fine man."

"He did his best," she whispered into the ground. Then she looked back up at Milo. "So, are you going to buy the place or not?"

"I'll need to think on it," Milo said. "But I promise you'll have my answer no later than tomorrow."

"Okay, I guess that's fair," she said. "What did you do for work in Philadelphia?"

"I beg your pardon?" Milo said.

"I'm just asking because I'm going to be looking for work when I get there. Perhaps you have some advice, or maybe could give me the names of some people I could talk to?"

"I see. Yes, of course," Milo said. "I spent most of my time there in the financial industry."

"Banking?"

"Yes, to a degree," Milo said. "Numbers and ledgers. Very boring as you can imagine."

"After all this," the widow said, spreading her arms wide. "Banking sounds pretty exciting."

"Let me see if can come up with some names," Milo said, focusing on one of the cows slowly lumbering across the paddock toward them. "Interesting looking animals, aren't they?"

"There's nothing interesting about them," the widow said.

Melvin immediately began to clear his throat.

"We should probably get going, Milo," he said.

Milo ignored the tug on his arm and kept staring at the cow.

"They really need to be milked twice a day?"

"Twice a day, every day," the widow said, shaking her head. "Shorty always said he was going to become a millionaire by inventing a cow that took weekends off."

"That's funny," Milo said.

"It would have been if Shorty had been joking."

"I see," Milo said, giving her another small smile. "Again, I'm sorry for your loss. Either Mr. English or I will be in touch with you sometime tomorrow."

"I hope I didn't scare you off," she said.

"Not at all," Milo said. "I appreciate your honesty. And I must say, I find the prospect of owning this property fascinating."

"Are you sure you've never been on a farm before?" she said, frowning at Milo.

"I'm quite sure. Why do you ask?"

"Because if you find this place fascinating, I'd swear you'd been kicked in the head by a cow."

# An Island Beckons

**Melvin untied the boat** and slowly reversed his way out of the small cove. He worked his way around the shoal into deeper water then opened the throttle. The cool breeze and soft mist returned, and Milo closed his eyes to enhance the experience.

"She's an interesting woman," Melvin said.

"I think she's escaping just in time," Milo said, his eyes still closed. "Another five years there and she'd be a shell."

"If you're not in a hurry, I'm sure I can come up with some of other farms that are more profitable," Melvin said, wiping the spray off his face. "I really need to put a windshield on this."

"I like it," Milo said. "That spray makes me feel alive."

"So, would you like me to find some more properties to look at?"

"No, that place is perfect," Milo said, opening his eyes to stare at the shoreline as they sped past.

"Really?"

"It's just undercapitalized and understaffed," Milo said, then caught the odd look Melvin was giving him. "I may not know anything about dairy farming, but I do understand business. I'd just need to expand, upgrade some of the equipment, and hire experienced people to run it."

"Yes, of course," Melvin said, refocusing on the water in front of him with a frown on his face. "So, I guess that means that you wouldn't actually be working the farm yourself, right?"

"What do you think, Melvin?"

Melvin chuckled nervously and nodded.

"Yes, that's what I thought," he said. "Not working the farm is probably going to hurt your profitability. But, then again, you probably already know that. I mean, what with you understanding business the way you do."

"Melvin, there are only a few things I can handle doing twice a day," Milo said, above the roar of the engine. "And none of them involve cows."

"Yes, yes. Of course, I understand completely. The widow and I agreed that the price should be six thousand dollars."

Milo glanced over and listened closely as Melvin began to prattle.

"Now, I know what you're going to say. You think that's a lot of money since the going rate for improved farm land is fifty dollars an acre. But if you consider the house, and the new barn, I think you'll agree that getting a working hundred acre dairy farm for six thousand dollars is actually a bargain. And if you make some of the improvements you're talking about, the value of the farm can only go up, right?"

Melvin waited for a response, but after getting nothing out of Milo, he continued to talk.

"Now, you need to understand that the six thousand is only the asking price. Given her rather desperate circumstances, and her desire to get out of town as soon as possible, I'm sure we can negotiate that down. Let's say, five thousand, or maybe even forty-five hundred? Perhaps, even less. She's desperate to leave town, and I'm sure I can talk her into just about anything."

"Are you suggesting I take advantage of a grieving widow just for my own personal gain, Melvin?"

"No, of course not, Milo. I would never suggest…I'm only trying to get you the best possible deal on the property. If you're interested in it."

"I must say I'm a bit disappointed in you, Melvin. And if we didn't already have a handshake agreement to work together, I might be forced to use someone else to broker the deal. But since I always try to be a man of my word, we'll continue as is. I just hope you won't use the same strategy on the *grieving widow* who owns the island we're about to look at."

"No, there's no chance of that happening. There's no grieving widow involved with this one. I certainly won't be trying to low ball the owner of this island," Melvin said, chuckling nervously. "And that's because I own it."

"I see," Milo said, smiling off into the distance. "So, you're a land speculator as well. You do have your fingers in a lot of pies, don't you?"

"Well, times are tough, right? And I like to stay busy."

"Idle hands and all that."

"Exactly," Melvin said, slowing the boat as they approached the island. "Well, here we are. I renamed it when I bought it, but you can call it anything you like."

"What's the name?"

"I call it English Land Island," Melvin said with a touch of pride. "I thought using the family name was a nice touch."

Milo nodded and continued to study the remote island as Melvin slowly piloted the boat around the perimeter. It was thickly populated with pine and cedar trees, and whatever the terrain looked like above the rocky outcrop that surrounded the island was well hidden from view.

"It's about a quarter mile long and a couple hundred yards wide in most spots. It has around five flat acres of decent soil where you can plant crops or a garden if you like. And there's plenty of room to build whatever sort of house you'd like. The side we're on now is pretty much out of the wind most of the time, and if you're looking at building a boathouse, which I'd recommend, this would be the place to put it. Let me get the boat in over there, and we'll go take a look."

Melvin tied the boat to a tree, and they made their way up a makeshift path that led to the upper portion of the island.

"At one time, I had big plans for this place," Melvin said. "But it's so far from town, and I realized that I'd be spending most of my time going back and forth. Now I chalk the whole thing up as a young man's fantasy. I put this path in, and that was about as far as I got."

"So, I take it you're desperate to sell?" Milo said with a devilish grin.

"Oh, my. Absolutely not," Melvin stammered, then realized Milo was joking. "Oh, that was a good one, Milo. Actually, I'll be expecting to get fair market value for it."

The path ended, and Milo stared out at the flat grassland that opened up onto a majestic view of the River.

"You say the dirt is good?" Milo said.

"It's a bit rocky in spots, but nothing that can't be cleared. You could grow pretty much anything you wanted. But look at that view, Milo. You said you were looking for privacy. Well, this is about as good as it gets. On a busy day, you'd be lucky if you saw a dozen boats go by."

"I like it," Milo said, nodding. "How much?"

"Four thousand."

Milo smiled at him.

"Really, Melvin?"

"What?"

"You bought this island six years ago for a thousand dollars," Milo said. "From a grieving widow if I'm not mistaken."

"Where did you hear that?" Melvin said, stunned.

"It was just a rumor," Milo said, shrugging. "And do I need to remind you that we're just coming out of a world war?"

"What does that have to do with anything?"

"Prices are down all over," Milo said.

"At the moment, perhaps. But in a year or two, things will pick up, and the economy should be booming."

"Perhaps. But I seriously doubt it. In fact, I see the economy heading into a deep dive in the not too distant future."

"Now you're a fortune teller turned dairy farmer?"

"That's funny, Melvin," Milo said, smiling as he stared out at the expanse of water surrounding him. "Let's just say I feel it in my gut. And do I need to remind you that I'm not buying in a year or two? I'm buying today. And the price I'm paying is two thousand."

"Two? Well, I don't know if I can do that."

"It's a good price, Melvin. You'll have doubled your initial investment, and combined with your commission from the Wilson property, you'll make somewhere close to twenty-three hundred dollars today. That's four times what the average worker makes in a year. Nice work if you can get it, right?"

"Are you saying you're going to buy the dairy farm?"

"If you agree to sell me this island for two thousand dollars, that's exactly what I'm saying. If you won't, then I'm afraid I'll probably be forced to go straight to the widow Wilson and deal directly with her."

"I thought you said you were a man of your word," Melvin said, his eyes narrowing as he squinted into the sunlight.

"I said I always try to be. And my word is that, in a few short hours, you'll be holding eight thousand dollars in cash in your grubby little hands, and I'll be holding the deeds to the farm and this island. Or you'll be left holding the bag. An empty bag, Melvin."

"I guess I know where I stand then, don't I?" Melvin said, glancing around the island before shaking his head. "Okay, I've never really liked this place anyway. You're welcome to it."

"Then we have a deal," Milo said, extending his hand. "Let's head back to your office and get it done."

"But the bank will be closed by the time we get back," Melvin said.

"There's no need to worry about the bank, Melvin."

"You always carry around that much cash, Milo?"

"Sure, why not? It's not that heavy."

# Milo's Money Goes Missing

**Milo left Melvin English's office** as soon as he'd signed his name on both contracts and handed over the stack of cash. He watched Melvin lovingly place the money inside the safe behind his desk, and then politely refused his offer of a celebratory drink. Milo used the excuse of another meeting as the reason for saying no. Truth be told, Milo couldn't wait to get away from the prattling lawyer who'd started talking louder and longer ever since Milo had agreed to both deals. Milo made the short walk back to the Crossley and headed straight to the bar to celebrate.

"Milo, right?"

"You don't forget a name do you, Tom Collins?"

"In my business, it pays not to," Tom said, wiping down the bar. "Let me guess, a beer with a back of Midnight Miracle."

"Perfect," Milo said, drumming his fingers on the bar.

He watched Tom Collins pour his drinks, then tossed the shot back. Milo closed his eyes and felt the warmth surge through him.

"Remarkable," Milo said, pointing at the shot glass for another. "I bought a dairy farm today."

"Really? You don't waste any time."

"No, I don't. And I also bought an island with absolutely nothing on it."

"A blank canvas, huh?"

"Yes, indeed. I like that image, Tom Collins. A blank canvas on which to create my masterpiece."

"You planning on building a summer home on it?"

"I'm not sure exactly what it will turn out to be," Milo said. "But I do need to get a structure built before winter arrives. And I need to get a boat. And find someone to take care of my farm." Milo shook his head and took a sip of beer. "There's so much to do."

"It certainly sounds like it," Tom Collins said, then looked past the sitting Milo at the woman who was approaching. "Good evening, Daisy."

"Hi, Tom," Daisy said, coming to a stop next to Milo and staring at him. "I remember you. Milo, right?"

"Correct. It's nice to see you again, Daisy."

Daisy focused her charm on Tom who was already leaning forward with his elbows on the bar. Milo smiled to himself and tossed back his second shot of Midnight Miracle.

"Tom, I hate to do this to you again," Daisy said. "But I need a favor."

"Daisy, please, not that," Tom said. "The last time you called your mama from the bar you tied up the phone for almost half an hour."

"Please, Tom," she said, placing her gloved hand over his. "She's been sick. And if I don't call at least once a week, she worries."

"Why can't you call from Frannie's?" Tom said.

"There's no privacy there," Daisy said. "Besides, Frannie doesn't allow personal calls during business hours. Please, Tom."

"I can't help you, Daisy," Tom said. "I'm sorry, but I got in a lot of trouble the last time I let you use it."

"Oh, Tom," she said, tearing up.

Milo watched her performance and was impressed.

"Perhaps I might be able to help," Milo said, then waited until he had Daisy's attention. "Why don't you just use the phone in my room?"

"You want me to go to your room?" Daisy said, now flirting with him.

"Why not?" Milo said.

"To use the phone?"

"Of course. You'll have all the privacy you'll need," Milo said. "Tom, if you'll watch my drink, I'll be back shortly."

"But not too soon, right?" Daisy said, laughing. "Okay, Mr. Razner. Why don't you take me to the *phone* in your room?"

Milo stood and walked next to her as they headed across the lobby, then up the stairs to the second floor.

"People will talk," Daisy said, slipping her arm under Milo's.

"I'd be disappointed if they didn't," Milo said, making no effort to remove her arm.

Outside his room, Milo grabbed the key from his pocket and opened the door. He held it open and remained in the doorway.

"The phone is next to the bed," Milo said. "Take all the time you need. And I hope you mother is feeling better."

Daisy stood in the doorway and glanced around at the large suite in front of her.

"I thought you said you had a room," Daisy said. "It looks like there's several of them in there."

"Only three," Milo said. "I don't like being confined in one place."

"I can probably help you with that," Daisy said, squeezing his hand. "Let's go see how many confined places we can come up with."

She strolled inside and tossed her bag on a chair near the door. Then she looked back at Milo.

"Aren't you coming in?" Daisy said, confused.

"Perhaps, later," Milo said, bowing slightly. "After you make your call, please rejoin me downstairs. I'd love the chance to get to know you a bit better."

"You sure are a strange one," Daisy said, cocking her head. "Oh, now I get it. You think letting me use your phone is going to entitle you to a freebie."

Milo smiled at her then pointed at the phone.

"Your phone call. Please make yourself comfortable and take all the time you need. I'm sure your mother is dying to catch up and hear about all the wonderful things you've been doing."

"I doubt if my mama would like to hear anything about what I've been doing," Daisy said, removing her gloves.

"Yes, I imagine you're right. I'll see you downstairs later."

Daisy stepped back as Milo gave her a small wave and the door clicked shut.

"Thank you, Daisy," Milo whispered to the closed door.

Milo glanced up and down the hallway and found it empty. He walked briskly to the back stairwell and made his way down to the first floor, then out one of the back doors. Milo strolled across the street, not making eye contact with the few people he saw but careful not to appear like he was avoiding them.

Just a guy out for an evening walk after dinner, he decided.

Milo entered the small park that ran behind several shops and offices. He remained in the shadows until he reached Melvin English's back door. He quickly picked the lock, paused just for a moment to reflect on how easy it had been, then stepped inside and closed the door behind him. Milo headed straight for Melvin's office, slipped on a pair of thin leather gloves, and sat down in Melvin's chair facing the safe.

"Not very smart for a lawyer, Melvin," Milo said, spinning the dial on the outside of the safe.

Earlier, when Melvin had started prattling on about his big plans and how the twenty-three hundred he'd made today was going to help accelerate them, he'd entered the combination of the safe without paying much attention to Milo and where he was sitting. Milo hadn't gotten a clear look at the numbers but was sure he knew the combination as soon as Melvin stopped on the second number.

Milo spun the dial to the right a couple of times and stopped on four. Then he spun it left and stopped on one. April Fool's Day. Sounds about right, Milo decided with a smile. Then he spun the dial back to the right and stopped on eighty-nine. Milo thought that Melvin looked a lot older than thirty, and was pretty sure he'd age even more tomorrow morning. Milo turned the handle, and the door silently opened. Milo grabbed his eight thousand and what looked like another four from the safe, slid the bundles into his coat pocket, then closed the door and left the office.

He removed his gloves and checked his watch as he approached the back door of the hotel. Twelve minutes, he noted. Milo stepped inside and kept an eye out for others as he made his way back to the lobby and then into the bar.

"That was quick," Tom Collins said, laughing. "You're going to get a bad reputation."

"She's just using the phone," Milo said. "And if I were ever to succumb to Miss Daisy's charms, you probably wouldn't see me for days."

"There you are," a voice from behind Milo said. "I've been looking for you."

"Oh. Hi, Melvin," Milo said, turning around. "I was just upstairs in my room."

"We're going to have that celebratory drink," Melvin said.

"It sounds like you've already started celebrating," Milo said, nodding at Tom for a round of drinks.

"Right after you left the office. I haven't stopped since. What are we drinking?"

"Beer and a magical elixir called Midnight Miracle," Milo said.

"I'm very familiar with it," Melvin said, sliding into one of the barstools. "But don't let me have more than six of those, Tom."

Melvin roared with laughter and slammed a hand down on the bar.

"I take it you bought your properties from Melvin," Tom Collins said.

"I did indeed," Milo said.

"Wow. Talk about your horse kick," Melvin said after he recovered from his first shot of Midnight Miracle. "Yes, he most certainly did. And I gave him a great price on both properties."

"I find that hard to believe Melvin," Tom Collins said as he dried glasses with a towel. He glanced at Milo. "Did he?"

"I have no problem with the price I paid for them," Milo said. "In fact, it's almost like Melvin was giving them away."

"See?" Melvin said, pointing at his empty shot glass. "You know what's wrong with people like you, Tom?"

"What's that, Melvin?"

"No trust. In order to be successful in business - or even life when you think about it - you have to know who you can trust." Melvin reached out and placed a hand on Milo's shoulder. "The first time I laid eyes on this man, I said to myself, *this is someone I can trust.*" Melvin paused and frowned. "Where did we meet?"

"At the temperance meeting," Milo said, glancing at Tom Collins.

"Of course. The temperance meeting," Melvin said, raising his glass of beer. "To the beautiful Miss Peppin. For her, I'd probably consider giving up the drink."

"And if she had you, she'd probably think about starting," Tom Collins whispered.

"What?"

"Nothing, Melvin," Tom said. "I'm just thinking out loud."

"I do that sometimes," Melvin said. "Oh, don't forget. We need to stop by the widow Wilson's place - your place - in the morning to have her sign the deed over to you."

"And give her the money."

"Of course."

"What time?" Milo said.

"I thought we'd swing by around nine," Melvin said, then downed his second shot. He wobbled in his chair for a moment before placing both hands on the bar to steady himself. "Maybe we better make that eleven."

"I'll just meet you there," Milo said.

Melvin turned to look at Milo and struggled to focus on his face.

"Okay. You know, I think I should probably head on home."

"That sounds like a good idea, Melvin," Milo said. "You had a big day today. And who knows? Maybe tomorrow might even be a bigger one."

"That's right, Milo. In business, you never know, right?"

"You never know," Milo said, smiling.

"How much do I owe you for the drinks?"

"Don't worry about it. The drinks are on me, Melvin."

"That's mighty kind of you. Are you sure?"

"Absolutely. It's the least I can do."

# Milo Makes a Loan

**The widow Wilson placed a tray** of hot fried dough on the table and sat down and poured two glasses of sherry. Milo leaned forward to enjoy the smell coming from the tray then leaned back when the widow seemed to lurch for her glass.

"It's a bit early in the day, isn't it?" Milo said, nodding at the decanter.

"I'm celebrating," the widow said, downing half her glass before taking a piece of fried dough from the tray. "I like to put some butter on it and then add some of the strawberry jam. Try it, you'll like it."

Milo did and nodded as he chewed.

"It's very good. Did you make all of this?"

"Right down to churning the butter," she said, emptying and refilling her glass in one smooth movement. "And that's the last time I'll ever do that. You ever try your hand at churning butter?"

She held up two heavily callused hands for Milo to see.

"Actually, no," Milo said, taking a sip of sherry.

"Good for you. Take my advice and don't waste your time trying to learn," she said. "Where the heck is he?"

"I have a feeling that Mr. English might be moving a bit slow this morning," Milo said.

"Well, he better hurry up and get here," she said. "I'm getting a ride to the train station, but I need to get there by two o'clock. And tomorrow morning, I'll be waking up in Philadelphia."

"Oh, that reminds me," Milo said, reaching into his pocket. "I jotted down the names of some people that might be able to help you. Feel free to mention my name. I'm not sure what opportunities they'll have available at the moment, but I'm sure something will come up."

"Thanks for doing that. You're a kind man. Any idea what they'll expect me to do?" the widow said, chewing on a fingernail. "I'm not sure five years as a farmer's wife is going to cut much cloth in Philadelphia."

"My guess is that you'll have no shortage of offers for housekeeping services. Possibly as a live-in taking care of a rich family's home. Cleaning, shopping, cooking, maybe keeping an eye on their children. Something like that."

"I can do that," she said, nodding.

Then there was a knock on the front door.

"It's about time," she said, getting up from her chair.

Moments later, she returned with a chagrined and hungover Melvin by her side.

"Hello," Melvin said, sitting down across the table from Milo.

"You feel as bad as you look?" Milo said.

"You have no idea," Melvin said.

"Okay, let's get this done," the widow said as she sat back down.

"I, uh, I'm afraid there's a bit of a problem, Mrs. Wilson," Melvin stammered.

"Problem?" she said, sitting upright in her chair and staring at Melvin.

"Yes, a problem," he said, helping himself to a glass of sherry. "But it's my problem and only a temporary one."

"What's the matter, Melvin?" Milo said, leaning forward.

"My office was robbed last night."

"What?" Milo said. "Someone broke into your office?"

"They must have," he said, scratching his head. "But there's no sign of a break-in. There's no broken glass anywhere. And no damage to the safe. It's like my money just disappeared."

"You mean while we were celebrating at the hotel somebody went into your office and cleaned you out?"

"It certainly appears that way," Melvin said.

"Who has the combination to the safe?" Milo said.

"Just me. But I'm such a talker, especially when I drink. I must have said something to somebody."

"You're telling me you don't have my money?" the widow said.

"I'm so sorry, Mrs. Wilson. But I will have it a few days. I'll just need to… move some things around."

"A lot of good a few days is going to do me. I have a train to catch."

"I could wire it to you as soon as I get my hands on it," Melvin said.

"I'm not signing the property over until I get my money," the widow said, glancing back and forth at Milo and Melvin.

"That is going to be a problem for me," Milo said. "I have some things that need to be taken care of immediately."

"I understand, Mr. Razner. But I'm not signing anything until I get paid."

"Of course not," Milo said, gently patting her hand. "If I were in your situation, I'd be saying exactly the same thing." Milo turned in his chair. "We have a problem here, Melvin."

"Tell me about it," he said, running a hand through his hair. "I'm out over twelve grand."

"Ouch," Milo said.

"Yeah, it does kinda hurt."

"Mr. English," she said. "While I'm sure you're in some degree of pain over your current situation, let's get back to why you're sitting here drinking my sherry and eating my food in the first place. My money. I want my money."

"Yes, I know you do, Mrs. Wilson," Melvin said. "Two, three days, at most. Unless, of course, it doesn't happen before Friday and the bank closes for the weekend. If that happened, and that would be highly unlikely, we're looking at next Monday or Tuesday at the latest."

"A few minutes ago it was a day or two at most," the widow snapped. "Now, we're getting close to a week."

"You're going to get your money, Mrs. Wilson," Melvin snapped back, then grimaced and rubbed his temples. "I'm just going to need a little time."

"What you might need is to be arrested for trying to swindle a grieving widow out of her property."

"Oh, my. No, I swear, it's nothing like that. I just happened to hit a snag and am dealing with a bit of a cash flow problem," Melvin said, then looked at Milo with pleading eyes. "Do you have any suggestions, Milo?"

Milo leaned back in his chair and stared off into the distance. Then he leaned forward and put his elbows on the table.

"I think the way out of this is for you to take out a loan, Melvin."

"Take out a loan?" Melvin said. "But it would probably take longer to get a loan approved than it would for me to… move some things around."

"If you went to a bank, sure," Milo said. "But not if you borrowed it from me."

"From you?" Melvin said, frowning.

"What are friends for?" Milo said.

"Now there's an idea," the widow said. "How long would it take you to get your hands on the money?"

"About as long as it takes me to reach inside my coat pocket," Milo said, smiling at her.

"You're walking around with that much cash?" Melvin said.

"I went to the bank this morning," Milo said, shrugging. "I need to get a boat, and I need to find somebody to do some construction on my island property. Not to mention some of the improvements I need to make here at the farm. And since I'm going shopping today and like to pay in cash, I guess it's your lucky day, Melvin."

"Yeah, my lucky day," he said, exhaling loudly.

Milo reached inside his coat and removed a large stack of bills. He counted out six thousand dollars in fifties and twenties then slid the stack across the table to the widow Wilson.

"That's too much," Melvin said, then stopped when he saw Milo's reaction. "I mean, the sale was for six thousand, but you need to back out my commission of three hundred."

Milo gave Melvin a tiny smile and shook his head.

"I'm so sorry, Melvin," Milo said. "I just assumed that you'd want to wave your commission considering all the additional stress Mrs. Wilson has been forced to deal with this morning."

"Yeah, I sure do feel it," the widow said, nodding. "All these ups and downs are a lot for a grieving widow to deal with."

She got up from the table and grabbed the empty decanter. "Let me go refill this while you gentlemen talk."

Melvin took several deep breaths then glanced up at Milo and nodded.

"Okay, I'll wave my commission."

"And borrow the six thousand?" Milo said.

"Yes."

"Plus interest," Milo whispered.

"Interest?"

"Well, I do have to consider this a business loan," Milo said. "And I have a strict policy that all business loans carry interest. Now, if this were a personal loan that would be a completely different situation."

"We could call it a personal loan," Melvin said.

"I guess we could," Milo said. "But that really wouldn't be honest, would it?"

"Who am I gonna tell?" Melvin said. "And she's moving to Philadelphia."

"Like I've heard you say, Melvin. Business is business."

"Yeah, I gotta stop saying stuff like that. Okay, I'll write it up when I get back to my office. Six grand plus interest. I assume we'll be using the current bank prime for the interest rate."

"No, I'm sorry, Melvin," Milo said. "I try to avoid using any numbers the banks come up with whenever possible. I sort of have my own interest rate table."

"I was afraid you were going to say that, Milo."

"Don't worry, Melvin. I'm sure you'll get used to doing business with me."

"I can't wait."

"Me either," Milo said. "And just so we're clear, the juice on six grand is two hundred a week."

# Milo Cuts Frank Some Slack

**The first thing Milo noticed** when he stepped inside the large marina was the high ceiling. It reminded him of something you'd see in a church, but there wasn't much praying going on in here. Just a lot of pounding and sawing and a scraping sound Milo knew was the sound of sandpaper on wood. He glanced around at the collection of workers and waited until he was certain he'd identified the man he was looking for. Milo approached and waited for him to finish a detailed conversation with one of his workers. He was using terms like centerline and ballast and beam, and they rolled off the tip of his tongue as easy as a good morning hello. But the man might as well be speaking Greek as far as Milo was concerned. Milo tried to follow the conversation and was about ready to give up when he heard the man start talking about the draft.

Finally, Milo said to himself. Something I understand. Milo glanced around the inside of the marina that was open on both ends and waited to feel it. Then he frowned. I might consider it a cool breeze, Milo thought, but I sure wouldn't call it a draft.

The man finished his conversation and looked around as if unsure what was next on his list of things to do. Then he spotted

Milo and started walking toward him. Milo was impressed with the way the man kept his eyes focused on him, sizing Milo up, getting ready to deal with the well-dressed stranger who probably looked, to him, like someone from the government or somebody about to pick his pocket.

Or, Milo had to concede, even a bit of a dandy.

"I hate to interrupt since it's clear you're a very busy man," Milo said. "But are you Mr. Slack?"

"I am," the man said, still studying Milo's eyes. "People call me Frank."

"Milo. Milo Razner."

Milo extended his hand and Frank returned the handshake. Milo did his best not to flinch, but the man's grip was like a vise and Milo was intrigued by the thick layer of sawdust that clung to the man's thick sweaty forearms. But the man made no effort to brush the sawdust off. Milo wondered if it was because it would be pointless given all the sawing and sanding going on, or perhaps it was a sign of pride, the man saying without saying what he did for a living and wanted the world to know it.

"It's nice to meet you, Frank. I believe I am in need of your services. And you come highly recommended by Melvin English."

"I wouldn't put too much stock in anything Melvin has to say," Frank said, his eyes starting to soften.

"Oh, don't worry, I don't," Milo said. "That's why I asked my favorite bartender for a second opinion."

That one cut the ice and Frank laughed and started rocking back and forth on his heels.

"What can I do for you, Mr. Razner?"

"Please, call me Milo."

"Milo it is."

"Would it be possible for us to speak somewhere it's a bit quieter? While I'm sure your workers are an incredibly skilled group, they certainly make quite a racket."

"Sure. Follow me."

Milo followed him to the far end of the marina and outside onto a long dock that extended over the water. Milo turned around to look at the outside of the building and couldn't help staring at the series of double doors that extended up the side of the building that faced the water. He noticed Frank giving him a bemused look.

"I don't understand," Milo said. "Why would you put doors way up there? They have to be fifty feet above the water."

"You seem like a smart guy, Milo," Frank said, giving him a small smile. "See if you can figure it out."

Milo nodded and continued to stare up at the doors that got smaller until the set near the top of the roofline was no more than six feet wide.

"It's from the days of steamboats, isn't it?" Milo said. "They had those big smokestacks, and you figured out a way to bring the boats inside and work on them without having to take the smokestacks down."

"Well done. When I heard you speak at the meeting the other night, I knew you were a smart guy."

"Obviously not as smart as you, Frank. That is quite brilliant. You built your warehouse to accommodate the prevailing designs of the day rather than stick with old thinking and make your life a lot harder. Creative adaptability of that sort is a rare quality, Frank."

"Creative adaptability. I like that," Frank said, nodding. "My daddy thought I was crazy when I first mentioned the idea. I was about eight years old at the time."

"Lucky for your father he listened to you. Is he still running the business?"

"No, it's just me now," Frank said. "My daddy died several years ago."

"I'm sorry to hear that. But he obviously left quite a legacy."

"Yeah, my daddy had a good long run," Frank said, again rocking back and forth on his heels. "So, how can I help you, Milo?"

"I need a boat. I'll need two boats, actually. But just the one for now."

"Okay. What kind of boat do you need?"

"I need something that is sturdy and capable of towing considerable weight. It doesn't need to be fast, but I do need something with a powerful engine."

"I see," Frank said. "Can I ask you what you'll be towing?"

"Supplies. Construction materials. Stuff like that. I just purchased a farm and an island, and I want to get started on some improvements straight away. I figure I have about four months before winter sets in."

"Okay. I think I have something for you that will do the trick," Frank said. "Tell me a bit about the second boat you're going to need."

The way he said it caught Milo's attention and he gave Frank a small grin. Frank continued to rock back and forth on his heels as he studied Milo's face and did his best to give nothing away.

"The second boat will probably have to be built from scratch," Milo said.

"That's not a problem," Frank said. "It's generally how I keep busy in the winter."

"That makes sense. This boat will also need to be able to handle some weight, but everything it carries will need to be onboard." Milo cocked his head. "Did I say that right? Onboard?"

"Yes, that's right, Milo," Frank said, laughing. "How much weight will it need to carry?"

"About three thousand pounds. Not counting the two people onboard."

"That's a fairly precise number. You've obviously given this some serious thought."

"I give most things pretty serious thought, Frank," Milo said. "I find it tends to cut down on surprises and mistakes. What's that old carpenter saying?"

"Measure twice, cut once?"

"That's the one. It's good advice."

"I try to follow it all the time," Frank said. "What else do you need?"

"It needs to be fast," Milo said.

"How fast are you thinking?"

"Top end, sixty miles an hour," Milo said as calmly as if he were ordering a beer.

"Sixty miles an hour?" Frank stopped rocking on his heels. "Did you know that the world speed record for a boat was recently set?"

"I did not know that," Milo said. "How fast did the boat end up going?"

"About seventy miles an hour."

"Interesting. Well, since I don't have any plans to race my boat, we won't have to worry about beating their record, will we?"

Frank laughed.

"If you aren't planning on racing, I can only think of one reason why you'd want to go that fast."

"I can't wait to hear it, Frank."

"It would be to keep anybody from catching you and your three thousand pounds of cargo."

"Not counting the two people onboard," Milo said, grinning from ear to ear.

"Not counting them," Frank said, nodding. "You're going to need a couple of V8 engines to pull off that sort of speed. And we'd be looking at a total length of thirty, maybe even thirty-five feet."

"I knew you were the right man to talk to," Milo said. "So, you could build a boat like that?"

"I'm sure I can," Frank said, again rocking on his heels. "For the right price, of course."

"Of course. And what would the right price be?"

"You're convinced the President's veto is going to be overridden, aren't you?" Frank said, staring out at the River.

Milo flinched, then recovered and gave Frank a big smile.

"Well done. Yes, Frank. In fact, I'd bet my life on it," Milo said. "Now that I think about it, I am probably betting my life on it."

"All the more reason not to let anybody catch you," Frank said.

Milo laughed and decided that Frank Slack was definitely someone he wanted to be in business with.

"I've given the idea some thought myself," Frank said.

"Really? And?"

"And that kind of life isn't for me. Life's hard enough when you're looking straight ahead and trying to move forward. I can't imagine what it would be like always looking over my shoulder."

"Now you know why I need a really fast boat, Frank," Milo said, surprised at how easy the guy was to talk to.

"So when you are forced to look over your shoulder, the things behind you are getting smaller."

"Well put, Frank. How much are you going to charge me to build the boat?"

"Well, that's a bit hard to calculate on the spot," Frank said, scratching the stubble on his chin. "But a boat that special shouldn't necessarily carry a price tag. A boat like that should probably be seen as more of an *annuity*."

Milo let Frank's comment roll around in his head. Then he put his hands on his hips and studied the boat builder standing a few feet away.

"I like the way you think, Frank Slack."

"Creative adaptability?"

"Without a doubt," Milo said. "What sort of annuity do you think the boat should be able to provide?"

"I'm not sure, but I'm thinking about a little something for each case."

"Case?"

"You aren't going to be transporting by the case?"

"I'm going to be transporting milk, Frank," Milo said. "I'm no expert, but I don't believe it's sold by the case."

"Milk?"

"Yes. A very special milk."

"I see," Frank said, giving his chin a hard scratch. "Well, if we're talking about milk, then I guess we should be talking in gallons."

"Exactly. I was thinking about, let's say, fifty cents a gallon for the finished product."

"You mean the milk, right?"

"Of course," Milo said. "I'll be delivering three hundred gallons each trip."

Frank whistled softly, and it echoed across the water then faded.

"How many deliveries are we talking about?"

"To start, one or two a week," Milo said.

"That's a lot of milk. Three hundred bucks a week. And that's what I call an annuity," Frank said, rocking back and forth so hard it looked like he was about to fall over.

"I'll need the boat ready to go as soon as the River ice melts. That would probably be sometime in April, right?"

"Maybe March if we get an easy winter," Frank said. "And if the law goes into effect early next year that would probably be right around the time people are starting to run out of all the *milk* they got squirreled away."

"Yes, one would imagine."

"And people would hate going without their milk, right?"

"I know I would," Milo said. "If you have a minute, I have a few sketches I'd like to share with you."

"I'd love to see them, Milo," Frank said, strolling back down the dock. "Can I ask you where you're going to get your hands on that much milk?"

"At the moment, Frank," Milo said. "I wish you wouldn't."

"Okay, I get that. It's just that you're going to need some very special cows to pull that off."

"Only one, Frank. I only need the one."

"I'd really like to meet that cow," Frank said.

"All in good time, Frank. All in good time."

"I have a feeling that your milk is going to be the talk of the town."

"Oh, let's hope not, Frank."

# Milo Calls On The Crankovitches

**Milo studied the young man** standing in front of him and was surprised by how young he seemed. He was also surprised by the squalor of what the faded sign at the front of the dirt driveway had the audacity to call a dairy farm. At the moment, Milo and the man were standing in deep mud, and he chastised himself for not having the foresight to wear his boots. But Milo chalked it up as one more learning experience and let it pass without comment.

"Do I know you, sir?"

"No, we've never met, Billy. But I am familiar with your work."

"You've had our milk?" the man said, thoroughly confused.

"No, I don't drink milk, so I've never had the pleasure," Milo said, glancing at the group of cows munching grass in a small paddock. "Where's the rest of your herd?"

"That's all of them," he said. "We're trying to grow the place, but it's hard."

"Yes, I imagine it is," Milo said. "Is there someplace we could talk? Someplace away from all this mud?"

"The front porch will have to do," Billy said. "Ruby won't let us in the house with muddy feet."

"Obviously a wise woman."

Billy gestured toward the dilapidated structure that passed for a house and Milo, tiptoeing the whole way, followed him onto the porch and sat down opposite him in an old wooden chair.

"You know me," Billy said. "But I don't know your name. I find that a bit off-putting."

"My name is Milo Razner. Tom Collins said you were the man to talk to."

"Oh, Tom sent you," Billy said, relaxing a bit. "I'm sorry, but I'm all out of last year's batch. But if you stop back in about a month, I should have some ready."

"That's fine, Billy," Milo said. "I'm not here to buy a jar from you. My interests are, let's say, on a slightly grander scale."

"Well, if you're talking about buying in quantity, I charge twelve dollars a gallon for my good stuff."

"Ah, yes. The magnificent Midnight Miracle."

"You have been talking to Tom."

"To a point, yes. I'm here to discuss a business opportunity, Billy."

"Well, I appreciate that, Mr. Razner. But trying to scratch out a living on this farm pretty much takes up all my time."

"I imagine it does," Milo said, rubbing his feet together to get some of the mud off his shoes. "Do you own this farm, Billy?"

"No, at the moment we're renting. But someday I hope to be able to buy it."

"I understand, Billy. Dairy farming is a noble calling. Most honorable. But don't you think your true skill lies elsewhere?"

"My true skill?"

"I'm talking about your cooking abilities, Billy. I've never seen anything like them before. And believe me, I've been looking for a long time."

"It's just a hobby. But thanks. I take pride in my cooking."

"That's exactly what I thought the first time I tasted your Midnight Miracle. I said there's somebody who takes a lot of pride in his work."

The front door opened and a woman stuck her head out. Milo looked at her and couldn't help but notice how pretty she was. He also wondered how long that would last if she stayed in this place.

"I didn't know we had company, Billy. Who's this?"

Milo stood and tipped his hat.

"My name is Milo Razner, Mrs. Crankovitch. It's a pleasure to meet you."

She stepped out onto the porch and closed the door behind her. She leaned with her back against the railing and studied Milo closely.

"What can we do for you, Mr. Razner?" she said, folding her arms across her chest.

"Please call me, Milo. Can I call you Ruby?"

"Maybe," she said, shrugging. "Why are you here?"

"Tom told him to stop by," Billy said.

"You're about a month early," she said.

"Allow me to explain. Tom mentioned that you might still have some of last year's batch available, and while I was intrigued by the prospect of obtaining some of it, that's not why I'm here."

"He says he has a business proposition for us," Billy said.

"Okay," Ruby said. "Let's hear it."

"Right to the point. I like that," Milo said, smiling. "You've obviously married well, Billy. Getting right to it, you probably aren't aware that I've just purchased the Wilson farm."

"You're a dairy farmer?" Ruby said, busting loose with a wide grin that caught Milo by surprise and made his heart skip a beat.

"Actually, I consider myself more of a businessman. But I do believe that this area is in desperate need of a larger dairy operation that can operate on more of a regional level. And to operate on a regional level, some degree of scale is needed. If that concept makes any sense to you."

"I'm very familiar with the concept of scale, Mr. Razner," Ruby said. "As well as yield, acreage, feeding requirements, and the easiest way to get cow crap out of a hoof. But if you're looking at scaling up your operation, I'm afraid you're looking in the wrong place. Unless your plan is to scale mud."

"That's funny, Ruby. Yes, I can see that this isn't the place," Milo said. "You're woefully undercapitalized, and my guess is that you often wonder if milking the dozen or so cows you have is even worth the effort."

"Hey, we're doing okay," Billy said.

"Let him finish, Billy," Ruby said, continuing to study Milo closely.

"And since scale is what's necessary to make any real money dairy farming these days, I'm about to invest heavily in both improving my new operation as well as dramatically increase its capacity," Milo said, not taking his eyes off Ruby.

"And you thought you'd do the neighborly thing and stop by to tell us that you're about to put us out of business?" Ruby said.

"Oh, my, no," Milo said. "I'm here to offer you a way off this property and get you into something that will actually produce some real money without you having to kill yourself in the process."

"I'm not following," Billy said.

"Then let me be perfectly clear. I want you and your wife to manage my new dairy farm," Milo said, then paused before continuing. "And do some cooking on the side."

Ruby nodded, then broke into a wide grin.

"You're betting Prohibition gets passed, aren't you?" she said.

"I had no idea how smart a woman you were, Ruby. Trust me, I won't make that mistake again. She's remarkable, Billy."

"Yeah, I know," Billy said, not giving the compliment about his wife the attention it deserved. "But the President struck that new law down, right?"

"Mr. Razner believes the President's veto is going to be overruled, Billy," Ruby said, talking to him like he was a young child. "And he wants us to help him get into the illegal booze business."

"Really?" Billy said, scrunching his face into what appeared to be a grimace. "I didn't hear him say that at all."

"You should listen to your wife, Billy," Milo said. "She's sharper than the edge of my razor."

"But I only cook about twenty gallons a year," Billy said. "I don't care what you want to charge for it, you can't make a living off of that."

"He's talking about scaling up the volume, Billy," Ruby said, unable to take her eyes off Milo. "By how much?"

"A lot," Milo said, shifting his attention to Billy. "Let me ask you a couple of questions, Billy."

"Sure. Go ahead."

"How long are you letting your mash ferment before you start cooking?" Milo said.

"A couple of weeks," Billy said. "As long as the temperature stays warm enough, that's plenty of time."

"The lower the temperature, the longer it takes to ferment, right?"

"Yeah."

"When fermentation is done, do you start cooking right away?"

"Yeah, usually. I'll start cooking when the sun goes down, and I'm usually pretty much done by morning."

"It smells when you're cooking, doesn't it?"

"It smells awful. That's one of the reasons I like to cook at night. It draws less attention."

"Smart. When you cook your Midnight Miracle, what size container do you use?"

"It's a five-gallon copper still I made. It works real good."

"And how much Midnight Miracle do you get from the five gallons?"

"Well, I do a first run that produces about a gallon and a half. And then a second one that makes about one more."

"A two to one ratio? That's impressive, Billy. And you hit the mash with some more sugar and yeast before the second run?" Milo said.

"Yeah, if I want to keep the alcohol level up I have to. I use a lot of sugar and a special yeast I make myself. The corn gives it most of its flavor, but it's the sugar and yeast that really drive the ethanol up."

"A hundred and fifty proof if I'm not mistaken," Milo said.

"Yeah, that's close. Maybe a little higher."

"And your entire process takes about two weeks start to finish?"

"Yup. I shoot for a batch every couple of weeks until I run out of corn," Billy said. "But you'd want more, right?"

"Much more, Billy," Milo said.

"I don't know how that would be possible, Mr. Razner."

"Why not?"

"Because that five-gallon still can't handle it," Billy said. "I can only work with what I got, right?"

Milo glanced at Ruby who was shaking her head and giving her husband a sad smile.

"We'd be using slightly larger stills, Billy," Milo said.

"Oh. How big?"

"Six hundred gallons," Milo said.

"Six hundred gallons?" Billy said. "You want me to make you three hundred gallons of Midnight Miracle?"

"I want you to make three hundred gallons a week, Billy. Year round."

"What? I don't have anywhere near the ingredients to pull off something like that," he said. "And how do you expect me to cook in the winter up here? It's way too cold."

"You let me worry about all that, Billy. Except for the yeast. You'll need to handle that. But I'm sure that won't be a problem."

"No, I can make plenty of that. But how can I do all that cooking and work a farm at the same time?"

"Again, let me handle that. I'll be hiring some additional people to help you run the farm. And as far as anyone knows, running the dairy farm is all you're doing. Am I making that point clear enough?"

"Yeah, we get it," Ruby said. "How long before the government starts sticking its nose into what we'll be doing? We'd be looking at a long stretch in prison if we ever got caught."

"I believe that it will take the government at least a year to figure out how big the problems they're about to create are. Then it will take them another year or two to come up with some sort of plan to deal with them. And if I know anything about how the government works, when they do finally come up with sort of solution, they won't be willing to spend anywhere near what it would take to fix it. It's one of the things I love about our government."

"Incompetent, but predictable?" Ruby said.

Milo laughed.

"I'm going to have to borrow that one, Ruby. It's the perfect description."

"You've spent a lot of time putting all this together haven't you, Milo?" Ruby said.

"I have indeed, Ruby," Milo said. "And I've been looking long and hard for the right place to do it and the right people to do it with. I came here today convinced that Billy was the right man for the job. But I had no idea that I would also find a woman who would understand exactly what I was talking about from the jump. And I'm willing to bet that you're already coming up with some additional ideas to make it even better."

"How much are you willing to pay for the Midnight Miracle?" Ruby said.

"I was thinking about three dollars a gallon," Milo said.

"Three dollars a gallon?" Billy said, scoffing at the idea. "I already get twelve."

"Billy, please be quiet," Ruby said.

"But, Ruby-"

"Billy, do you know how much money he's talking about?"

"Yeah, he's talking about three dollars a gallon," Billy said.

"At three dollars a gallon, we're talking nine hundred dollars a week, Billy."

"We are? That's a lot."

"Yes, it is," Ruby said. "But it's not enough. We'll do it for five a gallon."

"So, you're a negotiator as well. I like that, Ruby. Let's say we split the difference and call it four," Milo said, extending his hand toward Ruby. "That would make it an even twelve-hundred a week. That's a nice round number.

"Four it is," she said, returning his handshake.

Milo felt a tingle on the back of his neck when she used her free hand to gently scrape her fingernails against the back of his wrist. Milo filed it away along with all the other reasons he already had for getting to know this woman better.

"As far as the farm goes, you'll be on the payroll as co-managers with a joint salary of a thousand dollars a year plus a share of the profits. Compared to what you'll be making on our other venture, it probably won't seem like much, but every little bit helps, right?"

"Yes, every little bit helps," Ruby said, smiling.

Milo shook hands with Billy, then looked around the decrepit property.

"I suggest you start packing. Mrs. Wilson has signed over the property to me and has left town. Feel free to move in whenever you're ready. I think you'll like the house. The widow Wilson called it cozy. I'm going to leave now and let you folks discuss some things. I'll swing by in a couple of days, and we'll talk in more detail."

"Okay," Billy said, still baffled by what had just transpired. "Thanks, Mr. Razner."

"Call me Milo, Billy."

"You got it, Mr. Razner."

"Okay, then," Milo said, shaking his head before smiling back and forth at them. "And if either one of you breathes a single word about any of this to anyone, you will both find yourself at the bottom of the mighty St. Lawrence. Have I made myself clear on that point?"

"Crystal clear," Billy said.

Milo beamed at him.

"Just like your Midnight Miracle."

# Beulah Peppin Bites Back

**Milo climbed the short flight** of stairs leading up to the front porch and knocked on the door. While he waited, he turned around to take in the view of the River. He admired the explosion of colors as the sun set over the calm water and again took comfort from knowing he was in the right place at the right time. The front door opened and Beulah Peppin, freshly bathed and wearing a robe, stared at him while toweling her wet hair.

"Mr. Razner," Beulah said, making no effort to let him inside. "I had a feeling it wouldn't be long before our paths crossed again."

"Good day, Miss Peppin," Milo said, removing his hat and extending the bouquet of flowers he was holding. "I saw these growing on my way over and thought of you."

"Flowers? Isn't that what a man gives a woman when he has courtship on his mind?" Beulah said, wrapping the towel around her head and tying it tight.

"I wouldn't call this a courting visit, Miss Peppin," Milo said, having a hard time taking his eyes off her exposed neck.

"What would you call it?" she said, cocking her head at him.

"Let's call it an opportunity for us to catch up."

"An update of sorts," she said.

"Yes. An update. Let's go with that."

Beulah took a step back and accepted the bouquet as she waved Milo inside. She headed for the living room and gestured for him to sit on the couch. Beulah sat down in a chair opposite him and tossed the bouquet on the coffee table between them.

"I hope I didn't interrupt your bath," Milo said.

"No, I was finished and just about to have supper."

"What are you having?"

"A beef roast with vegetables."

"Are you expecting company?" Milo said.

"No. Why do you ask?"

"That just sounds like a lot of food for one person."

"Is that an attempt to get invited to stay for dinner?"

"You see right through me, Miss Peppin," Milo said.

"Apparently, subtlety isn't one of your strengths, Mr. Razner."

She removed the towel from her head and shook it until her hair tumbled down and draped her shoulders.

"I'm sure you're right. I should probably work on that," Milo said, reaching inside his coat to remove the jar of Midnight Miracle Billy had given him from his own personal stash. He placed it on the coffee table next to the flowers.

"What's that?" Beulah said, eyeing the jar.

"That is the answer to a lot of prayers," Milo said, relaxing into the couch and draping a leg over the other.

"Maybe if you pray to the devil," Beulah said, then gave him a hint of a smile.

"I bought the dairy farm," Milo said.

"I heard."

"You heard?"

"Small town," Beulah said, shrugging. "You're going to need someone to run it for you."

"Already done. I hired Billy and Ruby Crankovitch earlier today."

"The moonshiner? Interesting."

"I was planning on looking for someone with more experience. Then I met the wife."

"I've heard that she's a smart woman."

"She is. Very smart. And definitely someone who can make a real contribution."

"Is she pretty?"

"Extremely so," Milo said, remembering the tingle on his neck.

"Then you should probably be careful, Mr. Razner. You wouldn't want to do anything that might upset Mr. Crankovitch since it appears that he holds the key to your future."

"There's no need to worry about that, Miss Peppin," Milo said, flashing a smile in her direction. "When it comes to matters of the heart, my interests reside elsewhere. But you make a good point."

"You do have quite the way with words, Mr. Razner."

Beulah stood and sat down next to Milo on the couch. She leaned in and kissed Milo long and hard. Milo slipped both hands inside her robe and returned her kisses as he explored north and south. He lowered his head and playfully nipped her shoulder with his teeth.

"Ow," Beulah said, laughing as she wiggled away and pulled her robe tight.

"I've missed you," Milo said.

"Get used to it, Milo. It wouldn't be good for business if people saw a bootlegger and the head of the Temperance Society making company together."

"But we can still do this, right?" Milo said, again reaching for the inside of her robe.

"Occasionally," Beulah said, getting up and sitting back down in the chair. "But only at night and always here. And you should probably start using the back door."

"Okay. Yeah, I can do that," Milo said.

"Is that stuff as good as everyone says?" Beulah said, nodding at the jar.

"Even better."

Milo headed for the kitchen and returned with two small glasses. He poured and handed one to Beulah.

"To us," Milo said, raising his glass in a toast.

They downed their drinks, and Milo waited for her reaction. Beulah took a few moments to catch her breath, then exhaled loudly as she put the glass down on the coffee table.

"My, my. I'm warm and tingly all over."

"Well, you were just on the couch with me," Milo said, grinning. "But I'm sure the booze has something to do with it."

Beulah laughed and leaned forward to pick up the jar. She held it up to the light, studied it, then put it back down on the table.

"Have you talked to the guy in Rockport yet?" Beulah said.

"No, but he's my next stop," Milo said, refilling both glasses. "You're sure he's the right man for the job?"

"Based on everything I've heard, he's the one you need to talk to."

"Good. You weren't wrong about Crankovitch or English, so I'm not gonna question your instincts."

"How is Melvin?" Beulah said. "I heard someone broke into his safe and cleaned him out."

"Yes, he told me," Milo said. "Most unfortunate. I'm afraid Melvin is a bit *downtrodden* at the moment."

"You got the farm and the island for nothing?"

"I did. Plus another four thousand," Milo said, giving her a coy smile. "And then he had to borrow the six grand from me to pay the widow. It was beautiful."

"Go easy with him on the juice," Beulah said. "That six grand is small potatoes, and we don't want to attract any attention by putting the squeeze on him."

"No, I won't," Milo said. "But I couldn't resist having a little fun with him. You know how I feel about lawyers."

"I do. But be gentle with English. He might be useful at some point in the future."

"I sincerely doubt that," Milo said. "But I'll play nice for now. I'm going to refuse his first payment next week. And I'm going to tell him I'm waiving the juice since I've reconsidered and am now calling it a personal loan. At some point in the future, I might even consider telling him not to worry about repaying the six grand."

"Good. That would be smart. We'd own him at that point."

"Yes, we would. So, it's something to consider. Unless he pisses me off."

"And if he does?"

"Then it's straight to the bottom of the River for Mr. English."

"Interesting choice. I wonder if fish eat lawyers."

"I doubt it," Milo said, reaching for the two glasses. "Let's have one more."

"I don't know if I should," she said, accepting the glass. "The way this stuff warms my body, I'll probably have to slip out of this robe and stretch out on cool sheets."

Beulah downed her drink and sat back down on the couch next to Milo.

"Close your eyes, Milo."

He complied, and he leaned his head back. He felt Beulah's lips and tongue against the side of his face, then bolted upright when she bit his neck hard.

"Ow, that hurts," he said, rubbing his neck.

"Now we're even," Beulah said, laughing. "Take me to bed, Mr. Razner."

"It will be my pleasure, Miss Peppin."

"Let's hope the feeling is mutual," Beulah said, her robe falling to the floor as she headed for the bedroom. "And bring the jar."

# Episode 2

## Friends and Enemies

"This new law is downright un-American. George Washington built his own brewery, Thomas Jefferson wrote the Declaration of Independence in a bar, and everybody who signed the thing drank booze. Instead of calling me a bootlegger, try to think of me as one of the new Founding Fathers."

Milo Razner

# A Little Birdie

**Milo, fighting back against a lack** of sleep and a mild hangover, stood on the dock and stared down at the wooden boat that had definitely seen better days. Frank Slack noticed the frown on Milo's face and chuckled.

"I know what you're thinking," Frank said.

"That I've lost my mind if I pay more than a dollar for this thing?" Milo said.

"It's a work boat, Milo. That's what you said you wanted."

"Yeah, but just look at it. Does it actually float, or is it just tied to the dock?"

"It's my own personal work boat, Milo," Frank said, shaking his head.

"Now you're just blowing smoke up my skirt."

"No, I'm not, Milo. Not only can it hold a lot of weight, but you could also tow a freight train behind it."

"That oughta come in handy," Milo said, squinting as the sun poked through a set of clouds.

"Well, yeah. If a freight train could float," Frank said, then waited for Milo's laugh. When it didn't come, he continued.

"Look, Milo, it's a great boat. It used to be my daddy's. You can use it as long as you need. No charge."

"Well, I do like the price," Milo said. "Okay. Thanks, Frank. I appreciate it."

They both turned around when they heard the sound of footsteps. A very small man with a bad limp was slowly making his way down the dock.

"There he is," Frank said. "Right on time."

"That's my driver?" Milo said, grimacing at the limp.

"That's him. Birdie knows the River better than you know your girlfriend's private parts."

"If I didn't know better, I might wonder who you've been talking to, Frank," Milo said, managing a small smile as he flashed back to last night with Beulah. "What happened to his leg?"

"Don't worry. I'm sure he'll tell you all about it," Frank said. "Hey, Birdie."

"Hi, Frank. Beautiful day for a boat ride."

"It is," Frank said, shaking the man's hand. "Birdie, this is Milo Razner."

"Hi, Milo. I'm Birdie Gray. It's nice to meet you. Frank says you're going to need a driver. Someone who knows his way around the River."

"I do indeed. It's nice to meet you, Mr. Gray," Milo said, sizing the man up.

"Mr. Gray is my daddy. Call me Birdie."

"Okay. Birdie it is. Frank says you know the River better than anybody."

"I do," Birdie said, nodding.

Milo liked the way he said it: No boasting, just a simple statement of fact.

"We should get going then," Milo said. "I need to go to Rockport. I assume you know how to get there?"

Birdie looked at Milo like he was a total idiot then glanced at Frank.

"Yeah, I can probably figure it out," Birdie said.

Frank laughed.

"You two have fun," Frank said. "Keep the boat as long as you need, Milo."

Birdie slowly made his way into the boat and started the engine. Milo untied the lines, climbed in, and sat down on the bench seat next to Birdie. They headed for deeper water and Milo was impressed when he watched Birdie roll and light a cigarette with one hand without taking the other off the wheel.

"Rockport, huh?"

"Yes. I need to speak with someone over there."

"Nice town."

"It's my first trip to Canada," Milo said, enjoying the cool breeze hitting his face.

"It looks the same as here," Birdie said. "But the flags are different."

"Thanks. I'll keep that in mind," Milo said, glancing over at Birdie who sat calmly driving the boat and smoking his cigarette.

"It's not a big thing. But it might come in handy in case you ever go on a bender and wake up not knowing where you are," Birdie said.

"You're a bit of a comedian, aren't you, Birdie?"

"Oh, you noticed," Birdie said, glancing over and giving him a smile.

Birdie opened the throttle, and the boat surged forward. Milo liked the way the boat moved through the water. It wasn't that fast, but you couldn't miss its power. They passed the back of the castle Milo had seen the other day from Melvin's boat and the further they got from the deep main channel, the more at ease Milo felt. He watched an eagle ride the wind and saw a fish jump. The eagle swung around for a second look, then gave up and disappeared from sight.

"It's nice back here, isn't it?" Birdie said. "Real peaceful."

"It's beautiful," Milo said, nodding. "How do you know when you're actually in Canada?"

"It's coming up soon," Birdie said. "I'll let you know."

"What happened to your leg?"

"I fell off the roof of a barn."

"There seems to be a lot of that going around," Milo said.

"So I've heard. I did it when I was a kid, and my parents didn't have the money for me to get it fixed," Birdie said.

"You've had to live with that limp your whole life?"

"Yeah. It cost me my ballet career," Birdie said, flicking his cigarette butt overboard.

"You are a funny man, Birdie," Milo said, frowning briefly at what Birdie had done with the butt.

"Well, when you walk like I do, having a sense of humor comes in handy," Birdie said, slowing the boat. "Here it comes."

"What?" Milo said, glancing around.

"The international line between the U.S. and Canada," Birdie said, pointing down at the water. "Right there."

Milo leaned over the boat and scanned the surface of the water.

"I don't see it," Milo said, staring down and squinting.

"A little to your left," Birdie said.

"No, I can't see it anywhere," Milo said. "What color is it?"

"I think it's chartreuse."

"Chartreuse?" Milo said, continuing to scan the surface of the water in vain. "That's an odd choice."

Milo heard Birdie cackle, then sat back down and glared at him.

"Very funny, Birdie."

"Works every time," he said, laughing. "Sorry, Milo. But I couldn't resist."

"I owe you one," Milo said, shaking his head at his own gullibility.

"But we are officially in Canadian waters now," Birdie said, then pointed at the horizon. "And there's Rockport dead ahead."

"It is close, isn't it?" Milo said, smiling.

"As long as you got a boat," Birdie said, opening the throttle.

Minutes later, Birdie pulled into the town dock, and Milo secured the boat to two metal cleats.

"Hey, not bad," Birdie said, watching Milo. "I thought I might have to teach you the proper way to tie a boat off."

"I'm a quick study, Birdie," Milo said, glancing around before spotting the sign he was looking for. "You wouldn't be looking for full-time work by any chance, would you?"

"It depends."

"On what?" Milo said.

"On whether or not I'd get to drive that new boat Frank's building for you."

"Of course. All the time, whenever you want, Birdie. It'll almost feel like it's your boat."

"Then I'm in," Birdie said.

"Don't you want to talk money first?"

"No. Frank said you were a straight shooter and more than fair with him. And that's all I needed to hear," Birdie said.

"I like the way you think, Birdie. Pardon the rather poor nautical pun, but welcome aboard," Milo said, surprised but pleased by the man's attitude. "Do you mind waiting here while I take care of business?"

"Not at all," Birdie said, stretching out on the front seat. "It's a good day for a nap."

"That's a good idea," Milo said, remembering last night that had turned into early morning by the time Beulah Peppin had let him get to sleep. "I could use one myself."

"Being well rested is important," Birdie said, his hat shielding his face from the sun.

"Yes, it is."

"Especially when you're going sixty miles an hour over water."

# Milo Does a Little Shopping

**Milo walked down the dock**, then turned left and headed for the store that sat on the edge of the River and advertised antiques and used furniture. He entered the dimly lit warehouse and, apart from the ratty couches and chairs and a large collection of wooden hutches and cabinets, found the place empty. At the main counter, he saw a small bell next to the cash register and tapped it once. Seconds later, an old man entered through a door behind the counter and shuffled toward Milo.

"Can I help you?"

"I'm looking for Clinton Farwell," Milo said.

"I'm Clint," the man said. "Are you looking for some furniture? I just got a nice living room set in you might like."

"No, thanks, Clint. I'm all set on furniture, but I do need your help."

Clint raised an eyebrow and stared at him. Milo liked the fact that the man was suspicious and took it as a good sign.

"If you ain't here for furniture, I probably can't help you, mister."

"I'm not so sure about that, Clint. Allow me to introduce myself. I'm Milo Razner."

"Nice to meet you, Mr. Razner. I don't think I've ever seen you before."

"No, I just moved to the area. And I live on the other side. In Alex Bay."

"Okay. How do you think I can help you?"

"I understand you used to own a distillery that you operated right here on this property," Milo said.

"I did. And I made some of the best whiskey Canada has ever seen," the old man said with a touch of pride.

"And then Prohibition arrived in Canada and put you out of business," Milo said.

"Yeah, 1916 was a bad year for the folks in Ontario," Clint said. "Now they've banned it across the country."

"But I hear they're already talking about repealing it," Milo said.

"A lot of good that's going to do me," Clint said. "It would take me three years to ramp up and get back in business. And as you can probably tell from looking at me, I might not have three years left."

"I'm sure you have decades left, Clint," Milo said, smiling at him. "You aged your whiskey for three years?"

"Yeah, for my basic product I did. I aged a lot longer for some of the top-shelf blends I made," Clint said, shaking his head. "But it's all gone. The big guys who were able to get export contracts are making out okay, but a lot of the little guys, like me, went under. Those bastards ruined me with that stupid law. Just wait till the Dries get their way on your side of the River."

"Actually, Clint, I can't wait," Milo said, grinning.

"I'm not following."

"How would you like to get even with those bastards, Clint?"

"Assuming I ever could, how would I go about doing that, Mr. Razner?"

"With this," Milo said, removing a glass jar from his coat pocket.

Clint picked up the half-filled jar and held it up to the light. "What is it?"

"It's the stuff miracles are made of, Clint. Do you still have all your distillery equipment?"

"I do. It's in the back. There's not much call for stuff like that. And I refuse to sell it any of the big companies."

"As a matter of principle," Milo said.

"Yeah, that's right," Clint said, still examining the contents of the jar. "Well, Mr. Razner, are you going to offer me a taste of this, or do I need to ask?"

"You read my mind, Clint. All we'll need is a couple of glasses."

"Follow me," Clint said, heading for the door that led to the back of the warehouse.

Milo followed him and stepped into another world. The high-ceilinged room was filled with distilling equipment and stacks of empty crates, and it was spotless. But what really caught Milo's eye were the two large copper stills sitting next to each other along one wall. Even in the dim light, the copper gleamed, and the stills almost seemed to be demanding his attention.

"I like to keep the place clean," Clint said, noticing Milo's expression. "Force of habit. Have a seat."

Milo sat down in one of the four leather chairs that surrounded a polished wood table. Clint returned carrying two shot glasses, and he placed them on the table before sitting down next to him. Milo opened the jar and carefully poured. He handed one of the shot glasses to Clint and held up his own in a toast. They touched glasses, and he watched Clint down his and waited for his reaction.

"Wow. Now that is something special," Clint said, again holding up the jar to the light. "Who makes it?"

"I think it's a bit early to have that conversation, Clint," Milo said, shrugging.

"Okay, so we're talking about a world-class moonshiner with no name," Clint said.

"For now, yes."

"I doubt if you came all this way just to have me taste it, Mr. Razner," Clint said. "What do you need from me?"

"I need you to make it different, Clint."

"I don't think I could do much to improve this stuff," Clint said, helping himself to another shot. "You want another?"

"No, thanks," Milo said. "And don't drink it all. You're going to need some to work with."

"I must be a little slow on the uptake today, Mr. Razner. I'm still not following you."

"I agree completely that it would hard to make it better. But what I said was I need you to make it *different*."

"Different how?" Clint said, thoroughly confused.

"I need you to turn it into whiskey. Or at least make it look and taste like whiskey. Canadian whiskey. Which, if I'm right, will be all the rage by this time next year."

Clint frowned, then a small smile appeared. Eventually, it turned into a wide grin.

"You're betting Prohibition is gonna get passed in the States, aren't you?"

"I'm doing a whole lot more than just betting on it, Clint," Milo said.

"What proof is this shine?" Clint said, tossing back the second shot. "Damn, that's good. Whoever makes this sure does know what he's doing."

"He certainly does. But he doesn't know anything about making whiskey. It's around 150 proof. Right now, my cooker is working on getting it up to 160."

"And since it's that strong, the number of people who'd enjoy drinking it is pretty small, right?"

"Yes, despite its remarkable qualities, I'm going to need a product that appeals to more of the general public."

"You want to cut it," Clint said.

"Yes, down to around eighty proof."

"That wouldn't be a problem. All it would take is water. And we've got plenty of that around."

"Yes. And very good water it is. But it will need some color and more of a whiskey flavor."

"Okay," Clint said, nodding.

"I was thinking that perhaps soaking it in oak chips might work," Milo said.

"That would do the trick. Maybe a touch of charcoal."

"And if you had a way to agitate it, you know, keep stirring it, it probably wouldn't take too long to give it some nice color and a hint of that smoky oak flavor people expect."

"No, it wouldn't," Clint said. "And it wouldn't be the first time I've tried to speed the process up a bit."

"How long?"

"I'd say around ten days, maybe a week. And then strain it, and, if necessary, finish it up with a touch of sugar to take the edge off."

"Or maple syrup?"

"Yeah, that would work. After that, all I'd need to do is bottle it and stick a label on it."

"Oh, no, Clint," Milo said. "I wouldn't expect you to bottle it here. I'll handle that on the other side."

"Then how the hell are you going to transport it?"

"In ten-gallon milk containers," Milo said. "You see, Clint, I'm a dairy farmer."

"Are you now?" Clint said, laughing.

"Yes, I'm just getting started," Milo said, smiling. "But I'm learning a lot already. Did you know that cows have to be milked twice a day?"

"Yeah, I think I heard that somewhere," Clint said, giving Milo an odd look. "How much product are we talking about?"

"As soon as the ice goes out next spring, my plan is to start bringing you three hundred gallons a week."

"And head back home with six hundred of the finished product?"

"Yes, but only three hundred gallons per trip," Milo said. "Hopefully, we'll get to two deliveries a week by the end of the first month."

"That's a lot of booze."

"Yes, it is. Fortunately, there's going to be a lot of thirsty Americans."

"It almost a crime to do that to something this special," Clint said, swirling the contents of the jar.

"I'm sure you'll come up with something almost as good," Milo said. "And feel free to keep a gallon of the original on hand just for you. What do you say, Clint?"

"It sure beats the hell out of selling furniture," Clint said.

"Oh, you'll still need to keep the furniture store open," Milo said.

"Yeah, I get that," Clint said, nodding. "And I assume you'll be transporting at night."

"I will. I couldn't help but notice that you have a set of doors that open directly into a boathouse."

"I do. I built it five years ago. It sure made my life a lot easier during the winter," Clint said. "You could just drive your boat in and load up out of sight of any prying eyes."

"That would be perfect. I also couldn't help noticing that you have a couple of very nice copper stills sitting idle."

"I do. Six hundred gallons each. I had them made during a time when business was booming."

"Of course," Milo said, nodding. "I hate to see them just sitting there."

"You want to buy them?" Clint said.

"Well, I was just about to special order two for myself, but seeing them here I can't help but ask myself why I should even bother."

"I'm sure I could part with them if the price were right."

"Oh, I'm quite sure you'll find that the price is definitely right, Clint. I'm so glad I stopped by today. I knew you were the man to talk to."

"How did you get my name anyway?"

"My business partner is very good at identifying talented people. You know, finding the right person for the job and all that."

"Have I met your partner?" Clint said.

"Oh, I doubt that very much, Clint," Milo said, glancing around the room. "So, let's talk money."

"Okay. I'm used to dealing with cases, so I'll need to do some translating."

"By all means."

"A case of whiskey is a dozen quart bottles. That's three gallons."

"It is."

"And a case of good Canadian whiskey will run you twenty or maybe thirty bucks if you don't know where to buy in bulk. And that will probably go up after Prohibition gets passed."

"I'm sure you're right," Milo said, nodding.

"But all I'll be doing is adding color and flavor," Clint said. "And water."

"Yes, we don't want to forget the water, Clint," Milo said, chuckling.

"Gee, now that I think about it, it's hard to come up with a good number."

"Let's try it this way. How happy would you be if I gave you a dollar for each gallon of finished product you deliver?"

"Probably not as happy as I'd be if you gave me two," Clint said, staring at Milo.

Milo laughed and poured two more shots of the Miracle.

"You read my mind," Milo said, handing him one of the glasses. "And would I be correct assuming that you'll be willing to throw in the stills as a good faith gesture?"

"You would," Clint said. "I'll even help you load them in the boat when you're ready."

"Perfect," Milo said, nodding as he glanced around. "Twelve hundred a week sounds like a nice round number to start with."

"I do like round numbers," Clint said, tossing back the shot.

"Yes, they're much easier to work with. You're going to make a lot of money, Clint."

"But nowhere close to what you're going to make, right, Mr. Razner?"

"No, Clint. Nowhere close."

# Oscar's English Lesson

**Oscar Hyde smiled and touched** his hat to a mother with two young children as she passed his office. He watched her walk past and admired the view as she strolled up the street then into the grocery store. Oscar noticed Melvin English making his way across the street heading in his direction, but hid his frown and gave him a small wave.

"Good morning," Melvin said, climbing the small set of steps that led up to the verandah.

"Hey, Melvin. Have a seat and tell me what's on your mind," Oscar said, gesturing to an empty chair.

"No, let's talk inside," Melvin said, heading for the front door of the police station.

Oscar followed him inside, poured himself a generous shot of whiskey, and settled into his chair.

"Isn't it a bit early for that?" Melvin said, nodding at the glass.

"Not if you haven't stopped from last night," Oscar said, tossing his drink back then putting his feet up on the desk.

Melvin shook his head and shuffled back and forth in front of the desk.

"You seem troubled, Mel," Oscar said, lighting a cigar and blowing smoke up at the ceiling.

"Can I have one of those? Things are a bit tight at the moment," Melvin said.

Oscar frowned, but reached into his pocket and tossed one of the cigars to Melvin.

"Sit down, Mel," Oscar said. "You're making me nervous. You're all…twitchy."

"You'd be twitchy too if somebody just emptied your safe and stole all your money," Melvin said, struggling to get the cigar lit.

"Yeah, I probably would," Oscar said, nodding. "Any luck finding out who might have done it?"

"Isn't that your job, Oscar?"

"I already looked into it, but I couldn't find anything suspicious."

"So, that's it? You looked into it, but now you're done?"

"What do you want me to do, Mel?" Oscar said, relaxing further into the chair and pulling the brim of his hat down like he was planning on taking a nap. "Are you sure you didn't misplace it?"

"Are you trying to be funny, or does it just come natural to you?"

"Most days, it seems to come natural," Oscar said, a chuckle escaping out from underneath the hat.

"I'm glad you can joke about it," Melvin said, finally sitting down. "You do know that this could set our plans back."

"Maybe your plans."

Oscar put his feet on the floor, sat up, then placed his elbows on the desk and grinned at Melvin.

"I can always find another partner, Mel."

"Don't start on me today, Oscar. I'm not in the mood."

"Hey, I'm just trying to think like a businessman. Isn't that what you're always telling me I need to do?"

"Yeah, I gotta stop saying stuff like that," Melvin said. "I'm going to need a little time to rebuild my nest egg. But I'll be ready to go in the spring."

"Speaking of rebuilding, you got the three hundred you owe me?" Oscar said.

"Haven't you been listening? I just told you I'm tapped out. And now I've got another creditor I need to take care of first."

"I don't think I like the sound of that."

"How do you think I feel about it?"

"Don't know, don't care, Mel. I just want my three hundred."

"Well, you're going to have to wait," Melvin said. "Milo Razner doesn't seem to be the sort of man who has a lot of patience."

"What the hell are you doing borrowing money from an outsider?"

"I didn't have a choice. I needed six grand to pay the widow Wilson for her farm."

"You're into this guy for six grand?" Oscar said, shaking his head.

"Yeah, and the weekly juice is two hundred," Melvin said, puffing hard on his cigar.

"Ouch. I haven't met the guy yet. What's he like?"

"He's smart. At least he thinks he is. Why he bought a dairy farm is beyond me, but he says he's a businessman and knows how to spot an opportunity. But what's worrying me is that I think he's hiding a real mean streak. And that can't be a good thing for a guy who owes him six grand."

"You want me to have a chat with him?" Oscar said. "You know, just a little friendly reminder that we don't like outsiders coming to town and taking advantage of the locals."

"It probably couldn't hurt," Melvin said. "If only he'd come to town a week or two later. I know I could have gotten the farm from her for a couple of grand at most. But then this guy Razner goes ahead and offers full asking price. Who does something like that?"

"Somebody with more money than brains, Mel. Don't give this guy more credit than he deserves. I'll talk to him."

"Thanks."

"Have you had any luck finding any product on the Canadian side?"

"Yeah, I talked to a guy the other day who can guarantee us five cases a week," Melvin said.

"Five cases? That's it?"

"That's just to start. He says he'll be able to do more in a couple of months after we get rolling. I imagine he can get his hands on all he wants. But he's a bit nervous about jumping in with both feet until he gets a chance to see how the law handles it."

"Did you tell him not to worry about that?" Oscar said, blowing smoke rings up at the ceiling.

"I did."

"But you didn't tell him *why* he shouldn't worry, right?"

"Yeah, I told him he'd didn't need to worry because the law will be the one smuggling the booze," Melvin said, shaking his head. "Of course I didn't tell him. Do I look stupid, Oscar?"

"Only on certain days, Mel," Oscar said. "Well, if he stays nervous, just tell that I'm the only lawman around, and I'm way too busy to worry about a few cases of whiskey. And if he's worried about the Coast Guard or Border Patrol sticking their nose where it doesn't belong, just remind him that the closest station is thirty miles upriver on Lake Ontario. I can't even remember the last time I saw one of their boats down here."

"Okay," Melvin said, nodding. "He wants thirty bucks a case."

"Thirty bucks?"

"He's not stupid, Oscar," Melvin said. "He knows what's going to happen as soon as that law gets passed. Just wait and see. A lot of people are going to be jumping into the booze business around here."

"Not while I'm top cop around here they won't," Oscar said, crushing out his cigar. "What do you think we'll be able to sell it for over here?"

"Probably fifty bucks a case. Maybe more after a bit of time passes."

"That's a tidy little profit," Oscar said. "Too bad all of yours might be going to pay this guy Razner the juice on the six grand."

"That's for reminding me. I need to get my hands on some money in a hurry," Melvin said.

"How do you plan on doing that?"

"I thought I might steal it."

"Sounds like a good plan," Oscar said, getting up out of his chair. "Now, if you'll excuse me, I need to get back to protecting the lives and property of our fellow citizens."

# Milo Builds a Barn

**Milo listened closely** as Ruby Crankovitch continued
to offer possible solutions to the long list of problems he was
trying to solve. His head was starting to hurt from trying to keep
track of everything he needed to get done, and he was making
every effort to stay focused. But his attention span was
challenged every time the wind whipped her thin cotton dress
tight against the back of her legs. Milo continued to nod as she
talked and gestured and did his best not to stare.

"Look, Milo," Ruby said. "It doesn't need to be that big.
And if we tuck it further back in the trees, it's going to help keep
the place out of the wind and a bit warmer during the winter."

"But if we go that small, Ruby, where the heck are we going
to put all the corn and sugar?" Milo said, frowning at the
drawing she was holding.

"We'll just take the roofline up about five feet, then we'll
add a platform running the length inside we can use for storage.
We'll build it about ten feet off the ground, and we can even put
in some sort of trough from the platform to the floor. All Billy
will need to do is shovel it on. If we get the angle right, the corn
will slide right down into the cooker. And we can build a

platform in this corner up off the ground where we can stack the sugar."

"Why off the ground?"

"To help deal with the field mice primarily. It'll be the dead of winter, and every critter on the island will be trying to get inside where it's nice and warm."

"It's always something isn't it?" Milo said, frowning.

Ruby laughed as Milo continued to study the drawing. Then he looked around at the stand of trees Ruby was talking about and nodded.

"I think you're right," Milo said. "That would work."

"And it'll save us at least a couple weeks building the thing," she said, shivering as a gust of wind bore into them. "I should have worn something warmer than this dress."

Milo flinched when she pushed her back and legs tight against him as she turned around to watch Billy heading their way.

"You probably shouldn't do that, Ruby," Milo said, taking a deep breath.

"It's just a matter of time, Milo," she said, not turning around. "But take all you need."

"You need to focus on making sure Billy stays happy."

"Take a look at him. Doesn't he look happy to you?"

Milo watched Billy approach and had to agree that he did appear to be quite content. As he got closer, Ruby took a small step forward, and Milo relaxed.

"Well, you were right, Ruby," Billy said. "If we pull the boat in on the other side, I think we'll be able to use some sort of pulley to hoist all the equipment and supplies up. It would sure beat trying to carry it all up that hill."

"I knew it would work," Ruby said.

"That's the thing you'll learn about my wife, Milo. Once she sets her mind to something, there ain't much you can do to change it."

"I'm beginning to see that, Billy," Milo said. "We were just talking about the barn."

"What about it?" Billy said.

"We're going to make it a bit smaller but raise the roof. And we're going to move it back inside the tree line a bit," Milo said.

"As long as I got room to cook, it don't matter to me," he said, shrugging. "But make sure you leave enough room for all the firewood."

"Firewood?" Ruby said.

"Uh, yeah, Ruby," Billy said. "I'm going to need a fire if you're expecting me to be able to cook."

"Billy, you can't use an open flame fire for this," Ruby said.

"Why not?" he said, frowning at his wife.

"Because you're going to be throwing off more fumes than you can shake a stick at. Cooking six hundred gallons is a whole lot different than cooking five."

"She's right, Billy," Milo said. "If that still ever exploded, they'd be picking pieces of you out of the River."

"What am I gonna cook with then?"

"Coal," Ruby said. "And you're going to burn it inside a cast iron stove with the door shut tight. All the time, every time. Do you understand, Billy?"

"Don't talk to me like I'm a kid," Billy snapped. "I hate it when you do that, Ruby."

"And remember to keep the place clean. Don't leave any corn or sugar lying around out in the open. That would be an invitation for everything with four legs to come inside. You need to be paying close attention to everything you're doing all the time."

"I said stop it, Ruby," Billy snapped. "Stop nagging and picking at me."

Ruby softened and gave him a sisterly hug.

"I just don't want you blowing yourself up, Billy. I want you safe and sound."

"Okay. I want the same thing. But try to go easy on me, huh?" Billy said, moving in for a kiss that Ruby half-heartedly returned. "Say, Milo, I've been wondering about something for a while now."

"Only one thing? Consider yourself a lucky man, Billy."

"What?"

"Nothing," Milo said. "What's on your mind?"

"Cooking during the winter," Billy said.

"What about it?"

"Well, for a couple of things, all the snow and ice."

"We're going to insulate the barn the best we can," Milo said. "And the coal stove I've got on order is going to do a great job keeping the inside of the barn nice and toasty. Don't worry, it'll be more than warm enough for fermentation."

"Yeah, that's great, Milo," Billy said, scratching his head. "But I was thinking more about me."

"What about you?"

"I get the fact that I'll be able to get the boat in and out of here a lot of the time during the early winter. But when the ice moves in, how am I supposed to get over here to cook? And then get back home?"

Milo had been wondering when Billy would finally put two and two together and ask the question.

"Well, I guess you'll just have to stay here on the island when the weather gets real bad, right?"

"But I could end up stuck here for weeks, Milo," Billy said. "That's a lot of time for us to be away from the farm."

"Us? No, Billy, I'll need to stay at the farm," Ruby said. "Given all my responsibilities, I can't run the risk of getting stuck over here."

"And I can?" Billy said, staring at her.

"You're the cooker, Billy," Ruby said, again sliding into her maternal tone. "That's your sole job."

"And just think about all the inventory you'll be able to build up over the winter," Milo said.

"Yes, that's a lot of money just waiting to be made, Billy," Ruby said, placing a hand on his shoulder.

"But what would I do over here all by myself?"

"Read. Maybe take up a hobby," Milo said, shrugging.

"Read? Read what?" Billy said, almost spitting the words out.

"Books," Milo said. "You can borrow some of mine."

Billy made a face like he'd swallowed a lemon.

"Or write long love letters to Ruby telling her how much you miss her," Milo said.

"Gee, that sounds like a lot of work," Billy said, now frowning. "I guess I could experiment with some new shine recipes."

"There you go," Milo said. "Say, why don't you head down to the dock and give Birdie a hand bringing up the supplies? I think he's brought lunch as well. And help him out on the way up. He's still struggling with walking up that incline."

They watched him head off, and Milo felt another gust of wind and snuck a quick glance at Ruby who was hugging herself as she stared at her husband making his way through the thick grass.

"Can I ask you a question, Ruby?"

"Of course, Milo," she said, still facing away from him.

"How on earth did you end up marrying Billy?"

"At the time, he was my only option," she whispered.

"Your only option to get out of where you were?"

"Yes," she said, inching closer until her back was pressed against him.

"Do you ever regret it?"

"Only on most days," she said, gently scratching the back of his hand with her fingernails. "In fact, I was just about to leave him when you happened to show up. You saw the life we were living. If you can call that living."

"Yeah, I get that. But you're staying, right?"

"You couldn't get rid of me if you tried, Milo. You rescued me, maybe even saved my life. You're like my Prince Charming. And now you're going to make me a rich woman," Ruby said, squeezing his thigh. "I have every intention of repaying you."

"Ruby, we need to make sure that Billy stays happy," Milo said.

"Or at least, keeps cooking."

"Yes. At a minimum."

"You let me worry about Billy, Milo," she said, arching her back. "Before long, I expect you'll be spending most of your time making sure I stay happy. Oh, shoot. I think a bug got me. Scratch my back, Milo."

Milo tentatively reached his hand out and gently scratched her shoulder.

"Is that my back, Milo?"

"Technically, probably not."

"Lower, Milo."

Milo complied.

"Lower."

Milo cleared his throat but again followed her instructions.

"You're getting closer, Milo. Lower."

Milo stopped scratching for a moment and glanced down.

"I think I just ran out of back."

"Yes, you have," she whispered into the wind. "Lower."

Milo exhaled as his hand resumed its exploration.

"Right there."

"That's not your back."

"I know. But that's where it itches. I'm going to need it a bit harder, Milo."

"I don't think that's possible, Ruby."

# Oscar Plays a Little Hyde and Seek

**Milo took a sip of beer** and waved off Tom Collins offer of a third shot of Midnight Miracle.

"You sure, Milo?" Tom Collins said. "I'm about out of it. It might be your last chance to get a taste for a while."

"I'm sure I'll manage," Milo said, giving him a big smile. Then he frowned into his beer glass.

"You're in an odd mood tonight, Milo," Tom said. "You seem really happy most of the time, but then you turn… perplexed. Yeah, that's the word I'm looking for."

"Yes, I guess I am perplexed," Milo said. "On second thought, maybe I will have one more."

"It's a woman, right?" Tom said, carefully pouring the shot.

"Oh, yeah. It's a woman all right," Milo said, scratching his stubble.

The sound reminded him of sandpaper on wood, and he remembered he needed to check in with Frank Slack to get an update on how the new boat was coming along. Then his thoughts went right back to the sight of Ruby's windblown dress wrapped tight around her legs.

"Let me ask you something, Tom. Have you ever been forced to deal with a woman who won't take no for an answer and is doing everything in her power to make you do something you probably shouldn't even be thinking about?"

"Not unless I was holding a stack of fives in my hand," Tom said, laughing. "Let me give you a piece of advice my daddy always gave me."

"Getting advice from a bartender? Now there's a novel idea," Milo said, tossing back the shot.

"Well, I know you don't just come in here to drink," Tom said, grinning. "My daddy always used to say that it's a lot easier to beg for forgiveness than it is to ask for permission."

"That's actually pretty good advice," Milo said, nodding. "Did it work for your daddy?"

"Yeah, for a while. Then he got shot climbing out our neighbor's bedroom window. So, I'd have to say the results were mixed."

The phone in the bar rang, and Tom Collins answered it before the second ring. He listened, then put his hand over the mouthpiece and looked at Milo.

"It's for you," Tom said.

Milo shrugged and took the phone from him.

"This is Milo Razner," Milo said, gesturing for another beer. "Oh, hello, Senator. How are you?"

Milo watched Tom stop in his tracks and turn when he heard who was on the other end of the line.

"Yes, I agree," Milo said. "I can't see any chance of it not passing either...What do I think? I think it's downright un-American, but you tell me, you're the Senator...No, sir, I'm done doing that. I appreciate the offer, but I've already started a new chapter up here...I'm a dairy farmer now...Yes, you heard right...I'm glad you find that funny, and, yes, they do need to be milked twice a day...Uh-huh...Yes, I know that. But don't worry, Senator, I won't forget you or all that you've done for me. Now, if you'll excuse me, I have some pressing business to attend to. Why don't you make yourself useful and go vote on something? Good day, Senator."

Milo handed the phone back to Tom and took a sip of beer. He waited for a question, but all he got from Tom Collins was a raised eyebrow.

"That was Senator Miller," Milo said. "I believe he's one of yours."

"He is. Although I like to blame all the people in New York who actually voted for him. Can I ask why he's calling you?"

"I used to do some work for him," Milo said, casually shrugging it off.

"Doing what?"

"A little of this, a whole lot of that. You know how it goes."

"No, I can't say that I do, Milo."

"Prior life. It's not important," Milo said. "It's strange, but I thought I heard somebody breathing on the other end of the line."

"Oh, that would be Violet," Tom said, drying a glass. "Violet Hollman. She operates the phone system. And she loves listening in on other people's calls."

"You're kidding, right?"

"No, I'm not. We've got a party-line system up here, and Violet considers it part of her job to keep her ears open about what's going on around town."

"And everyone just tolerates the intrusion?" Milo said, frowning.

"Hey, how else are we gonna stay current with what's happening?" Tom said, laughing. "But if you ever want to start a good rumor, Violet's your girl."

"I'll try to remember that," Milo said, starting to feel the effects of the third shot. "Hey, I almost forgot. I want to talk to you about something."

"Save it for later," Tom said, his eyes focused the entrance to the bar. "Asshole alert."

Milo did a half-turn in his chair and saw the man heading his way walking like he thought he owned the joint. It appeared he hadn't bathed in a week, and he walked slowly, taking in the room to see who was there, but also taking his time just so people wouldn't miss the fact that he'd arrived. The man was average height, at best, and Milo assumed there was a receding hairline hidden under the hat. And his eyes were beady and sunk back in their sockets making him look like a fat owl. But the main impression Milo was left with was that the guy, despite rapidly going to seed, had a very high opinion of himself. He stopped right next to Milo and grinned at Tom.

"Good evening, Oscar," Tom said. "What can I get you?"

"Beer. And a shot of Midnight Miracle," the man said, continuing to ignore Milo.

"Sorry. I'm fresh out of Miracle," Tom said, glancing at Milo.

"Then make it a whiskey."

The man turned and leaned with his back against the bar as he glanced around.

"A little chilly today, huh?" the man said, still not looking at Milo.

"Actually, what got most of my attention today was the wind," Milo said, taking a sip of beer.

"Yeah, we get all sorts of things that blow in and out of here," the man said. "They can be most annoying."

"Do you always have trouble making small talk, or are you the local weatherman?" Milo said, deciding to go straight for a little jab.

The man turned and finally acknowledged Milo's presence with a nasty glare.

"You don't know who I am? You must be new in town."

"I don't. And I am," Milo said, glancing up at him and extending his hand. "Milo Razner."

"Oscar Hyde," he said, ignoring Milo's offer of a handshake.

"Hide? As in, that's what you like to do at the first sign of trouble?" Milo said, reaching for a handful of peanuts.

"No, you won't catch me hiding from trouble, Mr. Razner. In my line of work, it's just the opposite."

"That usually means you're either a criminal or a cop," Milo said, casually dropping a peanut shell into a bowl. "Probably a little of both."

Tom Collins set Oscar's drinks down in front of him. Oscar tossed the shot back, took a long, slow pull from his beer, then wiped his mouth with the back of his hand and stared at Milo.

"Milo Razner, huh? You know, I was just talking with somebody this morning, and your name came up."

"You're going to have to be more specific. I've met a lot of people since I got here. It's a friendly town."

"Most times," Oscar said, turning back around and placing both elbows on the bar. "Unless we're dealing with an outsider we don't like."

"I'm just a dairy farmer trying to make a living, Chief Hyde," Milo said, then paused to look over at the man who continued to glare at him. "Is that the correct moniker to use? What should I call you? Chief? Sheriff? Or maybe you prefer Bodhisattva."

"What?" Oscar said, his glare turning into a confused frown.

"It's a Buddhist term for an enlightened being. But I guess if I have to explain it, I probably shouldn't be calling you that. Right, *Chief?*"

Despite the fact his face was turning beet red and didn't find Milo funny in the least, he gave Milo a soft chuckle.

"Melvin said you were somebody who considered himself to be a smart guy," Oscar said, nodding at Tom and pointing at his empty shot glass.

"Well, if anybody would understand that particular character trait, it would be Melvin."

"Are you bad mouthing a friend of mine?"

"Not at all. Despite his considerable shortcomings, I'm quite fond of Melvin."

"Especially now that he owes you money, right?"

"No, I liked Melvin just fine before that," Milo said, taking another sip of beer. "Chief Hyde, is there a point to this conversation? Or are you just here to do a little dick waving?"

Oscar recoiled like he'd been slapped, then quickly recovered. A tight smile formed on his thin lips. "You need to watch your step, Mr. Razner." He tossed back his fresh shot and drained what was left of his beer.

"I will certainly be doing that. And I hope you take some of your own sage advice. From what I hear, between your nonstop drinking and some of your other pursuits, the people who hired you are getting a bit worried that you're stepping out of line all over the place. And based on what I see, it doesn't look like you make much of an effort to clean yourself up after you make a mess."

Oscar leaned closer and whispered into Milo's ear.

"I'm going to enjoy making a mess of you, Mr. Razner."

"Chief Hyde," Milo said, just loud enough for others to hear. "I've just invested thousands of dollars of my own hard earned money in this town and have already provided six people with new jobs. And I have plans to hire a whole lot more. As someone who makes their living as a suckling on the public sector teat, maybe that doesn't mean much to you. But to the people who are doing everything they can to make this a viable place to live and raise their families, trust me, it means a lot. And whenever you'd like to have that conversation with those individuals, just let me know the time and place."

"I ain't talking about having a conversation," Oscar said.

"Oh, I see," Milo said, nodding. "You want to settle this in a *man to man* kind of fashion."

"Yeah, I do. It's nice to see that you're finally getting my drift."

"Are you suggesting that we do some sort of shootout at high noon, or should I just wait for you to shoot me in the back?"

"The choice is all yours, Mr. Razner," Oscar said through a low growl.

"Let me think on it a bit, and I'll let you know. Now, if you don't mind my asking, if you plan on staying any longer, could you at least move downwind?"

Oscar glared at Milo, then tossed two dollars on the bar. He nodded goodbye to Tom and slowly strolled out of the bar. Milo touched his empty shot glass, and Tom poured a shot of Midnight Miracle.

"Does he always waddle like a duck, or only when he's drunk?" Milo said.

"He's always drunk," Tom said. "And you might want to be careful with him."

"Don't worry about him. He's just a man who thinks he's doing his job but has obviously lost his way," Milo said, holding the shot glass up to the light.

"When it comes to Hyde, it's usually his way or the highway."

"Well, there's nothing I like about his way, and I have no plans to leave. But I'm sure Chief Hyde and I will eventually reach some sort of compromise. Or at least a mutual understanding."

"You like poking the bear, don't you, Milo?"

"Only if the bear deserves it, Tom. Now, as I was saying earlier, I need to talk with you."

"About what?"

"A business opportunity. What else?"

"What do you have in mind?" Tom said, leaning forward on the bar.

"How would you feel about working in Rockport?"

"Rockport? Doing what?"

"At first, learning, primarily. After that, I'll be offering you some very rapid advancement. But for now, I need to ask you a question."

"Sure. Shoot."

"What do you know about selling furniture?"

# The Wets Throw a Party

**When Congress overrode** President Wilson's veto in late October, Milo celebrated briefly with Beulah Peppin then ramped his activities up to a fever pitch. And by the time the calendar had rolled over into January, he was exhausted, but excited and chomping at the bit to get rolling. Milo was also more than ready to start replenishing his cash reserves.

After the barn was finished in November, and six months of cooking supplies had been brought to the island and stored, Milo, along with Billy, Birdie, and Tom Collins had disassembled both of Clint Farwell's stills and transported them to the island in the dead of night. The stills were heavy and cumbersome, but using the pulley system Ruby had come up with, they eventually managed to get them up the hill and into the barn where Billy went to work getting them ready.

As soon as he was comfortable with the progress being made on that side of his operation, Milo turned his attention to the dairy farm that, to his considerable surprise, was already close to breaking even. Ruby, displaying a work ethic that surprised and delighted him, had acquired fifty more cows, hired three more people to work the farm, and bought a brand new delivery truck with *Razner's Dairy* emblazoned on the side. But per his instructions, she left the hiring of the two people who'd be driving the truck to Milo.

Winter had arrived late, and the weather stayed manageable. As such, Billy, who'd started cooking in late November, was still able to make his way back and forth across the River on most days as long as he was careful and made the trip during the daylight hours. But the temperatures had stayed well below freezing the past week, and the ice along the shoreline was beginning to thicken and make its way further out into the River.

Milo had continued to successfully fight off Ruby's advances, but his protests were growing weaker by the day, and he was starting to obsess on the woman and ready to concede. And Milo, although he was no fan of winter weather, had to admit he was looking forward to an extended cold spell that would keep Billy preoccupied with the two things Milo wanted him doing more than anything; being stuck on the island with nothing to do but cook, and away from the farm.

He woke up from his afternoon nap around two, reluctantly leaving his dream of Ruby taking a milk bath, and opened his eyes to see Beulah Peppin staring back at him from the adjacent pillow. He smiled at her and stretched his arms over his head.

"I needed that," Milo said. "You wore me out, Miss Peppin."

"I couldn't help it. We won't be seeing each other for a while," Beulah said. "You had the biggest smile on your face. It looked like you were dreaming."

"Yes, I was," Milo said, grinning. "I was dreaming about you lying right in the middle of a pile of hundred dollar bills."

"Milo, I'd call you a filthy rotten liar if you weren't so good at it," she said, laughing as she lit a cigarette. "Who's going to be there tonight?"

"Probably everybody who doesn't know where their next drink is coming from," Milo said, accepting the lit cigarette from her. "What time is your party starting?"

"Around seven," Beulah said, climbing out of bed. "You should stop by."

"To have tea and crumpets with all the Temperance folks who helped make our new enterprise possible?" Milo said. "Thanks, but no. I'll leave it to you to thank them on my behalf."

"I can't believe we're this close. It's taken forever to get here," she said, sliding into her robe.

"It has. But everything has gone to plan," Milo said.

"You're welcome."

"We make a good team, Miss Peppin. I'm going to miss having you around," Milo said. "But I promise to get down there as often as I can."

"I hope you will," she whispered as she stared up at the ceiling. "How long will it take before we're able to walk away from all of it, Milo?"

"That all depends. How much money do you want to make before we call it quits?"

"Millions, Milo. I want to make millions."

"Well, since it's taken the government all these years to ban booze, I reckon it'll take them at least ten more before they get around to repealing it. And if we're not rich by then, we don't deserve to be in this business in the first place."

"Do you ever get scared about what might happen to us, Milo?"

"I'm doing my best not to. Don't worry, Beulah, we'll be fine," he said, trying to relieve her concern about the possibility of getting shot or going to prison, but thinking about Ruby Crankovitch.

Milo climbed out of bed, dressed, then gave Beulah a long kiss goodbye and headed back to his room at the Crossley to get ready for the party people were calling the Goodbye Booze Bash. Stretched out in a hot bath with a glass of whiskey over ice, he made a mental list of all the people he needed to talk with that night. Unable to turn his mind off after he finished, he focused on Ruby and eventually drifted off and didn't wake until the water was cold.

He made his way downstairs around eight feeling refreshed and looking forward to having some fun. The main ballroom was crowded, and a lot of the revelers were already slurring and staggering as they laughed and flirted with everyone who came within earshot. It was as if some of them thought, if they got drunk enough, it might last them through Prohibition.

"Are you still sure you don't want to sell locally?" Tom Collins said, approaching Milo from behind. "I'm seeing a lot of potential customers."

"Hey, Tom," Milo said, extending his hand. "No, we won't be selling around here. And feel free to remind everyone on the payroll that if I see an ounce of our stuff within fifty miles, I'll personally take them for a nice long swim."

"Got it," Tom said. "But you gotta admit, it is tempting."

"Just keep taking the long view, Tom, and you'll be fine," Milo said, taking the room in. "I'm glad you made it over."

"This is the last time for a while," Tom said. "It's getting too dangerous out there. I just missed hitting a chunk of ice earlier that would have sunk my boat. So I'll be staying in Rockport through the rest of the winter. Clint's all alone in that big house, so I'm renting a room from him."

"Good call," Milo said, nodding. "You got a cover story worked up in case people start wondering what you're doing there?"

"I'm there to help my Uncle Clint run his furniture store. After all, he's getting up in years."

"That'll work. But try to stay vague on the specifics," Milo said. "How's Clint doing?"

"He's starting to get a real spring back in his step," Tom said. "And he can't wait to get going. Yesterday, I had a sample of what he's been working on."

"And?" Milo said, his interest piqued.

"You're gonna like it," Tom said. "It'll never be mistaken for a ten-year-aged blend, but nothing else ever is, right?"

"Tell Clint not to get greedy when he's cutting the Miracle," Milo said. "We want people liking it and coming back for more."

"Oh, they'll be coming back," Tom said. "It's good."

"When you get a chance, start experimenting with something the women might prefer. Maybe one of those concoctions that got you your nickname. But stick with something that grows around here. Something that won't cost us a fortune to make."

"Apples."

"Yeah, that'll work. There's no hurry, but see what you can come with and maybe next fall we'll make a big apple buy."

"You got it," Tom said, glancing around. "Good party. You gonna get drunk tonight?"

Milo spotted Billy and Ruby Crankovitch standing off to one side of the room. Ruby had her hair up and was wearing a new dress that clung to her in all the right places. Milo's mind left the business world and started racing off in a completely different direction.

"No, I better not," Milo said.

**Oscar Hyde** placed an elbow on the bar then propped his head in his hand. Melvin English watched then laughed.

"You out already?" Melvin said. "It's not even nine o'clock."

"I started early. As soon as I got back from Rockport with the five cases," Oscar said.

"Try talking a little louder," Melvin whispered violently. "Please tell me you didn't open one of the cases."

"It was only one bottle, Mel. Relax. And I needed to make sure it's good stuff. Quality control and all that."

"How about we actually get this thing off the ground before you start drinking all the profits?"

"Relax, Mel," Oscar said, standing upright to glance around the room.

Melvin shook his head then stared at his business partner.

"Hey, wait a minute. We were going to take my boat on the first run and go together so we could map out the best route. Don't tell me you used the police boat."

"Why not? I use the boat all the time to go over there," Oscar said, doing his best to focus.

"Not to run illegal booze," Melvin whispered.

"It wasn't illegal this afternoon," Oscar said with a shrug.

"Unbelievable. Where's the booze?"

"I already unloaded it."

"What? Now, why did you do that?"

"Because Prohibition starts tomorrow in case you haven't noticed."

"How much did you get for it?"

"Thirty-five a case," Oscar said.

"That's it?"

"Five bucks a case profit. That's not a bad start."

"That's a terrible start, Oscar. And you know it. All you had to do was wait for a few weeks until people started running out. So, where's my cut?"

"I thought we'd reinvest," Oscar said, grabbing a fresh drink. "We'll head back over as soon as the weather warms up."

"You're talking about March, Oscar," Melvin said.

"Then I guess we're lucky I got over there today, don't you think?"

"What I think is that you should quit drinking, Oscar."

"You too, Melvin? You're starting to sound just like somebody from the government."

"No matter where it comes from, it's good advice. And I think you should take it, Oscar. Who'd you sell the five cases to?"

Oscar glanced around then located the man he was looking for. He nodded in the man's general direction then tossed back another shot of whiskey.

"Him. The guy talking with Razner and that bartender."

**Milo studied** the man called Willy Lawless as he continued to explain the situation and outline his plans for the immediate future. Milo liked the way the guy listened carefully to what he was saying, and he seemed to get things the first time. And although Milo hadn't worked with him before, Willy came highly recommended as someone who could carry his own weight and play a specific character when necessary. The role Milo had him playing at the moment was someone with deep pockets and on the prowl to buy a lot of bootleg liquor.

"I get what you want me to do, Mr. Razner," Willy said, frowning. "But I'm getting stuck on the why."

"First of all, Willy," Milo said. "This is a party, so there's no frowning allowed. The last thing we want is anybody thinking we're talking business. And we sure don't want anyone getting the impression that we're working *together*. So, lighten up and have a laugh. We're just three guys enjoying the party, having a couple of drinks, and getting to know each other."

Willy grinned and slapped Milo on the back, then shared a laugh with Tom Collins.

"The Senator sure was right," Willy said, laughing. "You do work in mysterious ways."

"That's much better," Milo said. "Look, I understand what I'm asking you to do sounds a bit strange."

"But you have your reasons, right?" Willy said.

"Of course I have my reasons," Milo said, annoyed but managing to force a smile. "Just keep buying all the booze those two get their hands on until I tell you to stop."

"And just store it in the house?" Willy said.

"Yes. And I don't want to see a drop of it anywhere in town. Just store it in the second bedroom for now. Beulah's leaving in the morning, so bring the five cases in with the rest of your stuff you're moving in. When that bedroom fills up, we'll figure out where to put the rest of it."

"I'm a little confused too, Milo," Tom said. "We're going to buy all of Hyde's booze and just sit on it?"

"For now, yes," Milo said. "But when the law eventually comes calling, I have a relocation plan all worked out."

"But Hyde is the law," Tom said.

"I'm talking about Federal law officers," Milo said.

"But there aren't any Federal officers around here dealing with booze," Tom said.

"There will be, Tom. Again, you have to start taking the long view."

"And you're going to keep paying thirty-five a case?" Willy said.

"Yes, for now. But don't worry, we'll get all of our investment back," Milo said.

"How are you going to do that?" Willy said, almost frowning but remembering to smile at the last second.

"We're going to steal it," Milo said.

"Gee, I don't know, Mr. Razner. I've never robbed a bank before," Willy said.

"Relax, Willy. I wouldn't ask you to do anything like that. Besides, robbing banks is for amateurs. Hyde and English won't be able to put that money in the bank. He's a low paid cop, and even he's not stupid enough to do that. It would raise too many questions. He'll hide it somewhere in his house."

"Or maybe put it in Melvin's safe?" Tom said.

"Oh, I doubt that," Milo said.

"It sounds like an awful lot of work, Mr. Razner," Willy said. "Wouldn't it be easier to just shoot him?"

"Of course it would be easier," Milo said, grinning. "But I hate killing people. Unless it's the only option available."

"Or unless they really piss you off," Tom said, laughing.

"Yeah, there is that," Milo said. "Besides, doing it my way is going to be a whole lot more fun."

**Ruby Crankovitch** left her husband chatting with a couple of acquaintances as soon as she spotted Milo standing by himself staring through one of the picture windows that looked out over the River. She sidled up quietly and brushed against him.

"Hello, Ruby," Milo said, not turning around. "You look beautiful this evening."

"And you're just looking at my reflection in the window," she said. "Why don't you turn around and get a good look at the real thing?"

"I saw you earlier when you first came in."

"You were waiting for me to get here, weren't you, Milo?"

"Yes, Ruby. I was."

"That's so sweet. I couldn't wait to see you either. But what I really can't wait for is tomorrow morning."

"Is Billy ready to go?"

"He's not happy about it, but I think I finally convinced him. You want to know how I did it?"

"No, that's okay. I'll just use my imagination."

"After that, I spent the rest of the day making sure the boat was packed with everything he'll need. He's got at least two months of food and supplies."

"Two months?" Milo whispered.

"Yes. Just think about where we'll be in two months."

"In a whole lot of trouble?"

Ruby laughed and took a step forward until she was standing next to Milo. They both stared out at the moonlight that was shimmering off the water.

"I can't imagine how cold that water must be," Milo said. "It's going to be hard next winter trying to get product back and forth without killing ourselves. Remind me to talk with Frank Slack at some point."

"Your brain never stops working does it, Milo?"

"Lately, it seems to head off in a different direction whenever it pleases."

"I wouldn't worry about it, Milo. I'm sure it's just a question of blood flow. And speaking of that, is there any chance we could slip upstairs to your room? I'd love to show you the rest of my outfit."

"Not a chance in hell, Ruby," Milo said, forcing himself to keep talking to the window.

"Then dinner. Tomorrow night. Let's say, around seven?"

"Okay. I'll be there. What are we having?"

"Does it matter?"

"I seriously doubt it."

"Come hungry, Milo."


**Tom Collins** ordered another beer then stood with his back to the bar watching the party that was turning more raucous by the minute. People were dancing and bouncing to fiddle and banjo, and the room was a hot, sweaty mess as the song ended, then people chanted a toast to the end of alcohol and the band immediately ramped back up.

Good party, Tom thought, nodding to himself. Deciding only one thing would make it better, Tom sharpened his focus and looked around the room with purpose. He spotted a young woman he recognized standing off by herself, and Tom wondered if he had the energy for the requisite amount of dancing and conversation it would take. Before he could make up his mind, he noticed Oscar Hyde and Melvin English heading his way. Unable to escape without appearing rude, Tom smiled and nodded as they approached.

"Tom Collins," Oscar said with a heavy slur. "My favorite bartender. The Miracle Man."

"Evening, Oscar," Tom said. "Hey, Melvin."

"Where have you been, Tom?" Melvin said. "I haven't seen you around in a couple of weeks."

"I'm over at Rockport at the moment. I decided to give up bartending and do something a little different."

"I was just in Rockport today," Oscar said, more to himself than anyone else.

"Nobody cares, Oscar," Melvin snapped, then focused on Tom. "What are you doing for work over there?"

"Selling furniture."

"Furniture?" Oscar said. "Well, I hope you brought a couch with you tonight because I could sure use one right about now."

Oscar found his comment funny, and he roared and slapped the bar with a hand.

"Did you get let go here because of the new law?" Melvin said.

"No, they actually wanted me to stay and tend bar in the speakeasy they're putting in behind that wall over there," Tom said. "But if it gets raided, I'm afraid the bartender will be the first one they arrest."

"Who's gonna raid it?" Oscar said, frowning. "They ain't gonna be hurting anybody."

"Yeah, you're probably right, Chief," Tom said, glancing at Melvin.

"Can you make any money selling furniture?" Melvin said.

"It's a little slow at the moment, but I'm expecting things to pick up soon," Tom said, smiling.

"Well, if you ever need to make a little extra cash, just let me know," Melvin said. "Oscar and I are starting a little operation on the side you might find interesting. And we'll be needing some extra hands at some point."

"You don't say?" Tom said. "Is it legal?"

"Of course, it's legal," Oscar said, swaying back and forth as he tried to focus. "As long as I say it is."

# Billy Tells a Bedtime Story

**Deciding he needed sleep** more than another drink, Milo slipped away from the party and headed upstairs to his room. He was just about ready for bed when he heard a soft knock on the door. Afraid of who he might find standing on the other side, he peered through the peephole and relaxed when he saw the familiar face. He opened the door and smiled.

"Hey, Billy. What brings you up here at this time of night?"

"I just wanted to have a quick word with you, Mr. Razner."

"Sure. Come on in. And I wish you'd call me Milo."

Milo closed the door and gestured at a chair. Billy sat down, removed a glass jar from his coat and placed it on the coffee table in front of him.

"Is that some of the new stuff?" Milo said, staring at the jar.

"It's the first pull from the first batch," Billy said. "I thought it only right that you should have the first taste. Well, the second one actually. I had to do some tasting of my own just to make sure the quality is there."

"Sure, I get that. And?"

"It's really good, Mr. Razner. A hundred and sixty proof, just like you asked for. I was a bit worried about cooking in big batches like we're doing, but it's gonna work out fine."

Milo held the jar up to the light then poured. He handed one to Billy and clinked glasses.

"To us," Milo said, downing his. "Wow. Billy, you are a genius."

"Thanks. I appreciate that. And I thought you'd want to know that I've been able to keep the two to one ratio going. And I've got three batches in inventory already and a new one coming every week just like we talked about. By the time the ice goes out, I think we'll be sitting on close to three thousand gallons."

"I'm glad to hear that, Billy," Milo said, fighting off the urge to do some quick math in his head. "Ruby says you're a little reluctant to spend that much time alone on the island."

"At first, maybe," Billy said. "But I'm actually looking forward to it."

"Really? I have to say I'm surprised to hear that."

"I've been telling Ruby I don't want to go because that's the only way I'm able to…get close to her these days. If you get my drift."

"No, I think you've officially lost me, Billy."

"The only time Ruby will let me touch her these days is when she needs to get me to do something. She thinks lying down with me is the only way I'll agree to do what she wants. And I let her think that."

"Because you love lying down with her, right?"

"It's the only thing I love about being with Ruby," he said. "The rest of the time she makes me feel like the dumbest person walking the earth. It's like I'm not worthy of even breathing the same air as her."

"Really?"

"You must have seen it, Mr. Razner. She's always on my case about something and talking down to me. I can't take it anymore. Two months away from her is going to seem like a vacation. But I will miss the lying down part."

"Yes, I imagine you will," Milo said, stunned by the revelation. "Why are you telling me all of this, Billy?"

"Despite my overall feelings about her and the way she treats me, I want to make sure she's okay while I'm gone. So, I was wondering if you'd be willing to keep an eye on her."

"Keep an eye on her?" Milo said.

"Look, Mr. Razner. I might not be the sharpest tool in the shed, but it's pretty clear that Ruby is very fond of you. And I know Ruby. Once she sets her mind on something, she doesn't stop until she gets what she wants. And you'd be doing me a favor if you'd be willing to go along with her."

"What on earth are you talking about, Billy?"

"As soon as I can, I need to get as far away from Ruby as I can," Billy said. "You see, I've met someone else. Somebody who likes me and treats me nice. With respect, if you know what I mean. And if Ruby is with somebody like you and happy about it, it will make it a lot easier for me to get out. You ain't seen it yet, but Ruby's got a mean streak a mile long when she's riled up."

"Let me get this straight. *You* want to get away from *her*?" Milo said, pouring two more shots of Miracle.

"As soon as possible," Billy said. "But I need to make sure Ruby's happy before I break the news to her. I'm afraid of what she might do if she isn't."

"I must say, this isn't a conversation I was expecting to be having tonight," Milo said. "Who's the other woman?"

"She's one of the girls from Fannie's place."

"You've fallen in love with a working girl?"

"Yeah, but that's just a temporary thing for her until we get enough money together," Billy said.

Milo's mind started racing, and he forced himself to stay calm as a thought popped into his head that sent chills down his spine.

"You're not talking about stopping cooking for me, are you, Billy?"

"No. Not at the moment. But, eventually, yeah."

"Well, let's not do anything rash. We're on the cusp of something really big here."

"I know we are. And you've been really good to me, Mr. Razner. But I'm going to be taking a lot of risks. If it's all the same to you, I'd like to keep our business arrangement profitable, but as short as possible."

"Tell you what, Billy. Let me talk with Ruby, and when you get back from the island, we'll sit down and talk it through. Maybe next winter, you'll be able to take your lady friend with you to the island just so you'll have some company."

"That might work. Let me think on it," Billy said.

"Well, where you're headed, you'll have lots of time to do that," Milo said. "I need to ask you something, Billy. You haven't said anything to this woman about what you're doing, have you?"

"No, sir. Not a word."

"That's good. Because if you did, it would carry some serious consequences."

"I know. That's why I haven't said anything. I told her I was heading south for a few months to tend to some family business. I hate lying to her, but I didn't see any other way around it."

"I wouldn't worry about it too much, Billy. In her line of work, I'm sure she's used to it."

"Yeah, she probably is. Another good reason for her to get out. Well, I guess I should get going," he said, standing and extending his hand. "Thanks, Mr. Razner. I'll see you soon."

"Be careful," Milo said. "And remember, no open flames while you're cooking."

"You sound like Ruby," he said, heading for the door. "Have fun, Mr. Razner. But be careful. If she gets her hooks in, you might never get loose."

"Thanks for the warning," Milo said. "Are you sure about this, Billy? I mean, she is your wife."

"Hopefully, not for much longer," he said, putting on his hat. "But I will miss the lying down part."

He left, and Milo closed the door behind him. Milo climbed into bed and stared up at the ceiling replaying the conversation. He removed the task of keeping Billy happy from Ruby's list and added it to his own. Regardless of whatever feelings he might develop for Ruby, keeping Billy cooking was the first priority. Milo also added having a chat with the new love of Billy's life to his list of things to do.

When he finally finished reviewing what he needed to take care of, Milo allowed his thoughts to drift back to Ruby. He found himself wondering just how far her hooks had already been set as well as how much further they'd sink in after tomorrow night's activities. Then his mind quieted, a condition Milo attributed to a change in blood flow, and he started to drift off with a surprisingly clear conscience. Just before he slipped into a deep sleep, another thought popped into his head.

Perhaps Tom Collin's daddy had it all wrong.

Maybe it wasn't always easier to beg for forgiveness than to ask for permission.

Especially when you didn't even have to ask in the first place.

# Episode 3

## Let the Games Begin

"If you really want to see how the criminal mind works, try banning something people enjoy."

Milo Razner

# It Might Take
# Some Getting Used To

**Milo walked along the dock** inside Frank Slack's place of business and fell in love at first sight for the second time since he'd arrived in town. But rather than the soft beauty and round curves of Ruby Crankovitch, this time it was the gleam of polished wood and skilled craftsmanship that made Milo's heart skip a beat.

"Frank, what have you done?" Milo said, kneeling down on the dock to run a loving hand along the top rail of the boat.

"It's beautiful, isn't it?" Frank said, nodding with pride.

"It's incredible," Milo said, climbing aboard.

"Take a look at this," Frank said, joining Milo on the boat. "You're gonna love it."

Frank, also paying homage to his creation, gently rubbed a hand along a raised section near the stern that was about three feet high. Then he knelt down and released two metal clasps that ran along the back. The hinged compartment opened, and Milo saw thirty circles that were about a foot in diameter and recessed into the wood floor.

"Your sketches worked perfect, Milo. All you need to do is set each container in one of the recesses, then close and lock the hatch. Your *milk* will be snug as a bug in a rug in there."

"And out of view of prying eyes," Milo said, nodding approvingly. "It's brilliant."

"Beautiful day for a boat ride."

Frank and Milo glanced up and saw Birdie standing on the dock and admiring the boat with a huge smile on his face.

"It certainly is, Birdie," Frank said, helping him climb down into the boat. "Okay, let's take her out for a spin. I've been waiting for this day for a long time."

Birdie made his way to the bow and sat down behind the wheel.

You ready, Milo?" Frank said.

"I'm chomping at the bit," Milo said, sitting down next to Birdie and softly clapping his hands.

Frank untied the lines and Birdie started the engine. A throaty roar filled the boathouse.

"Listen to that," Frank said. "She's purring like a kitten."

"If the kitten weighed eight hundred pounds, maybe," Milo said, suddenly feeling a bit edgy.

Birdie idled slowly out of the boathouse into the inner bay and slowly made his way to deep water. Early April had remained frigid, and the cloudy sky and wind weren't helping.

Milo buttoned his coat and hoped he'd dressed warm enough for what he anticipated would be a cold ride. But if the boat was troubled by the weather, it wasn't evident. To Milo, it seemed like the boat was anxious to show itself off, and the engine continued to emit a low rumble as it cut through the water with ease. Birdie glanced over at Frank who nodded, then Birdie opened the throttle just a touch. The boat responded, and the bow rose then planed over.

"What do you think so far, Milo?" Frank said, beaming like a proud papa.

"I can't believe you built this," Milo said.

"Thanks. It's the best thing I've ever done."

"You ready to see what this baby can do?" Birdie said, glancing back and forth at both of them.

"Go for it," Milo said, sitting forward on the edge of his seat.

"Now, I gotta warn you, Milo," Frank said. "This might take some getting used to."

Birdie turned into the main channel and pointed the boat downriver. Then he opened the throttle, and the engine roared to life. Milo, unprepared for the thrust, was thrown back against his seat as the boat accelerated and he felt a lump form in his throat. Birdie rolled and lit a cigarette with one hand on the wheel with a huge grin fixed on his face. Milo noticed, frowned, then yelled at Birdie over the roar of the engine.

"Shouldn't you have two hands on the wheel?"

"We're fine, Milo," Birdie shouted back. "This thing almost drives itself."

"Almost just isn't going to cut it, Birdie," Milo said, tightening his grip on the seat and hunkering down out of the torrent of cold air. "How fast are we going?"

"Forty-eight," Birdie said, glancing down at the speedometer. "You want to see what sixty feels like?"

"Sure, why not?" Milo yelled. "I can't imagine dying is going to feel any different than it would at this speed."

Birdie laughed and opened the throttle all the way. The boat seemed to be riding on top of the water, and it effortlessly cut through the small chop. Birdie turned away from the main channel and retraced the route they'd taken on their first trip to Rockport in Frank's work boat. As they entered a narrower portion of the River that was surrounded by various islands, Milo got a full appreciation of just how fast they were going as they sped past the shoreline in a blur. When the River opened up again, and they could see Rockport off in the distance, Birdie began to turn the wheel back and forth. The boat responded to his light touch, and it made a series of S's that left Milo's stomach in knots. When Birdie finally slowed the boat to a crawl, all three men were speechless.

"A boat like this is enough to make you believe in God," Birdie said as he lovingly ran his hands over the steering wheel.

"I don't know about believing, but I think I *saw* him when you made that last turn," Milo said, still trying to catch his breath. "How was this even possible, Frank?"

"It's just good engineering combined with a whole lot of power," Frank said, seeming somewhat surprised himself by what he'd just experienced. "I don't think you're going to have to worry about being caught, Milo."

"I'm not concerned about who might be sneaking up from behind," Milo said, still stunned by the experience. "It's the immovable objects in front of me I'm worried about."

"Relax, Milo. That's why you hired me," Birdie said. "You want to drive for a while? See if you can get a feel for how it handles?"

"No, that's okay. I think I'll wait a few days until I get used to traveling at the speed of light," Milo said.

"We've got company," Frank said, looking off into the distance. "That's Melvin's boat."

"Is that Oscar with him?" Birdie said.

"Yeah, our chief of police hard at work as usual," Frank said, waving to the approaching boat.

"They're probably coming back from Rockport with their five measly cases," Birdie said, laughing. Then he paused when he saw the looks Frank and Milo were giving him and explained himself. "Oscar told me the other night when I saw him at Fannie's. As usual, he was three sheets to the wind and couldn't stop yapping about how rich he was going to get."

"Well, between the way Oscar blabbers when he's drunk, and the way that Melvin, well, blabbers all the time, I don't like their chances," Frank said, shaking his head. "The Bumbling Bootleggers."

"From the way Oscar is scrambling to get something covered up with a tarp, I think you're right," Milo said. "But I have to give them credit. It takes a set of balls to be moving product in the middle of the day."

"No, what it takes is a brain to know better," Frank said, laughing.

"Oscar thinks he's untouchable," Birdie said. "That's probably a big mistake."

"I'm sure you're right," Milo said. "But let's not ruin this beautiful day by talking about Oscar."

"Doesn't the competition bother you?" Frank said.

"Not at all. I want as many small-timers running booze as possible. The more, the merrier," Milo said, waving to the two men as they slowed their boat.

"So when the government starts cracking down, they'll have some low hanging fruit within easy reach, huh?"

"Hey, they gotta have somebody they can catch, right?" Milo said, laughing. "Besides, the day I start worrying about competition from those two is the day I'll need to buy a rocking chair and sit on the porch reminiscing."

"Nice boat," Melvin called out as they drifted close.

"Thanks," Milo said. "This is her maiden voyage."

"That thing looks like a real gas-guzzler," Oscar said, eyeing the boat.

"You know, I was just thinking that, Bodhisattva," Milo said. "Everything and everybody is so damn thirsty these days. You guys been doing some shopping?"

"What?" Melvin said, immediately starting to fidget.

"I just noticed the tarp and figured you'd been shopping over in Rockport," Milo said.

"Yeah, well, we picked up some stuff we don't want to get wet," Melvin said.

"Smart," Milo said, nodding as he stared at the tarp that barely concealed what they were carrying.

"That sure is a beautiful boat, Milo," Melvin said.

"Yeah, Frank outdid himself," Milo said, smiling. "And with Birdie at the wheel, I figure I'll be safe and sound and not end up killing myself."

"Yeah, that would be a real tragedy," Oscar said. "Let's get going, Melvin. We got a meeting to get to."

"Oh, yeah. Sure, Oscar," Melvin said. "Enjoy your day, gentlemen."

He waved as he accelerated and the boat soon disappeared from view.

"You think they're selling their stuff locally?" Frank said.

"Beats me," Milo said, casually.

"It's warming up a bit. What do you say we head up the Canadian side for a while?" Birdie said, restarting the engine.

"As long as you promise to keep it under forty," Milo said. "Sixty is going to be a bit much for me for the time being."

"Okay, you got it, Milo," Birdie said with a tinge of disappointment.

"But it's sure nice to know it's there if we need it."

# Fannie

**Milo climbed the steps**, paused on the verandah to glance at the view, then stepped inside. Compared with other similar establishments he'd visited in the past, the place seemed smaller and a bit rundown. But it was furnished nicely, and the lighting was soft and not too revealing. But judging from the way several of the male visitors in the main room were hunkered down and keeping as low a profile as possible, the lighting, Milo conceded, might need just a touch of work.

He approached a counter that reminded him of one he'd see checking in to a hotel and noticed a bell identical to the one at Clint Raslo's furniture store. He tapped it once, and a woman soon appeared through a set of floor to ceiling curtains. She was bottle-blonde and past her prime, but Milo liked the way she carried herself and had to acknowledge that in her day she'd probably been a knockout. But her eyes were cautious, and she looked at him with genuine curiosity.

"I don't believe I know you," she said, evenly.

"No, we've never met. I'm Milo Razner, Miss Fannie."

"Milo Razner," she said, breaking into a smile. "I was beginning to wonder if you were ever going to stop by."

"I've been meaning to, but I have been so busy since I hit town. I'm sure you understand all too well the demands of running your own business," Milo said, glancing around. "And I must say you run a very nice establishment, Miss Fannie."

"Only debtors and grovelers call me Miss Fannie," she said, looking him over up and down.

"Fannie it is then," Milo said, laughing.

"Are you enjoying living up here?"

"Very much so," Milo said, then gave her a small frown. "But I do have to admit that the winter was long and a lot colder than I'm used to."

"All the more reason to stop by, Mr. Razner," she said. "This is the warmest place in town."

"Yes, I'm sure it is," Milo said, already fond of the woman.

"So, how's the dairy business?"

Milo liked the way she casually asked the question with no motives behind it other than a genuine interest in how another businessman was doing. From one entrepreneur to another and all that.

"It's surprisingly good," Milo said. "In fact, I'm about to expand into cheese."

"Cheese, huh?" Fannie said, nodding. "I sell pussy myself."

Milo flinched at her bluntness, but quickly recovered and smiled at her.

"Wouldn't the more accurate term be *rent*?

"I heard you were funny, Mr. Razner," Fannie said, overtly flirting with him. "These days, I'm pretty much out of *direct service*, if you catch my drift, but I'd probably be willing to make an exception for you. Most of these girls think they know everything there is, but I'm sure I have a few tricks up my skirt you'd find interesting. But if you're like most of the men who come in here, you're probably looking for something a bit younger."

"Fannie, I'm flattered," Milo said, gently placing a hand over hers. "And on any other night, I'd be honored to take you up on your generous offer. But tonight, I have someone specific in mind."

"And who might that be?" Fannie said, glancing around the main room.

"Daisy."

"Oh, so you're a top-shelf kind of guy," she said, giving him a nod of approval. "Good choice. And you're in luck. She just started her shift. But you probably knew that already, right?"

"As a matter of fact, I did," Milo said. "And I'd like to reserve her for the rest of the evening if that's okay with you."

"You want her all night? You're a brave man, Mr. Razner," Fannie said, raising an eyebrow. "Okay, but all night is going to cost you."

"Of course," Milo said as he removed his wallet and placed a fifty on the counter. "I trust that's sufficient to cover it?"

Fannie eyed the money, then nodded as she casually grabbed it and slid it into her cleavage.

"That's an interesting safe you have there," Milo said, smiling. "The next time I come in, maybe you'll share the combination with me."

"I might just do that, Mr. Razner. And if you happen to finish up a bit early tonight, stop back down. I've just opened a little Blind Pig in the back room. I've got some nice Canadian hooch I think you'll like."

"Now that you mention it," Milo said, removing a ten from his wallet. "If you could send up a bottle with two glasses and some ice, I'd appreciate it."

"I'll be more than happy to do that, Mr. Razner. Room two at the top of the stairs. Enjoy your stay and come back soon."

"I'm sure I will, Fannie. And it was a pleasure to finally get the chance to meet you," Milo said, starting to turn away from the counter before stopping. "That's an interesting term. Blind Pig. I've only heard the term speakeasy before."

"You're probably used to hanging out in higher-class joints. That's what they call a speakeasy. But places for the regular folks are usually called Blind Pigs. For a while, I tried to get people around here to call my place a speakeasy, but they resisted. I guess speakeasy sounded a bit too uppity for them. And if my customers are more comfortable with the swine reference, I gotta go with it."

"You need to keep your customers happy," Milo said.

"Sure, I get that."

"Exactly."

"But what does Blind Pig refer to? It's quite perplexing."

"I think it comes from the situation where people were supposedly paying their money to see some exhibit or carnival attraction. You know, something weird like a blind pig. And after they got inside and ordered, and went where they were told, their drinks would be waiting for them next to a statue of a small pig. That's how the story goes anyway."

"And since it was a statue, the pig saw nothing, and it was safe to drink there, right?" Milo said.

"You're a quick study, Mr. Razner."

"Please, call me Milo. You're a very good teacher, Fannie."

"Yeah, I've been told that before," she said, flirting heavily again.

"I'm glad I stopped by this evening. I've learned something new."

"Just wait till you've spent an evening with Daisy."

# Daisy Delivers

**Milo walked up the stairs** to the second floor and knocked on the door. He waited to be invited in then stepped inside and closed the door behind him. She was wearing silk and not much of it and reclining with her head propped up on a stack of pillows. When she recognized him, she sat up, surprised to see Milo, hat in hand, standing at the foot of her bed.

"Mr. Razner," she said, beaming at him. "I was beginning to wonder if you were even going to stop by."

"There seems to be a lot of that going around tonight," Milo said, smiling back at her.

"What?"

"Nothing. I hope you're doing well this evening, Daisy."

"I am," she said, beginning to slide out of her robe. But she stopped when Milo held up a hand. "You want me to leave it on?"

"For now, yes," Milo said, sitting down in a chair next to the bed.

"Okay, it's your money," she said, shrugging. "But I gotta warn you that the robe tends to get in the way."

"Yes, I'm sure it does," he said, chuckling as he glanced around the room. "This is very nice. Fannie takes good care of you."

"I'm her top earner," she said, reaching for a hair brush and running it through her long, thick hair.

Milo liked the way she said it as a simple statement of fact, not boasting at all. As he studied her he decided, given her looks and that smile, her success certainly wasn't a surprise, and she probably didn't feel the need to brag about herself. Milo took that as a good sign.

"So, what's your pleasure?"

"I thought we might talk for a while."

"Talk?" she said, frowning at him. "You ain't some kind of weirdo are you, Mr. Razner?"

Milo laughed and draped one leg over the other.

"No, I've been told in the past that I can be rather demanding, but I don't think you'd find any of my proclivities strange, Daisy."

"Yeah, I imagine you're right. I doubt if you could come up with anything I haven't seen or done before. But we should probably get started. The clock's ticking, right?"

"No, you don't need to worry about that, Daisy. I've paid for the entire evening."

"All night?" she said, shrugging. "Okay, it's your funeral. How much did Fannie charge you?"

"Fifty dollars. Does that sound about right to you?"

"I guess. But you're my first all-nighter. I just wanted to know how much you paid her to make sure I get my full cut."

"Business is business, right?"

"Exactly," Daisy said, nodding.

They heard a knock on the door. Daisy was about to respond when Milo held up a hand and walked to the door. He accepted the tray holding a bottle of whiskey and a bucket of ice then tipped the woman a dollar. Milo poured two drinks over ice and handed one to Daisy. She swirled the whiskey in the glass then took a sip.

"So, Mr. Razner," she said, stretching back out on the bed. "What do you want to talk about?"

"Billy Crankovitch," Milo said, taking a sip of his drink.

"You paid fifty bucks to spend the night talking about Billy?"

"Pretty much, yes."

"Maybe you are a weirdo," she said, setting her glass down on the nightstand. "What about Billy?"

"A few months back, he shared some information with me that I'd like to confirm," Milo said, taking another sip.

"Before he left town to take care of some family business?" Daisy said, laughing.

"Yes. Why do you find that funny?"

"Mr. Razner, I'm pretty good at recognizing when somebody is blowing smoke up my skirt. Since I tell so many lies myself, I guess I've just gotten good knowing when one is heading back my way."

"That's interesting. What sort of lies do you find yourself telling, Daisy?" Milo said, adding a bit more ice to his drink before topping it off.

"It pretty much runs the gamut," she said, examining her nails. "But most of them fall under what I like to call the Big Three."

Milo raised an eyebrow and waited.

"Size, expertise, and plans for the future," Daisy said, smiling at him.

"And did you end up lying to Billy about the *Big Three*?"

"Not all of them. Billy's plenty big enough, and his wife has taught him well, but I may have gone a bit overboard with the plans for the future."

"Let's talk about those," Milo said, lighting two cigarettes and handing her one.

"Thanks," she said, taking a puff. "I told Billy that I was desperate to get out of this life."

"Are you?"

"Do I look like a desperate woman to you, Mr. Razner?"

"No, but perhaps you have a quiet desperation you don't often share with the world," Milo said, glancing at her over the top of his glass.

Daisy laughed long and hard. Then she shook her head, took a sip of whiskey, and went back to work on her cigarette.

"You're funny. I like that. One thing you'll learn about me, Mr. Razner, is that I don't have any problems sharing my thoughts with the world."

"Well, I just thought I should check," Milo said, grinning. "One needs to be careful about whose bed they climb into these days."

"I like you," she said, nodding as she finished the cigarette. "Yeah, I think I like you a lot. There's something about you that really grabs my eye. I recognized it the first time we met at the Crossley. But I can't quite put my finger on it. You sure you don't want to help me figure it out?"

"I'll see what I can do," Milo said. "You want to use your finger or mine?"

"See. Right there," she said, sitting up on the bed. "That's exactly what I'm talking about." She sipped her whiskey and stared at him. "You don't pay for it very often, do you, Mr. Razner?"

"I think all men pay for it in some way, Daisy. But that's a whole other conversation."

"We got all night," she said, cocking her head and smiling.

"Yes, we certainly do. But for the moment, let's get back to Billy. Did you tell him that you'd love to run off with him?"

Exasperated, Daisy shook her head and pointed at Milo's pack of cigarettes. He tossed it to her, then rose out of his chair to light her cigarette then sat back down.

"Men," she said, blowing a smoke ring up at the ceiling.

"I'm probably going to need a bit more, Daisy."

Her mood brightened, and she laughed again. Milo found himself starting to get captivated by the young woman.

"Billy told me he was about to come into some serious money," Daisy said.

"Did he now?" Milo said, forcing himself to stay casual.

"Yeah, from his family. He said his mama was sick, and he was going to inherit everything when she passed. I knew it was bullshit, but I played along."

"You knew he was lying?"

"About the family part, yeah. It's pretty easy to find out a person's background if you know where to look. But you know all about that don't you, Mr. Razner?"

"Yes, Daisy. I do."

"But I figure he could be coming into some serious money given what's going on in the country right now," Daisy said, holding up her glass of whiskey. "Billy's a really good cooker, and that particular skill has to be in very high demand."

"I suppose there's a chance you could be right," Milo said, lighting another cigarette.

"Mr. Razner, we're having such a nice time," Daisy said. "Please don't start blowing smoke up my you know what."

Milo raised his glass in salute to her and smiled.

"You're right. Please accept my sincere apology."

"Apology accepted," she said. "All I said to Billy was, if he did happen to come into big money, a girl would have to be crazy not to give his offer of running off together some serious consideration."

"I see," Milo said, deep in thought.

"I get paid to tell men what they want to hear, Mr. Razner. What they decide to pay attention to and what they choose to believe is something I can't control."

"So, you don't worry about it, right?"

"Worrying about things I can't control has always seemed like a big waste of time," she said, shrugging.

She handed him her empty glass, and Milo added fresh ice and a healthy splash of whiskey. She took a sip, crushed out her cigarette, then stared at him.

"Can I ask you a question, Mr. Razner?"

"Of course. It's going to be a long evening if both of us don't hold up our end of the conversation."

Daisy sat more upright on the bed before continuing.

"Billy's cooking for you, isn't he?"

Milo did his best not to flinch and bought a little time by toying with his drink. He hadn't expected any make or break moments this evening, and he was caught completely off guard by the question. Milo stared back at her, but she wasn't giving anything away as she waited for his response.

"Yes, he is," Milo whispered.

It was Daisy's turn for deep thinking, and she stared off into the distance for several moments.

"And as soon as he told you about our conversation, you panicked and decided you'd head over here to find out exactly what we talked about, right?"

"Well, panicked is such a strong word," Milo said, grinning. "But, yes, I was somewhat concerned."

"I'm sure you were," she said, grinning back. "The last thing you want is your cooker walking away just when you're about to get started. Why did you wait a couple of months to ask me about it?"

"I thought I should wait until he got back in town. You know, hold off until I was certain our conversation this evening would even be necessary."

"He's back, isn't he?"

"Yes, he is," Milo said.

"Billy spent most of the winter on that island you bought, didn't he?"

Milo stared at her in disbelief.

"Remarkable," he whispered.

Milo drifted off as a thought came to him.

"You disappeared for a minute there, Mr. Razner. What's on your mind?"

"I was just sitting here thinking about some of the incredibly smart people I've met since I moved here and realized that most of them are women."

"I take it that's your way of paying me a compliment," she said, laughing.

"Yes. You're a very smart woman, Daisy. I like the way your brain works."

"Well, I'm sitting up at the moment. That's when I do my best thinking."

"You don't think well when you're lying down?"

"When I'm lying down, I do my best not to think at all, Mr. Razner."

"Occupational hazard, right?"

"Exactly. You're pretty smart yourself."

"Can I ask *you* a question?"

"Why stop now?"

"How did Billy ever afford you? When I met him, he was a dirt-poor farmer."

"He only paid me the first time, and I expect he'd been saving up for a while."

"I see," Milo said, confused. "And all the other times were free?"

"The other *time*," she said. "We've only been intimate twice."

"Really?"

"Yeah, all the other times we just talked."

"Here?"

"No, never here. Billy was always managing to run into me around town, and we'd start talking. After a while, he started opening up about his wife and how she was always running him down, making him feel like a fool. Stuff like that."

"Yes, he shared the same conversation with me," Milo said.

"Then I did something stupid," she said, finishing her drink.

"I find that a bit hard to believe, Daisy."

"That's sweet. But I can do stupid with the best of them. I made one of the biggest mistakes a girl like me can make. I ended up feeling sorry for him and gave him a freebie."

"And I assume Billy took it the wrong way," Milo said.

"Yeah, he sure did. But it's my fault. I broke my own cardinal rule. Freebies always give men the wrong impression and make them think there's something there that isn't."

"So, you don't have any plans to run off with him?"

"Well, I guess that depends, Mr. Razner," she said, turning coy. "How much are you paying him?"

Milo shook his head and laughed.

"How would you like to work for me, Daisy?"

It was her turn to be caught off guard by a question, and she fell silent. Milo sat quietly waiting for her to organize her thoughts and focused on his whiskey.

"Will I get to keep my clothes on?"

"If and when you take your clothes off, it will completely be your choice."

"Would I have to leave Fannies? I kinda like it here."

"No, actually, I'd prefer you to stay right where you are and keep doing what you do. This would be a second job of sorts."

"And something you'd like to keep just between you and me, right?"

"Yes. It would be our little secret."

"What exactly do you want me to do, Mr. Razner?"

"Keep Billy happy. It's your choice about how you decide to do that. You can gently cut him loose or string him along. Or promise that you're sure the two of you will eventually end up together. But for the foreseeable future, the message you need to send to Billy is that there is no way you can ever see yourself leaving the area."

"If I stay, he won't leave," Daisy said. "That's what you're betting?"

"I think it's more of a sure thing than a bet," Milo said, grabbing the bottle of whiskey.

"How much is it worth for me to keep him happy?"

Milo put the bottle down and reached for his wallet. He removed a crisp fifty and placed it on the bed.

"It's worth one of those every week for as long as Billy remains in my employ."

"And all I have to do is make sure he doesn't leave?" Daisy said.

"That's it," Milo said, again grabbing the bottle. "And if I ever need you to do anything else, you will be paid extra for those services."

"You sure you won't be expecting the occasional freebie, Mr. Razner?"

"I would hardly consider it to be free, Daisy," Milo said, nodding at the fifty. "But, no. Again, the choice of when and where you're going to get naked will be all yours."

"Like, right now?"

"Exactly. Would you prefer to get naked tonight?"

"No, I'm good. And I'm kinda enjoying myself. It's a nice change," she said, holding out her glass for Milo to refill.

"Then it's settled. Tonight is for talking."

"But what do I tell Fannie and the rest of the girls in the morning? They're gonna be dying to know how you were."

"Tell them anything you want," Milo said.

"I suppose I could tell them you were the best I've ever had and leave them guessing about the rest."

"That'll do."

# Milo and Ruby Take a Meeting

**Billy handed Milo a piece** of paper that contained a list of supplies he needed. Milo studied the list then looked up at Billy.

"Are you sure you don't need more sugar than that?" Milo said.

"No, we're good, Milo. I figured out a way to use a bit less on the second run of each batch, so our supply is lasting longer than I expected," Billy said.

"That's good," Milo said, nodding. "That'll bring down our production costs a touch."

"Well, like you always say, every little bit helps," Billy said.

"I do say that a lot, don't I?" Milo said, laughing.

"Well done, Billy," Ruby said, giving her husband's hand a quick squeeze.

"Thanks, Ruby," Billy said, smiling at his wife.

To Milo, the smile appeared genuine, but the two of them had been bending over backward trying to be nice to each other since all three of them had sat down for a chat. Soon after Billy had arrived back at the farm after the ice went out, Ruby had started in on him again about his lengthy list of shortcomings. And Billy, with a new sense of pride and stiffened backbone, had come back at her full force with several comments and complaints of his own.

Milo had tolerated the tension and hostility for three days, then decided to put a stop to it. Milo started the conversation with a strong reminder about their need to take the long view, then turned blunt. He'd made it clear that he not only expected them to keep working together, they'd also at least appear to be civil to each other while doing it. Milo was now at the point where he couldn't tell what was real when it came to them, but his strategy seemed to be working.

"And I'm going to start planting the corn at the island this week," Billy said. "If we can get three acres of a decent yield, I'll have just about enough corn to last all year. That will make things a whole lot easier than having to tote all those bags up that hill."

"You're doing a great job, Billy," Ruby said, beaming at him. "You've got everything so well organized."

"Thanks, Ruby. You're doing a real good job yourself," Billy said. "Well, that Miracle isn't going to cook itself, so I best get going."

"Birdie and I will be getting to the island no later than seven tonight. If you could wait for us to get there and help us load, I'd appreciate it," Milo said.

"No problem, Mr. Razner," Billy said. "I'll see you later. Enjoy your day, Ruby."

"You too, Billy. Be careful. And don't forget to take the lunch I packed for you."

Milo and Ruby followed him down the path and stood on the end of the dock and waved goodbye as he backed the workboat out of the boathouse and headed for the island to begin his work day.

"Now, was that so hard?" Milo said, glancing at Ruby.

"I figured out, if I just grit my teeth, I can get through it," she said. "But I don't think being nice to me is any easier for him."

"Just do your best to keep him on an even keel, Ruby," Milo said.

"And what about me, Milo?" she said, inching closer.

"Well, I guess keeping you happy has become my job, wouldn't you say?"

"I told you that would happen," Ruby said, pressing up tight against him. "How's your morning schedule?"

"What did you have in mind?"

"Oh, just our usual business meeting," Ruby said, strolling down the dock and onto the path that led up to the house.

Milo followed a few steps behind and enjoyed the view. A few minutes later, they were upstairs calling their standing meeting to order. As always, the first item on the agenda was assigned to Milo and consisted of him making sure Ruby was ready to begin item two. Milo was still a bit perplexed by the way business and pleasure had ended up co-mingling over the past few months. But he had come to the conclusion a few weeks back that if more business meetings were run this way, they'd start on time, and people would probably get a whole lot more out of them.

"You're all set for tonight's run?" Ruby said, climbing on top of him.

"Yeah, we're good," Milo said, closing his eyes.

"We're going to need a second milk truck pretty soon," she said.

"I know," Milo said. "Probably in a month or two."

"Milk yield is up about five percent this month," Ruby said. "I think it might be that special feed we're supplementing the hay with."

"I hate to complain, Ruby. But your agenda items are kind of all over the place this morning," Milo said, opening his eyes.

"Oh, you poor baby," Ruby said, laughing. "Am I not paying enough attention to you?"

"I suppose I could use a little more."

Ruby leaned forward and rubbed herself against his chest as she whispered in her ear.

"Is that better, Milo?"

"Much," he said, closing his eyes again and smiling.

"When are you meeting with your other partners?" she whispered.

"After I do the first delivery," Milo said. "I have a couple of meetings scheduled for that night, so I'll need to stay over."

"Meetings like this one?"

"I doubt if it would be possible to recreate this meeting, Ruby."

"That's sweet. So, when am I going to meet these mysterious other partners?" she said, placing her palms on his shoulders and picking up the pace as she closed her eyes.

"Ruby?"

"Yes, Milo."

"You do know that if you want something, all you have to do is ask, right?"

"Sorry, Milo," she said, opening her eyes to look at him. "Force of habit. Can I ask you a question?"

"It seems like as good a time as any," Milo said, running his hands up and down her back. "But it may take me a few moments to formulate an answer."

"What are we going to do?"

"Well, I thought we'd try to finish up here with a bang, then get back to work."

"No, you idiot," she said, laughing as she gave him a playful slap. "I'm talking about what we're going to do over the long-term."

"The long-term?" Milo said, opening one eye to look at her.

"Yes, after Billy finally convinces that whore to settle down with him. As soon as he does, I thought we might settle down ourselves into something a bit more permanent."

"Are you talking about getting married, Ruby?"

"Well, I'm sure not talking about doing this for another twenty years," she said, thrusting against him harder. "Although I sure do enjoy this."

"Gee, I don't know about that."

"Why not?"

"Ruby, we're successful business partners who just happen to like sleeping together. Why do you want to go and ruin a beautiful thing?"

# The First Run

**Just before sunset, Birdie steered** the new boat into a slip at the town dock where Milo was waiting. Milo climbed in and sat down next to him.

"Hey, Birdie."

"Beautiful evening for a boat ride, Milo."

"Birdie, you say that every time I see you. Are there ever any that aren't?" Milo said.

"No, probably not," Birdie said, shaking his head. "Anytime I can get out on the River, it's pretty much always beautiful."

"You don't ask for much, do you, Birdie?" Milo said, studying his new friend who'd quickly become one of his favorite people.

"I've got all I need, Milo," Birdie said with a shrug. "Asking for anything more would come across as me being greedy or ungrateful."

"Words to live by," Milo said, nodding. "Maybe you should have a little chat with Ruby."

"What's that, Milo?" Birdie said.

"Nothing. I'm just blabbering," he said, softly clapping his hands. "Okay, let's go move some illegal booze."

"If you don't mind, I'd like to open the boat up a bit on the way to the island," Birdie said, backing out of the slip.

"Okay, but keep it under fifty," Milo said, hunkering down a bit lower in his seat.

Birdie headed for the main channel as a majestic red and purple sunset began to form. They completed the trip to the island, one that had taken almost half an hour in Melvin's boat, in less than ten minutes. Billy was sitting on the dock that extended out of the boathouse and dangling his feet in the water. He stood as they approached and tied the boat off.

"Isn't that water freezing?" Milo said, nodding at Billy's bare feet that had turned a shade of bright pink mixed with purple.

"It sure is," Billy said.

"Then why the hell are you sticking your feet in it?"

"Ever since I've been a kid, it's something I do every year in the spring. I like to keep checking the temperature so I'll know as soon as it's warm enough for me to go swimming."

"Is it ever warm enough to swim in April?" Milo said.

"Oh, not a chance. It'll be weeks before you can get in the water and not freeze to death," Billy said.

Milo stared at his cooker then shook his head.

"Okay, thanks for clearing that up, Billy. All right, it's getting dark in a hurry. Let's get the boat loaded. Birdie, you just stay down here."

"You sure you don't need some help?" Birdie said.

"No, we're fine," Milo said. "But go ahead and open the back hatch."

After making several trips each using two dollies Milo had specially made, all thirty, ten-gallon milk cans weighing around a hundred pounds each were loaded. Birdie closed and secured the hatch and climbed back into the driver's seat. Milo remained on the dock with Billy.

"Okay, I guess that's it," Milo said, staring down at the stopwatch he was holding. "Thanks for sticking around."

"No problem. I decided to stay here tonight to get the jump on a new batch," Billy said.

"Do you need me to let Ruby know so she doesn't worry?"

"Nah, I mentioned this morning that I might just stay over," Billy said. "How was your *meeting* this morning?"

Milo flinched. Although Billy had been the one first to raise the issue, Milo was still uncomfortable discussing what he was doing with the man's wife.

"It was productive," Milo said. "We talked about getting a second milk truck."

"Before or after?" Billy said.

Milo considered the question, then exhaled loudly.

"Actually, it was during."

"She does that with you, too?" Billy said, surprised by the news. "I'm glad to hear that. I thought it was just me. You know, like I wasn't doing enough to keep her focused."

"No, I'm sure it's nothing you did or didn't do, Billy. Ruby seems quite capable of handling more than one thing at a time. In fact, she seems to prefer it."

"Daisy says Ruby does that because she has problems with intimacy," Billy said. "I don't know if I agree with her or not."

"Why not?"

"Probably because I'm not exactly sure I understand what the hell Daisy's talking about," he said, frowning.

"Tell you what, Billy. Next time you're with Daisy, instead of having her explain it to you, ask for a demonstration."

"You think that'll work?"

"I don't know. But I'm sure it'll be a lot of fun finding out," Milo said, patting him on the back. "Okay, be safe. I'll see you soon."

Milo waved goodbye and climbed aboard. He sat down next to Birdie who started the engine before Milo had gotten settled. Birdie glanced over his shoulder at Billy who was making his way up the incline. Then he stared at Milo.

"Is there something on your mind, Birdie?"

"Oh, you noticed."

"You're wondering about Ruby," Milo said.

"Among other things. I'm familiar with the concept of somebody sleeping with another man's wife, but this is the first time I've ever seen the two guys have a civil conversation about it."

"It's a long story," Milo said.

"I'd be shocked if it wasn't," Birdie said, chuckling. "I sure hope you know what you're doing."

"Yeah, me too," Milo said, pointing forward. "Let's go. Rockport. Dead ahead."

Birdie opened the throttle, and if the boat was bothered by the additional weight it was carrying, it didn't show it. They made their way back upriver until Boldt Castle appeared in the distance. Birdie steered the boat behind the castle, and they made their way through the scattering of islands and shoreline until the River again opened up and the lights of Rockport twinkled on the horizon. Minutes later, they pulled into Clint's boathouse where he and Tom Collins were standing next to the open doors that led directly into the warehouse.

"Good evening, gentlemen," Milo said, climbing out of the boat and tying it off. "How's the furniture business these days?"

"About to get a whole lot better I imagine. That is one beautiful boat, Milo," Clint said, accepting Milo's handshake.

"Thanks. It's pretty amazing," Milo said. "Watch this. Birdie, if you would do the honors."

Birdie limped his way to the stern and unfastened the clasps. Then he raised the hatch and the metal cans, in five rows of six, glistened from the overhead lights.

"Impressive," Clint said. "You guys want to come inside and have a drink and catch up?"

"Any other night but this one, Clint," Milo said, checking the stopwatch he was holding. "I'm trying to get a feel for how long each part of the run is going to take. So, let's get this unloaded and inside." Milo hopped back into the boat, then paused to look back up at Clint and Tom. "And don't scratch the boat."

Clint rolled a wheeled cart down the dock and Milo and Tom, working together, carefully removed all the milk cans from the hatch and gently placed them on the cart. It took two trips to get all thirty cans inside the warehouse and a total of eleven minutes.

Satisfied with the results, Milo arched his back and passed around his pack of cigarettes.

"You excited about finally getting started?" Milo said to Clint.

"I am," he said, nodding. "I can't wait."

"How did your flavor and color tests work out?" Milo said.

"I've got it down to a week," Clint said, proudly. "It's never going to be confused with a twelve-year blend, but it looks and tastes real good, Milo."

"A week? That's all?"

"I've been playing around with your idea to agitate the shine after I cut it with the water and add in the oak chips and some other ingredients."

"Like what?" Milo said.

"A bit of charcoal, a touch of rye, and a couple of other things."

Milo made a mental note to ask Tom to get the complete recipe Clint was using.

"I got an idea when I was doing a load of wash about a month ago," Clint said. "I pretty much ruined my washing machine, but I was able to get water to flavor and color in a couple of days. So then I added a motorized arm to a couple of my storage vats. I just let them run non-stop until we get the product where we want it."

"And you're convinced it's going to work?" Milo said.

"I'll let you decide that," Clint said with a big grin. "In fact, why don't you put that damn stopwatch away and hang on for a sec. I'll be right back with a test sample I'd like your opinion on."

A few minutes later, Clint returned carrying a bottle and four shot glasses. He poured the drinks and Tom passed them around. Milo held his up to the light and was impressed with the color. He smelled it and got a hint of smoked oak and nodded. Then he tossed the shot back, and a wide grin emerged.

"What do you think?" Clint said.

"I think the price of a case just went up," Milo said, holding out his glass for a refill.

"Can I ask you what you're going to be selling it for?" Clint said.

"No, Clint. You can't," Milo said, tossing back the second shot.

# Milo Takes a Road Trip

**Milo watched Elmer Fergin** and Roscoe Leach climb down out of the vehicle, a brand new black Model-T truck with *Razner's Dairy* written in gold letters on the side of the cab, and did his best to control his reaction. And while he did manage to avoid laughing out loud, he wasn't able to contain the wide grin that Elmer and Roscoe were obviously anticipating. They both scowled at Milo as they headed his way.

"Look at you two," Milo said, glancing up and down at their uniforms. "You make an adorable couple."

"Don't start, Milo," Elmer said, his voice low and gruff. "I feel like a damn fool in this getup."

Milo studied their all white, long-sleeved coveralls with their first names written in script above the heart and the matching white shoes. But it was the white captain's hat with the small black bill that made Milo want to laugh.

"You look great," Milo said, forcing his smile to move from mocking to friendly.

"We look like a couple of ice cream pushers," Roscoe said, stuffing a wad of chewing tobacco inside his cheek. "And you know it."

"Good. That's exactly the look I want. And try not to get any tobacco juice on your uniform, Roscoe," Milo said. "I want you looking like a professional and a man who takes pride in his work."

"Yeah, I'll try to be careful not to dribble on myself," Roscoe said, still glaring at Milo.

"Okay, gentlemen," Milo said. "If you're done pouting, let's see if we can get some work done today. And just so we're clear about your uniforms, the sillier you think you look, the less likely it is that people will think you're anything other than a couple of guys who deliver milk for a living. Am I making my point clear?"

Elmer and Roscoe nodded and followed Milo as he made his way along the wooden path that led down to the boathouse. Birdie was standing on the dock next to the boat about to light a cigarette and nodded when they stepped onto the dock. He smiled when he saw Elmer and Roscoe but turned to one side to block the wind and hide his grin. The hatch in the stern was open, and the first thirty milk cans of finished product sat waiting in plain view.

"Okay, these need to be loaded into the truck. They go in first, six to a row, and then fill the rest of the truck with cans of milk from the barn. Make sure they're secured and don't overload the truck until we get a few trips under our belt and get a feel for how it handles the road."

"Got it, Milo," Roscoe said, climbing down into the boat.

"And don't forget rule number one," Milo said.

Confused, Elmer and Roscoe glanced at each other then looked at Milo.

"Don't scratch the boat," Milo said. "Birdie, I need a word with you."

Birdie followed Milo as he walked away from the boat and out of earshot of the two men who were already lifting the milk cans onto the dock.

"What's up, Milo?"

"Do you think you can handle tonight's run by yourself?"

"Sure. As long as Clint and Tom are there to help me load up, I'll be fine. But I thought you wanted to wait a few days before you did the next run."

"I did," Milo said, lighting a cigarette of his own. "But Clint has another three hundred gallons ready to go, and since I'll be staying overnight, I thought I'd just stick around until the truck arrives tomorrow. I want to see if we can handle consecutive days without overtaxing Beulah or her workers."

"Smart," Birdie said, flicking his cigarette butt into the River.

"Don't do that, Birdie," Milo said, frowning.

"Do what?" Birdie said.

"Throw your shit in the River."

"It's just a cigarette butt, Milo."

"And if everybody living around here cops that same attitude, pretty soon we'll all be swimming in garbage and drinking dirty water. Besides, the birds and fish could end up eating them. Try to show a little respect for what Mother Nature has given us."

"You're an odd duck, Milo."

"I'm just a man who's ahead of his time, Birdie," Milo said, staring out at the water.

"So, what should I do with them?" Birdie said.

"Put them in your pocket or swallow them," Milo said. "I don't care. Just don't throw them in the River."

"Whatever you say, Milo," Birdie said, shaking his head.

"That's what I like to hear," Milo said, smiling. "And remember, nice and slow with the boat this evening."

**As soon** as Elmer and Roscoe had the truck loaded, Milo climbed in the passenger seat and waited impatiently for Elmer to start the truck. They were soon rumbling out of town and onto what passed for the highway that led to Watertown, thirty miles south. Traffic was light, but the road was rough in spots, and several potholes filled with water and spring mud slowed their progress at times. But Milo was pleased as he glanced down at his stopwatch when they arrived at the outskirts of Watertown and saw that they'd made the trip in a little over an hour and a half.

"An average of twenty miles an hour," Milo said, glancing over at Elmer. "Not bad."

"We could go a lot faster," Elmer said.

"There's no need to go any faster, Elmer," Milo said, his voice firm to help emphasize the point he was making. "Got it?"

"I know, Milo," Elmer said. "But I'm gonna die of boredom doing this every day."

Milo removed his hat and twirled it around a finger as he shook his head.

"Our first delivery, and you're already whining, Elmer?"

"Nah, it ain't that, Milo," Elmer said. "It's just that when you called us to come up here and help you, Roscoe and I were expecting to see a bit more..."

"Action," Roscoe said from the backseat.

Milo turned around to respond but stopped when he saw the machine gun lying across Roscoe's lap.

"What the hell are you doing with that thing?" Milo said.

"You said we needed to be armed," Roscoe said.

"Not in plain view, you idiot," Milo said, glaring at him. "You two are supposed to be representatives of a family farm that sells milk to working families and their kids. What kind of reaction do you expect to get if some young mother sees you toting a machine gun?"

"That I'm someone not to be trifled with," Roscoe said.

"As in, put the milk and butter down, lady, if you know what's good for you?" Milo said.

"He didn't mean anything, Milo," Elmer said. "Did you, Roscoe?"

"I thought I was pretty clear," Roscoe whispered as he shoved the machine gun under the seat. "All I said was that I wanted a little action. Otherwise, what's the point of being a gangster?"

"You want to know the biggest problem with getting action is, Roscoe?" Milo said.

"What's that?"

"People usually aren't very fond of getting shot at, and, as such, they have a tendency to shoot back."

"Well, I guess that's just an occupational hazard then, isn't it?" Roscoe said, turning petulant.

Milo glanced back and forth at them until he was sure he had their undivided attention.

"I'm only gonna say this once, so pay close attention. And if I have to say it a second time, it'll be the last words you ever hear," Milo said, draping an arm over the seat and turning to make sure they could see him clearly. "I'm paying both of you about ten times what an average worker makes in this country, and if you want to bitch and moan, I'll be more than happy to help you find jobs digging coal or milking cows for a living. Or, if you really piss me off, we're gonna find out if you can swim the length of the St. Lawrence River. The only thing I'm asking you to do six days a week is get up in the morning with a smile on your face, load the truck, and drive thirty miles to make one, I repeat one, delivery. Then after you've unloaded the truck with a *smile on your face*, you drive back home, gas up and wash the truck, and then you're done for the day. Most days, you'll be finished work by two in the afternoon. And if that isn't good enough, or doesn't provide enough *action* for you, just let me know and I'll find a couple of other guys from the list of several hundred others who'd sell their own mother to have your job."

Milo paused, fixed a glare on Roscoe, then moved it over to Elmer who was gripping the steering wheel tight with both hands and staring out at the road.

"Have I made myself clear?" Milo whispered.

A hush fell over the truck, and the only sound was the rumble of the engine for several seconds. Then Elmer and Roscoe both nodded.

"I'm sorry, Milo," Elmer said.

"Yeah, me too," Roscoe said.

"Try to take the long view, gentlemen."

Milo adjusted his hat as he turned back around in his seat and stared out the window deep in thought. He continued to silently observe the emerging city landscape until he heard Elmer's voice.

"Did you say something, Elmer?" Milo said, glancing over.

"I just asked what was on your mind. You drifted off for quite a while there," Elmer said.

"I was just sitting here thinking that what Alex Bay needs is an ice cream parlor."

**They entered** the city, turned onto Arsenal Street, then drove around the elaborately designed Public Square and made their way to State Street. Milo smiled when they were driving past the shops that dotted the street, and he looked up and saw the sign that read *Beulah's Cheese Emporium.*

"Make a right into that alley up there," Milo said, pointing. "Beulah said we'll see a brick building with a big red door," Milo said.

Elmer slowed the truck when they saw the building, and Milo hopped out as soon as it came to a stop. He knocked loudly on the door, and moments later it opened, and a worker waved the truck inside. Milo walked inside the well-lit room and waved to Beulah who waved back and smiled at him, then finished her conversation before strolling toward him.

"It's nice to see you, Miss Peppin," Milo said, extending his hand.

"You as well, Mr. Razner," she said, shaking hands with him. Then she caught a glimpse of the gold lettering on the side of the truck. "Well, it's not exactly the same as seeing your name up in lights, Mr. Razner, but I guess everyone has to start somewhere."

"It's nice to see you haven't lost your sense of humor, Miss Peppin. Are you ready for us?"

"We are indeed," she said, waving to one of her workers standing nearby. "Charlie, I need you for a minute."

Beulah introduced the two men and the man named Charlie led the way as they walked toward another section of the warehouse. He unlocked a door and waited for them to step inside before following and closing the door behind him. Milo glanced around the windowless room and saw a large metal vat on a platform about three feet off the floor with three nozzles at the bottom of the vat about four feet apart from each other. He also saw two long tables, and several large stacks of what he assumed were collapsed cardboard boxes.

"So, after all our back and forth debating it, you decided to go with cardboard," Milo said.

"Yes, you were right, Milo. We didn't need to go with wood boxes. And they're easy to stack and a lot lighter," Beulah said.

"It's nice to win one once in a while," Milo said.

Beulah laughed and looked at Charlie.

"Don't worry, Charlie. He'll grow on you."

"Okay, take me through the process," Milo said.

Beulah nodded at Charlie.

"Sure, Beulah," Charlie said. "Since the product is all ready to go, Milo, all we'll need to do is roll the milk cans in, and empty them into the vat. We put it up on the platform to keep folks from having to bend over all the time."

"Smart," Milo said, nodding.

"We'll have three people filling bottles and two more handling corks. After that, everyone will work together on labeling and packing. What ratio of pint versus quart bottles did you decide on?"

"We're going to start with an eight to two ratio of quarts to pints," Milo said. "Most of the speakeasies will want to deal with quarts, but I'm expecting that they'll want some pints on hand for people to take home with them. If that changes, we'll let you know. But each case will be twelve quarts or twenty-four pints. Either way, it's the same amount of booze."

"Got it," Charlie said. "Three gallons a case. You'll be bringing in three hundred gallons each trip. By my math, that's a hundred cases."

Milo liked the way the guy seemed to know his numbers and the way he'd broken down the bottling process.

"I like dealing with round numbers. And I've got the second half of the first batch ready to go, so I thought we'd do another delivery tomorrow to see if your process can handle a daily bottling," Milo said. "I have a feeling this thing could grow in a hurry, and I don't want to make any promises I can't keep."

"I like a man who thinks ahead," Charlie said, giving Milo a look that made him a bit nervous.

"What did you come up with for labels?" Milo said.

"We found a local printer," Beulah said, then noticed the look Milo was giving her. "Relax, Milo. He's Charlie's cousin."

"Yeah, you don't need to worry about Sammy. He'll be printing the labels as a favor to me. It's just a sideline from his usual business."

"What's he do?" Milo said.

"He's a counterfeiter," Charlie said, laughing.

"Then I'm going to cross your cousin off the list of things I need to worry about," Milo said, laughing along. "You got something I can take a look at?"

Beulah walked to one of the tables and returned carrying one of the labels. She handed it to Milo, and he examined both sides.

"Genuine Canadian whiskey from the plains of Red Deer," Milo said, reading from the label. "Where the hell is Red Deer?"

"Somewhere way out in Alberta," Charlie said.

"Do they grow grain out there?" Milo said.

"They do. But I don't have any idea if anybody makes whiskey there."

"If they grow grain, don't worry, somebody's making whiskey," Milo said, then shrugged. "Well, if anybody gets curious and wants to travel all the way to Alberta to find out if there's a distillery in town, more power to them," Milo said.

"You didn't happen to bring a sample for us to taste by any chance, did you, Milo?" Beulah said.

"I thought you'd never ask, Miss Peppin," Milo said, removing a pint bottle from his coat.

Beulah walked to a cupboard and returned with three small glasses. Milo poured, handed the bottle to Charlie, and raised his glass.

"Here's to big ideas," Milo said. "And even bigger money."

He downed his drink and waited for their reaction. When they both broke into big grins, Milo shrugged and spread his arms wide.

"Good, huh?"

"Remarkable," Beulah said. "And this is the same stuff I drank before?"

"Identical," Milo said. "It's just been played with a bit."

"Well done. My compliments to the chef," Beulah said, helping herself to a second taste. "Charlie, would you mind chatting with Milo's guys for a few minutes and make sure everyone is clear on how we'll be handling things?"

"Sure, Beulah," Charlie said. "It's a pleasure finally getting the chance to meet you, Milo. Beulah has told me a lot about you."

"Yeah, she can be a bit of chatterbox at times," Milo said, smiling at her. "Just wait until she starts waxing poetic about the evils of alcohol."

They watched Charlie depart and then they came together for a deep kiss and long embrace.

"I've missed you, Miss Peppin."

"The feeling is mutual. And we've got some catching up to do tonight."

"Charlie seems like a sharp guy," Milo said. "Where did you find him?"

"He came with the cheesemaker I found up in Montreal. They were sort of a package deal."

"Brothers?"

"Guess again," Beulah said, giving him a coy smile.

"Childhood buddies?"

Beulah kept looking at him with the smile plastered on her face and waited.

"Really?" Milo said when the lightbulb finally went off. "You don't say?"

"It doesn't bother you, does it, Milo?"

"Beulah, you've known me a long time, and I'm surprised you even need to ask. Of all the reasons there are for not liking or looking down on somebody else, who they choose to lay their head next to at night is way down at the bottom of the list."

"Everybody deserves to be happy, right?"

"Exactly," Milo said, then cocked his head when a thought popped into his head. "I thought he was giving me a funny look."

"Well, you are pretty cute, Milo," Beulah said, laughing. "Speaking of happy, how's Billy doing?"

"He's settled down for the moment. And I've got a new insurance policy in place to make sure he stays that way."

"Good. And how's Ruby?" she said, raising an eyebrow at him.

"Ah, Ruby. Ruby is going to be a problem at some point," Milo said, rubbing his chin.

"I warned you about sleeping with her," Beulah said.

"Yes, you did. But between you not being around, and Ruby's considerable charm and rather overt advances, she wore me down."

"You're a weak man at times, Mr. Razner," she said, shaking her head. "What sort of problem are you talking about?"

"Ruby seems to be considering our current situation as the initial stages of something that will lead to a more permanent arrangement," Milo said, choosing his words carefully.

"Geez, Milo. What am I going to do with you?"

"Are you talking about the long view, or later on tonight?"

"Both. Or maybe neither if you don't learn to control yourself," Beulah said, laughing.

"Hey, I'll have you know that I recently spent fifty dollars to spend all night with a lovely working girl and didn't lay a finger on her. That has to count for something."

"Yes, Milo. I'm sure that demonstrates some real personal growth on your part," Beulah said, giving him a peck on the cheek. "Is Ruby doing a good job running the farm?"

"She is. She's got a very good head for business."

"I'm glad to hear that. We're going to need as many smart people as we can find."

"Yeah. And I really like the way she runs a meeting."

# The Senator Comes Calling

**Milo knocked on the door** and glanced at Beulah while they waited. Her hair was down, and she was wearing a dark red jacket over white cotton, and a pair of ankle-high stiletto boots Milo hoped he could convince her to keep on later that evening.

"You look beautiful, Miss Peppin, Milo said, giving her a quick squeeze.

Beulah smacked his hand away and smiled at the man who opened the door.

"You must be Beulah Peppin," the man said, beaming as he looked her over.

"And you must be Senator Miller," Beulah said, extending her hand.

The Senator took her hand and gently kissed it before looking at Milo.

"You weren't joking, Milo," the Senator said. "She is beautiful. How are you?"

"I'm just fine, Senator," Milo said, returning the handshake before stepping inside the hotel suite. "And you?"

"Oh, you know. Dealing with all the usual pressing problems of state," the Senator said. "What are you drinking?"

"I thought we might have some of what I've brought with me," Milo said. "That is why you're here, right?"

"Among other things, yes," the Senator said, glancing at the bottle Milo handed him. "I've been waiting a long time for this night. I'm excited." The Senator glanced at the label on the bottle and read from it. "Red Deer. Interesting name. Alberta?" He looked at Milo and frowned. "You're moving the booze all the way from Alberta?"

"What about it?" Milo said.

"Aren't your transportation costs killing your profit margin?"

"With all due respect, Senator, my transportation costs really aren't your concern," Milo said, heading for a table that held several glasses. "I thought your partner was going to be here tonight."

"He's in the bathroom. He'll be right out."

Milo nodded and set four glasses out in a row. The Senator handed the bottle back to Milo, and he poured the drinks. The bathroom door opened and a well-dressed man with a large handlebar mustache entered the living room of the suite drying his hands on a towel. He took a quick look at Milo and then ignored him after he got his first look at Beulah. The man continued to stare at her long past what Milo considered proper.

"You must be Beulah. Please excuse my staring at you, but I find myself caught completely off guard. We are going to have to come up with another word to describe you because beautiful doesn't do you justice," the man said, holding her hand with both of his. "I'm Ben Green."

"It's nice to meet you, Mr. Green," Beulah said, blushing.

"And you must be, Milo Razner," Ben Green said, finally acknowledging Milo's presence. "I've heard many things about you from the Senator."

"That's interesting," Milo said, staring back. "I haven't heard a word about you other than you're the Senator's business partner."

"Yes, Ben and I go way back," the Senator said. "But we do our best not to be seen in public together. And as far as this enterprise is concerned, you will be dealing solely with him. For obvious reasons, I'm sure you understand why I need to, shall we say, keep my distance."

"We understand, Senator," Milo said. "And you wouldn't want to be caught doing anything that might, shall we say, undermine the public's trust in you."

The Senator laughed nervously and proceeded to hand everyone their glass.

"I've always liked the way you get right to the point, Milo. No, I certainly wouldn't want that to happen."

The Senator raised his glass in a toast, and they all downed their drink.

"This is good," Ben Green said, crossing to the table to examine the bottle. "Alberta? That's a long way to go for Canadian whiskey."

"Yes, that's what I thought," the Senator said.

"It won't be long before cops in both countries start watching every distillery near the border. But I doubt if anybody is going to be too worried about keeping a close eye on somebody located a couple thousand miles away," Milo said, shrugging. "That should help keep us way off the radar."

"Maybe for a while," Ben Green said, pouring another round of drinks. "Eventually, someone could put two and two together."

"We'll deal with that if and when it happens," Milo said.

"Your transportation costs must be exorbitant," Ben Green said, savoring his second mouthful.

"That's not your problem," Milo said, tossing back his shot.

"No, you're absolutely right, Mr. Razner. How you get the product here and how much you pay to do that is none of my business. So, let's say we talk about what is my business, shall we?"

"That's why we're here, Mr. Green," Beulah said, glancing at the Senator.

"Relax, gentlemen," the Senator said. "You've just met, so let's try to keep things civil. You've got all the time in the world to grow to hate each other."

Ben Green gestured at a couch, and Milo and Beulah sat down. Green and the Senator sat down across from them.

"The Senator tells me that we'll be the only ones you'll be delivering product to," Ben Green said.

"Yes, we prefer dealing with only one customer," Milo said. "The fewer number of people involved, the less chance any of us have spending the next several years locked up."

"I must say, Milo," the Senator said. "I thought that was one of your strongest selling points when we first discussed the deal."

"Why draw any unnecessary attention to yourself, right?" Milo said.

"You might find this odd coming from a politician," the Senator said, laughing. "But I have to agree with that sentiment."

"What sort of quantities can you promise?" Ben Green said, again examining the whiskey bottle.

"I'm guaranteeing one hundred cases per delivery for the next four months," Milo said.

"I assume this would be a weekly delivery?" Ben Green said.

"Yes, but I'll be doing a second run tomorrow of another hundred cases just to demonstrate our ability to consistently deliver a high-quality product," Milo said.

"And make a little extra money to recoup some of your initial investment?" Ben Green said, smiling.

"In part," Milo said. "But I have some plans for expansion I'd like to get started on. Before long, I'll be upping my guarantee to two deliveries a week."

"Two hundred cases every week?" the Senator said. "Impressive. Can you assure us it will all be as good as this?"

"It's all going to be the same product, Senator," Milo said.

"What about top-shelf brands?" Ben Green said.

"What about them?" Milo said.

"Well, this is a fine three-year-old blend, but some of our customers are going to want something more high end."

"I can understand that," Milo said. "And feel free to offer all the top-shelf stuff you want in your speakeasies. But you won't be getting it from us."

"Why on earth not?" Ben Green said.

"Because we don't need to," Milo said. "This is exactly what most of your customers are going to want. A consistent product they can enjoy and trust that doesn't break the bank."

"Trust?" the Senator said.

"You still remember that concept don't you, Senator? Pretty soon everybody with a bathtub is going to be making all kinds of different hooch. And my guess is that a lot of that stuff is not only going to taste awful, but it will be downright dangerous for people to drink. We want folks to see the label on that bottle and say I'll have a shot of Red Deer."

The Senator and Ben Green looked at each other and nodded.

"That makes a lot of sense, Milo," the Senator said. "Okay, if we can agree on a price, I think we have a deal."

"It's sixty-five a case," Milo said, flatly.

"Sixty-five?" Ben Green said. "Isn't that a bit high, Mr. Razner?"

"I think you're getting a bargain, Mr. Green," Milo said, leaning back into the couch. "It's a high-quality product, and the masses are going to line up to get their hands on it. And even if you only sell it for four bits a shot, you'll be tripling your money."

"I see you've been doing some math, Mr. Razner," Ben Green said.

"It's kind of a hobby of mine," Milo said. "And don't forget that you'll only have to make one pick up a week. No running back and forth dealing with small quantities and multiple suppliers. That cuts your exposure way down. And if you have a clever way to get it into the hands of the people who run your speakeasies, you shouldn't ever have to worry about getting caught."

The Senator and Ben Green both found Milo's last comment funny. Milo looked back and forth at them.

"Sorry, Milo," the Senator said. "But we were having that conversation just before you and Beulah arrived. Yes, we do think we've come up with a clever way to distribute on our end."

"We just bought a business that deals in fresh produce," Ben Green said. "And since all forty of our speakeasies are within a five-mile radius of Watertown, the people who operate them will simply drive in and pick up their *vegetables* as needed."

"Smart," Milo said. "We're using a cheese store as a front."

"Cheese? Very good, Milo," the Senator said. "Am I correct assuming that the cheese will be made from the milk that comes from your dairy farm?"

"You are," Milo said, smiling.

"Aren't you worried about carrying cases of whiskey in a milk truck?" Ben Green said.

"Not in the least," Milo said.

"Cheese," the Senator said, for some reason finding the idea funny.

"We think we're going to make some good money from the cheese store," Beulah said. "I'll make sure to give some samples to your driver when he does his pickup."

"Making money from a legitimate business operation?" the Senator said. "It's a bit of departure for you, isn't it, Milo?"

"Well, Senator, times are tough all over," Milo said. "And every little bit helps, right?"

"It does indeed."

"Can you guarantee that price?" Ben Green said.

"We can guarantee you the sixty-five a case through the end of the year," Milo said. "We may need to revisit it at some point down the road."

The Senator and Ben Green again looked at each other and nodded.

"So, I take it we have a deal?" Milo said.

"We do," Ben Green said, nodding and extending his hand.

"That's music to my ears," Milo said, shaking hands.

"I feel like singing a bit of a tune myself. And I can't wait to see you again soon, Beulah," Ben Green said, again staring at her way too long for Milo's comfort. "Then I suppose all that's left to do is give you some money for the first delivery."

"Since the next delivery will be here tomorrow, let's just settle up right now for the first two hundred cases," Beulah said. "If *my* math is correct, I believe that's thirteen thousand."

Beulah's direct approach caught Ben Green off guard for a moment, but he eventually smiled at her.

"Of course," he said, getting up out of his chair. "I'll be right back."

He headed out of the living room, and Milo gently squeezed Beulah's hand.

"How much are we clearing?" Beulah whispered to Milo.

"Around ten grand," Milo whispered into her ear.

That piece of information produced a contented sigh from Beulah. Milo, anxious to get on with the rest of the evening, glanced at his watch.

"While we have a minute, I have some information for you," the Senator said, pouring himself another shot.

"Is it good news?" Milo said. "I'm having a pretty good day, and I'd hate for you to ruin it."

"It's not necessarily bad news. But I think you'll find it interesting. I had committee meetings this week for both Treasury and Judiciary," the Senator said, then glanced at Beulah with false modesty. "I'm on both committees."

"Impressive," Beulah said, giving the Senator a coy smile.

"And being on both is going to come in very handy," he said. "As I'm sure you know, Milo, when the Volstead Act was passed, it contained provisions for enforcement."

"And?" Milo said, suddenly interested in what the Senator was saying.

"And the government has finally got around to putting some meat on the bones, so to speak."

"Any time you're ready, Senator," Milo said, gesturing for him to get on with it.

"The Prohibition Unit will be attached to the Bureau of Internal Revenue, which is something I find rather ironic since Prohibition is going to be taking away the revenue that used to be generated by the tax on alcohol."

"It's good to know that we can always count on our government to show a lot of foresight," Milo said, grinning.

"Yes, well, that is a topic for a whole other discussion," the Senator said. "During our committee meetings this week, we received a variety of updates on the progress of the law since it went into effect. And one of the updates dealt with the selection of the Prohibition Agents who've been hired to enforce the law."

"Let me guess, there aren't going to be enough of them?" Milo said.

"Not even close," the Senator said. "They'll be woefully understaffed, and their budgets will be way below what they would need to do the job adequately."

"We had this conversation a year ago," Milo said.

"We did. And you were right."

"Did you get a chance to learn how many of these Agents will be assigned to my neck of the woods?"

"I did," the Senator said, smiling. "As a New York senator, the head of the Prohibition Unit was very interested in getting my opinion since his understanding of the geography of our great state is somewhat limited."

"And since you are a man of the people," Milo said. "You did your best to provide sage counsel."

"I did. And I told the head of the Unit that the most likely places where alcohol would be smuggled across the border were on Lake Ontario, and around Ogdensburg which is about thirty miles downriver of your current location. If my memory serves me well."

"Your memory is perfect, Senator. How many agents are we talking about?"

"Initially, there will be four assigned at the Lake, and they'll work closely with the Coast Guard who has a station located there. I believe the Border Patrol also has an outpost somewhere around there. And there will be three more agents posted near Ogdensburg."

"I can live with that," Milo said.

"And there will be one more located in Alex Bay," the Senator said. "I'm sorry Milo, but they felt the need to have some minimal presence between those two locations."

"Don't worry about it, Senator," Milo said. "That won't be a problem."

"Are you sure?" the Senator said. "I suppose I could talk with the head of the Unit, but sticking my nose too far into his business makes me a bit nervous."

"No, don't do that," Milo said. "We can deal with one guy easy enough. What sort of equipment are they giving them?"

"The guy who'll be assigned to your town will get a car and a boat. And he'll have a small budget to hire some locals part-time when he feels he needs them."

"What sort of boat?"

"Apparently, a pretty fast one. It's supposed to be able to do forty miles an hour. Is that fast for a boat?"

"I think it used to be," Milo said. "Don't worry, we'll be fine. Anything else?"

"Yes, as a matter of fact, there is," the Senator said, grinning. "I got the name of the man who'll be assigned there."

"You got his name? Well done, Senator."

"A man by the name of Roland Doyle."

"Roland Doyle?" Milo said, leaning forward with a frown on his face.

"Judging by your reaction, I take it you know the man."

"I think I might," Milo said, nodding.

"Who is he?" Beulah said.

"I used to know of a cop with the same name when I was living in Philadelphia," Milo said.

"You mean when you were robbing banks in Philadelphia, don't you?" the Senator said.

"Ancient history based on unfounded rumor and innuendo, Senator," Milo said, waving it off. "I'm a dairy farmer now."

"Does he know you, Milo?" Beulah said, frowning.

"We've never met," Milo said. "But he could know me by reputation."

"This could be bad," the Senator said.

"No, it's not a problem, Senator. It's just a situation that will need to be managed," Milo said.

"You'll need to keep me updated on a regular basis," the Senator said. "He could cause us some serious problems, Milo."

"Relax, Senator. I'll handle it," Milo said, chewing his bottom lip as he stared off at the wall.

"I don't want any surprises."

"I said I'd handle it," Milo said, continuing to stare off into the distance. "Well, what do you know? Roland Doyle."

# Episode 4

## Enter the Revenuer

"The immigration laws must have been recently loosened up. All of a sudden I'm seeing millions of Hypocrites walking around."

Milo Razner

# A New Man About Town

**Roland Doyle glanced up and down** the bustling
street lined with shops crowded with customers trying to decide
how to best spend their hard-earned money and looky-loo
tourists killing time until their tour boat departed. After arriving
in town yesterday, Roland had handed over four bits of his own
hard-earned money and given the guy selling tickets a dirty look
when he first heard the price. Roland thought fifty cents was a
small fortune to spend just to look at water and a bunch of way-
too-big houses built for rich people. Then he wondered if the guy
selling the tickets thought he was a rube and was trying to
overcharge him. But nobody was complaining, so Roland stayed
quiet but steamed inside.

He got a dirty look back from the ticket guy when Roland
had the audacity to ask for a receipt, momentarily interrupting
the constant flow of looky-loos lined up like a flock of sheep on
their way to the slaughterhouse and all too eager to part with
their money. Even though the boat tour was something for the
tourists, Roland considered it part of his on-the-job training and

a legitimate business expense. Hopefully, the people who processed his expense reimbursement claims would agree and not give him a hard time about it.

But the boat tour was enjoyable and confirmed two things Roland had been told when he'd first learned he'd be posted way up here on the Canadian border; it was a beautiful part of the country, and there was no way in hell he'd be able to stop the flow of illegal booze as a one-man operation. He'd be lucky to slow it down enough to make a dent in what was, in Roland's opinion, a government-sponsored license for criminals to print money.

Already desperate for a way out of this remote outpost, Roland knew there were only two ways to manage that short of him outright quitting and then trying to catch back on with a police department in any place other than Philadelphia. He knew his days in the City of Brotherly Love were over, but there were a lot of other cities around that sounded nice. New York was big, but a possibility. And he'd heard good things about Chicago. And since both of those cities would be at the center of illegal booze, they'd be great places for him to rebuild his reputation.

But before he could take his place on the podium as one of the great Prohibition agents of his day, Roland needed to figure out a way to get promoted. Moving up in the Prohibition Unit was his only way out of the wilderness and back to where all the real action was taking place. To make that happen in a timely fashion, as well as impress the people in Washington, Roland would either need to arrest a whole bunch of small fry or land a very big fish.

Spending countless hours trying to catch some local yokels smuggling a couple cases of Canadian sounded like a lot of work to Roland, and the number he'd need to get the right people's attention wasn't worth the paperwork. But catching one of the masterminds Roland was sure were lurking in the shadows and pulling all the strings sounded like a winning strategy. And he could already see the picture in the newspaper of him standing next to a big stack of whiskey cases with his best narrow-eyed glare on full display, saying this is what you get when you try to mess with Roland Doyle.

Yes, catching a big fish was the way to go. No, Roland said, silently correcting himself. Make that catching *the* big fish.

And if his bosses in Washington didn't like his strategy, they could take the $1,200 a year they were paying him and stick it. To be fair, Roland did have to admit that he liked the car that came with the job. But it was the boat that really got his juices flowing, and he was already envisioning spending many an afternoon out on the River fishing and relaxing.

But, first, he'd need to learn how to drive it.

Roland made his way through the crowded street with his head up, and his eyes fixed on a spot off in the distance. He was still developing his *look* and knew it still needed work. Roland wasn't shooting for friendly, but he would at least have to appear approachable if he expected anybody to ever talk to him and maybe tip him off about upcoming booze runs. But he couldn't try to come across as one of their own either, so he had decided to try adding a touch of citified-gentleman to his usual street-cop demeanor. And if he forced himself to smile once in a while, and ask a few questions instead of trying to have all the answers before he knew the facts, maybe he could pull this thing off after all.

That is if he could get a handle on his drinking.

Roland climbed the small set of steps and knocked on the front door of the police station. Why he was knocking instead of just walking in and introducing himself to the police chief he wasn't sure. But maybe being extra polite should also be part of his new look, so Roland decided to at least give it a shot. A gruff voice invited him in, and he walked inside the small space and saw a man sitting behind his desk putting something away in a drawer.

"Good morning," Roland said. "I take it you're Chief Hyde?"

"I am," Oscar said, wiping his mouth with the back of his hand. "Who the hell are you?"

"Friendly, huh?" Roland said, grinning. "I'm Roland Doyle. I'm the new Prohibition agent who's been assigned here."

"Yeah, I heard you were on your way," Oscar said, reluctantly rising out of his chair to shake hands. "When did you get in?"

"Yesterday. But it was too late for me to stop by to introduce myself."

"That's okay," Oscar said, sitting back down. "I wasn't here anyway."

"Out fighting crime and all that, right?"

"Yeah, probably something like that. I don't really remember much of what I did yesterday," Oscar said. "You want a drink?"

"I beg your pardon?" Roland said, doing his best not to sound eager.

"A drink. You do drink, don't you?"

"Chief, you do know that alcohol is illegal, right?"

"Not for personal consumption," Oscar said. "And this comes from my own stash. I started stocking up right after that stupid law was passed."

"I see," Roland said. "Still, in my opinion, it seems to be a bit of a stretch as far as the new law goes. Especially for an officer of the law."

"Mr. Doyle, with all due respect, I really don't give a shit about your opinion," Oscar said, pulling a bottle out of his desk drawer along with two glasses. "You want one or not?"

"No, I really shouldn't," Roland said, eyeing the amber liquid in Oscar's glass and feeling a lump in his throat start to form.

"Your loss," Oscar said, downing the drink and pouring another. "And more for me."

"No, I really shouldn't," Roland said, even though the man hadn't offered a third time. "Don't you think it's a bit early in the day?"

"Says who?" Oscar said, knocking back his second drink.

"Prevailing public opinion I would imagine," Roland said, sneaking another glance at the half-filled bottle.

Oscar snorted and poured himself another drink.

"One thing I've learned is that nobody ever gets anywhere in life worrying too much about the prevailing public opinion."

"Yes, well, I'd love to sit down with you at some point to discuss that," Roland said. "But for now, I was wondering if I could ask you a few questions."

"Knock yourself out," Oscar said, putting his feet up on his desk.

"How many people have boats up here?" Roland said.

"Most of them. There's not much point living up here if you're not going to spend as much time as you can out on the River."

"What types of boats are we talking about?"

"What types?" Oscar said, scrunching up his face into a confused scowl. "There's all sorts of boats around. Big and small. Boats you have to row yourself, and boats with big engines that'll really get you where you want to go. What kinda question is that?"

"I'm just curious to learn what I might be dealing with," Roland said.

Oscar laughed and downed his drink.

"You're dealing with a bunch of people who know a whole lot more about the River than you ever will, and who are going to hate your guts for trying to deprive them of one of their favorite activities."

"Yes, I imagine you're right," Roland said, feeling his hands starting to shake. "Have you had much luck tracking down any booze smugglers?"

"I reckon I would, if I ever spent any time trying to find them," Oscar said, sliding the bottle back into the drawer.

"You don't see that as part of your job?"

"I thought that was your job, Mr. Doyle," Oscar said, staring at him.

"It is. But I also see it as part of all of law enforcement's job these days."

"Again, says who?"

"Well, for one, the United States government," Roland said.

"I don't work for the U.S. government, Mr. Doyle. And until the people I do work for tell me otherwise, I'll keep doing what I've been doing since they hired me."

"Which is?"

"Fighting crime and protecting the safety and security of our local residents, what else?" Oscar said, grinning.

"You don't consider smuggling booze to be a crime?" Roland said.

"I guess I'd consider it a Federal crime, maybe. But I don't have any Federal jurisdiction now, do I?"

"I could deputize you."

"Yeah, you probably could," Oscar said, nodding. "And you could also kiss my lily white ass. But neither one is gonna make any real difference when it comes to bootlegging. Or my own level of personal involvement in that particular activity."

"I see," Roland said. "So, I guess I can't count on any cooperation from you?"

"Oh, I'll be glad to help out, Mr. Doyle. As soon as you arrest somebody, feel free to bring them by. And I'll be happy to lock them up until you can find somewhere else to put them."

"I'll bear that in mind, Chief Hyde," Roland said, already tired of the man. "I was also wondering if you've had any recent arrivals in town."

"Recent arrivals of what?" Oscar said, frowning.

"People. Perhaps a group of unfamiliar tourists, or maybe some new residents who recently relocated here."

"Most tourists are unfamiliar, Mr. Doyle. That's why we call them tourists."

"Yes, of course."

"And as far as new residents are concerned, I can only think of a couple people who've moved here in the last year."

"Who might they be?" Roland said.

"Are you always going to be asking this many questions, or is it just part of your getting to know folks strategy?"

"I'm sure my questions will become less frequent over time," Roland said. "Now, if you don't mind, anything you could tell me about these new residents would be greatly appreciated."

"Well, let's see," Oscar said, fiddling with his empty glass. "The new schoolteacher arrived just before the start of the school year. She's cute and single if you're looking for some companionship. And I hear she makes you stay behind to practice until you get it *just* right."

Roland watched as the man roared with laughter at his own joke. Eventually, he began a coughing fit and hacked up a glob of tobacco. Oscar spit into a trashcan, and Roland took a small step back from the desk.

"Well, they always say repetition is key. And while she does sound lovely, thanks, but no," Roland said. "I find myself solely focused on my work at the moment."

"Yeah, I figured that," Oscar said, nodding as he tried to concentrate. "About the only other person I can think of is a guy who moved here last year and bought a dairy farm."

"I see," Roland said, nodding. "I assume there are a lot of dairy farmers around here."

"Yeah, they tend to show up in places where cows congregate."

"Good one, Chief Hyde," Roland said, fighting the urge to punch the guy in the throat and walk out with his bottle of whiskey.

"This farmer isn't what you'd expect to see in a guy running cows for a living," Oscar said. "But I have to admit I was wrong about his chances for success. From what I can tell, he's making a killing."

"What makes him different from the others?" Roland said.

"He's just odd and has a very high opinion of himself. But he's creating jobs, and my bosses like people who do that."

"Of course. I've found that the private sector does tend to look favorably upon the job creators," Roland said.

"Do you always talk like that?"

"Like what?" Roland said, confused.

"Like you just bought a dictionary and are trying to get your money's worth."

"Another good one, Chief," Roland said, forcing a smile. "What makes this dairy farmer odd?"

"He's just different. It's hard to put my finger on it."

"What's his name?"

"Milo Razner," Oscar said, again removing the bottle from the desk drawer. "You know, I've always liked the way his name rolls off the tip of your tongue. *Mi-lo Raz-ner.*"

"Milo Razner," Roland whispered, doing his best not to let on that he might know the man. "Do you know where he's from?"

"Philadelphia, I think," Oscar said. "How he ever ended up here I have no idea."

"I imagine that would make for an interesting story."

Roland decided against asking him for the location of
Milo's farm. The way the chief was acting Roland wasn't clear
what side of the law Oscar was actually on. And since he seemed
to be saying nice things about Razner, anything was possible
when it came to who might be working together running booze
across the border. But if the man in question was the same Milo
Razner, Roland was pretty sure he could add him to the list of
big fish that were just waiting to be caught.

"Well, I suppose I should probably get out of here and let
you get on with the rest of your day," Roland said.

"Yeah, as you can see, I'm pretty busy today," Oscar said,
pouring another drink. "But thanks for stopping by. It's a small
town, so I'm sure I'll be seeing you around."

"It was nice meeting you, Chief Hyde."

"Yeah. And if I could offer you a piece of friendly advice,
the next time somebody offers you a drink, you might want to do
the neighborly thing and accept it."

"I'll keep that in mind," Roland said, opening the door into
bright sunlight that further seared his already parched throat.

# A Flower in Full Bloom

**Fannie picked up the** twenty-dollar bill Milo placed on the counter and tucked it securely into her cleavage. Milo smiled as he watched her readjust the top of her dress until her breasts were back where she wanted them, and the twenty had disappeared from sight.

"Either business is booming, or I do believe they're getting even bigger, Fannie."

"It's gonna cost you to find out just how big the safe is, Milo," she said, giving him a coy smile. "But you already know that, don't you?"

"Yeah, I know that," Milo said, smiling back.

"I've already delivered a nice bottle of Canadian and some ice to Daisy's room," Fannie said.

"Thanks, I appreciate it. As always, your customer service is outstanding."

"You sure you only want an hour tonight?"

"Yes," Milo said, shrugging. "Any longer than that with Daisy and I'm simply worthless the next day at work."

"That's not what she says," Fannie said, winking at him.

"Well, she is a chatty one at times," Milo said, then turned around when someone tapped him on the shoulder. "Hello, Melvin."

"Hey, Milo," Melvin English said, nodding hello to Fannie. "I just dropped by to grab a drink. Are you here to get horizontal, or would you like to join me?"

"I'm afraid I have other things on my mind than alcohol this evening, Melvin. But thanks for the offer," Milo said, waving as he headed for the stairs.

"Hey, Milo," Melvin said, calling after him.

Milo stopped, walked back to the reception desk and waited patiently for Melvin to get to the point.

"I was just wondering if you've met the new Revenuer," Melvin said.

"No, I haven't had the pleasure. Have you?"

"Yeah, I met him today. He stopped by my office for a meet and greet."

"What's he like?" Milo said, casually.

"About what you'd expect. Real serious about himself and what he calls his important work. And he asks more questions than a three-year-old."

"That's probably a good thing, Melvin."

"What? Him asking a bunch of questions?"

"Yes. If he wasn't asking you a lot of questions, it could mean he's suspicious about what you're up to," Milo said. "You know, keeping his cards close to the vest and all that."

"Why would he be suspicious of me?" Melvin said, frowning.

"No reason at all," Milo said. "I'm just saying if he were suspicious he might not say much and let you do all the talking. But I'm sure you don't have anything to worry about, Melvin."

"Yeah. Why would this guy worry about anything I'm doing?" Melvin said, laughing nervously. "Thanks, Milo."

"Is this Revenuer gonna have the right to come in here and raid the place?" Fannie said.

"Yes, I'm afraid he might," Milo said. "It's a rather intrusive law."

"Would I be within my rights to just shoot him?" Fannie said.

"Probably not your best option, Fannie," Milo said, laughing. "Let's see how it all plays out before you start panicking. He probably has his sights set on bigger targets. But if you feel he is starting to overstep his authority, let us know, and Melvin and I will have a chat with some of our local leaders."

"Okay," Fannie said. "Or maybe I'll just mention it to them the next time they're in."

"Fannie, I'm shocked," Milo said, grinning at her. "Are you saying you'd use their visit here as an opportunity to manipulate our town leaders at a weak moment?"

"That's what I'm saying," Fannie said.

"You're talking about blackmail?"

"Exactly."

"I knew there was a reason I liked you," Milo said, tipping his hat as he headed for the stairs.

**Milo found** Daisy as he always did; sprawled out on the bed wearing a smile and not much else. She looked up pleasantly surprised to see him.

"Oh, it's you. I was expecting someone else," Daisy said. "How are you, Milo?"

He removed his hat and sat down in a chair next to the bed and poured two glasses of whiskey over ice.

"I'm doing well, Daisy. I do hope you're not disappointed to see me."

"Not at all," she said, accepting her drink and raising it in a toast. "I'm glad you stopped by. I could use a break."

"I believe you're making an assumption, Daisy," Milo said, grinning. "How do you know I'm not here to ravage you?"

"Let's call it an educated guess," she said, sitting up to light a cigarette. "What's on your mind, Milo?"

"What on earth is that you're wearing?" Milo said, taking a closer look at the robe that hung off her at an odd angle.

"It's hideous, isn't it?" she said, hopping off the bed and letting the robe fall to the floor. "Oscar bought it for me. That's who I was expecting to drop by."

Milo caught himself staring at her from head to toe with repeated trips in between, then forced himself to glance down at the cheap tiger-print robe that looked like it was made of crepe paper.

"He wants me to wear it whenever he visits," Daisy said, scratching her bottom as she walked to the closet. She slipped into a silk robe but didn't bother to tie it. "The thing itches like hell."

"That's the least of its problems," Milo said, draping a leg over the other and taking a sip of whiskey. "But Oscar is on my list tonight, so let's start with him. I need an update on how you're doing with him."

"He's pretty much mine for the taking now," she said, scratching her arms. "And I can't wait until I get everything out of him you need. He creeps me out."

"That's completely understandable," Milo said. "But Oscar can't be the worst creature you've ever had to lay down with, Daisy."

"No, he's not," she said, focusing on her cigarette. "But he's a lot like him."

"I do like your sense of humor," Milo said, chuckling. "How did he react when you told him he didn't need to pay you?"

"Like a kid at Christmas," she said, blowing smoke up at the ceiling. "But since he's convinced himself he's a gift to every woman walking the earth, he didn't seem surprised when I let him know." She seemed to shudder at the thought of him. "He's disgusting, Milo, and he's a drunken creep. I still don't understand what your plans are for him, but I sure hope it doesn't take long for them to bear fruit."

"Don't worry, it won't be much longer," Milo said, topping off their drinks. "I have another job for you."

"Does it have anything to do with Oscar?" she said, frowning.

"No, actually this one deals with the new Revenuer, Roland Doyle," Milo said, lighting his own cigarette.

"I heard he was in town," Daisy said. "What do you need?"

"The usual," Milo said, tossing a crisp fifty on top of the bed. "Find out what you can about him. Get him to divulge some of his plans for clamping down on bootlegging. And at some point, I'm going to need you to slip something into your conversation," Milo grinned as he rattled the ice in his glass. "During one of your *quieter* moments, if you catch my drift."

"Yeah, I got it, Milo," she said, laughing. "So, what's the message you want me to give to Mr. Doyle?"

"I'll let you know. But it will be something about Oscar."

"Oscar?" she said, frowning.

"Yes," Milo said, nodding. "Actually, a message about his garage."

"Okay, Milo. That sounds like an odd topic of conversation, but I'm sure you've got your reasons," she said, shaking her head. "What else is on your mind?"

"Billy. How's he doing?"

"Billy's fine," she said, shrugging. "And he's stopped talking about leaving. At least for now."

"Good. Keep him happy, Daisy. You can do that, right?"

She leaned back against a stack of pillows and let her robe fall open. She spread her arms wide, bent her legs at the knees and wiggled her toes. Milo watched her then exhaled loudly.

"Dumb question. Forget I asked."

# Can You Hear Me Now?

**Violet Hollman wasn't at all** what Milo had expected. After hearing all the stories about her propensity to listen in on other people's phone calls, he'd assumed she was an older woman, perhaps even a grandmother with nothing better to do than sticking her nose where it didn't belong. But Milo was surprised to see a young, attractive woman, somewhere in her 30s, sitting in front of a switchboard and efficiently maneuvering various cables that enabled the calls to connect to the correct party. She was wearing a headset and paying close attention to what was being said. As such, she didn't hear Milo come in. He stood patiently at the front counter studying her, and when she did finally turn around, she jerked back in her chair, startled.

"Oh, you frightened me," she said, clasping her chest with her free hand. "I'm so sorry to keep you waiting."

"Don't worry about it. I was more than happy to watch and wait for you to finish what you were doing," Milo said, smiling. "And I must say, you were certainly focused. I assume it was an interesting conversation."

Violet's face flushed a color that almost matched her name, and her bottom lip quivered.

"I'm sure I don't know what you mean, sir," she stammered.

"Oh, let's not get off on the wrong foot by lying to each other, Violet," Milo said, continuing to smile at her. "Allow me to introduce myself. I'm Milo Razner."

"Oh, Mr. Razner," she said as some of the redness in her face receded. "It's nice to finally meet you."

"And you as well, Violet."

"What brings you to my office? Is something wrong with your phone?"

"No, my phone is working quite well, thank you," Milo said, glancing around. "Do you work here all day by yourself?"

"I do at the moment," she said as she moved some cables in and out of different holes in the switchboard. "I have someone who handles nights. And I had somebody helping me out during the day, but she moved on recently."

"That must make it difficult to stay current with all the different things going on," Milo said, staring at her.

Violet's face again began to turn a shade of bright red.

"Relax, Violet," Milo said. "I'm not here to make trouble for you. In fact, I'm here to present you with a business opportunity."

"Okay," she said, staring blankly at Milo.

"You see, Violet. I, like most people in town, are aware of your fondness for eavesdropping. And while I personally consider it to be a rather distasteful invasion of other's privacy, I believe it would be beneficial to have someone on my payroll with your access to information."

"You want to pay me to listen in on other people's phone calls?" she said, frowning.

"Why on earth would you want to keep doing it for free, Violet?" Milo said, grinning.

Violet started to protest then stopped and giggled. She placed a hand over her mouth and stared wide-eyed at Milo.

"What exactly are you looking for, Mr. Razner?"

"I assure you that it's nothing tawdry if that's what you're thinking. I have no interest in who might be keeping company with someone they shouldn't, or who might be working the other side of the street when it comes to matters of the law. Unless those things happen to intersect with my own interests."

"Okay. I think I'm following you," she said, nodding as she moved several mores cables in and out of the switchboard.

"There's a man who has just moved here. A gentleman by the name of Roland Doyle."

"Sure. The new Revenuer," Violet said. "I've heard a few things about him. Most people who've crossed paths with him already seem to hate him."

"That doesn't surprise me. He's a rather deplorable individual," Milo said. "Unfortunately, Mr. Doyle and I have, as you say, crossed paths in the past, and he continues to harbor a grudge for things he erroneously believes I was responsible for. And I can assure you, he is incorrect on all counts. But I believe Mr. Doyle has plans to do everything he can to tarnish my good reputation and do damage to my new business enterprise."

"The bastard," Violet said. "But what else would you expect from a Fed, right?"

"I'm glad to see we're on the same page, Violet."

"So, what do you need by way of information?" she said.

"For now, pretty much everything you hear from and about Mr. Doyle," Milo said. "And I will also need your help sowing a few seeds from time to time."

"You mean helping you *fabricate* a tale or two?"

"Well done, Violet," Milo said, nodding. "You catch on fast. There truly is a remarkable collection of young women residing in this area."

"What?"

"Nothing. I'm just thinking out loud," Milo said, waving it off. "So, what do you think of my offer, Violet?"

"I'm not sure, Mr. Razner," she said, staring at him. "I haven't heard it yet."

"Oh, so you're ready to talk money? Getting right to it. I like that."

"Information I have. Money, not so much."

"I was thinking about fifty dollars a week to start," Milo said, then waited for her to connect another call.

"Fifty a week just to keep my ears open for you?"

"Yes. And sow a few seeds when necessary."

"Well, I'm not much of a gardener, Mr. Razner," she said, laughing.

"Don't worry. I'll be giving you a lot of help with the planting," Milo said, his stare intensifying. "As well as keeping an eye on how things are growing. And keeping a close eye on you as well. You know, just to make sure you're adding the correct amount of fertilizer."

Violet blinked back at him until Milo's stare forced her to look away.

"And, of course, any information you come up with is for my ears only. Unless I tell you otherwise," Milo said, continuing to stare hard at her.

"Of course."

"Our arrangement will have to be our little secret, Violet. That point is non-negotiable."

"I understand, Mr. Razner," she said, finally managing to maintain eye contact. "I can handle that. I'm a much better listener than I am a talker."

"Well, like they always say, practice does make perfect," Milo said, smiling. "Very good. I'm glad to hear that. So, do we have a deal?"

"Well, Mr. Razner, the way I see it, right now I have three options available."

"Oh, do tell. I'd love to hear them."

"It's pretty obvious that you probably don't like it when people refuse what you consider to be a generous offer."

"You're right, Violet. I don't like it at all."

"So, my choices seem to be me saying no and probably having to leave town for my own personal safety, staying here and working for you, or finding out if I'm capable of swimming the length of the St. Lawrence," she said, shrugging.

"Funny you should say that. I use that swimming reference all the time," Milo said, grinning.

"Yeah. So I've heard."

# A Little Spin Leads To
# A Sudden Stop

**Roland had thought he was** getting the hang of things until the boat got broadsided by a heavy set of choppy waves that tossed him out of the driver seat and onto the deck. The boat rocked violently and began a hard-right turn toward shore as soon as he let go of the steering wheel. Roland scrambled back to the driver seat on his knees and managed to pull the throttle back to neutral, and the boat slowed then drifted.

Still dealing with a massive hangover produced by a quart of something that was called whiskey but tasted like pine tar, Roland decided, since he was already on his knees, to take advantage of his current position. He crawled to the side of the boat, draped his head over the edge, and threw up. When his eyes finally cleared and his stomach stopped churning, he turned around and sat with his back against the boat. Roland let the breeze wash over him hoping it would make him feel better, but another round of pine tar surged up his windpipe, and he managed to hang his head over the side just in time.

Roland gagged and retched several times then wiped his mouth with a sleeve when his breathing returned to normal. He staggered to his feet and sat down in the driver seat. Roland gently accelerated, headed downriver, and, a few minutes later when he was pretty sure he was done throwing up, pushed the throttle down and gripped the steering wheel tight.

**Milo watched** Elmer and Roscoe wheel the final two cans of last night's shipment up the incline to where the delivery truck was parked. He waited for the sound of doors slamming and the rumble of the truck driving off, then caught a glimpse of Birdie out of the corner of his eye just as he was about to flick a cigarette butt into the River. But Birdie remembered at the last second, and he crushed the butt out with his fingers and slipped it into his shirt pocket.

"Almost forgot," Birdie said, chuckling as he limped his way down the dock to where Milo was standing.

Willy Lawless gently closed the cover of the storage area in the stern and latched it shut. Then he sat down on the padded leather top and looked up at Milo.

"You said you wanted to talk with me about a business opportunity?" Willy said, trying to hand roll a cigarette and failing miserably.

"Give me that," Birdie said, shaking his head. "You're wasting good tobacco."

Willy watched Birdie expertly roll three cigarettes in rapid succession, then climbed out of the boat to light all three. Milo took a long drag from his and nodded his approval.

"How many cases of booze have we bought from Oscar and Melvin?" Milo said.

"We just hit two hundred," Willy said. "And I'm running out of places at the house to store it."

"Perfect. Two hundred is a nice round number. I think it's time we helped Roland Doyle get to know our police chief a bit better," Milo said, grinning. "And make a little money in the process."

"What did you have in mind?" Willy said.

"Well, first, I need to get Ben Green off my back. He's driving me nuts," Milo said.

"The guy who runs the speakeasies with the Senator?" Willy said.

"That's him," Milo said. "Some people are never happy. Every time I see him, he starts bugging me about top-shelf whiskey."

"So?" Willy said.

"So, I think this is the perfect time to set you up in your own sideline," Milo said.

"You want me to sell this guy Green all of the booze we bought from Oscar and Melvin?"

"No, only half of it," Milo said, catching a glimpse of a boat that seemed to be heading their way.

"What do you want me to do with the other half?" Willy said.

"Put it in Oscar's garage," Milo said, still staring out at the boat. "But not until I tell you."

"His garage? I think that's where he parks his car, Milo."

"You don't say? He parks his car in the garage?" Milo said, giving Willy a blank stare.

"No, I mean, with his car in there, there isn't going to be room for a hundred cases of booze," Willy said.

"Then I guess you'll have to do something about his car, won't you?" Milo said.

"Yeah, I guess I will," Willy said, grinning. "And you want me to sell the other hundred cases to Green?"

"I do," Milo said, nodding. "But you'll be doing it without me, Willy. And if I ever hear that you've mentioned my name to him, we're gonna have a big problem. Are we clear on that?"

"We are," Willy said.

"And you're going to have to figure out your own transportation. You can't use any of my equipment, my distribution network, or anybody who works for me. And stay far away from Beulah's cheese shop. You're going to be out there on your own, Willy. But this is your chance to start making some real money."

"Okay, I got it, Milo," Willy said, nodding. "How much should I charge him?"

"Seventy bucks a case," Milo said. "And we'll split the seven grand fifty-fifty. After that, you can charge whatever you want, and you'll keep everything you make."

"That's more than fair," Willy said, then raised an eyebrow at Milo. "In fact, it's such a good offer, a person might wonder why you're making it."

"Would you believe me if I said that I just wanted to do everything I could to help you get ahead?" Milo said, grinning.

"Do I look like I just fell off the milk truck, Milo?" Willy said, exhaling smoke.

"Good answer, Willy," Milo said. "I like doing business with people who tend to be skeptics. A healthy dose of suspicion is one of the keys to a person's longevity. But let me be clear, I do want you to succeed. And I also have some long-term plans for you I think you're going to like. But to address your immediate concerns, I think having a man with your skills running booze is just what we need around here."

"You mean, one more person to get Roland Doyle's attention and keep him from focusing on you?" Willy said.

"You are a quick study," Milo said, finishing his cigarette and sliding the butt into Birdie's shirt pocket.

"Hey," Birdie said, glaring at Milo.

"You're already using your shirt as an ashtray," Milo said. "Why ruin two?"

"They can try all they want, Milo, but nobody is ever going to catch me," Willy said. "Especially some rube Revenuer like Doyle."

"Well, let's hope you're right. But if Roland Doyle ever happens to catch you, you do know how to respond when he starts asking questions about me, right?"

"I sure do," Willy said, grinning. "I'm sorry, Mr. Doyle, but who's this Milo Razner you keep asking me about?"

"Perfect," Milo said.

"Do you think this guy Doyle is any good at what he does?" Willy said.

"I think you're going to get a chance to find out real soon," Milo said, nodding at the boat that was rapidly getting closer.

"Is that him?" Willy said, squinting through the sunlight.

"Yes, I believe it is," Milo said.

"He's going a little too fast for a landing don't you think?" Birdie said, studying the approaching boat.

"I do. And if he scratches my boat, he's a dead man."

**Roland couldn't** help but notice the dock and boathouse that were beginning to dominate his field of vision. He reached over to pull the throttle back to slow down, but got confused and pushed it the wrong way. The boat sped up, and Roland panicked. He let go of the steering wheel and pulled the lever back to the neutral position with both hands. But the boat's momentum continued to propel it forward, and the steering wheel spun. The boat made a forty-five-degree turn left, and the last thing Roland saw were three men standing on the dock staring at him in disbelief.

The boat slammed into the end of the dock head-on and came to an abrupt stop. Roland was launched over the bow and soared through the air. He bounced off the dock twice, then landed with a splash in the shallow water on his back.

Milo stared down at the unconscious Revenuer, then glanced at Birdie.

"Now do you understand what I'm talking about when I tell you not to throw shit in the River?"

**Milo and** Willy hopped off the dock into the water and dragged the man to shore. They stretched him out on the grass, and Milo found himself taking a bit too much pleasure as he slapped the Revenuer several times to wake him from his stupor. Eventually, Roland started blinking rapidly, then tried to sit up.

"Whoa, easy does it there, cowboy," Milo said, using both hands to help him sit upright. "You took quite a tumble there. But I have to say you make one hell of an entrance."

"Did I break anything?" Roland said, examining himself with both hands.

"Yeah, my dock," Milo said. "And I expect you to pay to get it fixed. Your boat is also probably going to need a bit of work. Birdie's over there right now taking a look to see if it's taking on water."

"My head hurts," Roland said.

"You're probably concussed. You might want to get it checked out when you get back to town. But just try to relax for now. Willy will be right back with some refreshments."

"I'm bleeding pretty badly," Roland said, examining his blood-stained hands.

"It's okay," Milo said. "You can bleed all you want on the lawn."

"You're Milo Razner, aren't you?"

"I am, Mr. Doyle. It's nice to finally meet you after all these years," Milo said.

"Yes, after all these years," Roland said, groaning. "I thought we were going to meet when I arrested your partner, Jimmy Sleaze. But you somehow managed to slip away. My guess is that you went out through the ventilation system of that bank."

"You must have me confused with somebody else, Mr. Doyle. Jimmy Sleaze used to be a buddy of mine, but I put some distance between him and me as soon as I figured out some of the things he was up to."

"And then you headed up here?" Roland said, climbing to his feet and struggling to maintain his balance.

"Not straight away," Milo said. "But as soon as I discovered this beautiful place, I decided to take up residence."

"And now you're a dairy farmer?" Roland said, trying to raise the eyebrow that was dripping blood.

"I am," Milo said. "I find it to be a most honorable occupation."

"Do you now?"

"I do. And I haven't stopped learning since I bought the place," Milo said. "For example, do you know that cows have to be milked twice a day?"

"I did not know that," Roland said, patting his head and checking his hands for signs of fresh blood.

"See, you're learning stuff already," Milo said, grinning. "Aren't you glad you, if you'll pardon the expression, dropped in? Which brings me back to my real question. Why are you here, Mr. Doyle?"

Roland looked around in all directions as if he was trying to get his bearings. He glanced at his boat that had a long crack near the top of the bow, grimaced at the damage, then glanced back at Milo.

"I'd like to talk with you about the illegal booze business that's operating in the area," Roland said.

"Well, I'd be happy to offer my two cents, Mr. Doyle, but if it doesn't come out of a cow, I don't think I can be much help these days when it comes to local beverages of choice," Milo said. "But why don't we grab a cold beer and have a chat?"

"What?" Roland said, again touching his forehead to check for blood. "I just asked you about illegal booze, and now you're offering me a beer?"

"The beer isn't illegal. It's made right here on the premises for home consumption. And anybody who's read the new law knows that permitted. Our latest batch is a German pilsner I think you'll like."

Milo and Roland watched Willy head down the path that led back to the boathouse. He was carrying a bucket packed with ice and several bottles. Milo gestured for Roland to walk back to the dock and he gingerly made his way to where the bucket sat waiting. Birdie finished inspecting the damage to Roland's boat and limped over and helped himself to a beer. Milo grabbed two beers from the bucket, opened both, and offered one to Roland.

"I really shouldn't," Roland said, staring at the bottle that was dripping ice water. "Perhaps another time."

"You sure about that, Mr. Doyle?" Milo said, grinning. "You just did a header off your boat and almost killed yourself in the process. Who knows how much time you've got left?"

Roland thought about it, then nodded and accepted the bottle from Milo. He tipped his head back and drained the bottle in one long gulp. He burped loudly, then exhaled and glanced down at the bucket.

"Yeah, I imagine you worked up quite a thirst during your flight," Milo said, reaching into the bucket and handing Roland another beer.

Roland nodded, grabbed the second beer, and drank half. He blinked several times, shook his head to clear it, then finished the other half.

"Good beer. Well, I suppose I should get going," Roland said. "I think I need to get to a doctor and have my head checked out."

"That's a good idea," Milo said, taking a sip of his beer. "We'd hate to have you walking around with a concussion thinking up all sorts of crazy ideas."

"Yeah, that would be tragic. Thanks for the beer, Mr. Razner," Roland said, staggering a bit as he made his way back to his boat. "I look forward to continuing our conversation as soon as I'm feeling a bit more coherent."

"Feel free to drop in anytime," Milo said. "But the next time, you might want to come in a bit slower. And you should try to remember that immovable objects have a tendency to come out ahead when you try to run them over."

"Yeah, thanks. I'll try to remember that," Roland said, frowning at Milo before glancing at Birdie. "Is my boat leaking?"

"I noticed some water in the bilge, but it's nothing I would worry about," Birdie said, shrugging.

"Okay. I appreciate you taking a look at it," Roland said, climbing aboard. "I'll see you around, Mr. Razner."

"Where do I send it?" Milo said.

"Send what?"

"The bill for fixing my dock," Milo said, pointing at several boards that had been split in half.

"Oh, yeah. Well, just drop it off at my office. I'll include it with my next expense reimbursement claim," Roland said.

"I'll do that, Mr. Doyle," Milo said, touching the brim of his hat.

"When they see the bill for that, I doubt if they'll worry much about the four bits for the boat tour," Roland said, more to himself than anyone else.

"I'm not following you," Milo said, frowning.

"I'm babbling. It must be the concussion. Okay, I'm off. I'll catch you later."

Roland eventually managed to get the boat in reverse and slowly backed away from the dock. He turned the boat around and drove off with a wave. All three men watched him until he became a speck on the horizon.

"Is it my imagination, or is he riding a bit low in the water?" Milo said.

"Oh, he's riding low all right," Birdie said, grinning as he watched the boat plow through the water.

"I thought you said it wasn't leaking," Milo said, staring at Birdie.

"No, what I said was I wouldn't worry about the water in the bilge."

"You mean, *you* wouldn't worry, but he probably should?" Milo said, a grin starting to appear.

"Oh, yeah," Birdie said, limping over to the bucket to grab a fresh beer. "If I were him, I'd be worrying a lot."

"Do you think he can make it back to town?"

"Before the boat sinks?" Birdie said.

"Yeah."

"If he keeps his speed up, I reckon he's got a chance of making it home dry. I'd probably give him a fifty-fifty shot."

"Well, maybe Mr. Doyle will do us a favor and drive real slow," Milo said, finishing his beer and placing the empty bottle back in the bucket. "Did you happen to catch the look in his eyes when he was downing those beers?"

"I did," Willy said. "It reminded me of the look my daddy used to get when he was on a bender."

"I do believe our Mr. Doyle may have a bit of a drinking problem," Milo said. "That could come in very handy at some point."

"A Prohibition agent who's an alcoholic?" Willy said. "That's funny."

"I believe the word you're looking for is ironic," Milo said. "But I agree, Willy. It is hard to miss the humor."

"Is he going to be a problem, Milo?"

"I'm not sure, Birdie. But I am certain he's going to be a total pain in the ass. Don't worry, it's nothing we can't handle."

"I gotta say, Milo," Willy said. "I'm a little worried. I hope you've got a plan to deal with him."

"That would be good," Birdie said, nodding.

"Gentlemen, you can both relax," Milo said. "By the time we're done with Mr. Doyle, slamming into that dock is going to feel like a mosquito bite."

"Good. I don't like him," Birdie said. "Is there anything you want me to do to help?"

"As a matter of fact, there is. I need to you come up with a map of some immovable objects that are lurking and just waiting to be discovered. If you catch my drift."

"Oh, I caught it, Milo," Birdie said, grinning. "And I assume you'll want me to drive?"

"Of course," Milo said, sitting down on the dock and dangling his feet in the water. "Willy, why don't you head up to the house and grab some more beers and a jar of Miracle? Thanks to our new friend, Mr. Doyle, I'm suddenly in the mood to spend the rest of the afternoon enjoying the sunshine and getting drunk."

# Taking One For The Team

**Daisy opened her eyes** as soon as she heard the man on top of her begin to snore. She silently cursed Milo, then remembered the crisp fifty he'd left for her and decided to give him a pass. But the dead weight of the snoring man crushing the air out of her lungs was a different story and wouldn't stand. If the guy had done enough to deserve a nap, she might have let it go, but he'd hadn't lasted long enough to start breathing heavy, much less work up a sweat. Insulted, as well as repulsed by the man, Daisy worked an arm free then flicked a finger hard against the thick bandage that was wrapped around the sleeping man's head.

"Ow," Roland said, waking up and rolling off her onto his back. He gently rubbed the tender spot and glared at her. "Damn, girl, take it easy. I'm dealing with a serious injury here."

"Oh, I'm so sorry, sweetie," Daisy said. "I was trying to get my arm loose, and my hand must have slipped."

"Feel free to let your hands slide anywhere they want, except my head," Roland said, sitting up in bed. "Where's that bottle?"

Daisy grabbed the whiskey bottle off the nightstand and handed it to him. He took a long pull straight from the bottle then wiped his mouth with the back of his hand. He took a moment to catch his breath then took another long pull. He handed the bottle back to her and stretched back out.

"Normally, I'd be thinking about another go-round," Roland said. "But I don't think I'm gonna be up for up tonight."

"That's okay, sweetie. I guess I wore you out. Besides, you shouldn't push yourself too hard," she said, climbing out of bed and slipping into her robe. She tied it tight and sat down in a chair and lit a cigarette.

"I guess it was a stroke of good luck to find you at the doctor's office, huh?" Roland said.

"It was pure kismet," Daisy said, recalling the phone call she'd gotten from Milo earlier commanding her to hurry up and get her butt over there.

"By the way, what were you doing at the doctor's office? You haven't caught anything I should know about, have you?"

"I beg your pardon?" Daisy snapped.

"I was just wondering...never mind."

"I was there to get a prescription," Daisy said, glaring at him. "I'm occasionally troubled by migraines."

"Yeah, I get a lot of headaches," Roland said. "But nothing like the one I've got today."

"I think mine are an occupational hazard."

"I would have thought you'd have to worry about injuries in other places," Roland said, frowning. "Anyway, I'm sure glad we met and hit it off so well. I gotta ask you a question though. Why would a working girl like you decide to climb into bed with me for free?"

"Temporary insanity?" Daisy whispered as she tipped her head back and blew smoke up at the ceiling.

"What?" Roland said, reaching for the bottle of whiskey.

"Nothing, sweetie," Daisy said, flashing him a big smile. "I was just ruminating out loud."

"Well, I sure did enjoy myself. And I certainly hope we can make this a regular thing," Roland said, draining what was left in the bottle. "Do you have any other suitors around that I might consider competition?"

"One or two, maybe," Daisy said, casually. "I've been known to keep company with Oscar from time to time."

"Oscar Hyde? The police chief?" Roland said, frowning. "I'm surprised to hear that. He seems to be a rather unpleasant man. And from what I've seen, quite the heavy drinker."

"He has his moments," Daisy said. "And as you probably noticed, I don't mind being with a man who enjoys a drink or two."

"Are you saying I drink a lot?" Roland said, glaring at her.

"For someone whose job it is to arrest people with illegal booze, I'd have to say, yeah, I am."

"I'm after big fish," Roland said, gingerly sitting up on the edge of the bed. "Besides, if folks can figure out a way to get booze into their house, who am I to quibble about that?"

"Noble," Daisy said, crushing her cigarette out.

"Yeah, I like to think so. What is it about Oscar you find appealing?"

Daisy casually sat back in her chair and looked off into the distance.

"Oscar always surprises me. One minute, he's all cop-like and no-nonsense. Then he'll turn into a little boy and be cute as hell."

"Oscar? Little boy cute?" Roland said, frowning. "Maybe if little boys chewed tobacco and chugged whiskey."

"Those are just some of the things that show how manly he is," Daisy said. "You probably wouldn't understand the little boy traits. Only another woman would get that."

"I'll take your word for it."

"But what I love the best about Oscar is how he's always trying to surprise me. Just the other day he said he couldn't wait to show me what was in his garage. He says we're going to have a lot of fun enjoying it."

"A new car?" Roland said.

"I don't think that's what he was referring to," Daisy said, brushing a strand of hair away from her face. "His car is nice enough, but it certainly isn't new."

"What do you think he was talking about?" Roland said.

"I'm not sure," she said, starting to slowly reel him in. "But he was acting all mysterious about it. And then he mentioned that he'd like to take me on a trip. A long weekend in New York. Broadway shows and fancy restaurants. That's hard for a girl to say no to."

"That sounds like an expensive weekend," Roland said, leaning forward.

"I guess," she said, again staring dreamily off into the distance.

"Especially on a small-town cop salary."

"Maybe he's come into some money and wants to share it with me," Daisy said, locking eyes with Roland.

"Yeah, that was going to be my guess as well," Roland said, then whispered. "I knew it."

"What's that, sweetie?"

"Nothing."

"I hate to do this, but would you mind if we called it a night?" Daisy said. "All of a sudden, I'm starting to feel a migraine coming on."

"I hear that turning all the lights off and lying down and staying real still with your eyes closed is a good way to deal with one of those."

"Yeah, I've tried that strategy in the past," Daisy said, giving him a weak smile.

"Does it work?"

"I'd probably say the results are mixed, but I'll let you know for sure the next time I'm forced to use it, sweetie."

# Milo Bites Back

**Twenty minutes after Milo** had slipped in the back
door and found Oscar sprawled out on the couch and snoring
loudly, he gave up searching the house and went back outside.
Feeling a bit giddy as the old juices started flowing, he headed
straight for the garage. He slowly opened the unlocked door and
turned on his flashlight. He pointed the beam at Oscar's car, a
Model T in decent shape, then scanned the rest of the garage.
Milo shook his head at the mess.

"What a pig," he whispered.

Various gardening tools, stacks of old newspapers, and
small piles of junk that should have been thrown away a long
time ago ringed the garage floor. Milo focused the flashlight on
three shelves attached to a side wall. Several paint cans were
lined up on the bottom shelf, and Milo continued right past them.
Then he had a thought and shined the light back on the cans.

"Huh," Milo grunted softly. "Could he be that stupid?"

Milo walked toward the shelves and tucked the flashlight
under his arm. He lifted a paint can and gently shook it. He
repeated the process as he made his way along the row. Most
were heavy and made a sloshing sound, but one softly rattled

when he shook it. Milo set the flashlight down on the shelf and used his pocketknife to open the lid. He whistled softly when he saw the bundled stacks of cash inside the can.

"To protect and serve indeed," Milo said, shaking his head. "Geez, Oscar. You need to lift your game. You're taking all the fun out of it."

Milo quickly counted the money that totaled a little over nine thousand dollars. Seven of it had come from Milo, and Oscar had gotten it from Willy as payment for the two hundred cases of whiskey. Milo couldn't care less where the rest of the money had come from, and he tucked all the bundles into his coat until the pockets bulged. He was about to put the lid back on the paint can when he had an idea that brought a smile to his face.

"Why the hell not?" Milo whispered.

He found a scrap of paper in one of the piles of junk and grabbed a pencil from his pocket. He jotted *Thanks, Oscar* on the paper and put it in the paint can then sealed the lid. Milo turned off the flashlight and slipped out of the garage and headed back to his suite at the Crossley.


**Milo entered** the hotel and stopped by reception to check for messages. He had one from the Senator, and the clerk gave Milo an admiring glance when he handed him the phone number.

"Impressive. You've got a senator calling you," the clerk said, smiling at Milo. "I wonder what he wants."

"There's not much to wonder about, Dudley. He's a politician," Milo said. "He either needs a favor, or he's looking for money."

Milo tipped his hat at the clerk and headed up the stairs two at a time. He removed all the bundles of cash from his pockets and tossed them on the bed. He chortled when he saw the size of the final pile then poured himself a drink. He sat down on the edge of bed, placed the call, and played with the bundles while he waited.

"Hello, Senator," Milo said. "I believe you called earlier."

"Hey, Milo," the Senator said. "I just called to get an update about our mutual friend. Can we talk freely over this line?"

"Actually, we can, Senator. Up to a point," Milo said. "I just had the hotel install a private line for me in my suite."

"That was smart, Milo. And probably worth every cent you paid for it."

"It better be, Senator," Milo said. "It cost me a small fortune."

"Oh, well. The cost of doing business, right? I was just checking in to see if you've crossed paths with our friend yet?"

"Actually, I have. In fact, just this afternoon."

"Really?"

"Yeah, he sort of dropped in unexpectedly," Milo said, taking a sip of whiskey.

"Is he everything we thought he was?"

"Actually, he's a bit less than we thought. But he seems dedicated to his job. And I'm sure he'll be doing everything he can to control the problem."

"I see. Well, that's good," the Senator said, clearing his throat. "He's doing very important work."

"He is. But I'm worried that he might not be able to handle it."

"Why is that?"

"Because he's an alcoholic," Milo said, riffling one of the bundles through his fingers.

"Really? How ironic."

"Yes, that's what I thought," Milo said. "But we should know more by later this evening. There's a rumor floating around that he might be called in tonight to crack down on one of our local smugglers."

"A rumor? Can you trust the source?"

"Yes, I'm sure I can. It's pretty much first-hand information."

"Oh, I see," the Senator said. "Okay, Milo, I'll let you go. But please keep me informed and let me know if you need anything."

"I will do that, Senator. Thanks for calling."

The Senator hung up, but Milo tucked the phone under his chin as he topped off his drink.

"Did you get all that, Violet?"

"Every word, Mr. Razner."

**Milo took** a long bath with a glass of whiskey then headed back down to the first floor. He headed for the main ballroom and turned down a long hallway until he stopped in front of a door manned by a large man wearing a uniform that probably left him embarrassed every time he put it on and looked in the mirror.

"Good evening, Howard," Milo said, reaching into his pocket and handing over a five.

"Evening, Mr. Razner," Howard said, bowing slightly. "Sir, again, you don't need to tip me just for letting you inside the speakeasy. You're one of our favorite customers."

"Howard, please indulge me," Milo said. "It's the least I can do to repay you for your outstanding service."

"Sir," Howard said, laughing. "All I do is open the door and make sure I keep all the riff-raff out."

"Exactly. And never underestimate the importance of riff-raff prevention," Milo said, giving the man's shoulder a friendly squeeze. "Speaking of which, are we dealing with any law enforcement inside this evening?"

"No, there's not a cop in sight," Howard said. "Usually, Oscar is here by now, but I haven't seen him all night."

"He's probably dealing with important police matters at the moment," Milo said.

"Oscar?" Howard said. "Are you sure we're talking about the same guy, Mr. Razner?"

"Well, hope springs eternal, right?" Milo said, stepping through the open door.

He looked around the crowded room and noticed a mixture of locals he knew and several tables of visitors who were all having a great time. If any of the patrons were concerned about being caught with illegal booze, none of them were letting on. Milo saw Melvin sitting at the bar by himself, and he walked over and sat down next to him.

"Good evening, Milo," Melvin said, giving his barstool a quarter turn. "Nice to see you. What are you having?"

"No, Melvin, drinks are on me tonight," Milo said, smiling across the bar at the bartender. "I'll have my usual, Wendell. Please, bring another for Melvin, and keep them coming until I tell you to stop."

"The milk business must be booming," Melvin said, tossing back the last of his beer.

"It's a remarkable thing, Melvin," Milo said. "Hundreds of those wonderful creatures producing a delicious and healthy beverage for us to enjoy. And all we need to do is use gentle hands to coax it out of them."

"You mean by squeezing their tits, right?"

"I was trying to wax poetic, Melvin," Milo said, frowning at him. "I take it you've been here a while."

"Yeah, probably too long," Melvin said, trying to focus on someone who'd just walked through the door. "I'm supposed to meet up with Oscar later on, and I want to make sure I'm drunk enough to deal with him."

"You know, Melvin," Milo said. "On my way through reception a few minutes ago, I overheard someone saying that there was some sort of ruckus going on near Oscar's house."

"A ruckus? Who said that?" Melvin said, immediately going on point.

"I didn't recognize the men," Milo said. "But they had that look."

"Feds?"

"Well, I can't say for sure. They could have been a couple of cheaply dressed businessmen. Regardless, it might be a good idea for you to keep your distance from Oscar this evening. I've heard some rumors that he may be involved in some rather nefarious activities."

"You sure do hear a lot of rumors, Milo," Melvin said, taking a long sip from his fresh beer.

"What can I say, Melvin? People just seem to enjoy talking to me."

"That's because you're a good guy, Milo," Melvin said, deep in thought. "Who else would have waived the six grand I owed him?"

"You were just caught in a bad situation, Melvin. And I wouldn't have felt right making you pay for the sins of others."

"Well, you didn't have to do it, but I sure appreciate it. And thanks for the heads up about Oscar. Maybe I will keep my distance tonight," he said, refocusing on the man who'd just arrived. "Hey, isn't that Tom Collins? I haven't seen him in ages."

Milo turned around and caught the look Tom Collins was giving him as he started walking toward Milo.

"Hello, Tom," Milo said.

"Hi, Milo. Melvin. How are you doing this evening?" Tom said.

"Very good, Tom," Milo said. "What brings you to town?"

"There's a small problem with the living room suite you ordered for the farm," Tom said. "We may need to make a slight change, and I wanted to discuss it with you before I went any further."

"Of course," Milo said. "I appreciate you making the trip over. Melvin, if you'll excuse us for a moment."

"Sure," Melvin said, handing his empty glass to the bartender. "I'll be right here."

Milo and Tom headed for a quiet corner of the room.

"What's going on?" Milo said.

"It's Clint," Tom said, shaking his head. "He's getting out of control."

"The drinking?"

"Yeah, there's that," Tom said, nodding. "He's pretty much hooked on the Miracle. But I can deal with that. It's the way he's starting to run his mouth about some things that have me concerned."

"Oh, I don't like chatty employees," Milo said.

"I know you don't, Milo."

"What's he talking about?"

"He's ranting and raving every day about how he's getting screwed on the deal. He says he should be getting a lot more than two dollars a gallon since he's the one who's made the product what it is. And now he's starting to make it personal."

"With me?" Milo said, rubbing his forehead.

"Yeah. He's calling you a steaming bag of you know what."

"I've been called worse," Milo said, shrugging. "That ungrateful prick. And to think I even bought him a new washing machine."

"He's usually whacked out on Miracle when he starts going off, so maybe he's all talk and no action. But I thought you should know."

"Thanks, Tom. Good call on your part."

"So, should we take him for a nice long swim?" Tom said.

"No, not yet," Milo said. "We need to wait a bit. How long before you completely understand his process?"

"A couple of weeks max. He does something during the final filtration I'm still trying to figure out. But I've got the recipe down pat."

"Okay, keep working on that as fast as you can without making him suspicious," Milo said. "And while you're at it, I'm going to need you to plant a seed for me."

"What sort of seed?"

"An idea seed," Milo said. "If Clint has decided he deserves to make more money, let's help him along. As you know, I also have a couple other employees I'm a bit concerned about. Maybe we can come up with an idea that will help us find out just how far all three of them are willing to go in one fell swoop."

"I get it," Tom said, nodding and grinning. "I think I can make that happen."

"I have no doubt, Tom Collins," Milo said, starting to head back to the bar before turning around. "Oh, and if Melvin does happen to ask, tell him we decided to go with taupe for the living room furniture."

"Taupe? That's an awful color," Tom said, scowling.

"Yes, you're right. It is," Milo said, giving it some thought. "Then let's go with the imaginary light blue."

Tom Collins laughed then checked his watch.

"I need to run," Tom said. "I'm supposed to meet Willy in a half-hour."

"Go forth and conquer, Tom Collins," Milo said, spreading his arms wide. "But be quick. And unseen."

"You're sure in a good mood tonight."

"Yes, I am," Milo said. "I had a bit of a windfall earlier today. And I just can't wait to see how the rest of the evening plays out."

# Everyone Earns Their Money

**Willy gave Birdie a hand** opening the garage door, then helped him get Oscar's car in neutral and rolling down the gentle slope of the driveway. When the car reached the street, Birdie started the engine and slowly drove away. Willy peered through the living room window and saw Oscar snoring in a deep sleep. He closed the garage door and trotted through the woods that ran off the back of Oscar's house until he reached the truck he'd *borrowed* earlier in the day. Tom Collins was already sitting in the passenger seat waiting for him.

"When did you get here?" Willy said.

"A couple of minutes ago," Tom said. "As soon as I finished up with Milo at the Crossley, I cut through the park and headed over. Did I miss anything?"

"No, Birdie just left with the car, and Oscar is still out like a light. It looks like he's in a coma. I hope he hears the phone."

**Violet started** to get nervous after the phone still hadn't been answered after a dozen rings. Eventually, a groggy, cranky voice answered.

"Yeah?"

"Chief Hyde?"

"Yeah?"

"It's Violet Hollman. From the phone company."

"Oh, sure. Hello, Violet. Why are you calling me at this hour?"

"Well, I just saw something and wanted to check to see if you were home. Now that I know you are, I think there might be a problem."

"What sort of problem?"

"Well, it's just that I saw your car go past my office. And it looked like a couple of kids were driving it."

"My car? Are you sure?"

"I think so. I thought I recognized the license plate, and you have those big fuzzy things hanging from your rear view mirror, right?"

"Yeah, I do," Oscar said. "And for the record, those big fuzzy things are genuine Indian artifacts I won playing bingo."

"I didn't know the Indians paid homage to fuzzy dice," Violet whispered.

"What?"

"Nothing, Chief."

"What direction were they headed?"

"I'm pretty sure they went north. They're probably just taking your car out for a little joyride, right?"

"I don't know," Oscar said. "But I'm sure gonna find out."

"Do you need me to do anything? Maybe call somebody else?"

"No, I'll handle it," Oscar said. "Thanks for the call, Violet."

"Anytime. And good luck, Chief Hyde."

**Oscar headed** for his bedroom to get dressed. He grabbed his gun and a pint of whiskey, packed his jaw tight with tobacco, then headed outside. He climbed into his police car and headed for town, then made his way north keeping a close eye out for his precious Model T.

**Birdie drove** the car for three miles, then parked behind a thick stand of pines about a hundred yards up from the River. He limped his way down to a dock, climbed in Milo's boat, and opened it up full throttle on his way back into town. He parked it in its slip at Frank Slack's marina, then slowly made his way to Fannie's with the extra twenty Milo had slipped him earlier burning a hole in his pocket.

**Oscar downed** half a pint of whiskey, then grumbled and dribbled tobacco juice all over his shirt as soon as he opened his mouth. He brushed at it angrily with the back of his hand and continued to drive slowly as his eyes swept both sides of the road for any sign of his car.

**Willy backed** the truck up to the garage and waited for Tom open the door. Then both of them quickly began unloading the hundred cases from the back of the truck and stacking them inside the garage. It took them a few minutes to figure out an efficient process, but they soon got a rhythm going. Fifteen minutes later, the truck was empty, and Tom Collins closed the garage door and hopped back in the truck. Willy slowly drove down the driveway, headed for the far side of town, and returned the truck to the exact spot he'd taken it from earlier in the day.

"That was easy," Willy said.

"Yeah," Tom Collins said. "Hey, it's still early. You want to swing by Fannie's place for a nightcap?"

"Just for a drink, right?"

"Yeah, just a drink. I don't think Daisy is working tonight," Tom said. "Her working hours have been pretty spotty lately."

"Figures," Willy said. "Just when you finally start making enough to afford her, she turns flaky."

"Yeah, it's always something, right?"


**Roland was** woken by the sound of the phone that was ringing off the hook. He sat up too quickly, felt nauseous and wobbly, and he gently grabbed the bandage on his head to help him get his balance. Eventually, he managed to tiptoe across the room to the phone.

"Roland Doyle speaking."

"Hi, Mr. Doyle. This is Violet Hollman from the phone company. I'm sorry to disturb you, but I didn't know who else to call."

"Violet? Oh, yes. Of course. How can I help you?"

"Someone just called me and said there was some sort of disturbance going on at Chief Hyde's house."

"Why would they call you?"

"They couldn't get in touch with him," Violet said. "But that's understandable since his car was stolen earlier, and I think he's out looking for it."

"I see," Roland said, grimacing from his headache.

"And since nobody can reach Chief Hyde, I thought I should call you since you're an officer of the law."

"Actually, Violet, a disturbance at a personal residence doesn't fall under my responsibilities," Roland said, anxious to get rid of the woman.

"Yes, I know, sir," Violet said. "But if someone was trying to break into your garage, I imagine you'd appreciate someone trying to look after your interests while you were away."

"His garage?" Roland said, holding the phone closer to his ear.

"Yes, that's what the person said."

"Who was the caller?"

"I didn't recognize the name, Mr. Doyle," Violet said. "It was somebody named Miss Smithson, Smytheson, or something like that. She was calling from the ice cream parlor."

"Probably a tourist," Roland said, nodding to himself.

"Yes, I believe so. Apparently, she and her friend were going for a walk when they went past the chief's house and saw something that made them suspicious."

"What did they see?"

"She wasn't very clear about the details. It was something about a delivery truck."

"A delivery truck? At this time of night?" Roland said, feeling the juices starting to flow.

"Yes, she thought it was odd and decided to call. Imagine her surprise when she described the house, and I told her it was where our chief of police lived."

"Yes, it does seem odd. Well, thanks for calling, Violet. I think I will go check it out. You know, one officer of the law helping out another."

"That's very kind of you, sir. Have a good evening, but please be careful."

"I will. Good evening."

Roland placed the phone back in its cradle, then headed off to get dressed. He grabbed his gun, searched in vain for whiskey, then headed outside to his car.


**Oscar caught** a glimpse of reflected chrome, then came to a stop and turned his police car around and headed back. He located his car a few minutes later and parked about fifty feet behind it. He left the car lights on, drew his gun, and slowly approached the vehicle. Oscar expected to find a couple of teenagers going at it in the back seat, but the car was empty, and he spent the next few minutes scanning the immediate area. Unable to locate the thieves, Oscar removed the car keys and slid them into his pocket. Then he climbed back into the police car and headed for home.

**Roland parked** in the driveway, climbed out of the car, and glanced around. It was dead silent, and all the house lights were off. He turned on his flashlight and slowly approached the garage. Right before he pulled the door open, Roland decided he should have his gun drawn just in case. He reached for it, then wobbled on his feet as another round of nausea hit him. He fumbled the gun while pulling it from its holster, and it fell to the ground, bounced off the driveway, then discharged and shot Roland in the foot.

"Son of a bitch," Roland said, grimacing as the pain emerged then spread.

He dropped the flashlight, dropped to his knees, then rolled around on the driveway in agony with one hand grasping his foot, the other holding his bandaged head. Roland rolled over onto all fours and grabbed the flashlight. Then he sat down and shined the light on his foot. Apart from serious damage to his right boot and some surface blood, all of Roland's toes were still attached and appeared to be working. But his foot hurt like hell.

He collected his gun then pushed himself upright. Another wave of nausea washed over him, and he stumbled forward and almost fell down. Roland stood still, breathing deeply with his eyes closed, and waited until his stomach settled and his temples stopped pounding.

Then he refocused on the garage. It took him a few minutes to work out the logistics, but he eventually managed to get the door open while holding his gun in one hand and the flashlight in the other.

When he saw the hundred cases of whiskey stacked neatly inside the garage, he whistled softly to himself. Roland felt a tickle in the back of his throat and slid the gun back into its holster. He turned the flashlight off and limped down the driveway. Roland looked up and down the empty street to make sure he was free of prying eyes, then limped back to the garage. He proceeded to load five cases of the whiskey into the back seat of his car. He covered them with a tarp, then backed the car down the driveway and parked it on the street.

Roland had just closed the garage door and was about to try and figure out his next steps when he saw the lights of Oscar's police car heading up the driveway. Oscar turned the car off but left the lights on. He climbed out and stared at Roland with a confused look on his face.

"What the hell are you doing here?" Oscar said.

"I got a call."

"Okay," Oscar said, frowning. Then he nodded at the bandage. "What happened to your head?"

"I had a little boating accident," Roland said.

"It looks nasty."

"It could have been worse," Roland said, flashing back to his ride home that afternoon where he'd managed to land the boat at Frank Slack's marina just before it sank.

"Hey, you're bleeding all over my driveway," Oscar said, scowling at Roland.

"Yeah, I got shot in the foot."

"You got shot as well?"

"Yeah, it's been quite a day," Roland said.

"Who the hell shot you?"

"Uh, at the moment, an unidentified assailant," Roland said, his temples pulsing hard.

"Okay, we need to back up for a sec. I've completely lost the plot. Tell me again what you're doing here," Oscar said.

"Well, you see, Chief Hyde," Roland said. "The call I got was about somebody making a delivery here."

"A delivery? Of what?"

Roland drew his gun, pointed it at Oscar, and walked backward until he reached the handle of the garage door. Oscar was staring at him like he'd lost his mind. Roland pulled the door open without taking his eyes off Oscar, and the car's headlights illuminated the stacked cases of whiskey."

"What the hell?" Oscar said, staring in disbelief into the garage. "It's a little early for Christmas. Where on earth did that come from?"

"That's a question we'll have plenty of time to discuss, Chief Hyde," Roland said.

"You don't think I had anything to do with that, do you?"

"There are a hundred, uh, ninety-five cases of illegal Canadian whiskey stacked in your garage, Chief," Roland said, hoping his math was correct. "What else would I think?"

"This is insane," Oscar said, heading for the front door of the house. "Let me make a couple of calls."

"Hold it right there, Chief. You're under arrest."

"What?"

"I'm sorry, but this much product can only indicate one thing. Intent to distribute."

"Maybe I'm just really thirsty," Oscar said, scowling. "Home consumption and all that, right?"

"I need you to drop your gun, drop to your knees, and put your hands behind your head."

"Yeah, like that's gonna happen," Oscar said, laughing.

"Or maybe you'd like to get shot," Roland said, pulling the hammer back on his revolver.

Oscar heard the *click* and got the message. He muttered under his breath as he removed his gun and tossed it on the lawn. He slowly made his way down to his knees and waited for Roland to snap the handcuffs on.

"I want to talk to my lawyer," Oscar said.

"You have a lawyer?" Roland said, surprised by the news.

"I do. Melvin English."

"Melvin? I didn't know he handled criminal cases."

"Well, he does now," Oscar said, climbing to his feet. "Where are you taking me?"

"You know, that's a really good question," Roland said, frowning as he rubbed his head. "How about your office?"

**Although it** was almost two in the morning by the time Milo entered the police station, he was still wide awake and had a bounce in his step. He'd been waiting anxiously for an update from Violet, and when she finally called to let him know that Oscar had been arrested and Roland was back from the doctor's office, Milo enjoyed a cigarette and a few sips of whiskey, then got dressed and made the short walk to the police station.

As soon as he stepped inside, he saw Oscar stretched out a narrow bed in a small jail cell, and Roland limping toward the desk carrying a cup of coffee.

"What are you doing here?" Roland said, giving Milo an odd look.

"I heard about what happened and wanted to check to make sure both of you are okay," Milo said, then glanced at Oscar who was now sitting up on the bed. "Aren't you on the wrong side of that door, Oscar?"

"That's what I tried telling Wyatt Earp over there," Oscar said, then yelled across the room. "I'm gonna sue your ass off, Hopalong."

"What happened to your foot?" Milo said, nodding at the fresh bandage.

"One of Oscar's business partners decided to take a shot at me," Roland said, gingerly sitting down behind Oscar's desk. "Fortunately, my training and skills enabled me to escape any real damage."

"Too bad your boating skills aren't the same high quality," Milo whispered.

"What?" Roland said, gently probing the bandage on his head.

"Nothing," Milo said. "Just a little late night babbling. You got shot in the foot?"

"I did. I'm afraid my work is inherently dangerous," Roland said.

Oscar scoffed loudly from inside the cell.

"Just try to relax, Oscar," Milo said. "I'm sure this is all a big misunderstanding."

"Not that it's any business of yours, Mr. Razner," Roland said. "But it is certainly not a misunderstanding. I found ninety-five cases of Canadian whiskey in Chief Hyde's garage."

"Ninety-five?" Milo said, raising an eyebrow.

"Or thereabouts," Roland said, shrugging. "It was dark, and I only had time for a quick count."

"Before you got shot in the foot?" Milo said.

"Yes. That's correct," Roland said, then noticed the expression on Milo's face. "What's the matter, Mr. Razner?"

"Ninety-five is such an odd number," Milo said. "But I guess some of the shipment could have gone missing during transport. Or maybe got tossed overboard."

"Yes, thrown overboard. I was just sitting here thinking the same thing," Roland said, nodding. "Great minds think alike, right?"

"Gee, I sure hope not."

# Episode 5

## A Changing Landscape

"Always try to avoid people shouting at the top of their lungs that the things you enjoy the most are inherently evil. Unless listening to people like that is one of your favorite things. If that's the case, knock yourself out."

Milo Razner

# Roland's On A Roll

**It was well past midnight** before Roland finished completing all the paperwork associated with Oscar's arrest. And figuring out where to put the corrupt chief of police had taken even longer than filling out the stack of forms his bosses needed for their filing cabinets.

Thinking out loud at one point, Roland had suggested that Oscar could stay right where he was for the duration of whatever sentence he ended up pulling. But Milo Razner had interrupted Roland by speaking up without even being asked for his opinion and saying that option was probably out of the question. After Razner had jokingly suggested that they leave Oscar right where he was and charge tourists four bits to stare and throw peanuts at him like they would at a monkey in a cage at the zoo, he'd reminded Roland that the town leaders wouldn't be pleased by the idea of their police chief being locked up in one of his own jail cells. A town heavily dependent on tourists handing over their hard-earned money wouldn't instill a lot of visitor confidence if the town's top cop, arrested on felony charges, was sitting on display as a cautionary tale for others to see. No,

Razner had said, it was better to get Oscar out of town, out of sight, out of mind, and all that.

As much as Roland hated agreeing with the bank robber turned dairy farmer, he had to concede that Razner had a good point.

Roland had been so preoccupied with finding a good home for Oscar that he'd completely forgotten about the five cases of whiskey he'd loaded into the back seat of his car. But that changed quickly after he arrived home. He stored the cases outside behind a stack of firewood, then remembered to bring a couple of bottles inside with him. After finishing half of the first, Roland was finally able to forget about his headache and the gunshot wound to the foot. He'd passed out on the couch and didn't wake up until he heard the phone ringing.

He sat up on the couch, took a long pull from the half-full bottle just to get his bearings, then squinted at the sunlight streaming through the window. Roland pulled the curtains shut, enjoyed the darkness for a moment, then limped toward the phone. Two steps in, his bad foot slammed into the coffee table, and Roland dropped to the floor in severe pain as tears formed in his eyes. The incessant ringing of the phone set his hangover on fire, and by the time he managed to answer it, his morning mood had turned as dark as the living room.

"Hello," he said, breathing heavily into the phone.

"May I please speak with Roland Doyle?"

"Speaking."

"Oh, hi, Roland," the man said. "Did I catch you at a bad time? It sounds like you've been running a foot race. Or maybe you've got company, and I caught you right in the middle."

The man chortled into the phone at his own joke.

"Who the hell is this?" Roland snapped, reaching for the bottle.

"It's Vernon Adams."

At the sound of his boss's name, Roland snapped to attention and put the bottle down.

"Mr. Adams," Roland said. "It's good to hear from you. What can I do for you, sir?"

"I just called to congratulate you."

"You did? For what?"

"For the arrest you made last evening. You've only been on the job up there for a few days, and you've already caught a corrupt cop red-handed with a garage full of illegal whiskey. Well done, Roland."

Roland was surprised and relieved that a boss of his wasn't calling to complain about something he'd done. Or, as was more often the case, hadn't gotten around to doing. Roland grabbed the bottle and took a long pull.

"How did you hear about it so soon?" he said, wiping his mouth with the back of his hand.

"I just received a call from Senator Miller," Vernon Adams said. "Usually, I get a bit nervous when a senator finds it necessary to do that, but he was just calling to congratulate me on the Unit's excellent work."

"He was? Well, that's great news, right?"

"It is indeed. And since the Senator sits on committees that have a major impact on our funding, your arrest couldn't have come at a better time. We're right in the middle of trying to get next year's budget approved."

"Well, I'm glad I could help, sir," Roland said, his mood beginning to improve despite the hangover.

"I knew you were the right man for that job," Vernon Adams said. "I know it must be hard being a lone wolf, but it seems to fit your...personality."

It sounded to Roland like a backhanded compliment, but he let it go. He took another sip from the bottle and waited.

"Yes, I knew you would be perfect for that location," Vernon Adams said. "And last night's performance is certainly worthy of a written commendation for your personal file."

"That's nice of you, sir," Roland said. "And I sure do appreciate it. But I was wondering if it would be possible for you to perhaps consider a promotion? Or at least a transfer."

"Why on earth would I do that?"

"Because I'm doing such a good job here?" Roland said, then chastised himself for making it sound like a question instead of a simple statement of fact.

"But you've just gotten started, Roland. Just imagine all of the wonderful things that lie ahead of you," Vernon Adams said, his voice rising with excitement. "Chasing down bootleggers in the dead of night. Shutting down establishments selling illegal booze. And doing all of that while being in constant personal danger. I must say that I'm rather envious, Roland. What I wouldn't do to change places with you and become an agent who's actually out there in the field where all the action is."

"I'd be happy to share some of my responsibilities with you, sir," Roland said. "I sure could use the help."

"Yes, yes. Of course," Vernon Adams said, clearing his throat. "Perhaps right after I get through this nasty budget process."

Roland scowled into the phone then took a longer pull from the bottle.

"So, what would it take to get promoted out of here, sir?"

"Well, it's a bit early to even be talking about that," Vernon Adams said. "But if you were able to track down the source of the police chief's whiskey, that would be one hell of a one-two punch. You know, capture both sides of the transaction."

"Yeah, I got it," Roland said, ready for the call to end. "And if I were able to get the guy selling it on the Canadian side, that would be enough for you to approve me getting out of here?"

"I thought the area was supposed to be incredibly beautiful," Vernon Adams said.

"Yeah, it is."

"Then why the rush to get out?"

"I just learned that I hate the water, and I'm scared to death of boats," Roland said, then silently cursed himself. "But that's just between you and me, right?"

"Of course."

"So, what do you think?" Roland said, squeezing the phone tight.

"Well, Roland," Vernon Adams said. "I can't promise anything, but I'd have to say that it would be hard to ignore an accomplishment like capturing the source working on the Canadian side. Or if you were able to bring down another major player like the police chief, that would certainly get a lot of people's attention."

"I think I could make a real contribution in New York, sir. Or maybe Chicago."

"Yes, I'm sure you could, Roland. But look at it this way. Up there, you get all the credit for everything that happens."

"And all the blame."

"Not if nothing bad happens, Roland," Vernon Adams said. "By the way, have you had any luck yet tracking down who shot you last night?"

"As of the moment, no. He's still officially listed as an unidentified assailant," Roland said, then decided it was as good a time as any to mention it. "By the way, you're going to be getting a bill for repairing a dock. And another one for fixing my boat."

"You ran into a dock with your boat?"

"Yeah. Long story. Some guy was trying to run me over, and I had to… take corrective action."

"I see. Do you think it was the same guy who shot you?"

"Yes, sir. I'm positive."

"Well, I'm sure you'll track the bastard down in the near future. And I hope you and your foot are doing well. Look, I need to run. Good work, Roland. And I'll make sure to send you a copy of the commendation I'll be putting in your file."

"Thank you, sir," Roland said, shaking his head. "Goodbye."

Roland hung up and sat back down on the couch. He gently probed the bandage on his head until he was satisfied he didn't need to go back to the doctor, then rubbed his throbbing foot. Deciding he had a few hours before he needed to meet the people who'd be transporting Oscar, Roland stretched out on the couch and went back to sleep.

# Twitchy and Grumpy

**Milo, on too little sleep** and already looking forward to his morning meeting, woke tired and twitchy to the sound of a ringing phone. He managed to answer it without having to get out of bed, and he tucked the phone up against his ear as his head sunk back into the pillow.

"Milo Razner. Oh, hi, Violet," Milo said, closing his eyes. "I see. Okay…No, I seriously doubt he's going to be promoted anytime in the near future…No, actually, that's a good thing, Violet…Think it through…Yes, exactly. The devil you know and all that. Is there anything else? I need to get to a morning meeting…Yes, as a matter of fact, it is payday. I'll swing by your office later on this afternoon. Thanks for calling, Violet.

Milo put the phone back in its cradle and was about to go back to sleep when he heard a soft knock on the door. He climbed out of bed and slipped his robe on before heading to the door and looking through the peephole.

"Perfect." Milo shook his head as he opened the door. "Good morning, Clint. Do come in."

Clint Farwell strode past Milo with purpose and sat down in a chair without waiting to be invited.

"I was just about to order some coffee," Milo said, heading back to the phone. "Would you like some? Or maybe some breakfast?"

"No. I've already had my breakfast," Clint said.

Milo studied him closely while he waited for room service to answer. It looked like Clint hadn't eaten in a week, and Milo was pretty sure that whatever he had consumed for breakfast was of the liquid variety. Milo placed his coffee order then sat down across from him.

"I'm just here to pick up my pay, and I'll be off," Clint said.

"I guess I won't have any problems locating my employees today, huh?"

"What?"

"Nothing," Milo said, getting up and grabbing an envelope off his desk. He sat back down and tossed the envelope on the coffee table.

Clint reached for the envelope, flipped through the bills inside, then nodded and slipped it into his coat pocket.

"You seem troubled, Clint."

"Yeah, I guess I am a bit, Milo."

"Well, if twelve hundred in cash doesn't cheer you up, I'm out of ideas, Clint," Milo said, lighting a cigarette.

"I want more money, Milo."

"Sure. All you need to do is starting cranking out more product, Clint," Milo said, giving him a small smile. "I'll be more than happy to pay you for all of it."

"I'm talking about more money per gallon," Clint said.

"Clint, we have a deal in place. And that deal is for two dollars a gallon."

"It ain't enough."

"I'd say that thick envelope you just stuffed in your pocket says something different, Clint," Milo said, yawning.

"I'm telling you it ain't enough," Clint said, his voice rising as he started to get up out of his chair.

Milo held up both his hands and motioned for Clint to sit back down.

"Clint, it's way too early in the morning to be yelled at," Milo said, softly. "So, how about you settle down and explain why you feel you aren't adequately compensated?"

"I'm doing all the work," Clint said.

Milo stifled another yawn as Clint sat back down in his chair.

"Are you now?"

"Yes. Without me, your whole operation would have never gotten off the ground. And here I am making two lousy bucks a gallon while you're probably selling the stuff for thirty, maybe forty bucks a case."

"Clint, I have no idea where you came up with those numbers," Milo said, chuckling. "But I can assure you that I'm not selling the product for anywhere near forty bucks a case."

"Well, then maybe you should start thinking about finding somebody who'll pay you what it's worth," Clint said. "After all, aren't you supposed to be this big businessman?"

"Clint, I'm happy to sit here and discuss your concerns, as well as move my morning meeting back, but I don't think I like your tone."

"I really don't care if you like my tone or not, Milo."

"Clint, is there something about the boss-employee relationship you don't understand?" Milo said.

"No, it's very clear, Milo. We do all the work, you make all the money. And I'm not the only one who feels this way."

"I see," Milo said, getting up to answer the door.

A waiter rolled a cart into the room, and Milo tipped him and sent him on his way. He poured himself a cup of coffee, took a long sip, topped the cup off then sat back down. He took another sip and watched as Clint pulled a flask from his pocket. Clint tipped his head back and poured into his mouth.

"Miracle in the morning?" Milo said, looking at Clint over his coffee cup. "Do you think that's a wise choice?"

"It's the best idea I could come up with."

"So, these other employees who aren't happy with the way I'm running things?" Milo said. "Would you like to talk about them?"

"Nah, I'm just blowing off some steam. I wouldn't want to get anybody in trouble."

"I'm very aware of who my disgruntled employees are, Clint," Milo said. "At least I thought I was until you arrived this morning. I had no idea you were this unhappy."

"Well, it's been building for a while," Clint said, taking another sip from the flask.

"You shouldn't let things build up, Clint. It's not healthy. And I consider myself a pretty good listener. I've already talked with Tom Collins about his concerns. And I think we've got things worked out," Milo said, then paused until he'd locked eyes with Clint. "But I have no idea how Elmer and Roscoe are feeling these days. They're harder to read than a Chinese newspaper."

Clint flinched when Milo mentioned the drivers' names.

"So, you say you've talked with Tom?" Clint said.

"I did. He had some concerns about how a situation should be handled, and he and I worked through it. You'd be well-advised to use Tom's approach. You'd be amazed at the solutions you can come up with if you're willing to take the long view and have civilized conversations with the people who don't necessarily share your opinion."

"That's why I'm here, Milo."

"Really? I must have missed that," Milo said, staring at Clint.

"Yeah, well, like I said, I was just blowing off some steam."

"I see. And is there any more steam you want to share with me, or can I get on with the rest of my day?" Milo yawned again, then poured himself another cup of coffee.

"No, that's about it. All I need is an answer," Clint said, leaning forward in his chair.

"I'll be happy to do that," Milo said, staring back at Clint.

"Well, what is it?"

"I'm going to need a question, Clint."

"Oh. Okay, let's try this one. Are you willing to pay me four dollars a gallon?"

"Is that it? That's the question you need answered?"

"That's it, Milo."

"Geez, Clint, I thought you were gonna give me a hard one. Something like a math problem or maybe a physics question."

"Funny, Milo," Clint said. "So, what's your answer going to be?"

"No."

"I see. Can I ask you why?"

"Because the way I see it is like this, Clint. Since you aren't involved in the actual creation of the alcohol, aren't responsible for paying for any of the supplies or equipment, don't have to deal with transportation, and have no role in the distribution process, I would say that you are more than adequately compensated. And while I truly appreciate your contribution in helping us turn out a delicious product, I have to disagree with your earlier statement that I couldn't have done it without you."

"Then I guess we're just going to have to agree to disagree on that," Clint said, taking another sip from the flask. "I'm sorry you feel that way, Milo. But I'm telling you, things need to change."

"Things constantly change, Clint. They never stay the way they are. And things are either getting better, or they're getting worse. Fortunately, you have a lot of control over which way they go."

"What would you do if you were in my position, Milo?"

"Apart from enjoying the massive windfall you've received late in life? A windfall from me if I remember correctly."

"Yeah, apart from that," Clint said, a trace of spittle forming in the corner of his mouth.

"Well, I guess if I were you, Clint, I'd probably talk with the person I spend most of my day with to see how I could make my time at work, if not more profitable, at least a bit more enjoyable. I'd talk to Tom."

"And you'll be able to live with whatever Tom comes up with?"

"I'm sure of it, Clint."

# Willy Sticks a Toe In

**Willy climbed the steps** two at a time, removed his hat, then rang the doorbell. While he waited, he glanced around at the empty street and the immediate neighborhood. The houses were nice enough and well-kept, but not showy. And judging by the lack of horses and the number of automobiles parked outside most of the houses, Willy was left with the impression that the people who lived here were either on their way up or doing everything they could to fool their neighbors.

The door opened, and a man with a large handlebar mustache stood in the doorway giving Willy the once over.

"You must be Mr. Lawless," the man with the mustache said.

"I am. And you're Mr. Green," Willy said, extending his hand.

"Come in," Ben Green said, stepping back from the doorway to give Willy room. "I was just about to have coffee."

Willy followed him into a sitting room and sat down. He twirled his hat around a finger as he glanced around the room. Everything seemed new, and the place smelled of fresh paint.

Ben Green poured two cups of coffee, handed one to Willy, then sat down and studied him as he sipped his own.

"I must say that I was surprised to get your call, Mr. Lawless."

"That wasn't my intent, Mr. Green. To surprise you, that is," Willy said, tossing his hat on the coffee table. "But I figured you were the man to call."

"Well, you figured right, Mr. Lawless," Ben Green said, still keeping a close eye on Willy's movements and facial expressions. "Tell me again how you came to get my name."

"There's nothing special about it," Willy said, shrugging. "I was having a couple of pops in a speakeasy last night when I overheard the bartender talking about how he'd really like to get his hands on some top-shelf product. So, we started talking."

"And you informed the bartender that you were a man who could get his hands on this so-called *top-shelf product?*"

"Yes, sir. I sure did," Willy said, nodding.

"So, why didn't you just sell it to him?" Ben Green said.

"Well, Mr. Green," Willy said, giving him a small smile. "That thought never crossed my mind."

"Really? Why not?"

"I try to think like a businessman, Mr. Green. Like an owner, so to speak. And I wondered how I'd feel if some stranger off the street started selling illegal booze in one of my establishments without me knowing anything about it. I don't reckon I'd take that news well."

"I see. And what would *you* do if you caught someone doing that?"

"I'd have a little chat with him first, then I'd probably shoot him," Willy said, shrugging.

"Interesting choice," Ben Green said, smiling as he lit a cigarette. "Did this bartender give you my name?"

"No, sir. He was real careful about not doing that," Willy said. "After all, he didn't know me from Adam, and I could be anybody. You know, a cop working undercover. Or one of those new Prohibition agents they've got roaming around now."

"Yes, you could, Mr. Lawless. In fact, I was just sitting here thinking the same thing."

"I'd be surprised if you weren't, Mr. Green."

"Then how did you get my name?"

"I've been trying to figure out who was running all the speakeasies in the area. You know, asking a few questions, keeping my eyes and ears open. And I've had the idea that it was you for a while, but I couldn't confirm it until last night."

"And someone, maybe this bartender, told you my name?"

"No," Willy said. "It was when I heard the passing reference for the third time. That's when I knew."

"Passing reference?"

"Yeah, I heard a couple of folks who are running speakeasies for you talking. And they were wondering out loud if they should do something. Then one of them said to the other that they should *run it past The Mustache.* That's when I was sure."

Ben Green laughed.

"That's quite amusing, Mr. Lawless. But it still doesn't convince me that I can trust you."

"I get that, Mr. Green. And I wish I had someone who could vouch for me, but I'm doing all of this on my own. Nobody knows, and I mean nobody."

"You're doing all the work by yourself?"

"Yup. I drive the booze across the River all by myself, then load and drive the truck. You name it, I do it."

"And get to keep every nickel of profit, right?"

"Exactly, sir," Willy said, smiling. "It's a lot of work, but I think it's worth it."

"Okay, Mr. Lawless," Ben Green said, studying Willy for a long time before nodding. "I'm going to give you a shot to prove yourself. What sort of deal are you proposing?"

Willy grinned and sat forward in his chair.

"I've got a hundred cases of top-shelf Canadian just waiting to be delivered."

"A hundred? That's a good number," Ben Green said. "Can you guarantee that every week?"

"A hundred a week? It might take me some time to ramp up to that, Mr. Green. You see, the hundred is inventory I've had laying around until I found the right buyer. But I'm willing to guarantee you…fifty cases a week for now. And I'll do everything I can to get up to a hundred in the near future."

Willy had no idea how he was going to get his hands on fifty cases a week, but he wasn't about to let the opportunity pass.

"How much do you want per case?" Ben Green said.

"Seventy-five bucks," Willy said, doing his best not to flinch when he tossed the number out.

"Seventy-five?"

"It's a twelve-year-old blend, Mr. Green. And you won't believe how good it is. You should be able to get at least a buck a shot for it."

"Why does everyone seem to think they know what I should charge for a drink?" Ben Green said, frowning.

"What?"

"Nothing," Ben Green said, toying with his mustache. "Okay, seventy-five it is. But if the product isn't what you say it is, Mr. Lawless, we're going to be having a serious conversation."

"Yeah, I get that."

Ben Green grabbed a notepad from his pocket and scribbled on a page. He tore it out and handed it to Willy.

"Make your delivery tomorrow morning to this address. Drive around back and ask for Jugs. He'll be the one inspecting the shipment and paying you."

"Sounds great, Mr. Green. Don't worry. You can trust me."

"If I can't, don't worry, Mr. Lawless. I'll be the first person to hear about it."

They both turned when they heard someone enter the sitting room. Willy looked up and saw a woman wearing a robe and drying her hair with a towel.

"Ben, are you coming back to bed or not? I need to get back to the shop in about an hour," she said, then glanced up to see Willy. "Oh, I'm sorry. I didn't know you had company."

Willy stared at the woman way past the length of time a gentleman should. He had never seen her before, and he hoped it wouldn't be the last time he did.

"Beulah, I'd like you to meet, Mr. Lawless," Ben Green said.

"It's nice to meet you, Mr. Lawless," she said, flashing Willy a quick smile.

"The pleasure is all mine, Miss Beulah," Willy said, getting up out of his chair.

"I seriously doubt that," Ben Green said, grinning at the woman. "Now, if you don't mind, Mr. Lawless, off you go. Beulah and I have some other business to tend to."

# Running Late

**As soon as he finally** got Clint out of his suite with a promise to talk again soon, the phone rang, and Milo answered it on the second ring.

"Milo Razner," he said, refilling his coffee cup. "Oh, hi, Ruby. Yes, I know I'm late...I'm sorry...I said I was sorry, Ruby. I had an early morning drop in...No, it wasn't Daisy. Geez, Ruby, take it easy."

Milo put the phone down to light a cigarette. When the voice on the other end of the line finally slowed down and turned softer, he picked the phone back up.

"I'll get there as soon as I can...Probably an hour...Geez, Ruby...I don't know. You run a dairy farm. I'm sure there must be something you can do to stay busy until I get there...Like what? I don't know. Maybe go milk a couple of cows...Hello? Hello?"

Milo shook his head and put the phone back in its cradle. He headed for the bathroom and started to run a hot bath. Then he heard another knock on the door. He tightened his robe and padded across the floor. He peered out through the peephole and frowned, but he pulled the door open and stepped back to let her in.

"Good morning, Fannie," Milo said, forcing a smile. "What a pleasant surprise."

"Surprise being the primary word, right?" she said, glancing around the suite. "This is a real nice setup you've got here, Milo."

"Yeah, I like it. And the hotel treats me very well. Have a seat," Milo said, gesturing at the chair Clint had just vacated.

Fannie sat down and removed the shawl that was draped across her shoulders. Milo flinched at the amount of cleavage she was showing.

"Wow. That's quite a dress, Fannie," Milo said, forcing himself to make eye contact.

"I wore this just in case you decide not to listen to reason, and I have to work you over a bit," she said, grinning.

"If I don't get to my meeting pretty soon, I just might let you," Milo whispered.

"What?"

"Nothing. How can I help you?"

"It's about Daisy," Fannie said, reaching for one of Milo's cigarettes.

"Daisy? What about her?"

"Her earnings have dropped off."

"Really? I must say I find that hard to believe," Milo said.

"Oh, I'm sure she's still raking it in, but my cut has dropped off since she started doing what she calls special favors for others."

"I see," Milo said, lighting a cigarette.

"And I think you're the one she's doing these special favors for," Fannie said. "My, that's a big bed."

"Yes, it is. One can get lost in there."

"Oh, I'd find you, Milo," Fannie said.

"Yes, I'm sure you would," Milo said, flashing her a smile. "So, you're here to discuss what sort of *special favors* Daisy might be doing for me?"

"No, I don't give a squat about what she's doing for you, Milo. I just want my cut."

"Is that all? I thought you were going to want me to start talking out of school," Milo said. "We can fix that easy enough, Fannie. And I must apologize. Not factoring in your cut was an oversight on my part."

"You're going to agree just like that?"

"Of course. Daisy is your employee and, as an entrepreneur like yourself, I should have kept that in mind. How much are you down?"

"Somewhere in the neighborhood of fifty bucks a week," Fannie said, casually.

"I seem to be spending a lot of time in that neighborhood," Milo said, getting up and heading to his desk. He returned moments later and tossed four crisp fifties on the coffee table.

"There's a month in advance. Again, I apologize for the oversight. It won't happen again."

Fannie reached for the money, then glanced up at Milo.

"Should I put this in the safe, or are we going to consummate our new deal with something other than a handshake?"

"While that offer sounds most inviting, Fannie, I'm actually drawing a bath, and then I need to get to a meeting I'm very late for."

"Our timing never seems to be right, does it, Milo?" Fannie said, sliding the fifties into her cleavage then standing up. "Oh, well. One of these days, huh?"

"I can't wait, Fannie," Milo said, getting up to open the door. "Thanks for stopping by."

"I'll see you around, Milo," she said, then grabbed the back of his head and pulled him in close for a long, deep kiss.

She eventually broke the kiss and released him. Milo stared at her in disbelief.

"Yeah, I know. Good, huh?" she said, laughing as she waved goodbye and left.

Milo closed the door and exhaled loudly.

"Wow. Now I'm awake."

Milo walked to the bathroom and turned the water off. He was just about to ease his way into the hot water when the phone rang. Cursing, he headed for the phone.

"Milo Razner. Oh, hi, Ruby. Yeah, I'm still here…No, I am not avoiding you…Geez, Ruby. You're like a rabid wolverine this morning…Hello? Hello?"

# A Meeting of the Mindless

**Melvin followed the guard** who'd made it perfectly clear that he would rather be doing anything else other than escorting Melvin down the long hallway. The guard's keys jingled with every step, and he burped and farted as he casually strolled along the cement floor looking like he owned the joint. Melvin did his best to stay upwind as they kept walking until the guard stopped short directly in front of Oscar's cell and pointed.

"Is that the asshole you're looking for?" the guard said.

"Oh, so you've met Oscar?" Melvin said, chuckling. "Yup. He's definitely the asshole I need to speak with."

Oscar was sound asleep and snoring loudly. The guard looked through the bars and nodded at him.

"You know, it's funny," the guard said. "The guilty never seem to have any problem falling asleep."

"Actually, I'm sure it's the effect of the alcohol rather than any presumed level of guilt," Melvin said, staring through the bars at Oscar.

"Whatever," the guard said, starting to walk away, then calling out over his shoulder. "Keep it short."

"That's certainly my plan. And it was nice talking to you, Officer," Melvin said, then whispered. "Prick."

Melvin whistled softly, and Oscar stirred. Eventually, he opened his eyes and sat up on his bunk.

"It's about time you got here," Oscar said. "You bring a bottle?"

"No, I didn't bring a bottle. Damn it, Oscar. How about you try to get a little perspective? If Roland Doyle gets his way, you're looking at up to a year in here. Maybe more if you end up pissing off the judge."

"I got set up, and you know it," Oscar said. "In fact, I'm wondering if this whole thing might have your fingerprints all over it."

"Pissing off the judge is one thing, Oscar," Melvin said, shaking his head. "But you might want to think carefully before you do that to your lawyer."

"We'll discuss that further after you get me out of here," Oscar said.

"I just came from the courthouse. They've set bail at five hundred."

"Then pay it."

"I don't have five hundred dollars, Oscar."

"Why the hell not?"

"Because you've been holding onto all our profits and reinvesting, remember?" Melvin snapped.

"Oh, yeah," Oscar said, scratching the two-day stubble on his face. "Damn."

"Do you have any suggestions, or would you prefer to sit here until your trial starts?"

"Gee, I really don't want to do this," Oscar said, frowning. "But I guess I don't have a choice."

"Let's go, Oscar," Melvin said, drumming his fingers on the bars. "I've got things to do."

"Okay," Oscar said, motioning with his head for Melvin to come closer. "You need to go to my garage."

"You mean the scene of the crime?" Melvin said, breaking into a smile.

"Keep it up, Melvin," Oscar snapped, then leaned in close and whispered. "Slip in the back door, and along one wall you'll see a shelf with some paint cans. In one of the cans in the middle of the row, you'll find my money."

"Don't you mean our money?" Melvin said.

"Yeah, our money. Relax, Melvin. Grab the money and get back down here before the court closes. I can't spend the night in here."

"You expect me to drive all the way back home, get the money, and then drive all the way back?"

"That's exactly what I expect you to do."

"Before I do all that, we need to discuss my fee," Melvin said.

"You already owe me three hundred."

"And you owe me thirty-five hundred from the two hundred cases," Melvin said. "What's your point, Oscar?"

"My point is since we're business partners and all, I was sort of thinking you'd be waiving your fee," Oscar said.

"Well, you thought wrong," Melvin said. "And my bill rate is five dollars an hour."

"Five dollars an hour? Are you out of your mind?" Oscar said. "I ain't paying five bucks an hour."

"Okay, Oscar, whatever you say," Melvin said, stepping back from the cell. "Enjoy your stay."

"Wait. Okay, I'll pay it. But you're going to have to cap it at two hundred bucks."

Melvin shook his head.

"Oscar, do you really think you're in a strong negotiating position?"

"You bastard," Oscar said. "Keep it up and I'm gonna be forced do a little tap dance on your face."

"You know, Oscar, this place is really depressing, and I think a change of scenery might be called for," Melvin said, staring off and using his hands to help him paint the picture. "I see a paint can, full of cash, in my immediate future. And that can is sitting on a long stretch of sand just waiting to be opened." Melvin squinted and conjured up another image. "And what do you know, the can is sitting right next to me." He dropped the pose and gave Oscar an evil grin. "Remember to think of me during those long, lonely nights in here."

Oscar glared at Melvin through the bars but eventually nodded in agreement.

"Go get the money and get me the hell out of here, Melvin. Please."

"Ah, the magic word," Melvin said, laughing. "Okay, I'm going. I should be back in three to four hours."

"Hurry up."

"I'll do my best, Oscar. While you're waiting, why don't you see if they'll let you go outside and get some exercise? Or take a long hot shower and maybe make a new friend."

"You're not funny, Melvin."

"But don't tell anybody you're a cop. I have a feeling that wouldn't go over too well with some of the other guests."

# A Bad Day Turns Long

**Milo, finally comfortable with** the water temperature, had just closed his eyes and was about to drift off when he heard another knock on his door. He tried ignoring it, but the visitor was insistent. Milo climbed out of the tub, pulled his robe on, and headed for the door dripping water. Again, he peered through the peephole, then opened the door.

"I almost didn't recognize you with all your clothes on, Daisy."

"That's funny, Milo," she said, giving him a peck on the cheek as she walked past him.

Instead of sitting in a chair, she kicked her shoes off and stretched out on the bed.

"Make yourself comfortable," Milo said, shaking his head.

The phone rang, and Daisy sat up.

"You want me to get that?"

"No, you better not," Milo said, grabbing the phone. "Milo Razner. Hello, Ruby…Well, it's a little hard to get ready when you're calling me every five minutes for an update. Hello? Hello?"

Milo tossed the receiver on the desk and left the phone off the hook. He sat down behind the desk and rubbed his temples with both hands.

"Somebody's in trouble," Daisy said in a singsong laugh.

"Yeah, I guess you could say that. Are you here for your money?"

"Well, since I'm already here," she said, glancing at the stack of envelopes on the desk. "Why don't you toss me one of those big fat ones?"

"How about I just give you the one with your name on it?" Milo said, tossing her the envelope.

"You're grumpy in the morning," she said, examining what was inside the envelope before dropping it into her purse. "I could probably help you out with that, Milo."

"I have no doubt, Daisy, and if my day continues the way it's going, I may be taking you up on your offer," Milo said, lighting a cigarette.

"You're talking like I'm some sort of consolation prize," Daisy snapped.

"I'm sorry, Daisy," Milo said, exhaling audibly. "Okay, apart from wanting your pay, is there another reason for your visit?"

"I came here to give you some information, but I don't think I like your attitude, Milo," she said, pouting.

Daisy rolled over onto her stomach and buried her face in a pillow. Milo got up and sat on the edge of the bed. He was about to try consoling her when he heard another knock on the door.

"I need to move to an island," Milo said, heading for the door.

He opened it and saw one of the hotel staff staring back at him.

"I'm sorry to bother you, Mr. Razner," the man said. "But there's a Ruby Crankovitch on the phone who says she needs to talk with you. And she sounds a little cranky."

"Only a little? Tell her to call me on my private number."

"She said she already tried that, but all she got was a busy signal. That's when she called the hotel's main number."

"Well, I've been on another call," Milo said. "Tell her I'm done and to try my number again."

"Okay, sir," the man said, studying Milo's face. "Are you all right, Mr. Razner? You seem…troubled."

"I'm fine. Just tired and a little twitchy."

"Well, if you don't mind my saying, if anybody could help you out with those two, it would be her," he said, nodding at Daisy.

"Sound advice," Milo said, nodding. "Thanks. I'll bear that in mind."

Milo closed the door and headed for the desk. He put the receiver back in its cradle, then sat back down on the edge of the bed.

"Daisy?" Milo whispered.

"Yeah?"

"What do you need to tell me?"

"Nothing."

"Do you want to sit up and talk, or am I going to have to take one of those fifties back?"

Daisy rolled over and sat up with a grin.

"Here I was thinking you were gonna do something nice to make me feel better," she said.

"Let's go," Milo said, gesturing with a hand. "Start talking."

"Well, you'll never guess what Billy told me last night."

The phone rang, and Milo got off the bed and headed for his desk.

"I'd like to meet the guy who invented this infernal contraption and put a bullet in his head," Milo said, snatching the phone and holding it up to his ear. "Milo Razner. Oh, Ruby. What a nice surprise…Yeah. Uh-huh…Okay…Got it…Will that be all, or would you also like my balls on a platter?"

Milo flinched at her response, then gently placed the receiver back in its cradle.

"Okay, you were saying something about Billy?"

"Didn't she want them?" Daisy said.

"Want what?"

"Your balls."

"Oh. Yeah, she did. But just not in their present form," Milo said, again gesturing for Daisy to get on with it.

"Anyway, Billy and I were talking last night, and he said, as soon as he got home, he was going to ask Ruby for a divorce," Daisy said, hopping off the bed to grab a cigarette from Milo's pack. She lit it and climbed over Milo on her way back.

"Yeah, I've been waiting for that shoe to drop. What did you say when he told you?" Milo said, stretching out next to her as another wave of fatigue washed over him.

Daisy tucked her head against his shoulder and handed Milo her cigarette. He took a puff, exhaled smoke at the ceiling, then crushed it out.

"This is nice," she said, snuggling closer. "I did what you told me to do. I told Billy that it probably wasn't a good idea, and even if it was, it wasn't the right time. But he's not listening to me anymore."

"Since when?" Milo said, opening his eyes and turning his head to look at her.

"Since last night," Daisy said, placing a hand on Milo's chest inside his robe. "Billy's met someone else."

"What? Who on earth has he met that even comes close to you, Daisy?"

"Oh, aren't you sweet," she said, dragging her nails across his chest. "It's the new schoolteacher. Billy says that she's the best thing that has ever happened to him."

"If I didn't know better, I'd have to say that you're slipping, Daisy," Milo said, closing his eyes as he felt Daisy's nails gently sliding across his stomach.

"He said she treats him nice and is looking for the same thing he is," Daisy said.

"And what would that be?"

"Settling down and raising a family," Daisy said. "Just our luck, Milo."

"How's that?"

"What Billy says he wants more than anything is the only thing I can't give him."

"Billy doesn't even know what he wants for lunch, Daisy," Milo said.

"Sure, I get that. But what are we going to do?"

"Is the schoolteacher talking about leaving the area?" Milo said, sitting up.

"No, apparently, she likes it up here just fine," Daisy said, fluffing up a couple of pillows and stretching back out.

"Okay, that's good. Well, for now, just keep doing what you're doing with Billy. But don't put any pressure on him. I'll deal with the schoolteacher."

"What are you going to do about her, Milo?"

"I have no idea," Milo said, the mood completely shattered. He climbed out of bed and started pacing.

"Oh, and Billy said he was planning on having a talk with you," Daisy said, propping her head up using an elbow for support.

"What does he want to talk about?"

"Money. And more of it," Daisy said. "He said that when he gets divorced, Ruby is probably going to want half of what he makes."

"Perfect."

"What?"

"I was going for sarcastic."

"Oh. Did I do good, Milo?"

"Yeah, you did great."

"I could do more," she said, giving him the smile that made him melt.

"I believe you."

"Yes, I noticed."


**Melvin slowly** opened the back door that led into the garage and glanced around before stepping inside. He closed the door behind him and waited for his eyes to adjust to the light. He spotted the row of paint cans and quickly located the one that rattled softly when he shook it. Melvin pried the top off with a screwdriver and reached inside. He removed the note and studied it. He started to laugh but stopped when he remembered that half of the now missing money was his. Melvin slipped the note into his shirt pocket, climbed back into his car, and headed for Watertown wondering how he'd break the news. Melvin took some comfort in the fact that Oscar would be locked up on the other side of the bars when he heard it.

**Five minutes** after Milo had reluctantly shooed Daisy out of the suite, he heard another knock on the door. Officially classifying the day a complete disaster, he didn't even bother checking to see who his latest visitor was. He opened the door and saw Frank Slack standing at the doorway with a big smile on his face.

"Frank," Milo said. "I completely forgot I asked you to stop by. Come on in."

"I hope I'm not disturbing you," Frank said, stepping inside and admiring the suite. "Now, this is living."

"You want it?" Milo said. "It's going cheap today."

"What?"

"Nothing? Have a seat."

"Did I wake you?" Frank said.

"No, I've been up for hours," Milo said, then remembered his robe. "Oh, this. Yeah, I've been meaning to get dressed, but something keeps coming up."

Milo walked to the desk, grabbed the envelope with Frank's name on it, and handed it to him. Frank took a quick glance, then slid it into his pocket.

"I've got an update on the other boat you wanted," Frank said. "It's not pretty, but it was cheap."

"That's great. I'm not sure when or even if I'll need it, but it's good to have. Are you sure you don't mind storing it at your place out of sight?"

"Not a problem," Frank said. "It's not as fast as the one I built for you, but it'll do the trick. And I removed the windshield and painted everything jet black like you wanted."

"You're sure it'll be hard to spot at night on the River?"

"As long as there's no moon, it'll seem like it's invisible."

"Thanks for the reminder. I'll need to check the calendar," Milo said, heading to his desk to jot a note down. He sat back down and glanced at Frank.

"Is it too early for a drink?" Milo said, yawning.

"Yeah, probably," Frank said, giving him a weak smile.

"That's what I figured."

"So, how's everything working out with the new boat?"

"It's beautiful. And there's not a scratch on it. Apart from you and Birdie, it's about the only thing in my life that is currently working the way it's supposed to."

"Anything I need to worry about?" Frank said, cocking his head.

"No, everything's fine," Milo said, sitting down across from him. "I'll get it all sorted out. There are just a couple of things that have suddenly got their wires crossed."

"It's probably because of the full moon," Frank said.

"There's a full moon?" Milo said, frowning. "I did not know that."

"You have been busy," Frank said, laughing.

"I gotta ask you, Frank. Did you ever have one of those days when everything just seemed to be slipping a gear?"

Then the phone rang.


**Oscar stared** down at the slip of paper, then glared at Melvin.

"Thanks, Oscar? Is this your idea of a joke, Melvin?"

"No, I found the paint can, and that's what was inside."

"Maybe I should compare your handwriting with the note," Oscar growled.

"Oscar, I've spent all day dealing with your shit. Keep busting my balls, and you're gonna have to start doing your own shoveling," Melvin said. "Why would I take all our money and then leave you a thank you note?"

"To throw me off the trail, why else?" Oscar said, scowling at Melvin through the bars.

"Yeah, you caught me, Oscar. Nothing gets past you. You're such an idiot."

"Well, if it wasn't you, who the hell took it?"

"Probably the guy who put the booze in your garage," Melvin said. "I get somebody wanting to steal the money, but I'm not sure why they decided to set you up."

"To get me out of the way, obviously."

"Yeah, I'm sure you had them on the run, Oscar. They probably felt their world closing in on them," Melvin said, laughing. "You know, what with you doing all those detailed investigations you're so well known for."

"Shut up, Melvin."

"But you have to admit, the note was a nice touch."

"Yeah, I'm cracking up on the inside," Oscar said. "Okay, now what?"

"Well, I'm going to have to come up with five hundred bucks to get you out of here," Melvin said, scratching his stubble. "But that sure isn't going to happen today."

"Where are you going to get the money?"

"I don't have a clue, Oscar. But I do know I'm not gonna find it standing around here talking to you," Melvin said, glancing around. "This place gives me the creeps."

"You know, Melvin, it would only take one word from me, and you'd be right in here with me," Oscar said.

"Oscar, do I need to remind you that I'm the only person who is capable of getting you out? Wouldn't that be impossible if I were sitting in there with you?"

"Forget it. Just forget I said anything," Oscar said, breathing heavily. "Has the mayor said anything yet?"

"I knew there was something I forgot to tell you. He fired you this morning."

"The bastard. Damn. Now I've lost everything."

"Maybe, maybe not. But half of everything you lost was mine, Oscar. And that's the second time I've been robbed in the past six months. You'll have to excuse me if I sound less than sympathetic."

"You need to get me out of here, Melvin," Oscar whispered. "I can't stay in here with these animals. You won't believe what the guy in the next cell said he wanted to do to me."

Melvin glanced into the adjacent cell and saw a drooling man staring back at him with a lopsided grin and eyes that seemed to point in different directions.

"How ya doin'?" Melvin said to the man, then ducked when he flicked a handful of drool through the bars.

"You see what I'm dealing with?" Oscar said.

"Well, I guess, in the end, we're all judged by the company we keep, right?" Melvin said, waving goodbye as he headed back down the hallway.

**"Hello? Hello?** Is anybody here?"

"Oh, hi, Willy," Milo said, looking up from the shirt he was buttoning and turning away from the mirror. "Come on in."

"Did you know your door is open?" Willy said, frowning as he glanced around the suite.

"Yeah, I was trying to save a bit of time," Milo said, refocusing on his shirt.

"You lost me, Milo," Willy said, shaking his head.

"Long story," Milo said. "What's up?"

"I just thought I'd stop by and give you an update," Willy said, sitting down.

"Ah, yes. Your meeting with Ben Green," Milo said, grabbing an envelope off the desk as he walked past. He sat down and tossed the envelope to Willy. "How did it go?"

"Thanks for this, Milo."

"You earned it."

"Green's pretty much what you said he is. He tries to come off like he's a good guy, even a gentleman who's a bit of a dandy. But I could tell straight away that, deep down, he's one mean son of a bitch."

"Yes, I'm sure he is," Milo said, nodding. "Did he agree to seventy a case?"

"I talked up the quality of the booze and got him to pay seventy-five," Willy said, grinning.

"Well done, Willy. I'm impressed."

"Thanks. I'm making the delivery tomorrow, so I'll have your cut after that."

"That's fine."

"And Green wants me to guarantee him fifty cases a week," Willy said, then glanced up tentatively at Milo. "I agreed."

"Really? Oh, Willy," Milo said, staring at him. "What did I tell you was the most important fundamental of being a successful businessman?"

"Don't make promises you can't keep."

"Exactly," Milo said, lighting a cigarette. "Do you have any idea where to get your hands on fifty cases a week?"

"Not a clue," Willy said, shaking his head. "I think I'm screwed, Milo."

"Okay, I guess that's a start. Understanding the problem is the first step in solving it," Milo said, chuckling.

"What am I gonna do?" Willy said, squeezing the life out of his hat.

"Didn't I say you were going to have to fly solo on this one, Willy?" Milo said, fiddling with a button he'd fastened in the wrong hole.

"Yes, you did, Milo. But it's not like I'm asking you to do any of the work. All I need are a couple of suggestions."

"Coming up with the right idea is about eighty percent of the work, Willy. The rest is simple execution."

"If you help me out, Milo, I'll give you a cut of the profits," Willy said, still massaging the hat with his hands.

"Again, Willy, I don't want a cut. I don't want anything to do with your deal. The only reason I have for helping you out is because I'd hate to see you get shot."

"Yeah, that wouldn't be good," Willy said, his hands trembling as he tossed the hat aside and tried to light a cigarette. "So, what do you think I should do?"

"The answer is right in front of you, Willy."

"It is? Can you give me a hint?"

"Let me ask you a question, Willy. You desperately need to find a supplier who can guarantee you fifty cases of whiskey a week, right?"

"Correct," Willy said, leaning forward.

"Who do you know that is currently smuggling booze across the River?" Milo said.

"You mean apart from you, right?"

"Yes, Willy. Apart from me," Milo said, shaking his head.

Willy frowned and thought hard. Then he smiled and snapped his fingers.

"Melvin English."

"Very good, Willy."

"You think he can get his hands on fifty cases a week?"

Milo crushed his cigarette out and stared at Willy.

"Okay, right. It's my deal, not yours. Maybe now with Oscar locked up, Melvin might be looking for somebody else to work with. That's good news because I can't stand that cop. Yeah, Melvin," Willy said, rapid-fire. "He's the guy I need to talk to. I suppose he might be able to either get fifty cases a week from his current supplier or have some ideas about where to get his hands on more. I wonder what sort of cut he'd be expecting." Willy finally stopped to catch his breath. "What do you think, Milo?"

Milo continued to stare blankly at Willy until he got the message.

"Yeah, sorry, Milo," Willy whispered. "My deal, not yours, right?"

"Okay, Willy. Meeting over. You need to go, and I really need to see if I can salvage what's left of my day. I'm sure you and Melvin will have no shortage of things to talk about. And don't forget to leave my name out of it," Milo said, getting up to hold the door open for Willy.

"Anxious to get rid of me, Milo?" Willy said, laughing as headed for the door. "You got a hot date?"

"Yeah, I'm pretty sure her temperature is rising," Milo said.

"Well, if she's even close to the one that was with Ben Green this morning, you're a lucky man."

"Ben Green had a woman with him?" Milo said, holding the door half-open.

"He sure did," Willy said. "And she was a real beauty."

"You didn't happen to catch her name, did you?"

"Yeah. Beulah. I didn't get her last name."


**Clint tied** his boat off and headed down the dock into the warehouse. Tom Collins was standing along one wall organizing milk cans into groups of thirty. He stopped when he heard Clint close the door and turned around.

"Hey. How did it go with Milo?" Tom said.

"About what I expected," Clint said, sitting down at the table and pouring himself a shot of Miracle. "He said we'll talk again later, but he's not going to give me any more money."

"Well, you did agree to the deal, Clint."

"Things change, Tom," Clint said, tossing back the shot.

"What else did he say?"

"He said I should talk to you."

"About what?" Tom said, sitting down at the table and pouring a shot for himself. He refilled Clint's glass, then drank and sat back in his chair.

"He said, since my situation wasn't going to be more profitable, I should talk with you about making the workday more enjoyable," Clint said, laughing. "Classic Milo, huh?"

"It's actually not bad advice," Tom said, shrugging. "Maybe you need a vacation."

"What I need is more money," Clint said.

"You can't spend what you're making now, Clint."

"It's the principle of the thing, Tom," Clint said, getting up and pacing back and forth next to the table. "And Elmer and Roscoe agree with me."

"Elmer and Roscoe don't even agree that the earth is round," Tom said.

"I know they're not the sharpest tools in the shed, but at least they see things my way," Clint said, pausing to stare at Tom. "Unlike you."

"Don't get me wrong. I'm sympathetic to your problem, Clint," Tom said. "But Milo has been good to me, and I'm pretty happy with my deal. And I seriously doubt if I'm making anywhere near what you are."

"I sure hope not," Clint said, resuming his pacing. "That would just be more salt in the wound. No offense."

"Oh, of course not. None taken," Tom said. "Well, you know what Milo always says at times like this."

"Don't give me any of that *take the long view* crap, Tom. If I hear that again, I'm gonna puke."

"If you do puke, it'll probably be because of all the Miracle you've swallowed since you got up this morning. How much have you had today?"

"Not enough," Clint said, reaching for the jar. "Is that it, Tom? I ask for advice, and all you do is try to monitor my drinking?"

"Drink all you want," Tom said, stretching out in his chair and putting his feet up on the table. "Well, if you can't take the long view, and you can't let it go, I guess the only thing you can do is to try to make your point using more of a direct approach."

"You're suggesting I try something a bit more…confrontational?"

"I'm not suggesting anything. But if you do decide to do something stupid, you need to be prepared to deal with the consequences."

"I'm not afraid of Milo," Clint said, finally sitting back down. "But I will need to get a handle on his distribution system before I go much further."

"I thought that's what you had Elmer and Roscoe for?" Tom said.

"Sure, they know the general outline of how it works, but I'm sure Milo is holding some things back."

"As long as Elmer and Roscoe know who to introduce you to, you should be able to figure out the rest of it from there. You're a smart guy."

"Yes, I am, ain't I? What do you say, Tom? You feel like getting your hands dirty?"

"No, I'll be sitting on the sidelines watching how this one plays out."

"This is your chance to come in as a partner, Tom. If I end up taking over, I won't be asking you a second time."

"That's fine with me, Clint. I'm satisfied with my current role for the moment," Tom said, grinning at him.

"Your loss," Clint said. "But I can count on your silence, right? You're not going to say anything to Milo?"

"What could I tell him he doesn't already know? You're pissed off about your current deal and want something better."

"Yeah, you're right. Milo already knows I'm not happy," Clint said, toying with his empty shot glass. "So, I guess I should be careful. I just need to come up with something clever."

"Well, have another shot of Miracle. I'm sure something will come to you."

# Milo Lends More Than An Ear

**Milo half-listened to Ruby's latest** harangue, waited until she slammed the phone down, then gently placed the receiver back in its cradle. Then he picked the phone up and called room service to order a bottle of aspirin. Overloaded with a long list of things to think through and worry about, Milo stretched out on the bed in his underwear, socks, and half-buttoned shirt, and closed his eyes. He drifted off, then was woken by a soft knock. He climbed out of bed and grabbed a dollar off the desk to tip the guy bringing him his aspirin, then headed for the door. Milo opened it and stared at who was waiting.

"Melvin?"

"I take it you're surprised to see me, Milo."

"Actually, I was expecting something to fix this headache," Milo said, taking a step back to give him room.

"I'll see what I can do," Melvin said, walking in and glancing around at the plush surroundings. "Wow. Nice digs, Milo. How much does the hotel charge for this place?"

"Did you come all this way to discuss my rent, Melvin?" Milo said, gesturing for him to sit down.

"No, of course not," Melvin said, embarrassed. "It's none of my business. But it sure is nice."

Milo listened as Melvin launched into a lengthy babble that rambled in several directions. When he started to repeat pieces of the conversation, Milo held up his hands for Melvin to stop. Melvin nodded and sat quietly staring at Milo. Then he turned in his chair when he heard a knock on the door.

Milo got up and soon returned holding a bottle of aspirin. He poured two glasses of whiskey over ice, handed one to Melvin, tossed a small handful of aspirin into his mouth, and washed them down. Milo lit a cigarette, exhaled loudly, then nodded at Melvin.

"Okay, now I'm ready for you," Milo said. "But let's see if we can take it one step at a time."

"Sure, Milo. As I was saying, Oscar's locked up, and his bail has been set at five hundred dollars."

"Which you don't have because somebody stole all of Oscar's money."

"Yes. I know that probably sounds strange," Melvin said, glancing nervously at Milo.

"I wouldn't worry about it, Melvin. It seems to be the day for strange."

"And as his lawyer, I'm sure you understand why I want to get my client out of jail as soon as possible."

"Why the hell would you want to do that?" Milo said, raising an eyebrow. "It seems like the perfect spot for Oscar."

"Yes, I suppose you're right," Melvin said, laughing as he reached for one of Milo's cigarettes.

"Help yourself," Milo said.

"Sorry. But thanks. Anyway, despite Oscar's rather unpleasant nature, I'm bound by my professional ethics to do everything I can on his behalf."

"I thought you said you were a lawyer."

"What?" Melvin said, confused. Then he laughed. "Good one, Milo."

"You said something about Oscar's garage being robbed?"

"Yes, Oscar felt that this particular sum of money wasn't appropriate for a bank. You know, all those people asking way too many questions."

"I see. Perhaps some ill-gotten gains?" Milo said, smiling.

"Yes, well, I really shouldn't say any more about that," Melvin said, then couldn't stop himself. "Can I let you in on a little secret, Milo?"

"I'd be disappointed if you didn't feel you could trust me, Melvin."

"Oscar and I have been running a little business on the side," Melvin whispered as he leaned forward.

"I see. It doesn't have anything to do with dairy farming, does it?"

"Of course not."

"Then it's none of my business, Melvin. Whatever you two are up to makes absolutely no difference to me."

"I'm glad to hear you say that, Milo. And I know I can count on you to keep all of this confidential."

"Absolutely, Melvin," Milo said, topping off their drinks.

"Oscar and I have been dabbling in illegal hooch," Melvin said, grinning at Milo. "Yeah, we're dabbling."

"Really? I did not know that," Milo said. "So, the hundred cases they found in Oscar's garage were yours?"

"No, they weren't. That's the weird part. And it was ninety-five cases."

"Oh, right. Ninety-five," Milo said, silently chastising himself and blaming his fatigue. "If they weren't yours, where do you think they came from?"

"Oscar is convinced that somebody set him up," Melvin said. "But who would want to do that?"

"Well, it had to be somebody with an ax to grind. And when it comes to Oscar, there must be a conga line of people carrying grudges."

"Sure. It would probably take a month just to compile the list," Melvin said, then frowned. "What's a conga line?"

"It's a dance they do in Cuba."

"Huh. I've never heard of it before," Melvin said.

"You will. I'm sure it'll get here soon enough."

"You've been to Cuba?"

"Yeah, I did some work down there a few years ago. Beautiful place."

"Farming?"

"Finance," Milo said, smiling. "Well, whoever put the booze in Oscar's garage had to be somebody who knew what the two of you were up to. Have you been talking out of school again, Melvin?"

"I don't think so," Melvin said, staring off into the distance. "But it's a small town, right? People are bound to talk."

"Yeah, I'm starting to develop an appreciation for that," Milo said. "Maybe it was another bootlegger who's worried about the competition."

"That's what Oscar thinks," Melvin said.

"What do you think?"

Melvin took a long drag on his cigarette then disappeared momentarily behind a cloud of smoke.

"I don't think that's it. We're not a threat to anybody, and there's more than enough illegal booze to go around. Everybody I know who's running hooch seems to be doing pretty well."

"So, other people do know about you and Oscar, right?"

"Yeah, now that I think about it, I guess they must," Melvin said. "But I still don't think that's who set Oscar up."

"Well, if it wasn't one of them, I can only come up with one other possibility."

"Who's that?" Melvin said, topping off his drink.

"My guess is that it's a certain local Revenuer looking to make a name for himself."

"Roland Doyle?" Melvin said, stunned. "Of course. That makes perfect sense. It would make quite an impression with his bosses if he was able to bring down a corrupt cop."

"Yes, I imagine it would," Milo said, nodding.

"But where would he get his hands on all that whiskey?"

"Getting his hands on illegal booze is kind of his job, isn't it, Melvin?"

"Yes, of course. Silly me."

"Roland Doyle," Milo said, chuckling as he got up and headed to the desk. "I must say, he's already full of surprises."

Milo returned holding a large stack of cash. Melvin stared with his mouth open as Milo began counting out fifties. When he got to ten, he handed the five hundred to Melvin.

"That's for Oscar's bail," Milo said, then resumed counting. "And here's another five hundred to help you get by until you get your cash flow heading in the right direction."

"Why would you do this, Milo?"

"I'm just helping out a friend, Melvin," Milo said, folding the remaining bills and sliding them into his shirt pocket. "And if you want to hold onto Oscar's bail for a while, it won't bother me in the least. He can rot in jail for all I care."

"You're so good to me, Milo," Melvin said, then sat quietly for a long time. "You know, maybe some extended jail time might be just the thing Oscar needs to smarten up and fly straight."

"You make a good point, Melvin."

"Yeah, that is a good point, isn't it? I'm glad I stopped by," Melvin said, finishing his drink and getting up out of his chair. "Thanks again, Milo. I'm gonna pay you back as soon as I can."

"I know you will, Melvin."

"But I have no idea how I'm gonna do that."

"Don't worry, Melvin. I'm sure something will turn up."

"Yeah, you're right. But that's just me. Always worrying about something." Before he could launch into an extended babble about his personal idiosyncrasies, Melvin shifted topics. "So, I guess we're going to need a new police chief."

"Indeed," Milo said, trying to remember if he'd already added talking to the mayor to his to-do list.

"I wonder who they're going to hire. Somebody pleasant would be a nice change. Yeah, that's the ticket. Pleasant, but incompetent," Melvin said, smiling and nodding to himself. "Say, you want to head downstairs to the speakeasy? Maybe have a couple of drinks and check out the ladies? I'm buying."

"Any other time I would, Melvin. But right now, I find myself in desperate need of a nap."

Milo gave Melvin a wave then closed the door just as the phone started ringing. He prepared himself for the worst and picked it up on the second ring.

"Milo Razner," he said, holding the phone away from his ear. "Oh, hi, Violet. It's so good to hear your voice...Why? Because it's soft and quiet...Yes, I suppose those are good qualities for a telephone operator to have...I see. And he called her from my farm?... No, thanks, Violet. I'll handle it from here... I'm sorry I haven't had a chance to drop off your envelope... You want to swing by and pick it up? Sure, why not. Everybody else is. I'll be heading out in a couple of hours, but I'll leave it at reception for you... You're very welcome. And thanks for calling."

He hung up and felt the knock coming before he heard it. Milo trudged across the room and caught a glimpse of himself in the mirror. Deciding he looked ridiculous, he stopped to remove his socks, then opened the door. He flinched when he saw who it was, but she was smiling and gently stroked the side of his face as she passed him on her way in. She was wearing the ankle-high stiletto boots he'd bought for her and a long wool coat that was buttoned from top to bottom.

"Ruby, I'm so sorry," Milo said. "You won't believe the day I'm having."

"No, I'm the one who's sorry, Milo. I've been way too hard on you all day. Billy and I had a big fight last night, and I've been taking it out on you."

"How about that? Wonders never cease," Milo whispered as he closed the door.

"What's that?"

"Nothing," Milo said. "I'm glad you stopped by. And I must apologize for my appearance."

"There's no need to apologize," she said, remaining on her feet and smiling at him.

"What did you and Billy fight about?"

"Our divorce," she said, quietly.

"I see. I assume he was the one who raised the issue," Milo said, pouring a drink for her.

"He was. Apparently, Billy is in love with another woman."

Milo thought about divulging what he already knew but decided to keep his pipeline with Daisy to himself.

"Sure. We already know that. He's in love with Daisy."

"Not anymore," Ruby said, glancing around the suite. "He's fallen for the local schoolteacher."

"Has he now?" Milo said. "But that's not necessarily a problem, right? As long as Billy stays here and keeps cooking, we don't really care who he's in love with, do we?"

"Normally, no," Ruby said. "But this woman is going to be a problem, Milo."

"She's not talking about leaving the area, is she?"

"No, she's not," Ruby said. "The problem lies more in her belief system than where she lives."

"You lost me, Ruby," Milo said. "You sure you don't want to sit down?"

"Not yet," she said. "Our local schoolteacher's mother has an interesting job that I'm afraid her daughter has taken to heart."

"Okay," Milo said. "I'm going to need a little more, Ruby."

"Her mother is one of the leaders of the national Temperance movement," Ruby said. "Surprise!"

"Yeah, no kidding. Man, I just can't catch a break today," Milo said, rubbing his forehead. "And her daughter, the schoolteacher, is a rabid proponent of Prohibition?"

"If a dog were as rabid as she is, you'd shoot it," Ruby said.

"Who knows? It may come to that."

"Indeed. And in addition to her hatred of all things alcohol, she's also a devoted, God-fearing Christian."

"I've never had much luck dealing with that combination," Milo said, frowning. "Why the hell would Billy leave Daisy for a woman like that?"

Milo realized his mistake and flinched as he looked at Ruby. She glared at him but remained silent.

"What I meant to say was I guess we shouldn't be surprised. Billy is very impressionable," Milo said.

"Impressionable is a word for it," Ruby said. "We both know he's dumber than a box of rocks."

"Does she know what Billy does for a living?"

"I don't think so," Ruby said. "But he's planning on telling her in the near future. That's what we were fighting about last night."

"Really? I would have assumed you were arguing over money," Milo said.

"Not at all. I'm not going to worry about getting my hands on any of Billy's money," Ruby said.

"You're not?"

"No. Why would I? As soon as we settle down together, I'll have full access to half of yours," she said, laughing. Then she stopped when she saw the look Milo was giving her. "I'm joking, Milo."

"I'm really not in a joking mood, Ruby."

"I see," she said, starting to unbutton her coat. "What are you in the mood for?"

"Sleep."

"Maybe you'll be able to catch some shut eye in a bit," she said, removing the coat and letting it fall to the floor.

Milo blinked at her milky-white skin and the tiny silk ensemble she was wearing under her coat. He exhaled and whistled softly as he stared at her, then rediscovered his ability to speak.

"Is that new?"

"Well, it was this morning," Ruby said, putting her hands on her hips. "So, do you want to talk about your day some more, Milo?"

"No."

"You want to talk about what we're going to do about the schoolteacher?"

"No. I'll deal with her later," Milo said, unable to take his eyes off her.

"Then what do you want to do, Milo?"

"I'd like to call the meeting to order."

# Understanding the Gravity of Things

**Two hours later**, still tired but in a much better mood, Milo entered Fannie's and headed straight for the counter. He tapped the bell and glanced around while he waited. Off in the distance, he heard muffled laughter and loud voices, and Milo decided that Fannie's Blind Pig must be enjoying a big night. She poked her head through the curtain and was obviously relieved to see Milo standing there.

"Where have you been? I've been trying to call you for a couple of hours," Fannie said.

"I had the phone off the hook," Milo said.

"We need to talk. Hey, wait a minute," she said, frowning. "Then how did you know I wanted to see you?"

"Uh, I didn't," Milo stammered, then recovered quickly. "I just thought I'd stop by for a drink. What's up?"

She gestured for him to come around the counter and into her office. Milo stepped through the curtains and into a bizarre collection of antique clothing and dozens of photos of a young

Fannie covering the walls. He sat down in an overstuffed chair and studied the old photos.

"You were very beautiful when you were a young woman, Fannie," Milo said. "And, apparently, quite often naked."

"In case you haven't noticed, Milo, I still am. Beautiful, that is. Naked's gonna cost you."

"No, I didn't mean it that way. Of course, you're still beautiful," Milo said, stifling a yawn. "I'm sorry, Fannie. I'm not at the top of my game today."

"Relax, Milo. I'm just messin' with you," she said. "I need to show you something."

"I think I've already seen everything," Milo said, grinning up at the photos.

"Keep that sense of humor close by," Fannie said. "You're gonna need it."

She walked to the other side of her office and removed a sheet that was draped over an object about three-feet high. Milo's mouth dropped open when he saw the milk can shining in the light.

"What the hell?"

"That's exactly what I said when I got home this afternoon and found it sitting outside my back door," she said, sitting down across from him. "That is one of your milk cans, isn't it, Milo?"

"It certainly appears to be," Milo said, his mind racing.

"At first, I thought you might have lost your mind, Milo. I said, why the heck does he think that my place would know what to do with ten gallons of milk?"

"Yes, that is a good question."

"And then I opened it," Fannie said, lighting a cigarette and holding out the pack to him.

Milo took one and lit it. He exhaled smoke and forced himself to relax.

"What did you find when you opened it?"

"Well, it sure wasn't milk," Fannie said, grinning.

"I see. Can I ask you what's in it?" Milo said, softly.

"C'mon, Milo," she said, tapping ash off her cigarette. "I thought we were friends. Let's not start blowing smoke up each other's skirts, okay?"

Milo sighed audibly then nodded.

"It's really good whiskey," Fannie said. "I had a little taste earlier."

"Thanks," Milo whispered. "It is good, isn't it?"

"Yeah. And the guy who called earlier said I was really going to enjoy it," Fannie said.

"Do you know who it was?"

"No, I didn't recognize the voice," Fannie said. "But he did have an interesting proposal for me."

"I imagine he did," Milo said.

"The first can is free, then I can get all I want going forward."

Milo got up out of his chair, grabbed two glasses from the desk, then opened the milk can. He dipped both glasses, wiped the outsides dry with a handkerchief, then handed one to Fannie and sat back down.

"No sense letting it go to waste, right?" Milo said, touching glasses with her.

"I like the way you think," Fannie said, taking a sip.

"Oh, don't worry, Fannie. I'm thinking."

"I'm sure you are, Milo," she said, laughing.

"How much was he going to charge you?" Milo said, sitting back in his chair and draping one leg over the other.

"A hundred bucks a can. By my math that works out to around thirty bucks a case," she said, finishing her cigarette.

"Your math is correct," Milo said.

"That's a very good price."

"It certainly is."

"But not as good as the price you're going to offer, right?" Milo grinned at her.

"No, probably not," he said, then stared at her with a sheepish grin. "Did you know all along what I was doing?"

"To tell you the truth, Milo, I didn't have a clue," she said, giving him a look of admiration. "I pride myself on being pretty sharp when it comes to what people are doing and what their motives are. But you slipped that one right by me. And since I missed it, my guess is that everybody else did, too. Except for the people working for you, of course."

"Ah, yes. My workforce," Milo said, taking another sip. "They're a delightful assortment of personalities."

"So, somebody working for you has either decided to start stealing from you, or they're trying to set you up," Fannie said.

"Probably both," Milo said. "I'm lucky they picked you, Fannie. Another proprietor might not have had the same perspective as you."

"You mean someone who likes to take the long view?" she said, giving him a coy smile.

"Exactly."

"Do you know who might be dumb enough to pull a stunt like this?" she said, reaching for the pack of smokes.

"I have several possible candidates in mind," Milo said.

"Far be it for me to comment on how you run your business, Milo, but it sounds like you might need to tighten up your hiring practices," she said, raising an eyebrow at him.

"Yes, I'm sure you're right. And I've already started working on some improvements in that area," Milo said, grabbing both their glasses and refilling them.

"Which are about to be accelerated based on what's just happened?"

"You're very astute, Fannie. And so much more than just a pretty face," Milo said, handing her one of the glasses.

"Aren't you sweet?" she said, raising her glass at him. "One thing you learn running whores is how to understand people and what makes them tick."

"On that note," Milo said, leaning forward in his chair. "How did you know that I wouldn't just shoot you?"

"I thought about that possibility," she said, nodding. "But then I decided that you aren't a violent man by nature. You're someone who likes to come up with mutually beneficial solutions to problems. And since we already have an agreement in place, I thought that if I proved you could trust me, all we would need to do is sit down and make a slight modification to our existing deal."

"Define slight modification."

"Two free cans a week," Fannie said, casually blowing smoke up at the ceiling.

"Twenty gallons a week? Geez, Fannie, just how thirsty are the people who drink here?"

"Parched, Milo. They're absolutely parched."

Milo burst out laughing then began to cough.

"Okay, you've finally managed to do it, Fannie," he said when his breathing finally returned to normal.

"What's that?

"You did what you've wanted to do to me since we first met," Milo said, raising his glass to her.

"Yeah, I guess I kinda did," she said, grinning. "Was it good for you?"

"I'm sure it's not as good as the real thing, but it wasn't bad," Milo said. "Well played."

"Why thank you, Mr. Razner. I look forward to taking the long view with you."

"The *silent* long view."

"Of course," Fannie said.

"And I'll have to figure out something else to deliver it in. I can't have my milk cans sitting around here for everybody to see."

"I understand, Milo. Monday and Thursday will work best for my needs."

"Monday and Thursday it is. But you'll have to handle your own bottling. Will there be anything else at the moment? I need to run."

"No, I think that's it, Milo," she said, getting up from her chair.

Milo also stood and extended his hand. After the handshake, Milo again studied the photos of the younger Fannie.

"You truly were remarkable when you were younger," Milo said. "And the photographer obviously knew what he was doing."

"Yeah, I liked him," she said, staring at the photos of herself. "But he wanted more than I could give him."

"There seems to be a lot of that going around," Milo whispered, fixated on one of the photos.

"What?"

"Nothing," Milo said, pointing at one of the photos. "Your breasts are perfect in this one."

"They're perfect in all of them," she said, chuckling. "But the twins just happened to come out particularly good in that one."

"They certainly did," Milo said, unable to take his eyes off the photo. "They're gravity defying."

"Well, that was a long time ago. These days, I have to admit that gravity is winning. But I'm sure not going down without a fight."

Milo turned away from the photos to look at Fannie.

"I think we're going to enjoy working together," he said.

"I have no doubt about that, Milo. And who knows where it will lead, right?"

"Exactly. Whatever direction it takes us, Fannie."

"I think it should head in a southerly direction soon."

"Absolutely. We definitely need to do that in the near future," Milo said, nodding. "But I need to clean a few things up first. And I've got a lot on my mind at the moment. You know, things that are weighing me down."

"I wouldn't worry about it too much, Milo. It's probably just gravity."

# Episode 6

## *Entrepreneurial Spirits*

"The Dries like to get on their soapbox and rant and rave about all the headaches alcohol creates for society. What the hell do those people know about hangovers?"

Milo Razner

# Milo Lands A Big One

**The sun was hot**, the beer was cold, and the fish were biting. At least they were for Birdie. Milo reeled his line in for about the tenth time in the last half-hour and checked to see if the bait was still on his hook.

"You know, Milo," Birdie said, holding his pole in one hand and rolling a cigarette with the other. "I've always found that I catch more fish when I actually leave my line in the water long enough for it to get wet."

"Gee, thanks, Birdie. I'll try to remember that," Milo said, casting. "How is it possible for you to catch nine fish while I can't even catch a cold? Our hooks have to be sitting right next to each other down there."

"It because you're not holding your mouth right," Birdie said, focused on his fishing line.

"What?" Milo said, confused.

"Your mouth."

"What about it?"

"I just told you. You're not holding it right," Birdie said, giving Milo a quick glance. "Your lips need to be tighter. But you also need to give it a little grin just so the fish know you're friendly."

Birdie went back to his fishing. Milo continued to stare at him.

"What the hell difference would that make?" Milo said.

"Hey, if you want to argue with the guy who's already caught nine fish, knock yourself out."

Milo frowned but started working on his facial expressions feeling foolish the entire time. When Birdie finally glanced over, he let loose with a loud cackle.

"Sonofabitch," Milo said, glaring at him. "I fell for it again. Well played."

"It's like taking candy from a baby, Milo," Birdie said, still laughing as he switched fishing poles with him. "Here, try mine for a while."

Milo accepted the fishing pole and immediately felt a tug on the line.

"Hey, I think I've caught something," Milo said, grasping Birdie's fishing pole with both hands.

"No kidding?" Birdie said. "How about that? It's like the fish was just waiting for you to grab that pole."

"You're saying it was already on the hook?" Milo said, reeling the line in.

"I'm just saying there was no way you were gonna agree to stop until you caught at least one fish," Birdie said, putting down his pole and grabbing the net. "So, don't lose him. Easy does it, Milo. Easy."

Milo continued to reel the line in until a smallmouth bass broke the surface. Birdie leaned over and scooped the fish into the net.

"Hah!" Milo said, reaching into the net and removing the hook. He held the fish up with both hands and examined it. "He's a nice one." Then he gently tossed the fish back into the water. "Okay, we can go now."

"Why the hell did you do that?" Birdie said.

"I like catching them, but I can't stand the thought of killing them," Milo said. "Besides, you have nine. That's plenty."

"You're an odd duck, Milo," Birdie said, packing up both fishing poles. "But it kinda works for you."

"Odd is very underrated," Milo said, then drained half of his fresh beer. He stretched out and let the sun hit his face. "This is living."

"No argument there," Birdie said, starting the engine. "You want to stop by the island on the way home to check in on Billy?"

"No, I'm trying to take the whole day off," Milo said. "And if I have to deal with Billy, it'll just ruin my mood."

"Okay. Do you feel like taking the long way back? It's a beautiful day for a boat ride," Birdie said.

"Actually, I do," Milo said. "There's an island I've been keeping an eye on. And I told her we'd be there by three."

"Who? Keeping an eye on it for what?"

"Drive, my good man," Milo said.

Birdie opened the throttle a bit, and the boat surged forward effortlessly through the water. Milo sat up to enjoy the breeze.

"I have plans for the island we're going to take a look at," Milo said.

"What sort of plans?"

"Plans to buy it, of course," Milo said. "Take that small inlet right after we go past my island. Then make a left. You'll know it when you see it."

"No way. You're planning on buying Whisperer Island?" Birdie said, glancing over at Milo as he began rolling a cigarette.

"Maybe," Milo said, grinning widely. "Roll me one of those, will you?"

"I can't believe it," Birdie said. "I didn't know it was even for sale."

"It's just come onto the market," Milo said.

"Can I ask you how you know that?"

"I wish you wouldn't, Birdie," Milo said, accepting and lighting the cigarette.

"That is one beautiful island," Birdie said. "What are you going to do with it?"

"I've been thinking that it's about time we expanded our operation. And it's also getting close to the time when we might need to do a little *misdirection*."

"As usual, you lost me, Milo," Birdie said, shaking his head. "But I imagine you'll explain it all to me when the time comes."

"I certainly will."

"You thinking about spending the summers there? The house looks amazing from the water," Birdie said.

"I would love to live there. But that's going to have to wait. For the immediate future, it's going to be used for another purpose."

"You're going to do a little cooking there, aren't you, Milo?" Birdie said, grinning at him.

"Actually, Birdie, I'm going to do a whole lot of cooking."

**Melvin English** veered toward the far wall as he approached the drooling man's cell and kept an eye out for the handful of slobber he knew was on the way. It came and fell harmlessly onto the cement floor.

"How ya doin'?" Melvin said. "You've been saving that up just for me?"

The drooling man with the multi-directional stare snarled at him, then began humming a show tune. Melvin briefly pondered the decline of the judicial system then counted his blessings. He stopped in front of Oscar's cell and waited for the verbal assault to begin.

"Where the hell have you been?" Oscar growled as he sat up on his bunk.

"Busting my hump trying to figure out how to get you out of here, Oscar," Melvin said, peering through the bars but staying out of reach.

"It's been a week since I've seen you, Melvin. What the hell are you trying to prove?"

"Apart from your innocence, not much, Oscar. I'm doing everything I can, but I'm having major problems coming up with the five hundred for your bail."

"Steal it."

"And end up in here with you and Quasimodo over there?" Melvin said, nodding at the adjacent cell. "Not gonna happen, Oscar."

"Then borrow it."

"From who?"

"Obviously from someone who's got an extra five hundred dollars laying around," Oscar snapped.

"Well, sure. Why didn't I think of that? There aren't a lot of people like that around, Oscar. And I doubt if any of them are particularly anxious to do you a favor."

"Bastards," Oscar said. "I'm going stir crazy in here, Melvin. There must be somebody you could ask."

"Well, there is one guy," Melvin said, rubbing the side of his face. "But, no, it's probably not a good idea."

"Who are you thinking of?"

"Milo Razner."

**Birdie idled** the boat into the massive stone boathouse, and Milo hopped out to tie the boat off. He helped Birdie climb out of the boat, and they both stared in awe as they walked down the long dock taking in the high-ceilinged structure that was bigger than most of the houses in town.

"Wow," Birdie said.

"Yeah, that's the word for it," Milo said, continuing to take in his surroundings. "You sure you're up for the walk up that path? It looks like quite a hike."

"You think I'm gonna miss seeing this place?" Birdie said, limping his way onto the path.

"Well, take your time. There's no hurry," Milo said, following closely behind.

They slowly made their way up the path that wound through a well-tended lawn, past a large stone structure, and onto a set of stone steps that led to a wraparound verandah that provided a 360-degree view of the River.

"Can you really afford to buy this place, Milo?"

"Birdie, I don't think I can afford not to," Milo said, staring off into the distance.

The front door opened and an elderly woman with some spring in her step stepped out onto the verandah.

"Are you, Mr. Razner?" she said.

"I am. Mrs. Alexander?" Milo said, bowing slightly as she approached.

"Yes, I am. It's nice to meet you, Mr. Razner. Senator Miller had some very nice things to say about you," she said, smiling.

"Well, the Senator and I go way back, and the feeling is mutual. The people of New York are very lucky to have someone like him looking out for their best interests."

"Are you sure we're talking about the same Senator Miller?" she said, cocking her head at Milo.

Milo chuckled.

"Well, like every other politician, the Senator does have his moments."

"Yes, I'm quite familiar with many of them," she said, nodding. She looked at Birdie. "I'm Janice Alexander.

"It's nice to meet you. I'm Birdie."

"You just have the one name?" she said.

"Yeah, since people always seem to know who I am, it's the only one I've ever needed," Birdie said, shrugging.

"Interesting logic," she said with a small shrug. Then she focused on Milo. "So, Mr. Razner. I understand you're looking to buy an island."

"Actually, Mrs. Alexander," Milo said, gazing out at the River. "Judging by this view, I think I'm looking to buy this island. It's magnificent."

"Thank you. Yes, it is. This place has been very special," she said, turning melancholy. "But now that Jeffrey is gone, the memories are just too much for me to deal with."

"I was sorry to hear about your loss," Milo said. "I never met your husband, but Senator Miller always sang his praises."

"Yes, I'm sure he did," she said, managing a small smile. "Those two were always up to something."

Milo understood all too well many of the things the two men had gotten into, but kept them to himself. He didn't know if the woman even knew what some of them entailed, but Milo was certain she didn't want to talk about them, especially with a complete stranger.

"Come, follow me. I'd love to show you the house," she said, gesturing toward the front door.

They walked inside, and Milo was speechless as he took in the combination of wood, stone, and glass. The front room was enormous, and a floor to ceiling fireplace dominated the far wall.

"I told Jeffrey right from the jump that it was going to be too big," she said, smiling at the memory. "But he was insistent. What he thought we would ever do with eight bedrooms I have no idea. But we did manage to fill them whenever we threw a party."

"It's unbelievable," Milo finally managed to get out.

"Yes, it certainly is," she said, tearing up. Then she exhaled and recovered quickly. "And there are two other structures on the island besides the main house and boathouse. One is the generator room. Jeffrey always had to have his electricity. And he loved leaving the lights on." She chuckled as another memory took her away, then continued. "And the other structure was always used for storage. You know, as sort of a catch-all for the things we didn't know what to do with."

"That's the building we passed on our way up the path, right?" Milo said.

"Yes, that's the one. It's quite large, and it has a very nice stone floor Jeffrey designed and built himself," she said. "That was Jeffrey. He always had to have a project going on, or he didn't know what to do with himself. Would you like to take a look at it?"

"No, not at the moment, Mrs. Alexander," Milo said. "I think I've seen all I need to."

"Oh, my," she said, frowning. "Have you seen something you don't like?"

"Just the opposite," Milo said. "It's perfect. And I always like to wait to be surprised when I least expect it. Does that sound strange?"

"Not at all, Mr. Razner," she said, placing a hand on Milo's forearm. "This place would be perfect for you. It's full of surprises."

"Yes, that's what I've heard," Milo whispered.

"What's that, Mr. Razner?"

"Nothing," Milo said, beaming at her. "I'm just overwhelmed by how beautiful the island is, Mrs. Alexander."

"So, are you saying that you're interested, Mr. Razner?" she said, suddenly turning all business.

Milo looked at her with a new appreciation. She might be a sweet, old lady, but she didn't miss a trick. And she obviously knew what the place was worth.

"Yes, I'm very interested, Mrs. Alexander."

"I'm so glad to hear that," she said. "I really would like to get this wrapped up soon. I have a trip to Europe coming up, and I would hate to have to postpone it."

"Of course," Milo said, nodding. "I understand. Paris?"

"Yes. And Venice," she said. "Have you been to Europe?"

"I have. I did some work in London and Paris a few years ago," Milo said.

"Dairy farming?" she said, frowning.

"No. Finance," Milo said, smiling at her. "Dairy farming has come to me later in life."

"I see," she said. "Well, as I was saying, I'd like to get the island sold as soon as possible. If you need more time, I completely understand. But I do have some other potential buyers who'd like to see the place."

"No, you don't, Mrs. Alexander," Milo said, shaking his head. "I believe your asking price is fifty thousand dollars."

"It is," she said, nodding. "I know it's an obscene amount of money, but that's what my advisors are telling me it's worth."

"Fifty thousand is just fine, Mrs. Alexander," Milo said, glancing around. "I assume that price includes all the furniture?"

"Yes, apart from a few personal items I'll be taking with me, it does," she said. "You've made your decision already?"

"I certainly have, Mrs. Alexander," Milo said. "Unfortunately, I don't have fifty thousand in cash with me at the moment."

"Well, of course not," she said, chuckling at the absurdity of the idea.

"But I do have some cash on hand that I'd like to leave as a down payment. You know, as a demonstration of my good faith."

"That would be fine, Mr. Razner," she said, nodding. "How much were you thinking?"

Milo reached into his coat pocket and removed a thick stack of hundred-dollar bills.

"I was thinking about twenty percent," Milo said, starting to count out ten thousand in cash.

Halfway through, Milo caught a glimpse of Birdie's open-mouthed stare, fought back the urge to laugh, and almost lost count. When he finished, he handed the stack to the woman.

"Here you go. Ten thousand dollars," Milo said. "I'll have the rest of it tomorrow, Mrs. Alexander."

"Very good, Mr. Razner," she said, looking down at her sudden windfall. "I'm impressed. I do like doing business with a man who knows what he wants. I'll get my lawyer working on the deed transfer right away. Let me get you a receipt for this."

She strolled off toward what appeared to be the library, and Milo glanced around his new home and felt a rush of adrenaline surge through him. Then he got another look at Birdie who was staring off into space with the same open-mouthed expression that appeared to be frozen on his face.

"Birdie, you're not holding your mouth right."

# Lending Leverage

**Milo scratched an itch** on his arm as he studied his reworked to-do list. He'd crossed three items out but added four new ones. At the rate the list was growing, he'd either need to hire more help, or stop thinking up shit to do. The phone rang, and he answered it on the first ring.

"Milo Razner. Oh, hello, Senator," Milo said. "Thanks for getting back to me…Yeah, I bought it today…Probably about a week. She said she was heading off to Europe…Yes, she is a lovely woman…You're coming to Watertown next weekend? Yeah, that should work…Yes, I see. Good. I'm looking forward to catching up."

The Senator hung up, and Milo smiled as he waited.

"Are you still there, Violet?"

"Yes, Milo."

"Do you have any questions?"

"Uh. Like what?"

"Aren't you wondering what I bought today?"

"Maybe a little."

"But you weren't going to ask?"

"I didn't think it was any of my business."

"Really? I find that odd coming from you, Violet."

"Yeah, I imagine that is kinda strange," she said, laughing nervously.

"I bought an island," Milo said. "But please keep that to yourself, okay?"

"You got it, Milo. Mum's the word. Just let me know if you need anything. I'm only a phone call away."

"That's funny. Goodbye, Violet."

Milo hung up the phone then got up to pour himself a drink. Halfway through his first sip, he heard a knock on the door. He looked through the peephole and frowned, then forced a smile and opened the door.

"Melvin. This is becoming a rather frequent occurrence wouldn't you say?"

"I'm sorry to drop in on you unannounced, Milo," Melvin said, sitting down.

"It's not a problem. Would you like a drink?"

"Yes, please," Melvin said. "And a cigarette."

"Help yourself," Milo said, tossing the pack to him.

Milo poured the drink and sat down across from Melvin who appeared ready to burst.

"Okay, Melvin. What's on your mind?"

"I want to pay back five hundred of what I owe you."

"That's great. My cash flow took a bit of a hit today," Milo said, lighting a cigarette.

"But I'm going to need to borrow it right back," Melvin said.

"Let me get this straight," Milo said, frowning. "You're paying me back five hundred, but then you're going to turn right around and borrow it again?"

"Actually, it will be Oscar who's borrowing it back," Melvin said, grinning.

Milo was caught off guard for a moment, concentrated hard, then grinned.

"What are you up to, Melvin?"

"Nothing, really. But Oscar is pretty agitated about still being locked up, and he suggested I borrow the money for his bail."

"And you didn't feel the need to tell him that you'd already done that?" Milo said, raising an eyebrow.

"No. The way I see it," Melvin said, exhaling smoke. "If I'm the one borrowing the bail money, there's a good chance Oscar will never pay me back. But if he borrows it from you, I'm out of the picture, and he'll be forced to deal with you. And the juice."

"And you thought I might enjoy having some leverage over Oscar?" Milo said. "Interesting idea."

"Well, I have to admit that the thought did cross my mind," Melvin said, grinning at Milo. "But Oscar's worried about the juice on the five hundred."

"As he should be," Milo said. "Okay, Melvin. I'll play. Consider your debt to me officially halved."

"Just like that?"

"Sure, why not? I'm in a good mood today. And if the two of you are ever going to be able to pay off what you owe me, you need to get back to work."

# School Daze

**Milo approached the woman** who was sitting by herself on a park bench eating an apple and tossing peanuts, one at a time, to a small group of nervous but hungry squirrels. The woman laughed as the squirrels squabbled over each peanut, and the winner scurried off while the losers regrouped and waited for her next toss. Milo studied the woman as he drew nearer and decided that she was pretty, but not showy. He stopped a few feet away from her, then removed his hat and cleared his throat.

"Excuse me, ma'am," Milo said. "Are you Annabelle Caffey?"

"Why, yes, I am," the woman said, glancing up at Milo and squinting into the sun. "I don't believe I know you, sir."

Milo took a small step to the right to block the sun and smiled down at her.

"No, we've never met. I'm Milo Razner."

"Mr. Razner. Yes, I've heard your name," she said, smiling and nodding. "You're a local dairy farmer."

"Yes, I am. I find it to be a most honorable occupation. Would you mind if I had a word with you?"

"That would be fine," she said, sliding to the far end of the bench to give him more than enough room to sit down. "Please, have a seat."

Milo sat down and placed his hat between them on the bench. She went back to tossing peanuts and laughing at the results.

"It's like an experiment," she said, not even waiting for Milo to ask the question. "I've always been fascinated by what creatures are willing to do to get what they want. Or think they need."

"That sounds like something a scientist would be interested in, Miss Caffey," Milo said. "But here you are teaching school."

"Actually, I love science," she said, looking up from the squirrels to smile at him. "But I was called to teaching."

"I see," Milo said, laughing at two squirrels who were wrestling over a peanut. "Called by the Lord, I presume?"

"Of course," Annabelle Caffey said, brushing her hair back from her face. "Are you close to God, Mr. Razner?"

"Well, it's not like we're on a first-name basis, but I think we've come to an understanding."

"I'm sure that's what you believe, Mr. Razner," she said. "What can I do for you?"

"I heard some disturbing news recently and wanted to see if there was something I could do to help," Milo said.

"What did you hear, Mr. Razner?" she said, throwing the last peanut and crushing the bag. She put the bag in her pocket and glanced down at the squirrels who were staring up at her waiting for the next peanut. "I'm sorry. But that's all I have today."

"They all look like they've had enough," Milo said, chuckling. "Especially that chubby little guy."

"Yes, some creatures never seem to know when to stop," Annabelle said, catching his eye. "I believe you mentioned you've heard something that's disturbed you?"

"Yes, I did. I heard that a lot of the kids, especially the little ones like you teach, come to school without eating breakfast. Is that true?"

"Unfortunately, it is," she said. "A lot of families in the area are struggling."

"Well, that isn't right," Milo said. "How is a child supposed to learn anything on an empty belly?"

"I couldn't agree with you more, Mr. Razner. Is there something you'd like to do about it?"

"Well, yeah. I'd like to feed them," Milo said, frowning at her. "What else would I want to do?"

"You want to provide breakfast for all the kids at school?" she said, locking eyes with him.

"Sure. I got more milk and eggs than I know what to do with," Milo said. "You got a kitchen at the school? Someplace to cook and keep the milk cold?"

"We do."

"Well, that's great," Milo said. "Who would I need to talk to about getting something like that set up before school starts back up in the fall?"

"You'd need to speak with our principal, Mr. Cowley," she said, sliding just a touch closer to Milo.

"I'll have the manager of my farm get in touch with him," Milo said.

"Ah, yes, Mrs. Crankovitch," Annabelle said.

"Yeah, Ruby. Do you know her?"

"Only by reputation. But I do know her husband, Billy."

"Really? Billy also works for me."

"Yes, I know," she said with a small smile that made Milo nervous. "Can I ask you a question, Mr. Razner?"

"Sure."

"Will Billy remain in your employ after his divorce is finalized?"

"He better," Milo said. "I mean, I imagine he will. Why do you ask?"

"I'm just wondering," Annabelle said. "Lately, Billy seems so disheartened. It's like he's lost his passion for…farming." She smiled and winked at Milo. "I'm beginning to think that he might want to try something else."

"Well, dairy farming isn't for everybody," Milo said, suddenly on edge. "Are you and Billy close? If it's okay for me to ask you that."

"Billy and I are quite close," she said. "I'm not sure we have the sort of relationship he's searching for, but I guess things like that take time, right?"

"Of course," Milo said, nodding. "Billy's always talking about raising a family, but Ruby doesn't seem to want that quite yet. But that's about all I know. It's hard enough just being their boss. I don't have the energy to get involved in their personal problems."

"I can understand that," Annabelle said, looking at Milo like she was getting ready to try him on for size. "I take it the milk business keeps you busy."

"Pretty much," Milo said, nodding. "But I try to make time for social activities whenever I get the chance."

"I guess that's important."

"What do you do for fun, Miss Caffey?"

"Well, I like to read. Go for long walks. And pray, of course."

"What sort of things do you pray for?" Milo said, draping an arm across the top of the bench.

"Oh, just the usual," she said.

"Well, what do you know?" Milo said, waving at the man who was walking toward them.

"What is it?" she said, turning around.

"It's an old friend I haven't seen in a long time," Milo said, standing up. "Tom Collins. What brings you across the border?"

"Hi, Milo. How are you?" Tom Collins said, shaking hands. "I've got the day off from the furniture store, and I thought I'd take the boat out. Then I just decided to stop in town and say hello to some folks. How are you doing?"

"I'm doing great," Milo said. "Tom, I'd like you meet Annabelle Caffey. She teaches school here in town."

"Actually," Annabelle said, smiling up at Tom. "At the moment, I'm on summer break. You live in Canada?"

"Just across the River in Rockport," Tom said. "I work in a furniture store over there. Actually, I just got promoted to Assistant Manager."

"Good for you, Tom," Milo said. "You deserve it."

"Well, I think this is a good time for me to take my leave and let the two of you catch up," Annabelle said, standing up. "It was very nice meeting you, Mr. Razner. And thanks so much for your generous offer. I look forward to hearing how it all turns out. Mr. Collins, it was a pleasure to meet you as well."

"The pleasure is all mine," Tom said, bowing slightly. "How are you staying busy this summer, Miss Caffey?"

"Oh, a little of this, a little of that," she said, shrugging.

"Do you get out on the River often?" Tom said.

"No, I'm afraid I don't have a boat," she said.

"You can't spend your summer here and not be out there enjoying the river. Say, why don't you let me take you out on my boat sometime? I know I'm probably being way too forward asking. But who knows when I'll get the chance to see you again? I could pack a lunch. We could go fishing. Or maybe have a swim. How does that sound?"

"Actually, that sounds delightful, Mr. Collins. I would love to spend some time on the River," Annabelle said. "Thanks for your generous offer. I'll wait for your call then."

"Well, that's great news," Tom said. "How can I get in touch with you?"

"Oh, just call the main switchboard in town," she said, flashing a quick smile at Milo before turning back to Tom. "I'm sure Violet will know how to reach me. Good day, gentlemen."

Both Milo and Tom tipped their hats then watched her stroll up the street.

"She's very pretty," Tom said.

"Yes, she is," Milo said, continuing to watch her as she headed down the path. "Let me ask you a question."

"Sure."

"Have you ever seen a teetotaling, God-fearing woman have a walk like that, Tom?"

"You mean, the way her bottom sways back and forth?"

"Oh, you noticed," Milo said, laughing.

"Well, it's a little hard to miss, Milo," Tom said, laughing along.

"Yeah. And that's my point," Milo said. "I know a teetotal when I meet one, and she isn't. And I'm not buying the God-fearing part either."

"Why not?"

"Because that woman ain't afraid of anything," Milo said.

"You still want me to see if I can get close to her?"

"Oh, yeah. I want you to get *real* close, Tom."

"You really think she's going to be up for that?"

"I do," Milo said. "My radar is way up on her, Tom. And if I didn't already have my hands full, I'd be happy to handle this one myself."

"Yeah," Tom said, laughing. "I imagine juggling Beulah, Ruby, and Daisy is more than enough."

"And Fannie," Milo said, scratching his chin stubble.

"Fannie? Really?"

"Long story," Milo said. "Miss Caffey is up to something, Tom, and it involves a lot more than trying to teach long division to a bunch of ten-year-old kids."

"You really think she's working undercover for the Feds?"

"That's my best worst guess for the moment. And until I can prove otherwise and relax a bit, we're gonna stay with that assumption. She's definitely honed in on how Billy makes his living. And I'm pretty sure she's started trying to tie me to his activities. We need to stop her, or at least put a crimp in her plans."

"And I'm the crimp?"

"I knew you were a smart guy," Milo said, draping an arm over Tom's shoulders as they started walking in the opposite direction from the schoolteacher. "I imagine she's been trained to focus on a man's weaknesses to get him talking. Billy's a simpleton, so you could pretty much go in any direction you want and have some success. My bet is that she decided to use the teetotaling Christian as a way to make him feel guilty about what he's doing then get him talking."

"That wouldn't work on me," Tom said, shaking his head.

"No, it wouldn't. And she knows that. So, I suppose that gives you some flexibility regarding how you want to approach it, Tom."

"Well, I always have found myself most talkative when I'm around whiskey and naked women," Tom said, grinning.

"Yeah," Milo said, grinning back at him. "That's how I would have played it, too."

# The Beauty of Expansion

**The speakeasy at the Crossley** was loud and busy, and Willy had to lean across the table to hear what Melvin was prattling on about. The guy hadn't shut up since their drinks had arrived, and Willy was beginning to have second thoughts about even mentioning the expansion of their current arrangement. Melvin finally stopped talking long enough to take a sip of his drink and grab one of Willy's cigarettes.

"Interesting story, Melvin," Willy said. "I had no idea law school could be that dangerous."

"Usually, it's not," Melvin said, exhaling smoke. "Until you're almost caught stealing final exams."

"So, I take it you ended up getting good grades?"

"Oh, yeah. Straight A's," Melvin said, grinning. "You mentioned something about expanding our business relationship?"

"Yes," Willy said, doing his best to be heard above the racket, but not too loud to be overheard by others sitting nearby. "I have a buyer on my end who wants fifty cases a week."

"Fifty a week?" Melvin said. "That's incredible."

"Yeah, he's got a bunch of thirsty customers," Willy said. "And he wants to get to a hundred cases a week as soon as possible."

"Can I ask you who he is?"

"It's probably better if you don't, Melvin," Willy said. "The man loves his privacy if you catch my drift."

"Caught and filed away, Willy," Melvin said, nodding. "How much is he willing to pay per case?"

"For top-shelf stuff…sixty bucks a case," Willy said, trying to keep a straight face.

"Sixty? That's great," Melvin said. "I can get my hands on it for…forty."

"Twenty bucks profit a case," Willy said, tossing back the last of his beer. "And ten of it coming in my direction. I can live with that."

"Actually, I think your math needs a bit of work, Willy," Melvin said, smiling across the table at him. "Twenty bucks a case divided by three is around seven a case."

"Why the hell would we divide it by three?"

"Because I have a partner," Melvin said.

"That's fine, Melvin. And you should feel free to have all the partners you want, but Oscar's take is gonna have to come out of your end. But you'd still be making five bucks a case. That's nothing to sneeze at."

"Now hold on a minute, Willy. That hardly seems fair. After all, all three of us will be lugging the whiskey in and out of the boat."

"Yeah, but we only need two people to do it, Melvin," Willy said. "In fact, I could do it all by myself if I didn't need you to handle the buy."

"But Oscar will be doing his part, too."

"Melvin, since we started running the five cases a week, from what I've seen, the only thing Oscar does is take up space and drink half the profits."

"I don't know, Willy. Oscar is already pretty cranky with me. And if I have to tell him he's cut out of our deal, I'm not sure what he'd do to me."

"I'm not saying you have to tell him anything, Melvin," Willy said.

"You lost me," Melvin said, reaching for another of Willy's cigarettes.

"All we'll need to do is let Oscar do what he always does."

"Which is?"

"Something stupid."

"Oh, that. Yeah, sure, I get that. So, what's the plan?"

"I need you to place an order for fifty-five cases to be delivered to your usual spot on the Canadian side."

"I thought you said fifty cases?" Melvin said, frowning.

"Fifty for us," Willy said. "Plus, the regular order of five cases for Oscar to deliver."

"Okay, I think I'm with you," Melvin said. "And we'll turn Oscar loose with the five cases and let things take their natural course."

"You got it," Willy said. "Now I see why you got straight A's in law school. Tell me, as a lawyer, what do you think the Feds are going to do when they get their hands on a two-time offender?"

"I'm sure it won't be pretty," Melvin said, then gave it some more thought and laughed. "Actually, Willy, I take that back. I think it's going to be beautiful."

# Different Schools of Thought

**Milo found Billy in the barn** stacking sacks of sugar. He was sweating profusely and humming a tune Milo didn't recognize. To Milo, he seemed to be perfectly content. Then he wondered if the source of his contentment was the prospect that he'd soon be doing something other than cooking corn and sugar in a barn on a remote island.

"Hey, Mr. Razner," Billy said. "I'm glad you stopped by."

"Hi, Billy. Is everything going okay?"

"Everything's great," he said, wiping his brow with one of his sleeves. "I've got three hundred gallons ready to go, and a new batch fermenting. I'm going to cook again on Friday night."

"Perfect," Milo said, glancing around and finding everything clean and in its proper place. "I heard a rumor that you've asked Ruby for a divorce."

"Yeah, I figured it was time," Billy said. "And I sure ain't gettin' any younger. By the way, how are the two of you doing?"

"Me and Ruby? Well, as you know, she can be quite *demanding*."

"You ain't seen nothing yet," he said, laughing as he tossed another sack of sugar onto the stack. "But I sure do miss lyin' down with her."

"Well, you have Daisy for that now," Milo said, gently probing. "I'm sure she's more than enough to take your mind off Ruby."

"Daisy and I have stopped doing that," Billy said.

"Why on earth would you do that, Billy?" Milo said.

"Because I've fallen for somebody else, Mr. Razner. A good Christian woman with a set of morals who understands the evils of alcohol."

"I see," Milo said. "And she's taking care of your lying down needs?"

"Oh, no way, Mr. Razner. Miss Caffey would never agree to do that. Not until we're settled down together and ready to raise a family."


**Tom Collins** draped his arms along the side of the boat and held on tight as the thrusting woman's movements churned and splashed water.

"I've never done it in water before," Tom Collins said, gasping for breath.

"It's fun, isn't it?" Annabelle Caffey said, picking up the pace. "After we finish up here, we'll take a break then have another go inside the boat."

"Practice makes perfect, huh?"

"How else are you going to learn, Tom?"

About to lose control, Tom Collins closed his eyes and started reciting his ABC's.


**Milo shook** his head and scuffed the dirt floor with his boot.

"Billy, two months ago, you were bound and determined to settle down with Daisy."

"I know, Mr. Razner. But Annabelle is different. She's the sort of woman who makes a man think with something other than his you know what."

"You should play to your strengths, Billy."

"What?"

"Nothing."


**Annabelle seemed** to pull herself up out the water with no hands, placed her feet on Tom's shoulders, and hopped into the boat. She shivered then grabbed a towel and began to dry herself off. Tom climbed in and stretched out on the bench seat in the stern coughing water.

"That was good," Annabelle said, opening a cold beer and downing half of it. She handed the bottle to Tom and resumed toweling her hair.

"Can I ask you a question?" Tom Collins said.

"I'd be surprised if you didn't," she said, wrapping the towel around her waist. "Let me guess, you're wondering why a supposedly good Christian girl like me would get naked on the first date and try to turn you into a wet pretzel?"

"Yeah, I suppose that's a good place to start," Tom said, shrugging, then downing what was left of the beer.

"I have needs, Tom. And I've been looking for someone who might be able to satisfy them."

"And you think I'm the guy who can?"

"Well, we're certainly off on the right foot," she said, grabbing another beer. "But I also need to maintain a certain public image. I'm a schoolteacher, and my mother is quite famous in the Temperance movement. I can't run the risk of doing anything that might jeopardize either of our reputations. So, in public, I act one way. But as you can see, in private, I'm something else altogether."

"You are definitely something else," Tom said, grinning at her.

"And I must insist that you keep my private inclinations between us," she said, taking a sip of beer. "That is if you ever want to do this again."

"I don't talk out of school," Tom said. "Pardon the pun. But what about you and Crankovitch?"

"What about him?"

"I heard the two of you were all hot and heavy and getting serious," Tom said, sitting up.

"If you did, it came from him," Annabelle said. "I'm merely helping Billy try to find himself."

"By doing stuff like this?" Tom said, frowning.

"God, no," she whispered, shaking her head. "If I ever slept with Billy, I'd never get rid of him."

"What?"

"I'm just saying that Billy is very impressionable."

"Yeah, that's what I've heard," Tom said. "And I know I'm never going to forget the impression you just made on me. Especially, the one between my shoulder blades."

"You're funny, Tom. I'm so glad I ran into you in the park the other day," she said, sitting down and laying her head in his lap. "I was just sitting there talking with Mr. Razner and feeding the squirrels. Then, all of a sudden, there you were."

"It must have been fate, huh?"

"I guess it could have been. If you believe in that sort of nonsense. So, tell me, how well do you know, Milo Razner?"

"Not very well," Tom said, trying to stay focused but finding himself increasingly distracted. "We've met at social occasions a couple of times. And he's bought some furniture from me."

"He's unlike other dairy farmers I've met," she said, wiggling to get more comfortable.

"I think Milo considers himself more of an entrepreneur rather than any specific sort of businessman."

"That must provide him with some degree of flexibility," she said, staring up at him.

"Well, if anybody would understand flexibility, I reckon it would be you, Annabelle."

**Milo fought** the urge to grab the man by the throat and try to beat some sense into him. But he forced a smile and waited.

"I'm sorry. But I can't keep doing this, Mr. Razner," Billy said.

"Doing what, Billy? Using your God-given talent to bring joy to people who need it? Not to mention making a small fortune in the process."

The God reference got Billy's attention, and he paused to give Milo's comment some thought.

"I guess it is a gift, isn't it?" Billy said, glancing skyward.

"Of course, it is," Milo snapped. "If anybody could do it, do you think we'd be standing here having this conversation?"

"I don't mean to make you mad, Mr. Razner. You've been so good to me."

"Then let me keep being good to you, Billy," Milo said, then softened. "It's what He would want you to do."

"You really think so?"

"Why would He give you the gift, if He didn't want you to use it, Billy?"

"I guess that's a good point," Billy said, nodding. "Maybe I'll run the idea past Annabelle and see what she thinks."

"Good God almighty," Milo said, rubbing his temples with both hands.

"Praise the Lord."

# Going Overboard

**Milo got the call** he'd been expecting for days around
five in the afternoon. By six o'clock, Birdie and Tom were
sitting in his living room at the Crossley where they spent the
next two hours listening to each other's stories and sipping beer
and whiskey. They stopped drinking at eight to sober up a bit
and review their plans for the evening. But since the plan had
been ready for several days, they mostly kept telling stories and
laughing, even after they switched to coffee.

"I can't believe they'd do something this stupid," Tom said.

"Well, Clint's been bathing in Miracle and is pretty much
fried," Milo said. "And Null and Void don't have two neurons to
rub together between them."

"It still doesn't make any sense," Tom said, frowning.

"That's because you're expecting them to be capable of
taking the long-view, Tom," Birdie said.

"What he said," Milo said, nodding at Birdie as he topped
off their coffee cups. "I'm sure Clint thinks he can get away with
it once, make some money in the process, and see if he can get a
feel for how I respond when somebody tries to screw with me."

"Big mistake," Tom said, shaking his head.

"They don't come any bigger," Milo said.

**Elmer stood** at the edge of the water marveling as the sun set amid a colorful display of reds and orange. Roscoe cleared his throat to get Elmer's attention, then tossed a small rock that bounced off the back of his head.

Elmer, more startled than hurt, turned around to glare at Roscoe. "Hey, knock it off."

"Then get your ass over here and help me unload," Roscoe said, opening the back door of the milk truck.

Elmer spotted a boat approaching the secluded section of shoreline and waved.

"There he is," Elmer said. "Right on time."

Elmer caught the bowline and maneuvered the boat into shallow water. Clint turned the engine off and hopped across some rocks until he reached shore. Elmer tied the bowline to a tree then joined Clint and Roscoe who were chatting nearby.

"Did everything go to plan?" Clint said, glancing back and forth at them.

"Just like you said, Clint," Elmer said. "I called Beulah at the cheese shop this afternoon and told her we were having engine trouble. And then I said that we'd either try to do a late run tonight after we got it fixed, or we'd do a double run tomorrow."

"Good," Clint said, nodding. "And she bought it?"

"Yeah, she didn't bat an eye," Elmer said. "She even said she'd have one of her folks stay late tonight just in case we made it in."

"Okay, what about Milo? What did you tell him?" Clint said.

"We didn't have to tell him anything," Roscoe said. "He was out in that damn boat with the gimp all day."

"Even better," Clint said, then drifted off deep in thought.

"You want to run it past me again, Clint?" Roscoe said. "I'm still having trouble keeping it all straight."

"Again? Really, Roscoe?"

"It's a confusing plan," Roscoe grumbled.

"It's actually very simple, Roscoe. As soon as you stop asking dumb questions, we're going to unload the three hundred gallons into my boat. Then you're going to drive the truck a few miles out of town and wait for me. When I get there, we'll drive back into town, and then I'll call Milo and tell him what happened. After that, you'll wait for Milo to show up, explain what happened, then you'll meet me over at my hunting camp as soon as you can."

"It still sounds confusing ," Roscoe said.

"Well, it's certainly better than your plan to sell twenty gallons to Fannie every week," Elmer said. "I'm still waiting for that shoe to drop."

"For the tenth time, relax," Roscoe said. "Fannie turned the deal down. She said she's already got more booze than she knows what to do with. But she thanked me for thinking of her and promised to keep her mouth shut about it. You know, I think she likes me. I wonder if I can get a freebie out of her."

"It was a stupid thing to do," Elmer said.

"Well, excuse me for wanting to branch out a bit," Roscoe said, pouting.

"Gentlemen," Clint said, tipping his flask to his mouth. "While I find your banter fascinating, perhaps we can get on with what we're here to do."

**Milo listened** carefully to Tom and Birdie as they discussed the routes each one would take later in the evening. Whenever they discussed the River and the most efficient way to navigate it safely, particularly at night, Milo found himself out of the loop and somewhat envious of their expertise, and silently wondered if he would ever be able to join a River conversation with something other than a question.

"Couldn't I just come in from over here?" Tom said, pointing down at a map they had stretched out on the coffee table. "That looks shorter than trying to come in from the east."

"It is," Birdie said, nodding. "But you said you aren't real familiar with that stretch of River."

"No, I'm not," Tom said, shaking his head. "I have a good idea where his camp is, but I've never been there."

"Then you definitely don't want to come in that way. Especially in the dark," Birdie said, pointing at a specific spot on the map. "There's a shoal that extends out a couple hundred yards that'll rip the bottom of your boat out."

"Don't forget rule number one," Milo interjected.

"Yeah, we got it, Milo," Birdie said, laughing as he glanced up from the map. "Don't scratch the boat."

"You sure you know how to find his place, Tom?" Milo said.

"Yeah, as soon as I get inside that cove, I'll be able to figure it out," Tom said, nodding at Milo. "Okay, let's get rolling. I'm ready to go catch some criminals."

**About four** miles out of town, Elmer slowed, then drove the truck to the farthest edge of the road and stopped when it was partially hidden behind a stand of pine trees. He hopped out and glanced around through the darkness.

"What do we do now?" Roscoe said.

"I guess we just wait for Clint," Elmer said.

"Okay," Roscoe said, leaning against the side of the truck. "How much you think we'll get for the three hundred gallons?"

"Clint says at least ten dollars a gallon," Elmer said.

"Do the math for me, Elmer," Roscoe said.

"You're kidding, right? Didn't you ever go to school?"

"I was too busy trying to build my career to waste my time schoolin'," Roscoe said, glancing up at the stars.

"Yeah. Good call on your part. At ten bucks a gallon, three hundred gallons works out to three grand."

"You sure?" Roscoe said, frowning.

"Yeah, I'm almost positive," Elmer said, sighing. "We'll end up with a thousand bucks each."

"Is that all?" Roscoe said. "It sure sounded like a lot more when we first came up with the idea."

"Well, we'd all had a lot of Miracle," Elmer said, then headed to the back of the truck. "C'mon, give me a hand."

"Doing what?" Roscoe said.

"Making it look like we got robbed, what else?" Elmer said as he climbed into the back of the truck and tipped over one of the ten-gallon containers of milk.

Roscoe hopped in the truck and emptied two more of the containers. They tossed the empty cans on the ground then climbed down and surveyed the scene.

"Not bad," Roscoe said, nodding. "But I know what would make it more convincing."

"What?" Elmer said, glancing around. "It looks fine to me."

"If we're going to convince Milo we were robbed, it's going to have to look like we at least put up a fight."

"Oh, yeah," Elmer said. "Good thinking. How do you want to do that?"

"Punch me," Roscoe said, taking a step closer.

"What?"

"Hit me. But not in the nose. Right here," Roscoe said, pointing at his jaw.

"Your funeral," Elmer said, throwing a quick, hard left that caught Roscoe right where he was pointing.

Roscoe dropped to the ground and rolled around moaning in pain.

"Like that?" Elmer said, laughing.

"Yeah, like that," Roscoe said, rolling over onto his knees and rubbing his jaw. "Damn that hurt."

"You should see my right jab," Elmer said, grinning as he bounced on his feet like a boxer.

"Okay, my turn," Roscoe said, climbing to his feet.

"No way. I ain't gonna let you hit me," Elmer said. "If Milo asks why I'm not hurt, we'll just tell him the robbers had guns and got the drop on me before I could do anything."

"That's not convincing enough," Roscoe said, heading toward the front of the truck.

"What are you doing?" He turned around and watched Roscoe rummaging underneath the driver's seat. Roscoe stood up brandishing a pistol. He waved it around, then pointed it at Elmer.

"Now that sets an all-time high for stupid."

"Where do you want it?" Roscoe said, pointing the gun with one hand and rubbing his jawline with the other.

"Put that down," Elmer said.

"You wanted Milo to believe us. I reckon this oughta do it," Roscoe said, as he continued to wave the pistol in the air. "I'm thinking the fleshy part of your thigh. Don't worry. The bullet will go right through. Come a bit closer."

Elmer stared at Roscoe in disbelief but took a small step toward him. Then he leaped forward and grabbed for the gun. Roscoe grunted, closed his eyes as he fought back, and twisted his arm free. He opened his eyes and was blinded by a set of headlights that were rapidly approaching. Roscoe flinched, held up his gun hand to block the glare and squeezed the trigger. Elmer screamed and clutched the side of his head as he dropped to the ground. Roscoe, unsure about his next move as well as who might be driving the car, panicked, dropped the gun, then frantically looked around for it. Elmer scrambled across the cool grass, grabbed the gun, then pointed it skyward and fired. Roscoe screamed, grabbed his shoulder and collapsed on top of Elmer. They remained in a heap, breathing heavily and bleeding all over each other.

"You shot my ear off, you damn fool," Elmer said, gently touching the side of his head.

"What about my shoulder? I'm bleeding like a stuck pig," Roscoe said.

"What the hell are you two idiots doing?" Clint said, as he climbed out of his car, headlights still blazing.

"Oh, hey, Clint," Roscoe said, climbing to his feet and examining his shoulder. "Sumbitch, that hurts."

"What the hell were you two fighting about?" Clint said, staring at their white coveralls that were quickly turning bright red.

"We weren't arguing," Elmer said, sitting up on the grass. "We were just trying to make it looked like we got robbed."

"I see," Clint said, shaking his head. "Then, well done. Mission accomplished."

**Milo answered** the phone on the second ring.

"Oh, hi, Clint," Milo said. "Hang on a sec." Milo held his hand over the receiver. "Okay, this is it. Tom, you head out. And when you find the place, just hang out about a hundred yards offshore. We'll find you. Birdie, go grab the boat and wait for me at Frank's place. And ask him if he's got something we can use to cover all the seats."

Milo waited until both men left the suite then held the phone up to his ear.

"Okay, I'm back, Clint. What's up?…Robbed? Where?…I see. Yeah, I guess they we're lucky that you just happened to be headed back from Watertown…They got shot? How the hell did they get shot?… No, that's okay. If you're running late, just bring them by the Crossley, and I'll take care of it from there…Yeah, I'll meet you in front of the hotel."

Milo hung up and frowned.

"How the hell did they got shot?"

Milo headed downstairs through the lobby and outside into the cool evening air. He found one of the bellmen standing outside.

"Good evening, Jimmy," Milo said, lighting a cigarette.

"Well, hello, Mr. Razner. Beautiful night," the bellman said.

"It's certainly shaping up to be that way," Milo said. "Would you mind bringing my car around?"

"Certainly, sir. I won't be but a minute," the bellman said, accepting the key.

Milo watched him trot off, then had an idea. He walked back inside and headed for reception.

"Good evening, Mr. Razner, the night clerk said. "Do you need something?"

"Actually, I do," Milo said, smiling. "I'm planning a little late night...well, let's call it an *excursion*."

"I understand, sir," the night clerk said, grinning back. "And you want me to see if I can find you a bottle of something?"

"No, I'm all set when it comes to that," Milo said. "Actually, I was wondering if you could bring me a couple of blankets."

"Of course, Mr. Razner," the clerk said, winking. "The grass can get wet and cold at this time of night."

"I knew you'd understand."

"I'll be right back with those, sir."

**Milo parked** at the bottom of the hotel driveway. While he waited for Clint, he carefully spread the blankets out in the backseat and tucked them in tight. He leaned against the side of the car until he saw Clint's headlights approaching. Clint came to a stop next to Milo's car and turned the lights off.

"Hey, Milo," Clint said. "Sorry to ruin your night."

"Don't worry about it. I appreciate you calling me," Milo said, peering into Clint's car and nodding at Elmer and Roscoe who were holding their wounds and avoiding eye contact. Then he turned to Clint. "Did they say what happened?"

"Apparently, three guys in a truck ran them off the road about four miles out of town and took all three hundred gallons," Clint said. "I asked them what the hell they were doing making a delivery in the middle of the night. They said they'd had engine trouble that took them all day to fix. When Elmer and Roscoe tried to put up a fight, one of the guys pulled a gun and shot them."

"I see," Milo said, staring at Clint. "How bad are they hurt?"

"It looks like they'll be fine," Clint said. "Elmer lost part of an ear, and Roscoe took one in the shoulder. They're still bleeding and need to see a doctor, but they're gonna make it."

"I'll take care of them from here," Milo said. "Thanks again, Clint."

"No problem, Milo. I'd stay and help out, but I'm running really late for something else."

"Sure. You get going," Milo said. "And remind me the next time we see each other that we need to talk some more about making a few changes to our deal."

"You mean that?" Clint said, his eyes wide.

"Absolutely," Milo said, forcing a smile. "We definitely need to have a chat about that."

"That's great news, Milo. Thanks. I was hoping you might start coming around."

"Well, let's just say that, lately, I'm starting to see things in a whole new light."

Clint started to smile but flinched when he caught the look Milo was giving him.

**As he** drove the boat toward his hunting camp, Clint replayed his conversation with Milo several times. But half a flask of Miracle removed any concerns he had, and he pulled the boat into its slip. He made sure the tarp covering the thirty milk cans was tied tight, then walked up the dock whistling. He walked into his hunting camp, lit three kerosene lamps, and settled down in front of the fireplace with a fresh pint of Miracle and dared to dream about how much more Milo might be willing to pay him.

**"If you** morons bleed on my seats, we're gonna have a problem," Milo said, glancing over his shoulder.

"No, we're good, Milo," Elmer said. "But we do need to get to a doctor."

"All in good time, Elmer," Milo said, starting the car. "But it's a beautiful night for a boat ride."

"Boat ride?" Roscoe said. "Does this doctor you're taking us to live on the Canadian side?"

"Sure, let's go with that," Milo said, staring at both men through the rearview mirror.

"You wouldn't believe what we've been through tonight, Milo," Elmer said.

"Try me," Milo said.

"Well, that was more of a figure of speech," Elmer stammered. "You know, a general observation about the situation we were facing."

"Yeah, it was downright frightening, Milo," Roscoe said.

"I'm glad you got some good practice in," Milo said through the rearview mirror. "You know, just so the next time you find yourself scared, you'll know how to respond."

"Milo, I'm picking up on something here," Elmer said. "Are you saying you don't believe we were robbed?"

Milo pulled into Frank Slack's parking lot and turned the car off.

"Let's go," Milo said, climbing out.

"I ain't getting in no boat," Roscoe said, holding his shoulder.

"Yeah, given our situation," Elmer said, nodding. "We should probably get these wounds cleaned up first. Maybe a boat ride tomorrow would be a better option. We could do a little fishing. Have a couple of beers. It's supposed to be nice and sunny."

"Get out of the car," Milo whispered.

"No, I don't think that's a good idea, Milo," Roscoe said, shaking his head.

"Birdie, would you mind racking a shell into that shotgun you're holding to see if these two gentlemen might like to reconsider?"

The unmistakable sound echoed, then the evening air again turned quiet. Roscoe and Elmer climbed out of the car and stood next to each other waiting for further instructions.

"It truly is an amazing teaching tool," Milo said, smiling at the shotgun Birdie had pointed at both men. "I wonder if Miss Caffey has considered using it with some of her slow learners."

Milo pointed in the direction he wanted them to walk, and Elmer and Roscoe headed for the long dock that ran the length of Frank Slack's marina. Birdie limped along behind them pointing the shotgun at their backs. Milo followed and stopped to chat with Frank about halfway down the dock.

"You're all set, Milo," Frank said. "I draped several paint tarps across all the seats. Just bring them back when you're done."

"Thanks, Frank," Milo said.

"You need anything else from me?" Frank said, nodding at Elmer and Roscoe who were climbing into the boat.

"No, I don't think you want to be involved in this one," Milo said.

"I was hoping you'd say that," Frank said, waving goodbye as he headed back toward the parking lot.

Milo strolled down the dock to the boat, untied the lines, and sat down in the passenger seat. Birdie handed him the shotgun then started the engine. The boat roared to life and accelerated away from the dock.

"Milo, you need to give us a chance to explain," Elmer said.

"I can't hear you over the engine, Elmer," Milo shouted. "So, just sit there quietly and enjoy the ride.

"What?"

"I said shut the hell up."

"What?"

Milo pointed the shotgun at Elmer. He got the message and nodded. Both delivery men stayed quiet for the rest of the trip.

# Night Swimming

**Birdie slowed the boat** as they approached the hunting camp, then nudged Milo and pointed at a boat that was drifting about a hundred feet away. Milo pointed a flashlight and flashed the beam on and off twice. He received the signal back, and Birdie idled until Tom Collins pulled alongside. He and Birdie both dropped bumpers off the sides to keep the boats from rubbing against each other.

"Any trouble finding the place?" Birdie said, rolling a cigarette.

"No, it was easy," Tom said. You sure do know your way around, Birdie."

"Just been doin' it a long time," Birdie said, lighting the smoke.

"Has our other friend arrived?" Milo said, nodding at the hunting camp.

"Yeah, he's all settled in," Tom said. "How do you want to do this?"

"Why don't you anchor here?" Milo said. "Then climb aboard. No sense bringing two boats in." Milo looked at Roscoe and Elmer. "Are you two gonna keep your mouths shut, or am I going to have to shoot you right here?"

"I thought you were worried about making a mess on your boat," Roscoe said.

"Geez, Roscoe, why don't you see if you can piss him off some more? What is the matter with you?" Elmer said. "Shut up."

"Sound advice, Elmer," Milo said, grinning. "And for the record, Roscoe, you'll already be in the water if I decide to shoot you. Okay, Birdie, shut it down. We're going to need to paddle in."

"Good idea," Birdie said, turning the engine off. "She does tend to announce her presence."

Tom and Birdie paddled the boat to the dock while Milo kept the shotgun pointed at Elmer and Roscoe. They tied the boat off and climbed onto the dock.

"What are you carrying?" Milo said to Tom.

"I stole one of Clint's pistols."

"Well played. I doubt you'll need it, but it's good to have," Milo said. "You go around back and come in that way. But wait until you hear me start talking, and don't shoot him unless you don't have a choice."

"You got it," Tom said, striding down the dock and then onto the grass.

"Okay, you two, lead the way," Milo said, handing the shotgun to Birdie.

"What do you want us to do?" Elmer said.

"I want you to keep your scheduled appointment, what else?" Milo said.

"I don't know, Milo," Roscoe said. "My shoulder is hurtin' something awful."

"Yeah, that tends to happen when you start *gettin' some action*, Roscoe," Milo said. "Walk."

When they reached the camp, Milo led the way up the wooden steps, knocked on the door, then stepped to one side out of sight. The door opened, and he heard Clint's voice.

"That was quick," Clint said, then noticed the blood-stained uniforms. "Hey, I thought you were going to go see a doctor."

"The plan changed, Clint," Milo said as he stepped in front of Elmer and Roscoe and glared at Clint. "These two decided, instead of a doctor, they wanted to see if they might be able to conjure up a little Miracle."

Clint recoiled at the sight of Milo and made a dash for the back door. He stopped when he came face to face with Tom pointing a gun at him. Clint held up his hands and turned around facing Milo.

"You two. Sit," Milo said, pointing at a couch near the fireplace. "Birdie, if Null and Void do anything other than check their wounds, feel free to shoot them."

"Who's Null and Void?" Roscoe whispered to Elmer.

Elmer dropped his head and stared down at the floor.

Milo glared at Clint and nodded at the chair in front of the fire.

"Have a seat, Clint."

"Is there a problem, Milo?" Clint said, easing himself into the chair.

"Not anymore," Milo said. "But didn't I tell you that the next time we spoke, we needed to have a little chat about our deal, remember?"

"Well, that was only about an hour ago," Clint said, laughing nervously. "It'd be pretty hard to forget."

"I was just wondering because you seem to have trouble remembering things," Milo said, draping an arm across the mantel.

"Like what, Milo?"

"Little things, Clint," Milo said. "Like trust and loyalty. Respect. Remembering which side your bread's buttered on."

"I'm not following, Milo," Clint said, staring up at him. "Really, Milo. I don't know what you're talking about. I just happened to be driving home, and I found those two on the side of the road."

"I see," Milo said. "Then I guess it was a miracle that you just happened to come along when you did."

"Yeah, that's it," Clint said. "I guess it was a miracle."

"It seems to be a night for them," Milo said, pouring himself a shot and tossing it back.

"I'm not following, Milo."

"A night for miracles," Milo said, wiping his mouth with a handkerchief. "Like how three hundred gallons of my booze just happened to miraculously appear in the back of your boat."

"Oh, that," Clint said. "Would you like me to explain how that happened?"

"Can you?"

Clint rubbed his forehead as he stared into the fireplace.

"No, probably not, Milo," Clint said, beaten.

"Are you the one who shot these two idiots?"

"No, of course not," Clint said, shaking his head. "They shot each other."

"What?" Milo said, laughing.

Tom and Birdie joined in.

"Now, I'd love to hear an explanation for that," Milo said, grinning.

"We were trying to make it look like a robbery," Elmer said.

"And you decided to shoot each other?" Milo said.

"It was his idea," Elmer said, nodding at Roscoe.

"It sounded like a good idea at the time," Roscoe said.

"I definitely need to work on my hiring practices," Milo whispered.

"What?" Roscoe said.

"Nothing. Whose idea was it to try to sell my booze to Fannie?" Milo said, glancing back and forth at his two drivers.

Elmer nodded his head in Roscoe's direction. Roscoe caught it out of the corner of his eye and glared at Elmer.

"Thanks a lot," Roscoe growled.

"It was a stupid idea," Elmer said.

"And trying to steal the three hundred gallons wasn't?" Milo said.

"I'm so sorry, Milo," Elmer said. "It won't happen again."

"Finally, you said something that makes sense," Milo said.

"Milo, please. We're family," Elmer said.

Tom and Birdie stared at each other then looked at Milo.

"We're cousins," Milo said with a shrug. "On my mother's side."

"And you told my mama, your favorite aunt in the whole world, that you'd look after me," Elmer said.

"Yeah, I gotta stop saying stuff like that. But we'll talk about that later," Milo said. "First, we need to deal with our friend, Clint."

"Milo, don't do anything crazy," Clint said. "After all, you're the one who's always saying we need to take the long-view. And if you kill me, there goes your ability to turn Miracle into gold."

"Actually, Clint. Tom and I have already been taking the long view on that. Haven't we, Tom?"

"We sure have, Milo."

"I'm not following," Clint said.

"You see, Clint," Milo said, pouring himself another shot. "The thing I've learned about Miracle is that people tend to run their mouth when they drink too much of it."

"And you've been downright chatty, Clint," Tom said. "Your recipe is a bit complicated but pretty easy to follow once it's written down."

"You bastards," Clint said, starting to get up out of his chair then quickly changing his mind. "What can I do to make this up to you, Milo?"

"Nothing, Clint."

"You're just going to shoot me?"

"No, that doesn't seem to be the best option. And I usually hate having to make a mess like that," Milo said, removing a document from his pocket. "But we'll get to that later. First, I'm gonna need your signature on this document."

"What is it?"

"A contract transferring ownership of your furniture store to Tom."

"What?" Clint said, glaring at Milo. "I'm not signing that."

"Oh, you're gonna sign it, Clint. The only question is how long it's going to take me to persuade you. And after you sign it, you'll be free to go to an unknown land to live out the rest of your years in luxury."

"Really?" Clint said, cocking his head at Milo.

"The choice of whether or not to believe me is up to you, Clint. But I'm telling you you're gonna have a chance to live out the rest of your life in peace and quiet. And I always try to be a man of my word."

Clint thought about it, then nodded and scribbled his name on the contract.

"Okay, we're done here," Milo said, glancing around.

"What do you want to do about this place?" Tom said.

"I guess it's all yours, Tom," Milo said, shrugging. "You don't have a problem with that, do you, Clint?"

"Would it matter if I did?"

"Now you're catching on," Milo said, laughing. "Okay, let's get them back in the boat."

Birdie and Tom herded all three men back down to the dock and waited for Milo.

"Okay, you three get all those cans out of Clint's boat back where they belong," Milo said. "And don't scratch the boat."

Birdie rolled cigarettes while Tom, shotgun in hand, supervised the transfer of the booze. When all thirty cans were secured, Birdie closed the latch. He started the engine, and they headed for Tom's boat that was anchored just offshore.

"We'll take it from here, Tom," Milo said. "You're clear on everything, right?"

"I am," Tom said, then tipped his hat to the three men sitting in the back seat that ran along the stern. "Goodbye, gentlemen."

"I don't like the sound of that," Elmer said.

"Okay, Birdie," Milo said, checking his watch. "Time to head for deep water."

Birdie accelerated, and the boat surged through the water. Milo kept the shotgun pointed toward the back of the boat and stifled a yawn as his mood darkened. Twenty minutes later, the River widened and the number of islands dotting the water dwindled. Birdie slowed the boat and drifted in the current that was strong and immediately began pulling the boat downriver. Milo stood and pointed the gun at Clint.

"What?" Clint said, staring at Milo.

"It's time to begin your retirement, what else? In you go."

"You expect me to swim?" Clint said, bewildered.

"I suppose you could try to float and drift," Milo said, shrugging as he pointed the shotgun at Clint's face.

"But all my money and clothes are upriver, Milo," Clint said.

"Well, then I hope you're good at swimming against the current," Milo said. "In you go."

"Milo, please."

"It's a little late to be asking for favors, Clint."

"Milo, don't do this," Clint said, scrambling over the back seat onto the transom.

"If you scratch my boat with those boots, I'm gonna get mad, Clint."

"That would seem to be the least of my problems at the moment. Get away from me."

Milo shook his head at Clint then nodded at Birdie. Birdie fired up the engine, accelerated quickly, then looked back just as Clint tumbled off the back of the boat. Birdie turned the boat around and idled closer until it was right next to Clint who was splashing water and coughing.

"I can't swim, Milo," Clint said, churning the water desperately with both arms.

"You lived on the River all this time and never learned how to swim?" Milo said, staring down into the water.

"No. I always meant to, but I never got around to it," Clint said, coughing violently.

"Tragic," Milo said.

"Milo…please."

He continued to watch Clint struggle until he'd gone under the water four times but only come back up three. Milo turned to Roscoe.

"You're next," Milo said, pointing the shotgun at him.

"I can't swim with this shoulder," Roscoe said, getting up from the seat.

"Don't worry about that," Milo said. "You're not going to have to swim."

"Then I ain't worried," Roscoe said, defiantly.

"Really? Do tell."

"Yeah, I'll be fine. You said you wouldn't shoot me unless I was already in the water. So, if I don't go for a swim, I reckon that-"

Milo fired a shotgun blast that caught Roscoe in the chest and knocked him backward over the transom into the water.

"Damn, that was loud," Milo said when the blast finished echoing across the water. "Hey, Birdie."

"Yeah, Milo?"

"I'm sorry, but I made one hell of a mess back here," Milo said, glancing around the stern.

"That's okay, Milo. I'll take care of it in the morning."

Milo pointed the shotgun at Elmer who was quivering in his seat.

"Okay, cousin," Milo said. "You've seen your two choices. What's it gonna be?"

Elmer clamored to his feet, hopped up onto the transom and dove into the water. Milo ejected the remaining shells and tossed the shotgun on the seat.

"How far is he going to have to swim before he makes it to shore or runs into an island?" Milo said, staring at Elmer who was rapidly disappearing in the darkness.

"In this stretch of River?" Birdie said, rolling a cigarette. "There's no way he's going to be able to swim to shore. Out here, that current has a mind of its own. He's going downriver in a hurry whether he likes it or not."

"How far down is the next island he might get lucky enough to run into?" Milo said, accepting the cigarette from Birdie.

"Maybe ten, twelve miles," Birdie said, shrugging. "But I don't like his chances."

"Well, at least he has a shot at making it. I had to give him that much, right?"

"Yeah, I get that. What with him being family and all."

"I figured it was the least I could do."

"He was really your cousin?"

"Yeah. But we were never that close."

# Gonna Need a Bigger Basket

**Milo stood on the dock** inside the boathouse, keys and property deed in hand, and shared a teary goodbye with Mrs. Alexander. The widow was overcome with emotion at having to say goodbye to her beloved summer home. Milo was weeping tears of joy. Birdie limped his way along the dock and stood next to him as they watched Mrs. Alexander climb into the boat. Her driver helped her into her seat, headed for deep water, then accelerated. Milo and Birdie waved goodbye, and they stood on the dock until the boat became a tiny speck on the horizon.

"Congratulations, Milo," Birdie said.

"Thanks, Birdie. I can't believe I own this place," Milo said, taking in his surroundings. "Okay, time to do a little exploring. Do you mind waiting down here with the boat?"

"Not at all," Birdie said, rolling a cigarette.

"I won't be long," Milo said. "Do we have a bag or something I could use to carry something?"

"Let's see," Birdie said, scanning the boat. "I guess I could empty the picnic basket and let you use that."

"That'll work," Milo said.

Birdie knelt on the dock and reached down into the boat. He removed the wrapped sandwiches and several pieces of fruit and placed them on the seat then stood and handed Milo the basket.

"Perfect," Milo said, starting to walk off. Then he stopped and turned. "On second thought, I want you to come along, Birdie."

"To do some exploring?" he said, giving Milo a frown.

"Yes."

"Okay, you're the boss," Birdie said, shrugging and limping toward Milo.

"And take your time," Milo said.

"Like I have a choice."

Milo laughed.

"Yeah, I definitely want you with me, Birdie."

They started up the path that led to the house. The heat was cut by a gentle breeze out of the north, but Milo removed his coat and hat.

"When we're done taking a look around, you feel like taking the boat out for a spin?" Birdie said, doing his best to keep up. "It's a beautiful day for a boat ride."

"Maybe. Let's see what we come across while we're exploring," Milo said, fighting the urge to run.

Halfway up the path, they reached another path that led to the large stone building they'd noticed on their first visit.

"Let's go have a look in there," Milo said, nodding at the building.

When they reached the door, Milo flipped through the key ring he'd been given and located the one marked *Storage Building*. He pulled the door open, and they stepped inside to total darkness. Milo located the light switch, flipped it on, and the large room was immediately bathed in light.

"She wasn't kidding. The guy loved his electric lights," Birdie said.

"Yeah, he sure did," Milo said, scanning the room that was stacked with boxes and assorted junk. "It's a big room."

"This is where you're going to cook, aren't you?" Birdie said.

"This is the place," Milo said.

"You're gonna need bigger stills if you want to fill this space."

"Way ahead of you, Birdie. I've already ordered three new stills. A thousand gallons each," Milo said, surveying the room. "Including the two I got from Clint, that will give us over four thousand gallons of capacity."

"That's a lot of milk," Birdie said.

"Yes, but that can all wait for now," Milo said, walking back to the door.

Milo glanced down at the octagon shaped stone tiles that comprised the floor, then walked straight ahead and counted out loud as he made his way across seven tiles.

"You playing a version of hopscotch, Milo?" Birdie said, laughing.

"Shhh."

Milo counted three tiles to the right, then two more up from that spot and stopped. He knelt down and blew the dust away. Then he worked his fingers under the stone tile and grunted as he lifted it a couple of inches. Milo managed to slide the heavy tile to one side. He stared down at the metal plate that had been installed underneath the tile, then glanced up at Birdie who was peering over his shoulder.

"It's right where he said it was," Milo said, grinning over his shoulder.

"I can't ask who you're referring to, can I?"

"No."

"What's under there?"

"Well, let's have a look," Milo said, unlatching the metal plate and sliding it back.

"Sonofabitch," Birdie whispered, staring down at the hole in the floor.

Milo whistled softly and began removing the bundles of cash. He tossed them on the floor next to him and Birdie and soon a large pile began to form.

"They're all stacks of ten grand, Milo," Birdie said, flipping through one of the bundles.

"Yeah, I noticed," Milo said, continuing to remove the packets of cash. "It's a nice round number, huh?"

"The widow didn't know this was here, did she?"

"I'm sure she didn't, Birdie."

"Why would her husband keep it a secret?"

"My guess is that he didn't think she'd approve of how he made it," Milo said. "I know I sure wouldn't have been happy to hear about it."

"What was the husband up to?"

"He was up to a lot of things. But this money came from the days when he was a smuggler," Milo said. "Or so the story goes."

"Smuggler? But not booze, right?"

"No, not booze," Milo said. "People."

"He was smuggling people?"

"Yeah, mostly illegal immigrants from Asia. And some from Europe."

"To do what?"

"To work for next to nothing and keep their mouth shut while they were doing it."

"Doing what?"

"Digging coal, primarily. And probably a whole bunch of other shit jobs nobody else wanted to do."

"How much did they charge?"

"Up to five hundred a head," Milo said. "And judging by the look of things, business was good."

"Running booze is one thing, but smuggling people crosses the line, Milo."

"Yes, it does, Birdie," Milo said, counting the bundles of cash. "It's way beyond the pale of decent human behavior. This wasn't business. It was slavery."

"And that's why you're not gonna feel bad about taking the money, right?"

"You are a man of great insight, Birdie," Milo said, nodding.

"It was nice of her to pay you all this money just to take the island off her hands," Birdie said, shaking his head.

"Yeah, it's funny how things work out sometimes."

Milo finished removing all the bundles of cash, then closed the compartment and eventually managed to slide the tile back in place. He sat down on the floor surrounded by the money.

"How much do you think is there?"

"About five hundred thousand," Milo whispered.

"You're gonna need a bigger basket," Birdie said.

Milo grabbed five of the bundles and held them out.

"What?" Birdie said, looking back and forth at the handful of cash and Milo.

"Take it," Milo said, gently shaking the bundles in his hand. "This is for you."

"No, Milo. All I did was drive the boat," he said, shaking his head.

"Birdie, I pay a lot more money to other people who aren't anywhere near the friend you are. And that's just not right. Take it. You can't breathe a word about where it came from, but you are going to take the money."

Milo shoved the money into Birdie's hands.

"This is fifty thousand dollars. What am I gonna do with all this money, Milo?"

"Go buy a bunch of property and set yourself up. Maybe find a nice woman to settle down with. Then spend all your time making a bunch of kids. You know, so you'll have somebody to leave it all to."

"It would be a nice change not having to pay for it," Birdie said. "You're saying I should start taking the long-view, right, Milo?"

"Exactly."

"I'll still be able to drive for you, won't I?"

"Of course, you will. That's not going to change, Birdie," Milo said, giving his shoulder an affectionate squeeze. "And remind me later that we need to talk about another evening drive we're gonna have to take soon."

# Episode 7

## All Hands On Deck

"Prohibition? Sure, why not? I'll drink to that."

Milo Razner

# Who You Gonna Trust?

**Milo placed the suitcase** on the bed, then poured himself a drink and sat down. He lit a cigarette and watched the Senator stare at the suitcase like he was afraid to open it.

"What are you waiting for?" Milo said.

"I'm not sure," the Senator said, glancing up. "I feel like a kid at Christmas."

"Well, Senator, you obviously did enough to stay off the naughty list," Milo said. "I think you'll find that Santa's been very good to you this year."

"Yes, well, I'm sure Santa just wasn't paying very close attention," the Senator said, chuckling nervously as he opened the suitcase. "Oh, my goodness. How much is in here?"

"Two hundred and fifty thousand," Milo said, softly.

"What? That bastard told me there's was only two hundred thousand total," the Senator said, examining one of the bundles.

"I guess he didn't get around to making the appropriate withdrawal before he died. Or maybe his math skills slipped away near the end," Milo said. "How did he die again?"

"It's not important," the Senator said, waving the question off. "I can't believe that bastard was trying to short me."

"Yeah, I know. You'd think you could trust a guy who was smuggling Chinese illegals across the border," Milo said, staring blankly at the Senator.

The Senator stared at back at Milo, stunned.

"Where the hell did you hear that? I mean, I have no idea what you're talking about."

"Nice try, Senator," Milo said, laughing.

"How the hell did you find that out, Milo?"

"Does it matter?"

"Well, yeah, to me it might," the Senator said, getting up out of his chair. "You're such a little shit sometimes, Milo."

"Relax, Senator. All your dirty little secrets are safe with me. But I must say that this one is particularly dirty, even by your standards."

"Don't start getting all moral with me, Milo," the Senator said, refreshing his drink. "You of all people should know better than that."

"It's a despicable thing to do, and you know it, Senator."

"Perhaps," the Senator said, closing the suitcase and sliding it under the bed. "But not despicable enough for you to refuse your finder's fee, right?"

"No, you're right about that. If there was ever a time I was gonna take my cut, this is it."

"By the way, how much is your finder's fee?"

"Half," Milo said, extinguishing his cigarette.

"Half? There was half a million buried under the floor?" the Senator said, stunned.

"There was," Milo said, nodding.

"That rotten son of a bitch. Boy, you think you know somebody," the Senator said, shaking his head. "And you think you're entitled to half of it? That's quite a finder's fee, Milo."

"Well, I did have to look pretty hard for it," Milo said, flashing a smile at him.

"You had to be able to count to ten and move a rock. Goddamn, Milo. You want to keep a quarter million for yourself?"

"Senator, two minutes ago, you were expecting to get a hundred grand. Then I walk in here and give you two hundred and fifty thousand, and you're still not happy."

"Well, I suppose if you put it that way."

"Not to mention that the money was found on my property," Milo said, grinning.

"That's right. You lucky bastard," the Senator said, shaking his head in disbelief when the lightbulb went off in his head. "You made two hundred grand just by *buying* the place."

"Yeah, I'm starting to enjoy the real estate game. I suppose I should feel guilty about not telling the widow about the money, but it didn't look like she needed it."

"You're right. She doesn't. To her, the fifty grand you paid for the island is walking around money," the Senator said. "Okay, well played, Milo. Well played indeed."

"Thank you, Senator," Milo said, raising his glass in a toast. "As always, it's a pleasure doing business with you."

"Speaking of which," the Senator said. "Where are you at with your expansion plans?"

"Now, that I've got the island, things are going to start moving pretty fast. My new stills should be here soon. And I've been buying up corn and sugar like you wouldn't believe."

"You're using different suppliers, right? We don't want to raise any eyebrows by buying massive amounts from the same people."

Milo glared at the Senator.

"Sorry, Milo. Forget I asked. Far be it for me to question the genius of Milo Razner," the Senator said, tossing back his drink. "By the way, the speakeasies are doing incredibly well. And the Red Deer is a major hit. People love it."

"Are you still adding new ones?" Milo said.

"Yes, we're getting close to a hundred. And that's why we're so interested in your expansion plans. We're starting to have a problem keeping up with demand. You know, until I started dabbling in the booze business, I had no real appreciation for just how much our citizens like to drink."

"How else are they going to forget all the problems our government is making for them?" Milo said, getting up to refresh his drink.

"Funny, Milo," the Senator said.

"When is Green getting here?" Milo said, taking a sip.

"It shouldn't be long. He's been running a little late these days. Recently, Ben has become a bit...*preoccupied*."

"Is that your Senatorial way of telling me that he's been getting horizontal with Beulah?"

"Oh, you know about that?" the Senator said, surprised by the news.

"Of course, I know. Beulah and I decided a long time ago, if we were going to be successful business partners, we couldn't be keeping a lot of secrets from each other."

"Ben says she's the best he's ever had," the Senator said, grinning at Milo.

"Mr. Green should be enough of a gentleman to keep his mouth shut about things like that."

"Well, Ben and I are business partners. So, I'm sure you understand why he might have mentioned it."

"Point taken, Senator," Milo said, glaring off into the distance.

"It doesn't bother you?"

"No, it was about what I expected would happen," Milo said, still staring off and doing his best to hide the small smile that was beginning to form in the corners of his mouth.

**Annabelle left** the train station in Syracuse by cab and soon found herself standing outside the Yates Hotel, a massive six-story structure that seemed to cover the entire block. She'd heard that the place had been a favorite watering hole for local politicians before the new law was passed, and reputed to have a bar so long it required patrons at opposite ends to shout if they wanted to chat with each other.

She doubted the bar was still open, and even if it had been converted into a speakeasy, there was no way she'd be showing her face inside. But with the bottle Tom Collins had given her just before she left on her trip, she knew she'd be fine for the evening.

That is if she could keep her meeting with Vernon Adams short and focused on the business at hand.

She checked in and followed a bellboy up to the second floor. Annabelle unpacked her small suitcase, drew a hot bath, then settled in for a long soak with a glass of whiskey and the newspaper. She dozed off, woke when the water began to chill, then reheated the tub and nodded off again. She woke looking like an hourglass-shaped prune but feeling refreshed.

The knock came at seven on the dot, and she opened the door and found Vernon Adams standing in the doorway with a goofy look on his face holding flowers and a briefcase. She stepped back and waved him in then closed the door.

"These are for you, Annabelle," he said.

"I get the flowers, Vernon, but what on earth am I supposed to do with your briefcase?"

Vernon Adams' mouth formed a perfect circle, then he got the joke and chuckled nervously.

"Oh, that's a good one, Annabelle. They're mums."

"As in, mums the word?"

"Yes," he said, nodding. "I'm so glad you caught the reference."

"Well, thanks for the flowers, Vernon," Annabelle said, accepting the bouquet. "That was very sweet of you."

"My pleasure," he said. "And I'm so glad you wanted to meet here in your room."

"Don't read anything into that, Vernon. It's just not a good idea for you to be seen in public with one of your undercover agents."

"Of course not," he said, giggling. "Just under the covers, right?"

"Vernon. No," Annabelle said. "We've already discussed that several times."

"I don't understand, Annabelle. You were more than happy to do it before."

"Just that one time, Vernon," Annabelle said, rubbing her forehead. "And you were just lucky enough to catch me on the right day."

"The right day indeed. I know I'll never forget it," Vernon said, grinning.

"Me either, Vernon," Annabelle said, glancing away to scowl at the memory before refocusing on her visitor. "Now let's get to work."

Annabelle poured herself a drink then held up the bottle and waited for Vernon to respond.

"Oh, yes, please," he said. "I'd love one. After that train ride, I'm parched."

"I'm sure you could have gotten a drink on the train," Annabelle said, handing him his glass as she sat down at the table.

"Not a good idea," he said, taking a sip. "I'm the head of the Prohibition Unit. How would that look?"

"Like one more example of the hypocrisy that's running rampant?"

"Hey, I didn't make the law. I'm just supposed to be enforcing it," Vernon said, swirling the ice in his glass. "I'm glad you wanted a face to face meeting. I've missed you."

"It wasn't my first choice, but we need to be very careful about what we say over the phone," Annabelle said. "The switchboard operator in town has her nose into everything."

"That could come in handy at some point."

"Yes, it could," Annabelle said, focusing on her drink.

"Okay, you had me travel all the way from Washington. What's on your mind?"

"Milo Razner."

**Milo looked** up when he heard the door open. Ben Green and Beulah entered laughing and holding hands. Beulah saw Milo, looked away, and let go of Green's hand. She removed the shawl draped over her shoulders then looked back at him and smiled.

"Hi, Milo."

"It's nice to see you, Miss Peppin," Milo said. "Mr. Green."

"Hello, Mr. Razner," Ben Green said, giving Milo a grin as he slipped his hand behind Beulah's back. Beulah jumped a bit when she felt the hand and gave Ben Green a coy smile. Then she tossed her shawl on a chair and sat down next to Milo on the couch.

"How's the milk business, Mr. Razner?" Ben Green said, pouring two drinks and handing one to Beulah.

"Business is good, Mr. Green," Milo said, holding up his empty glass for him to refill. "I take it you're selling a lot of fresh produce as well."

"As fast as I can get my hands on it," he said, glaring at Milo as he grabbed the glass. "Of course, allow me to refresh that for you. I understand that you might have a solution to our emerging supply problem."

"I believe I do, Mr. Green," Milo said, accepting the fresh drink and raising it briefly in a mock toast.

"I'm happy to hear that. Senator, before we get started with Mr. Razner, I need to have a quick word with you."

"Of course," the Senator said, gesturing toward the bedroom of the suite.

Milo waited until the door closed behind them, then glanced over at Beulah who was already climbing into his lap. She kissed him long and hard, then settled back into a sitting position and folded her hands in her lap.

"I've missed you, Milo."

"Are you sure about that, Miss Peppin?"

"Oh, don't be like that," Beulah said, playfully swatting away Milo's hand that was starting to work its way up her leg. "You're the one who told me to do whatever I needed to get close to Green."

"It's not what you're doing that bothers me, although I don't like it much. It's who you're doing it with."

"I'm just taking the long-view, Milo," she said, stroking the side of his head with the back of her hand. "How are things up there?"

"Not bad. But I had to make a few personnel changes."

"Yes, I noticed you've hired new drivers," Beulah said. "They've been good so far."

"I'm glad to hear that. Let me know if that changes. And I promoted Tom Collins."

"I see," she said, frowning. "What happened to Clint?"

"He decided to try his hand at something different."

"At his age? What on earth was that?"

"Long distance swimming," Milo said, lighting a cigarette.

"Oh, I see. How did he do with that?"

"Not well."

"I take it he did something stupid?" Beulah said, leaning over to nuzzle his neck.

"Very stupid. Are we going to be able to get together later tonight?"

"I'm not sure," she said. "Ben and I have dinner plans, and then he said he has something he wants to show me."

"I'm sure he does. But I imagine you'll recognize it by now."

"Don't be like that, Milo," she said, squeezing his thigh. "Just try to stay patient. We're right on track."

**"Are you** sure about that?" Vernon Adams said, frowning.

"I'm positive," Annabelle said, refilling her glass even as she reminded herself not to drink too much.

"But Roland is convinced Razner is the mastermind up there. Or at least one of them."

"Roland's a raging alcoholic," Annabelle said. "And a despicable human being."

Vernon Adams nodded then yawned.

"Tell me something I don't know," he said. "Why do you think I stationed him way up there on the border?"

"Why don't you transfer him to a place where he could do something useful? Like getting himself shot."

"He already got shot."

"In the foot. And I'm sure it was self-inflicted. Really, Vernon. The man is incompetent. And I'm worried that he's going to do something really stupid and do damage to your reputation."

"Now, you're worried about me?"

"Of course, I'm worried about you, Vernon," Annabelle said, patting his hand. "And Roland Doyle isn't the sort of person you want representing your interests up there."

"So, you're saying I should move him out and replace him with someone a bit more competent?"

"No, I'm saying you should just transfer him out," Annabelle said. "And don't worry about replacing him. You've already got me in place to keep an eye on things for you."

"Would you be willing to go public?" Vernon said.

"As a Prohibition agent?" she said, scowling. "Absolutely not. I'm in the perfect role right now. I'm just saying you don't need anyone else there."

"I can't do that, Annabelle. I need to maintain at least a semblance of a presence in that section of the River. And there has to be trafficking going on in the area. Roland has already made a major arrest."

"Yeah, I'm still not sure how he managed to pull that off," Annabelle said, lighting a cigarette. "It's just that he's such a bungling drunk, I'm worried he's going to completely screw things up and get in my way."

"Or maybe get all of the credit in the process?" Vernon said, grinning at her.

"That thought has crossed my mind. You know me so well, Vernon."

"Well, I'm sure they'll be more than enough credit to go around, Annabelle."

"I'm looking at this job as a way to set myself up for the future. And I don't want an incompetent sot like Roland Doyle screwing things up."

"I suppose I could transfer him."

"No, don't worry about it," Annabelle said, exhaling smoke. "If you have to leave an agent in place, it might as well be him. At least I'll know who I'm dealing with."

"Okay, if that's what you want," Vernon said, shrugging. "Now, getting back to Razner. Why don't you think he's involved?"

"He seems to have gone straight," she said. "I've heard all the rumors about his past, but it appears he's seen the error of his ways and has decided he can be just as successful running a legitimate business."

"And you're buying it?" Vernon said, topping off his drink.

"Yeah, it's strange, but I am. Perhaps, he just got tired of having to look over his shoulder all the time. Razner's a bit of an odd duck, but I have a good feeling about him," she said. "He's going to provide breakfast for all the local school kids on his own dime."

"A noble gesture," Vernon said, nodding. "But a lot of criminals are known for their generosity when it comes to things like that."

"Yes, I know. But I'm convinced Razner's hands are clean on the bootlegging front."

"Well, if it isn't him, who do you have in mind?" Vernon said, fiddling with his pen.

"I'm not sure. I'm beginning to wonder if there are any other major smugglers working in that section of the River now that Doyle has caught that corrupt cop."

"It would be very surprising if there weren't more of them," Vernon said. "Perhaps they're just extremely good at covering their tracks. That's what Roland believes about Razner."

"Roland's drunk by nine in the morning."

"You know, Annabelle, I've been thinking that maybe it's time you got to know Roland a bit better," Vernon said as he removed his jacket and loosened his tie. "You know, get a little closer and keep an eye on his drinking. And maybe come up with some ways to help him out."

"You're joking, right?"

"No, not that close," Vernon said, chuckling. "And you certainly don't want to let him know what your real job is. So, using your considerable skills as an undercover agent, I think it might be a good idea for you to figure out a way to lend him a hand."

"And then report back to you?" Annabelle said, finishing her drink.

"Well, that couldn't hurt. I don't trust Roland as far as I can throw him," Vernon said. "And it would be nice if I could get something out of it."

"Whatever you say, Vernon. You're the boss."

"Speaking of getting something out of it," Vernon said, refilling his glass. "See if you can get your hands on a couple of cases of good Canadian. I'm having a hell of a time finding any in D.C."

# Oscar Heads Home

**Melvin didn't recognize the drivers**, but knew the truck and waved as they passed each other heading in opposite directions.  Oscar turned around in the passenger seat and craned his neck at the truck.

"Razner is delivering out of town?" Oscar said, settling back into his seat.

"Yes," Melvin said, focusing on the road. "His business has really taken off. He's buying up small farms as well as all the surplus milk he can get his hands on. He's also gone into the cheese business."

"Cheese?" Oscar said. "Is there any money in cheese?"

"I suppose. I see people eating it all the time," Melvin said, shrugging. "And guess who he went into the cheese business with?"

"Who?"

"Beulah Peppin," Melvin said, glancing over.

"The woman who was leading the Dry effort in town?" Oscar said, frowning.

"That's her. Milo said that she was looking for something else to do after the law passed. He says she has a good head for business."

"Razner's a lucky man," Oscar said. "She's a real looker."

"Indeed," Melvin said, inching the car to the edge of the road to avoid a pothole. "They need to fix this road."

"You think Razner has figured out what we're up to?" Oscar said.

"No, he doesn't have a clue. And he's way too busy with his dairy farm to worry about a couple of guys running a few cases across the border."

"Good. I don't like the prick," Oscar said.

"He just bailed your ass out of jail, Oscar. You might want to show a little gratitude."

"Yeah, maybe. As long as he doesn't try to kill me with the juice on the five hundred," Oscar said. "And we need to start moving a lot more than five cases. I can't stand the thought of owing money to somebody."

"Really? You could have fooled me, Oscar," Melvin said, shooting him a dirty look.

"You'll get your money, Melvin. What does our supplier say about increasing the number of cases?"

"He said it won't be long," Melvin said. "Maybe after our next run."

"Good. Have you talked with Lawless lately about taking some more cases?"

"He's working on a few things. But he doesn't have any specific buyers nailed down yet."

"Well, next time you see him, tell him from me that he needs to lift his game," Oscar said. "He should be able to move at least ten, maybe fifteen cases a week easy."

"I'll do that."

"Let me know what he has to say. When do you think my case is going to go to trial?"

"Maybe a month," Melvin said, casually.

"A month? Damn it, Melvin."

"It could be worse, Oscar," Melvin said, drumming his fingers on the steering wheel. "You could be sitting in jail with the drooler waiting for your trial to start."

"Yeah, I know. But I can't have this thing hanging over my head forever. What the hell is taking them so long?"

"I think they're waiting to see if they can come up with any additional evidence."

"Well, they ain't gonna find it because there wasn't any in the first place."

"The ninety-five cases of booze in your garage notwithstanding, right?" Melvin said, grinning.

"Somebody stole my car just to get me off my property then slipped in behind me and put it there. And you know it, Melvin."

"Yes, I know that," Melvin said, glancing over. "And believe me, Oscar, I'm doing everything I can to make sure I can prove it."

"Can you?"

"Doubtful," Melvin said, giving Oscar a sad smile. "But as long as you don't give them any more reasons to come down hard on you, I'm sure I'll be able to negotiate probation for you."

"I can probably live with that," Oscar said, nodding to himself.

"Besides, now that you're a full-time criminal, what difference would being on probation make?"

"Yeah, I guess you're right. At least I could still work."

"That's the spirit, Oscar," Melvin said. "The glass is half-full, right?"

"That sounds good. Did you bring a bottle?"

# Water and Ice

**Milo stared in disbelief** at the item on display in Frank Slack's private work room. He did a slow lap around it, then repeated the move in the opposite direction. Finally, he sat down on a workbench and kicked his legs back and forth as he stared at Frank who was looking back at him with a goofy grin.

"Well, what do you think?" Frank said.

"I think you've got way too much time on your hands, Frank," Milo said, staring back at the odd-looking contraption that was suspended on a hoist about four feet off the ground. "What the hell is it?"

"It's the answer to our winter delivery problem," Frank said.

The penny dropped, and Milo hopped off the workbench nodding.

"Okay, I'm starting to get it," Milo said, doing another slow lap around it. "So, it's one-part boat, one-part airplane?"

"No, it won't fly, Milo," Frank said, laughing. "The propeller in the back moves it forward by producing air that pushes backward."

"Okay," Milo said, unable to take his eyes off it. "But I'm sure you can understand my confusion."

"It's beautiful, isn't it?" Frank said, his eyes shining with pride.

"Not the first word that comes to mind, Frank," Milo said, chuckling. "Actually, it's one of the ugliest things I've ever seen."

"I'm not talking about how it looks, Milo. I'm talking about what it will do."

"Okay, let's talk about that," Milo said, hopping back up on the workbench.

"You asked me to start thinking about how we could handle the problem of transporting product during the winter."

"Yes, I did. But I had no idea you'd come up with something that looked as goofy as that thing."

"Will you please forget what it looks like, Milo?" Frank said, his voice rising a notch. "We're talking about some serious *creative adaptability* here."

"Okay," Milo said, lighting a cigarette. "Enlighten me, Bodhisattva."

"It's an iceboat. And they've been around for a while. But they've always used a sail for propulsion. And while that's fine, the unpredictability that comes with the wind is something we want to avoid."

"I'm with you so far, Frank."

"I was reading an article about the airboats they use down in the Everglade swamps, and it mentioned that they'd been trying some interesting things with car engines. So, I took the engine from a Model T I had sitting around."

"And used it to turn that propeller you've got attached to the back," Milo said, nodding. "Smart."

"Yes, I thought so, too. But that only solved half of our problem."

"Let me see if I can figure it out." Milo sat quietly for several seconds concentrating hard. "The other problem is what to do when we're dealing with both ice and water, right?"

"Well done, Milo," Frank said, nodding. "Exactly. Dealing with ice or water is relatively straightforward. The problem comes in the fall and spring when the seasons change, and we're forced to deal with both at the same time."

"Yeah, I've been worried about that one for a long time," Milo said, again hopping off the workbench to take a closer look at the iceboat.

"Then I hit on the idea of attaching runners to the boat hull and putting the propeller on the back."

"They'll work like skis, right?"

"If I've built it correctly, that's exactly how they'll work," Frank said. "It'll float in the water, but over the ice, the runners will move it just like a kid's sled. It's not going to be that fast, but it'll get you back and forth safely."

"Don't worry about going fast," Milo said, shaking his head. "It's not like we're going to have to try to outrun anybody."

"Yeah, who else would be crazy enough to be out there in the middle of the winter?" Frank said, laughing. "It's just under twenty feet long, and I had to build it wider than I normally would for balance. Trust me, you do not want it tipping over. And it's still not going to be the most stable thing you've ever ridden in, so you don't want to try driving it yourself, Milo. Leave that to Birdie."

"No argument there," Milo said, now admiring the iceboat. "You like it?"

"You're right, Frank. It's a thing of beauty. Just one thing."

"What's that?"

"You need to figure out a way to put some sort of protective cage around the propeller. That thing will take your head off."

"Yeah, I can do that," Frank said. "Good call."

"You're a genius, Frank."

"Thanks, Milo. It was a lot of fun working on it. There's just one small problem. You'll only be able to transport fifteen cans per trip. I'm just not comfortable adding any more weight."

"Fifteen per trip?" Milo said, shrugging. "Ten trips a week. That won't be a problem."

"Ten trips? You sure you got your math right, Milo? That would be fifteen hundred gallons a week."

"Yeah, it is. We're about to expand our production capabilities," Milo said, grinning.

"So, I'm getting a raise?"

"We're all getting a raise, Frank."

# Loose Lips

**Billy examined the wooden object** he was holding, then looked at Milo with a confused look on his face.

"It's a croquet mallet," Milo said, glancing at it. Then he resumed surveying the room.

"What do you do with it?" Billy said, turning it over in his hands.

"It's for duck hunting," Milo said, giving his cooker a blank stare.

"Okay," Billy said, nodding as he tossed it back into a box of assorted junk. "That's probably more sporting than using a gun."

"Yes, I'm sure it is," Milo said, turning around as Tom Collins entered the new cooking room. "How are we looking, Tom?"

"We've almost filled the barge. But Birdie is rearranging some of the boxes to make a bit more room. If this is all that's left, we should be able to make it one trip," Tom said, glancing around. "The room looks even bigger empty."

"Yeah, it does," Milo said. "There's plenty of space."

"What do you want us to do with the stuff we're towing back to the farm?" Tom said.

"Why don't you ask all the workers if they want to take a look?" Milo said. "There's probably some things folks can use. Let them pick through whatever they want, and then have them find a spot in the feed barn for the rest of it. We'll figure out later what to do with the junk nobody wants."

"Most of it won't float," Billy said. "Why don't you just toss it in the River?"

"For the same reason you don't stay in bed in the morning when you have to pee," Milo said, glaring at Billy. "How many times do I have to tell you, Billy? Don't be throwing crap in the River."

"Got it, Milo," Billy whispered.

Ruby entered wearing a pair of dirty coveralls over a well-worn workshirt. She was sweating profusely, and she sat down on a box and removed her work boots. She rubbed one of her feet as she looked around at the now empty space.

"Not many women could look that good wearing that outfit, Ruby," Tom said, smiling at her. "Doesn't she look great?"

"Yeah, fine," Milo said, glancing around the room.

"I guess it's okay," Billy said, shrugging.

Ruby gave Milo and Billy a dirty look, then put her hands on her hips and continued to glare at them. Eventually, she got tired of being ignored and turned away.

"You're sweet, Tom. It's nice to see there's at least one gentleman present." Ruby switched feet and sighed contentedly. "Geez, I'm worn out. And I thought running the farm was tough. That's a whole lot of stuff to be lugging around."

"Thanks for helping out, Ruby," Milo said over his shoulder.

"A small price to pay for getting a tour of the house, Milo," Ruby said. "And I thought we'd just have our regular meeting while we're here. That is if you can make the time for me."

Billy snorted and nudged Tom with an elbow. Milo caught it, but let it pass without comment.

"Meeting? Yeah, maybe later. Okay, let's talk about the layout." Milo began moving to each section of the room he was referring to as he outlined his ideas. "I thought we might use this corner of the room for storing corn and sugar. To the right of that, I thought we'd put the five stills in a row down that side."

"Five?" Tom said, frowning.

"Yeah, I changed my mind and decided to order three new ones," Milo said. "We've got plenty of room and the way this thing is taking off we might as well cook as much product as we can. That's okay with the two of you, right?"

"More product, more money," Tom said.

"As long as I got what I need to cook, it doesn't matter to me, Mr. Razner," Billy said.

"That's what I like to hear," Milo said, grinning as he took a few more steps to his right. "And now that we're moving the entire operation over here, instead of having to fill all those damn cans, I thought we'd just run the Miracle straight into the storage vats from the tap. As soon as the Miracle is in, Tom can get started straight away turning it into Red Deer."

Milo paused and glanced back and forth between Billy and Tom.

"That'll sure save me a bunch of work," Billy said. "Dealing with those ten-gallon containers gets old in a hurry."

"Yeah, I like the idea, Milo," Tom said, nodding. "And we can use the wall right behind us for storing the finished product. It's closest to the door."

"I was thinking the same thing," Milo said, nodding. "But there's no way getting around the incline between here and the boathouse. It's gonna be a pain, and we'll just have to deal with it. But since you're both getting a big raise, I'm sure you'll be more than happy to suffer through it."

"Can you take me through the math, Mr. Razner?" Billy said.

Ruby sighed and shook her head as she continued to rub her feet. Billy turned to glare at her.

"Well, excuse me for not being a whiz with numbers," Billy snapped.

"Yeah, like that's your biggest problem," Ruby said, slipping her feet back into the work boots.

"Enough," Milo said. "You two are giving me a headache. All right, Billy. Let's try this again. You'll have slightly over four thousand gallons of capacity. But you'll only be cooking half that amount each week. The other half will be fermenting."

"Yeah, I get that," Billy said, nodding. "The same process we're using now, just with bigger stills."

"And your weekly target is eight hundred gallons of Miracle. At four bucks a gallon, you'll be looking at a little over three grand a week. Thirty-two hundred to be precise."

Billy frowned.

"What on earth is the matter now?" Milo said.

"It just sounds like an awful lot of money," Billy said.

"That's because it is, idiot," Ruby said.

Billy ignored Ruby and concentrated hard.

"Well, she did say I shouldn't feel bad about enjoying the fruits of my labor," Billy said, nodding to himself.

"*Who* said *what*, Billy?" Milo said, suddenly on edge.

"Annabelle," Billy said, looking at Milo. "Just after she told me that you were right about me having a gift for cooking, she said I should gratefully accept and enjoy the fruits of my labor."

"Billy, what have you done?" Milo said, sitting down on a box next to Ruby.

"Nothing, Mr. Razner. The last time we talked, I told you I was going to discuss it with her."

"To talk about your using your gift. And only in general terms," Milo whispered through a dark scowl. "I didn't tell you to give her the details of what you actually do."

"Don't worry, Mr. Razner. I didn't go into the details."

"Did the word Miracle come up?"

"Once or twice maybe."

"Did you talk about gallons?"

"Maybe a bit."

"Did you discuss cooking on the island?"

"Uh, yeah."

"How about money?"

"Yeah, that's when she made the comment about me enjoying the fruits of my labor," Billy said.

"Well, at least you didn't go into any detail," Milo said, rubbing his head with both hands. "Where's winter when you need it?"

"What?" Billy said.

"Nothing," Milo said, glancing at Tom.

Tom nodded then glared at Billy as silence filled the room. Eventually, Billy broke it.

"You ain't got nothin' to worry about, Mr. Razner. Annabelle said that what I was doing was between her and me and the Man upstairs."

"That was mighty Christian of her."

"Praise the Lord."

"Okay, Billy," Milo said, getting up off the box. "What's done is done. Why don't you take the last of this stuff down to the dock and help Birdie load then head for the farm? And tell Birdie to swing back to pick me up after you unload and he returns the barge to Frank."

"You got it, Mr. Razner," Billy said.

"And you should take the rest of the day off, Tom. Why don't you take your boat out? Maybe take a friend along and go for a swim?"

Milo looked at Tom to make sure he understood the inference he was making. Tom nodded back.

"Oh, that sounds great," Ruby said. "Do you mind if I tag along, Tom?"

Tom glanced at Milo before answering. Milo considered the idea, then gave him a slight nod.

"Sure, Ruby," Tom said. "That sounds like fun."

"You don't mind waiting to give me the tour of the house, do you, Milo?" Ruby said. "And maybe we can have our meeting tomorrow. That is if you can find the time."

"You made your point, Ruby. There's no need to use a sledgehammer on me. Have a nice swim."

"I'm going to see if I can wash a few layers of dirt off before we go, Tom," Ruby said. "I'll meet you down at the dock. Goodbye, Milo."

Ruby left without waiting for a return goodbye, and Milo stared at the doorway shaking his head.

"Why is she so mad at you?" Tom said.

"You want the long or the short list?" Milo said.

Tom chuckled.

"Damn," Milo said. "That kid is becoming a real problem."

"What are you going to do about him?"

"I don't know," Milo said. "But you need to start learning how to make Miracle just in case."

"Geez, Milo, given everything else I've got going on, that could take some time."

"Don't worry about that, Tom," Milo said, giving him a crocodile smile. "You'll have all winter to figure it out."

"Sure," Tom said, nodding. Then he frowned. "What?"

"Winter," Milo said as he twisted his head back and forth until his neck popped. "Ah, that's better. What's the matter, Tom? You're boring a hole in my head with that look."

"You expect me to spend the winter over here, don't you?"

"Well, you sure aren't going to be spending it in Florida."

"But, Milo."

"Tom, how can we double our output of product if one of my main guys isn't here to keep an eye on things?"

"Stuck all winter on this island with Billy? Geez, Milo, I could have more interesting conversations with a boat cushion. What the hell are we gonna talk about?"

"I just told you. How to make Miracle."

"I really don't like the idea of spending the winter stuck over here, Milo."

"I'd be disappointed if you did, Tom," Milo said, flashing him a grin. "Now, get going and have some fun today."

"You sure you're okay with me taking Ruby out on the boat?"

"Why wouldn't I be?" Milo said, again turning his head back and forth to get another pop.

"Well, it's Ruby," Tom said. "And she's kind of your girl."

"Tom, Ruby is her *own* girl," Milo said, grimacing. "Damn this headache. And one thing I've learned is that Ruby is going to do what she wants to do regardless of what anybody else says. As soon as I figured that out, I stopped worrying about it."

"But what do I do if she gets…ideas?"

"Do whatever you want," Milo said, frowning as he vigorously rubbed his temples. "Damn, my head feels like I drank a gallon of Miracle last night."

"Are you sure it wouldn't bother you if, you know, something happened?"

"What the hell did I just say, Tom? And if something does happen, it will be Ruby's call, not yours. So, if I were going to be upset with somebody, which I'm not, I'd be mad at her, not you. Are we clear?"

"Okay, okay. I won't mention it again," Tom said. "Not that I think anything is going to happen."

"New topic, Tom," Milo said as he continued to rub his temples. "I think I've got way too much on my mind. All those questions and ideas must be bumping into each other in there."

"Do you want me to see what I can get out of Annabelle?" Tom said.

"No, don't worry about it. We're going to need to shift gears when it comes to her. Now that Billy has gone and run his mouth, Miss Caffey is now officially my problem."

# Undercover Work

**Milo's headache had been corralled** with a
handful of aspirin, but it still nagged and felt like someone was
flicking a finger against his forehead a couple times a minute. He
was sitting at his desk trying to concentrate long enough to get
some work done when the phone rang. He glanced at his watch
and answered it on the second ring.

"Milo Razner…Yes, I'm expecting her. Just send her up.
Thanks."

Milo put the phone back and noticed his palms were sweaty.
He wiped them dry on his pants and waited for the knock on the
door. When it came, he crossed the room quickly and opened it.
He smiled and gestured for her to enter. She stepped inside,
removed her shawl and handed it to Milo. He gestured at a chair,
then hung the shawl on a hook near the door. Milo sat down
across from her and smiled.

"I'm sure you were surprised to hear from me," Milo said.

"No, actually, Mr. Razner, you got in touch pretty much
when I expected you would."

"Really?"

"Yes. You seem to be a man who doesn't like to let problems fester."

"And you think I have a problem?" Milo said, raising an eyebrow.

"No, I think you think you have a problem. Whether or not you actually do, I would suspect, is the top of mind question for you at the moment."

"Perhaps I just reached out to you for social reasons."

"Oh, so you'd like to get social with me?"

"I can think of worse things to do with you," Milo said.

"Yes, I'm sure you can," she said, laughing. "But you should know that I'm a very good swimmer."

Milo flinched at the swimming reference and caught himself staring way too long at her. He eventually broke eye contact and fumbled for his pack of cigarettes.

"What can I do for you, Mr. Razner?"

"I understand you had a conversation with Billy that may have confused you."

"No, it was perfectly clear to me," Annabelle said, smiling. "Billy tends to run a little slow, but he usually ends up making his point. As long as you give him enough time to organize his thoughts."

"Ah, patience," Milo said. "I suppose that's an essential skill for a schoolteacher like yourself."

"Absolutely. And Billy, bless his heart, does often remind me of some of my students."

"You mean, the fourth-graders?"

"Sadly, yes. But as you've told him time and time again, he has a gift that can't be taught in school."

Milo exhaled loudly and lit a cigarette. He held the pack out to her and, to his surprise, she accepted one and waited for him to light it.

"What am I going to do with you, Miss Caffey?" Milo said, settling back into his chair.

"What would you like to do with me, Mr. Razner?"

"At the moment, I find myself torn."

Annabelle laughed as she tilted her head back and blew smoke up at the ceiling.

"Let me guess. Torn between under the covers, or under the River?"

"A straight shooter. I like that," Milo said, nodding. "Yeah, those two options pretty much cover it."

"I understand under the covers, and I must say that I'm flattered. But why on earth would you want to turn me into fish food?" Annabelle said. "Is that a bottle of whiskey on your desk?"

"Yes, it is."

"Aren't you going to ask me if I'd like a drink?"

"I didn't want to presume," Milo said, getting up to grab the bottle and two glasses. He sat back down and poured.

"Presume all you want, Mr. Razner. I'll let you know when you've gone too far."

"You know, Miss Caffey, despite the fact that you scare the crap out of me, I find myself drawn to you."

"That's probably because I'm an odd duck," she said, raising her glass. "Just like you. And you seem to like being around people who cut across the grain. Despite the fact that they might…scare the crap out of you."

"Interesting observation," Milo said, taking a sip. "Okay, so how do you want to start? Should I go first?"

"It's your meeting."

"Hmmm."

"What?"

"Nothing. I was just wondering about something," Milo said, reaching for a fresh cigarette. "Okay, let's dive right in then."

"I can't wait," she said, reaching for the cigarette pack. "Let's hope the water's warm."

"You're an undercover Prohibition agent, aren't you?" Milo said, staring at her.

"Yes, I am," she said, returning his stare.

"Well, that was easy," Milo said, shrugging.

"We both know what each other does, Mr. Razner," Annabelle said, topping off both their drinks. "Why waste time getting to the point?"

"Which point is that?"

"The point about what we're going to do now that it's out there on the table."

"Okay, fair enough. I assume you're working with Roland Doyle?"

"Absolutely not," she said as her face contorted into a grimace.

"Doyle doesn't know what you do?" Milo said, leaning forward.

"No, and he's not going to know. He's a despicable human being."

"No argument there. So, who does know?"

"One man by the name of Vernon Adams," Annabelle said. "He's my boss in Washington."

"I see. Are you in regular contact with him?"

"Regular enough. In fact, I just met with him in Syracuse the other day," she said, looking at Milo over the top of her glass. "I felt that what we needed to discuss should be handled face to face."

Milo thought for a moment, then grinned.

"Violet, right?"

"Yes, I'm still trying to figure out how to best use Miss Hollman to my advantage," Annabelle said. "Until I do, discretion is probably my best choice."

"Try money," Milo said. "I've found that Violet responds well to the fifty."

"I'll remember that," she said, laughing.

"What were you and Vernon Adams talking about that required so much discretion?"

"Why you, of course," she said, casually tapping ash off her cigarette.

"Damn," Milo whispered.

"It shouldn't surprise you that your name has come up in discussions, Mr. Razner," she said, draping a leg over the other. "You relocated to the area just before Prohibition was passed. And Roland Doyle has had a great deal to say about some of the things you used to be involved in."

"Vicious and unfounded rumors."

"Of course," she said, smiling and nodding.

"So, you've already thrown me over to the Feds as a bootlegger?" Milo said, crushing out his cigarette.

"Why on earth would I do something stupid like that?"

"To build your career, what else?"

Annabelle started laughing and didn't stop until Milo's agitation boiled over. He downed his drink and slammed the glass on the table.

"Relax, Milo."

"So, it's Milo now?"

"The time seems right for us to move to a first-name basis," she said, refilling his glass. "Trust me, Milo. The thought of building a career as a Prohibition agent has never crossed my mind."

Milo sat back in his chair and studied her carefully. She sat patiently and waited for him to collect his thoughts.

"Well, if you aren't interested in rising the ranks of the Unit, and you're only teaching school to cover your tracks, the only other reason you'd be here would be to work the dark side of the street."

"That would be your side, right, Milo?"

"Yeah, it can get pretty dark," Milo said, nodding. "And you think working on my side of the street is the only way to make any real money?"

"My only other option for making a lot of money in a hurry would be to set up shop as a working girl."

"I know a couple women who are doing pretty well," Milo said. "I could introduce you to the right people."

"No, that's quite all right, Milo," she said, grinning. "I've always thought that what I have was too special to sell. But as I'm sure Tom has told you, I'm more than happy to share it with the right man."

Milo's face flushed a deep red.

"Uh, yeah. Well, we're business partners and don't have a lot of secrets."

"I see," she said, reaching for another cigarette. "So, do you enjoy water sports, Milo?"

Milo choked on his whiskey and coughed.

"You don't mess around, do you?" he said, wiping his mouth with a handkerchief. "So, what did you tell your boss about me?"

"I told him that it was clear, regardless of what Roland Doyle had to say, that you had gone straight and become a legitimate businessman. I even told him about your plans to provide breakfast for all the kids at school. He was impressed." She paused to make eye contact. "You were serious about doing that, weren't you?"

"Absolutely. Ruby's meeting with your principal next week," Milo said, coughing again. "I'm still finding all this a little hard to digest."

"Try washing it down with a little more whiskey."

Milo chuckled, then did take another sip.

"But your mother is one of the leaders of the Temperance movement."

"Yes, she is," Annabelle said, grinning. "And isn't that the perfect cover? It's almost as good as being a dairy farmer."

Milo beamed at her.

"Okay, Annabelle. I'll play. How dark do you want to go?"

"What do you have in mind, Milo?"

"Let's stick to our deal for now. We can get to the other things on my mind later."

"I can't wait to hear them. You know, Milo, I've been thinking that having someone on the inside with access to all the Unit's plans would be worth a small fortune to you."

"To be honest, I've been thinking the same thing. But I'm going to need a number, Annabelle. I can't build a stack of hundreds just from *small fortune*. I wouldn't know when to stop counting."

"I assume that your business is continuing to grow."

"It is."

"Then rather than put a hard number on it that would constantly have to be revisited, I thought we should probably talk percentages."

"So, I take it you're talking about a long-term arrangement."

"I am. For the duration of that ridiculous law."

"We're probably looking at a decade minimum."

"Are you worried we're going to get sick of each other's company?" Annabelle said, draining her drink.

"I doubt if we'll actually be spending that much time together."

"You're probably right," she said, crushing out her cigarette. "Keeping up appearances and all that."

"I'm thinking…five percent."

"Think some more, Milo."

"Yeah, I figured you'd say that," he said, grinning. "Okay, Annabelle, for keeping me in the loop and out of jail, I'll be happy to give you ten percent."

"That's a nice round number," she said, nodding.

"What about Roland Doyle?"

"Well, I suggested that he be transferred, but my boss said that he needs to maintain a public presence in the area. As such,

Doyle isn't going anywhere. But that's not necessarily a bad thing. We could end up with someone much worse."

"Yeah, someone sober and competent," Milo said. "By the way, how is Doyle's reputation since he arrested Oscar?"

"It's actually surprisingly good," Annabelle said. "I believe his star may be on the rise."

"That's what I figured. Would you be interested in knocking a bit of the luster off it?"

"Oh, I would love that," she said. "After all, a girl's got to earn her money, right?"

"So, I take it we have a deal?"

"We do."

Milo smiled at his new business partner then got up out of his chair and extended his hand.

"Oh, Milo. I'm sure we can do a lot better than a handshake."

# Appetite Interruptus

**Annabelle sat down at the counter** next to a man whose head was buried in a newspaper. She cleared her throat but received no response. She reached in front of him to grab a menu, but the man continued to stare down at the paper unwilling to even acknowledge her presence. Then she heard soft snoring. Annabelle frowned and glanced up at the waitress who was glaring at the sleeping man.

"He must have had a long night," Annabelle said.

"More like a long life," the waitress said. "That's the third time this week he's fallen asleep at the counter. The other customers are starting to wonder if we're watering down the coffee." The waitress picked up a spoon and smacked the man's knuckles. "Hey, Sleeping Beauty, your breakfast is getting cold."

Roland Doyle opened his eyes and blinked at the waitress. He started hacking and coughed up a mouthful of phlegm that, at first, he seemed unsure what to do with. He spit it into a napkin, then looked around for somewhere to put it. The waitress grimaced then reached below the counter and held up a trash container. Roland tossed it in, then glanced down at the counter, and then back up at the waitress.

"How can my breakfast be getting cold? You haven't even brought it to me yet."

"Look under your newspaper," the waitress said as she walked away.

Roland folded his newspaper and discovered his plate of bacon and eggs. He grabbed a fork, broke one of the yolks, and dipped a piece of toast. He chewed slowly then realized someone was sitting next to him. Roland glanced over at Annabelle through bloodshot eyes and a three-day growth.

"Do I know you?" Roland said, blinking at her.

"I don't believe we've met. I'm Annabelle Caffey."

"Sure. You're a schoolteacher, right?"

"That's me," Annabelle said, scanning the menu in the hope her appetite might return.

"I'm Roland Doyle."

"Oh, you're Mr. Doyle," she said, turning on the charm. "You work for the Prohibition Unit. I have to tell you that I think the work you're doing is vital to our country."

"Then you're about the only person around here that does," Roland said, munching on a slice of bacon.

"That's because everyone around here seems cursed by the evils of alcohol," Annabelle whispered.

"So, I take it you're an official member of the Dries?" Roland said, staring at her like she might be from another planet.

"Yes, of course. Just like yourself," Annabelle said, forcing herself to reach out and pat his arm. "Actually, my mother is a leader in the national movement."

"Is she now?" Roland said, raising an eyebrow.

"Yes, and while my primary job is teaching school, I'm always on the lookout for people who might be, let's say, bending the rules when it comes to the Volstead Act. It's sort of a hobby of mine."

"Is it now?"

"Yes, and if there is anything I can ever do to help you carry out your duties, please let me know."

"You want to help me?" Roland said, frowning.

"Well, if there was some way for me to be of assistance, of course."

"I'm always on the lookout for information," Roland whispered. "But I don't have a budget to pay informers."

"Oh, I wouldn't expect to be paid, Mr. Doyle," Annabelle said, cringing at the idea. "I just want to do the right thing as an American. And, of course, as a good Christian."

"You're a credit to both, Miss Caffey," Roland said, sipping coffee. "You haven't heard anything interesting, have you?"

"As a matter of fact, I think I might have," she whispered as she forced herself to move closer.

"Really?"

"Yes, I was at the grocery store yesterday, and I overheard that man you arrested a while back, talking about another shipment."

"Oscar Hyde?" Roland said, surprised. "He must have made bail. Who was he talking to?"

"I couldn't tell. The other man was hidden behind the produce section."

"I see. What were they saying?"

"It was all quite vague, and they were understandably speaking in hushed tones. But it was something about it being the big one that was really going to put them on the map."

"I guess the bastard hasn't learned his lesson," Roland said, then grunted. "I'm sorry about my language."

"That's quite all right, Mr. Doyle," Annabelle said, smiling. "I'm sure he's exactly what you say. And to think that he used to be a member of law enforcement. The thought makes my blood boil."

"Yeah, I guess some people just shouldn't be allowed to carry a badge," Roland said, dragging another piece of toast through his eggs. "Do you think you might be able to get some more information about what he might be planning?"

"Oh, I doubt it," Annabelle said, frowning. "I only overheard what I did by accident. And I'm afraid that I don't travel in those circles."

"No, of course, you don't," Roland said, chewing and talking at the same time.

"But I…no, I probably shouldn't even mention it."

"What?"

"I was just wondering if someone else might have their ear closer to the ground than I do," Annabelle said.

"Like who?"

"Well, I probably shouldn't be telling tales out of school, but I have heard that Violet Hollman is quite tuned in when it comes to what is going on around the area."

"Hollman? The name sounds familiar. Who's she?"

"She operates the phone system in town," Annabelle said. "You know, the person who handles all the connections when people want to talk with each other."

"Oh, yeah," Roland said.

"I thought that someone with access to that much information might be useful to someone in your line of work," Annabelle said. "Not that I approve of her sticking her nose into other people's business."

Roland let the idea roll around in his head as he chewed, then swallowed loudly and grinned.

"I'm so glad you stopped by, Miss Caffey."

"Me too," Annabelle said, getting up from her stool. "But I need to run. It was very nice meeting you, Mr. Doyle."

"Aren't you going to have breakfast?"

"No, for some reason, I seem to have lost my appetite."

# Down On The Farm

**Milo glanced out at the River** and enjoyed the view while he waited for Ruby to finish her conversation with one of the farm workers. She was gesturing with both hands and laughing, and Milo wondered if he'd be getting the same Ruby or if her mood would darken as soon as they started talking. Fearing the worst, Milo decided to let her set the tone and then just play it by ear. Ruby waved goodbye as the worker headed toward one of the barns and then approached Milo.

"He's good," Ruby said, nodding at the departing farm hand. "I'm thinking about promoting him."

"Sure, that's completely your call," Milo said, nodding.

"He's still a little green, but I think he's the guy who should run the place after I decide to do something different."

"I'm sure he'll come up to speed after a few meetings with you," Milo said, trying to lighten the mood.

"Funny, Milo," she said, glaring at him. "But I'm not joking about wanting to do something different in the future."

"I see. What do you want to do, Ruby?" Milo said.

"I guess that's going to depend, isn't it, Milo?"

"Things usually do."

"I'm going to put him in charge of getting all the hay and corn in."

"He doesn't know what we're doing with the corn, does he?" Milo said.

"Relax, Milo. Nobody knows anything," she said, not making eye contact. "Oh, and I just bought another hundred cows."

"A hundred?"

"I figured since we're ramping up on the booze side, we should make sure we're actually producing enough milk to explain the increase in deliveries just in case anybody starts asking questions or tries to do the math."

"Smart," Milo said.

"Yes, I am, Milo. Thanks for remembering."

"Geez, Ruby. Please, don't start."

"I don't have a clue what you're talking about, Milo."

"Okay, Ruby. Whatever you say. But what are we going to do with all that milk?"

"We're going to sell it, Milo," Ruby said, glaring at him. "What the hell do you think we're going to do with it?"

"I meant who are we going to sell it to?"

"Beulah said she can take some of it. And I'm negotiating with a couple of other places in Watertown. A bakery. And somebody who makes ice cream."

"Okay, but get another delivery truck," Milo said. "And make sure it's dedicated to those deliveries."

"Why?"

"Because if you're going to start selling milk to people outside our circle, I don't want to run the risk of getting our product deliveries mixed up."

"Smart," Ruby said, nodding.

"Yes, I am. And don't forget it."

"Oh, finally I get a stir out of you," Ruby said, gently punching him on the arm.

"I can't figure you out, Ruby. One minute, you want me stuck to you like flypaper, then the next you get a look in your eyes like you want to hit me with a stick."

"What can I say, Milo? I'm unpredictable."

"Probably not the word I'd use, but whatever you say."

"I beg your pardon?"

Milo watched her glance around and wondered if she was searching for a stick.

"I'm just saying that you don't seem comfortable getting too close. It's like we get right up to the edge, then you back away."

"Oh, so we're back to my fear of intimacy. Is that it, Milo?"

"Well, the thought has crossed my mind," Milo whispered.

"Who you been talking to, Milo? Billy? Or Daisy."

"What do you want from me, Ruby?"

"I want you to do your job, Milo. And that job is to make me happy."

"Maybe you could start by defining it for me," Milo said.

"If you don't know by now, Milo, I really don't like our chances," she said, tying her hair into a ponytail. "That's better."

"Do you want to get out of the wind?" Milo said, nodding at the house.

"And do what?"

"I thought we might take a meeting."

"Didn't we just do that, Milo?"


**Milo glanced** around the suite and waved a hand in front of his face.

"Tom, why don't you open a window? There's enough smoke in here to make an opium den proud."

"You got any?" Birdie said.

"Got any what?" Milo said, frowning.

"Opium."

"Birdie," Milo said, grinning. "You been holding out on me? What the hell do you know about opium?"

"I tried it a couple of times," he said, shrugging. "That stuff sure gets your attention."

"You been to the Orient?" Milo said.

"No, I smoked it here in town."

"Here?"

"Yeah, I got it from some Chinese folks who were passing through town," Birdie said.

"Really?" Milo said. "What were they doing here?"

"At the time, I didn't have a clue. But my guess is that they were on their way to start working in a coal mine," Birdie said.

"Oh, I see," Milo said, raising a finger to his lips.

"If they were, opium probably would've been my choice, too," Birdie said.

"What's all this about coal mines and opium?" Tom said, returning from the window.

"Ah, it's nothing. Birdie was just telling me about a book he read," Milo said. "That breeze sure feels good."

"Did you get everything sorted out with Annabelle?" Tom said.

"Yeah, I think so," Milo said, puffing on his cigar. "But we're gonna have to keep a close eye on her."

"You're going to have to handle it, Milo," Tom said. "She told me that I'm, in her words, officially cut off."

"That's too bad," Milo said. "She's an interesting woman. What happened?"

"She got mad when she found out that I told you we did a lot more than just go for a swim. It's my own fault. She warned me to keep my mouth shut."

"I see," Milo said, nodding.

"So, did the two of you...?"

"I don't think I have anything more to say about that topic, Tom," Milo said, grinning.

"Got it," Tom said, laughing as he raised his glass in a toast. "So, did you talk with Ruby today?"

"I did," Milo said.

"And?"

"Let's see, she's getting ready to cut the hay and corn. She just bought another hundred cows. Turned my request for a meeting down and yelled at me for a bit. And then she felt the need to tell me about your swim."

"I swear, nothing happened, Milo," Tom said.

"I told you not to worry about it, Tom. Do whatever she wants."

"I'm doing my best to hold out, but I'm about to fold like a house of cards. She's really persistent."

"Yes, I'm very familiar with the problem," Milo said.

"She just took off all her clothes and jumped in the water," Tom said, shaking his head.

"I'm sure she did. Ruby does have a way of getting your attention, doesn't she?"

"And then she just stretched out on the boat to dry off. How am I supposed to deal with that?" Tom said.

"With great caution, Tom," Milo said, grinning. "Okay, time to get to work. Birdie, did you remember to bring the map?"


**Roland Doyle** polished off the last of the bottle then headed outside to the woodpile to grab two more. He noticed he was down to his last two cases and realized he'd have to restock soon. Knowing where he could find several small-timers running booze around town, Roland decided that spending a couple of nights patrolling the shoreline would be the easiest way to get his hands on a few more cases.

That is if he could summon the courage to get back in the boat.

Holding a bottle in each hand, he headed back inside and heard the phone ringing. Roland set one of the bottles down, removed the cork from the other, and took a long swig before answering.

"This is Roland Doyle. Oh, hello, Miss Hollman…I see. That's very interesting…Yes, I'll be here."

Roland hung up confused. He glanced around at the mess and did his best to tidy up. Then he stood in the center of the living room chugging from the bottle as he examined the results of his work. He shrugged in defeat then took one more long pull from the bottle. He put the bottles away in a kitchen cupboard then sat down in the living room and waited for his visitor.

Fifteen minutes later, Violet Hollman announced her arrival with a soft knock. Roland ushered her into the living room and gestured for her to sit down. She seemed unsure where to sit but finally decided on the couch.

"Thanks for agreeing to meet with me, Mr. Doyle," she said, folding her hands in her lap.

"My pleasure, Miss Hollman," Roland said, already feeling the itch for another drink. "You mentioned that you heard something that disturbed you."

"Yes, I did," she said. "You wouldn't have anything to drink, would you?"

"You mean like coffee?"

"Actually, I was thinking about something a bit stronger, Mr. Doyle."

"Yes, well. I'm afraid I don't have anything like that in the house," Roland said, scratching his chin stubble.

"No, of course not," Violet said, chuckling nervously. "Silly me. Look who I'm talking to."

"Don't worry about it, Miss Hollman. What do you have to tell me?"

"I heard a conversation about something big that is being planned for Friday night."

"This Friday?"

"Yes."

"Can I ask you where you heard this conversation?" Roland said, giving her a small smile.

"Oh, I really wish you wouldn't, Mr. Doyle."

"Of course. I understand completely."

"I probably shouldn't be saying anything about it," she said, wringing her hands. "But the thought of that much booze being trafficked into our town is just too much for me to ignore. It's one thing for people to bring in some for their own personal consumption, but this crosses the line."

"And just how much illegal whiskey are we talking about?" Roland said, leaning forward in his chair.

"A thousand cases," Violet said.

"A thousand? Holy shit," Roland said, then frowned at her. "Please excuse my language."

"Don't worry about it. Those were my exact words when I heard the number. That's a lot of booze."

"Indeed. Did they say where it was going to be delivered on the Canadian side?"

"Yeah, they mentioned a hunting camp outside of Rockport. They weren't specific, but they mentioned the name of a cove. I can't remember it at the moment, but I'm sure it'll come to me."

"A hunting camp," Roland said, nodding. "Very clever."

"And then one of them said something really strange that still doesn't make any sense to me," Violet said.

"What was that?"

"The guy started laughing and said, *who would have ever known that the furniture business could be this lucrative*? That's a direct quote. I didn't get the joke, but he and his buddy sure thought it was funny."

"And you don't know who these men were?"

"No, the calls were from the payphone in the drug store, and another was from a restaurant over in Rockport. They must have been trying to conceal their identities, right?"

"Yes, I'm sure they were," Roland said. "Did they happen to mention a specific time?"

"I didn't hear one," Violet said. "But they did make a couple references to around midnight if that helps."

"It does. Who's handling the phone system at the moment?" Roland said.

"The person I've got working nights. Why?"

"I need to make a call to Washington."

"Well, he can certainly help you with that," Violet said.

"Do me a favor, Violet," Roland said, crossing the room to pick up the phone. He held it out to her. "Ask him to place a call to the number on this card."

"Sure, Mr. Doyle," Violet said, grabbing the receiver.

"And be sure to tell him, unless he wants to go to jail, not to listen in on the call."

# Roland's Road Trip

**As Roland made the drive** to Watertown, he did his best to remember Vernon Adams' instructions as well as come up with the most logical way to lay out his plan for the others at the meeting. But he was fighting a hangover, and his thoughts were jumbled. By the time he finally reached Watertown and headed west toward Sackets Harbor, he was cursing himself for not having written any of his boss's instructions down.

When the vast expanse of Lake Ontario opened up in front of him, the view, while impressive, was a stark reminder of the impossible task he faced. You'd need a thousand agents just to patrol this lake, he decided. But Roland forced himself to stay focused on the prospect of catching somebody with a thousand cases of whiskey and tried not to think about seeing his picture in the newspaper. Or how arresting a major supplier would be his ticket out of the hinterlands and back into civilization.

He parked his car outside the Coast Guard station, took a long swallow from his flask, then climbed out. The wind was whipping off the lake, and he buttoned his coat. Roland took another look at the body of water that seemed to go on forever, kept an eye out for busybodies as he took another pull from the flask, then headed inside.

He was escorted into a meeting room where several other people were already waiting. Roland was introduced to everyone, then immediately forgot all their names. But the guy at the head of the table was the local head of the Coast Guard, so Roland decided, since he was sitting in the guy's building, he would focus on him first and see where the conversation led.

"Mr. Doyle," the Coast Guard guy said. "Thanks for making the trip down. I take it this is your first visit?"

"It is," Roland said, nodding. "I've been so busy, and I just haven't had a chance to get out much, mister, uh, sir."

"Stanley. John Stanley," the Coast Guard guy said. "Okay, let's get right to it. I understand you've uncovered a booze run that is scheduled for later in the week."

"Yes, Friday." Roland started reciting slowly as he tried to remember Vernon Adams' exact words. "And I thought it would be in all of our best interests if we tried to use all of the available resources in a concerted fashion." Roland frowned, then forced a smile. "Or something like that."

"Did you now?" the Coast Guard guy said, giving Roland a look that he immediately wanted to knock off the guy's face. "Well, Mr. Doyle, as you can imagine, we're all pretty busy here as well. And we have a lot of areas to patrol."

"Yeah, I saw the lake when I came in," Roland said.

"Yes, well, it's a bit hard to miss," John Stanley said, chuckling.

The others around the table laughed along, and Roland felt his temper begin to flare.

"So, you'd like all of us to join you in this operation?" a man sitting next to the Coast Guard guy said.

"I would," Roland said. "Who are you again?"

"I'm Wilbur Montgomery. I'm with the Border Patrol."

"So, I take it you don't have any real responsibilities for hunting down bootleggers?" Roland said.

"Indirectly," he said. "But if this operation involves illegal entry, I'm sure I'll be able to justify our involvement."

"Oh, don't worry," Roland said. "It's plenty illegal."

"What exactly are we talking about, Mr. Doyle?"

Roland was again stumped by the identity of the new guy who'd joined the conversation. The guy studied Roland, seemed to pick up on his confusion, then spoke in a quiet voice.

"Johnny Matters."

"What?" Roland said, confused. "Oh, yeah. I'm sure he does."

"What?" Johnny Matters said, staring at Roland.

"You said Johnny matters."

"Yes."

"What?"

"I'm Johnny Matters," the guy said, bewildered. "I'm the head of the Prohibition Unit's Ogdensburg group."

"Oh, I see," Roland said, exhaling loudly. "Thanks for clearing that up. What was your question again?"

Johnny Matters exchanged looks with everyone else at the table, then focused on Roland.

"I asked you what this operation actually entailed."

"It's a big booze run," Roland said, starting to find his footing. "It involves a major Canadian supplier, and I'm sure the people bringing it in are the big fish I've been looking for."

"Mr. Doyle," Stanley said, frowning. "We're a very small outpost of a fledgling agency that is woefully understaffed. And don't even get me started on the outdated equipment and lack of resources as a whole."

The others around the table nodded and murmured their agreement.

"Not to mention having to enforce the law itself," Stanley continued. "A piece of legislation that is destined to go down in history as one of the stupidest things our government has ever done."

Another round of nods and murmurs followed.

"It's still the law," Roland said.

"Indeed," Stanley said. "And I will do my absolute best to enforce it. But I need to pick my battles carefully and focus on the ones that might actually make a difference."

"This is a big one," Roland said, glancing around the table.

"I see," Stanley said. "What sort of quantity are we talking about?"

"A thousand cases," Roland said, glancing around to let the number sink in.

"That's a lot of booze," Johnny Matters said.

"It sure as shit is. And I've got the location, and the approximate time it's going to go down on Friday night," Roland said.

"I don't know, Mr. Doyle," Stanley said. "The thought of bringing one of my boats into that area of the St. Lawrence in the middle of the night concerns me. If you don't know your way around, those local waters can be very dangerous. And Friday is a new moon. It's going to be pitch black out there."

"Bring a flashlight," Roland said, shrugging.

"Now, why didn't I think of that?" the Coast Guard guy said. "Have you spoken with law enforcement on the Canadian side?"

"Yes, I talked to the police chief in Rockport," Roland said. "He gave me a hard time at first, but he eventually agreed to help out."

"I see. What about the Mounties?"

"The Mounties?" Roland said, frowning. "Are they the ones with the funny hat?"

"Yes, that's the one."

"Yeah, I talked with them," Roland said. "They weren't interested in helping out."

"Who did you speak with?" Johnny Matters said.

"Some guy by the name of Sonny something or other."

"Sonny McWilliams. I know him. He's good. Sonny really said that?" Johnny Matters said.

"Actually, he said, go away, you're bothering me," Roland said. "But I might have been a little too persistent. He was getting mouthy with me and didn't like it much when I grabbed him by the neck."

"You assaulted a Mountie?" Johnny Matters said, staring at Roland in disbelief.

"Nah, I wouldn't call it assault. It was more of a love tap," Roland said, shrugging it off. "So, can I count on your help, Mr. Matters?"

"Yes, Mr. Doyle. I will be there. Along with one of my boats and two of my men."

"That's mighty kind of you," Roland said, grinning.

"Well, Vernon said that since I work for him, I don't really have a choice," Johnny Matters said. "Apparently, your arrest of that corrupt cop made quite an impression on Vernon and a certain senator from New York. People in high places are listening to you, Mr. Doyle."

"They are?" Stanley said, frowning.

"How about you, sir?" Roland said to the Coast Guard guy. "Can I count on your help?"

"Well, given the…visibility an operation like this will have, I suppose I could free up a boat and a few of my men to help out. And I'll be more than happy to be there to supervise."

And smile for the camera, Roland thought.

"I'll bring a boat along, too," the Border Patrol guy said. "You said Rockport, right?"

"Yes, there's a furniture store on the waterfront," Roland said. "It's the front they're using to cover their tracks."

"I know that place," the Border Patrol guy said. "There actually used to be a distillery located there."

"Really?" Roland said, more convinced than ever he was on the right track. "But the drop-off is going to be at a hunting camp about three miles upriver from Rockport. There's a secluded cove tucked away off the main channel they're going to use."

"Sure," he said, nodding. "I know it well. I fish that spot every year in late spring for smallmouth."

"Well, we'll be trying to catch a much bigger fish on Friday," Roland said, grinning.

"Yes, of course," Stanley said, giving Roland the look again. "Good one, Mr. Doyle."

Roland forced his mouth into a twisted grin and clenched his fists under the table as he wondered how much fun it would be to make a few alterations to the Coast Guard guy's expression.

"I thought that we should wait until after dark to meet," Roland said. "Sometime around ten behind Boldt Castle. Do you guys know where that is?"

"Yes, I think I've heard about it once or twice," Stanley said, grinning as he looked around the table. "And I'm sure we'll recognize it when we see it."

Roland waited for the chuckles to die down then stood up and stared down at Stanley.

"I'm glad it's going to be dark on Friday night when we hit that furniture store."

"Why's that, Mr. Doyle?"

"Because if I happened to see that look on your face one more time, I'd probably be forced to do some rearranging."

# Now We're Cooking

**All three men looked around** and admired the spotless room and the gleam of copper. Milo smiled and clapped his hands softly.

"It looks just like a real distillery," Billy said, walking around in a small circle as he took in his surroundings.

"That's probably because it is, Billy," Tom said with a sigh. "What do you think, Milo?"

"I think it's a thing of beauty, Tom. Did all the furniture arrive?"

"It sure did," Tom said. "And the place looks great."

"Good. Okay, gentlemen, let's get cooking," Milo said, grinning. "Oh, Billy. I almost forgot. A couple of sugar deliveries will be arriving next week. You'll need to stop by the farm and pick them up."

"Will do, Mr. Razner," Billy said. "Ain't you worried people are gonna start asking questions about what you need all that sugar for?"

"You can't make ice cream without sugar."

"No, I guess you can't," Billy said, shrugging.

"How are we looking on corn?" Milo said.

"Between what we'll get from the farm and the other island, we should be good. But I'll let you know before the snow starts if we're gonna need more to get through the winter."

"Sounds good."

"Uh, Mr. Razner?" Billy said. "Could I talk to you about something?"

"Sure, Billy. What's on your mind?"

"Winter."

"What about it?" Milo said, staring at him.

"Well, it's just that last winter I got real lonely on that island all by myself."

"I know," Milo said. "And that's why I've asked Tom to stay here with you, so you'll have somebody to talk to."

"Yeah, that's all well and good, Mr. Razner, and I do enjoy Tom's company. But that's not exactly the type of lonely I was talking about."

"Oh, I see," Milo said. "You're wondering about female companionship."

"I am."

"Okay, do you have someone specific in mind?"

"Well, at first, I thought that Annabelle might be interested. But then she reminded that she has a responsibility to her students."

"Of course," Milo said, nodding.

"And lately she's cooled off completely if you know what I mean," Billy said.

"Cooled off? No, I haven't noticed that at all," Milo said.

"Yeah, I guess I was wrong about her wanting to be more than just friends."

"Hey, don't worry about that, Billy. We've all made that mistake more than once."

"Yeah," Billy said, nodding. "And then I got to thinking that even if Annabelle did agree to stay over here for the winter, given her morals and all, she probably wouldn't be willing to help me out with my loneliness problem. If you catch my drift."

"Got it," Milo said. "So, do you have someone else in mind?"

"Well, I haven't seen her around much lately, and she might think it's the stupidest idea she's ever heard, but I was thinking about asking Daisy," Billy said.

"Daisy? Interesting."

"What do you think, Mr. Razner? Is there any chance that Daisy might be willing to take me back?"

"I gotta like your chances, Billy."

**Milo stared** up at the photo of the younger Fannie. Daisy leaned over his shoulder to also study the photo.

"She was something else in her younger days, wasn't she?" Milo said.

"Yes. But mine are better," Daisy whispered into his ear.

"Perhaps. But I'd need another look at yours just to be sure," Milo said, turning around to grin at her.

"Sure, anytime, Milo," she said, laughing. "It's your money."

Fannie entered her office and sprawled out on the couch.

"Sorry, I'm late," she said, yawning.

"Don't worry about it," Milo said. "We were just killing time by making some comparisons."

"While I'm sure that was a fascinating discussion, Milo, can we just get to it?" Fannie said, stifling another yawn. "I'm beat."

"Sure," Milo said, sitting down across from her. "I need to talk to you about the upcoming winter."

"It's gonna be long and cold, Milo. I don't know what else to tell you."

"I'd like to discuss the possibility of hiring Daisy for the winter."

"What?" Daisy said, staring in disbelief at him.

"All winter?" Fannie said, sitting up on the couch. "Geez, Milo, it ain't that cold."

# All Hands On Deck

**About a hundred feet offshore**, Melvin slowed the boat to a crawl and grabbed his flashlight. He pointed it at the shoreline and squinted as he tried to spot the location he was looking for.

"There it is," Willy said, pointing his flashlight at the truck that was parked in the trees about twenty feet from the edge of the water.

"Got it," Melvin said as he inched the boat forward then killed the engine.

Willy hopped into the water and grabbed the bowline. He wrapped the line around a large rock and waded back to the boat and gently turned it until the stern was facing the shore.

"All right. Let's get these loaded in the truck," Willy said. "What time are you supposed to meet Oscar?"

"Soon," Melvin said, hopping off the boat into the water.

"Well, we don't want you to be late," Willy said. "Just give me a hand getting them out of the boat, and I'll handle the rest of it on my own."

"Okay," Melvin said. "Do I look wet enough?"

Willy shined his flashlight on him.

"No, you'll need to be more convincing than that."

Melvin nodded then dove under the water. He resurfaced moments later drenched.

"That'll work," Willy said, nodding.

They proceeded to unload the fifty cases from the boat. Then Melvin hopped back into the boat and started the engine. Willy untied the line and tossed it into the boat then waved as Melvin slowly headed for deeper water.


**Melvin pulled** the boat into its slip and climbed out. He caught a glimpse of Oscar heading his way, then stretched out on the dock and waited.

"What the hell?" Oscar said when he got close. "Melvin, are you okay?"

"Hey, Oscar," Melvin said, groaning as he sat up. "I'm glad you're here."

"Where else would I be?" he said. "What the hell are you doing taking a nap? Hey, you're soaking wet."

"Yeah, I hit a shoal on my way back in. I got tossed overboard and almost drowned. I was barely able to get back in the boat and make it to shore."

"Damn," Oscar said. "Are you hurt?"

"Yeah, I'm hurting all over," Melvin said. "I need to head home, then maybe go to the doctor."

"So, what are we going to do about tonight?"

"You can still make the run. But you won't be able to take my boat. I did some real damage to the prop, and I think it might be taking on water. I need to have Frank take a look at it in the morning."

"Okay. You got another boat?" Oscar said.

"Yeah, I do," Melvin said, pointing at an adjacent slip. "It's never going to win any races, but it'll get you where you're going."

Oscar shined a flashlight on the small wooden boat. He snorted as he examined it, then shined the light on Melvin.

"You call that a boat?" Oscar said, laughing.

"I guess you could swim if you want to, Oscar," Melvin said, climbing to his feet.

"Are you sure this thing will make it?" Oscar said, again shining the light on the boat.

"Yeah, you'll be fine. It rides a bit low in the water, but it's safe enough. But you better get going if you expect to make it to that camp before morning."

"How much horsepower has it got?" Oscar said.

"One and a half."

"Shit. I can row faster than that," Oscar said, snorting.

"Knock yourself out," Melvin said. "It's an early Evinrude. Don't worry, it runs great."

"I'm sure it does. But I'm more worried about the boat," Oscar said, gingerly stepping down into the boat and almost falling in as it rocked back and forth. "Damn, Melvin. With me in it, this thing is only sitting about a foot out of the water."

"Just sit real still, and you'll be fine," Melvin said, untying the lines. "Now get going."

"I don't like this, Melvin," Oscar said, cranking the outboard motor to life and slowly heading away from the dock.

"I can't say that I blame you, Oscar," Melvin whispered into the night air.

**Annabelle thumbed** through the thick envelope Milo had given her then dropped it into her purse.

"Business is good," she said, grinning at Milo.

"Yeah, I thought you'd like that envelope," Milo said, pouring two drinks. "I still can't believe that Roland convinced all of them to tag along."

"I'm sure everyone involved is already seeing their picture in the paper," Annabelle said.

"Well, if it plays out like I think it will, instead of smiling for the camera, they'll be scurrying like rats off a sinking ship."

"I wish I could come with you," she said, taking a sip.

"You're just gonna have to be happy hearing all about it second hand," Milo said.

"Yeah, I know. But still," she said, shrugging. "You feel like stretching out for a while?"

"I'd love to, but I need to get going," Milo said, glancing at his watch. "But feel free to hang around until I get back."

"I might just do that, Milo," she said, leaning over to give him a kiss.

"All right. Duty calls," Milo said, getting up out of his chair and heading for the door. "I'll see you later."

"Be careful out there," Annabelle said. "Oh, I almost forgot. Grab me a couple cases of Canadian if you get a chance."

**Roland did** his best to appear like he knew what he was doing as he maneuvered his boat between the three others. But he bumped against the Border Patrol boat, then scraped the side of Johnny Matters' boat, and came to a stop inches away from the Coast Guard vessel that towered over him. Roland glanced around at all three boats and cleared his throat.

"Okay, we should get going," Roland called out. "When we get there, you guys ring the perimeter of the store's boathouse offshore and give me five minutes before you dock. I'm meeting the Rockport chief of police in front, and we'll go in and confront the owner. The man we're looking for is a Clinton Farwell."

"You sure you want to check out the furniture store first?" Johnny Matters called out from his boat.

"Yeah, since the delivery isn't supposed to be made until midnight at the hunting camp, I thought we might get lucky and find all the booze still there," Roland said. "And it would be good to grab the Canadian supplier before we raid the camp."

"Okay, your raid, your call," Johnny Matters said.

"Follow me, gentlemen," Roland said. "And remember we want them alive."

"Uh, Mr. Doyle," the Coast Guard guy called down from the bow of his boat. "Let's try not to compound a goofy decision with a very bad one. I really don't think you're going to have to shoot anybody tonight."

"You never know," Roland called back.

"Let's just try to leave our guns holstered, okay?"

"I'll do my best," Roland said. "But I can't make any promises. Now, let's go catch some bootleggers."

Roland fired up his engine, posed to point at the horizon amid the collection of spotlights and flashlight beams, and, once again, moved the throttle in the wrong direction. The boat roared backward, and he slammed into the side of Coast Guard vessel and fell out of the driver seat onto the deck. He clamored to his feet, pushed the throttle forward, and again scraped the side of Johnny Matters' boat on his way past.

**Milo untied** the lines, hopped into the boat, and slid into the seat next to Birdie.

"You're starting to look like a real pro around boats, Milo," Birdie said, rolling a cigarette with one hand as he piloted the boat away from the dock.

"Thanks. I've got a good teacher," Milo said, grinning as he looked around. "This boat feels different from mine."

"Yeah, it will," Birdie said, handing Milo the cigarette then began rolling a second. "It's shorter, and the hull has got a much deeper V. But it handles great."

"I can't see a thing," Milo said, glancing around in the darkness.

"If you think it's dark now, just wait until we get away from town," Birdie said, laughing.

"You sure you know where you're going?" Milo said.

"Yeah, I'm pretty sure."

"I'm gonna need more than pretty sure, Birdie."

"Relax, Milo. I could make this drive with my eyes closed."

"Go for it. Who could tell the difference tonight?" Milo said, hunkering down in his seat as Birdie accelerated.

"You might want to keep your mouth shut," Birdie said.

"I beg your pardon?" Milo said, glaring at Birdie.

"There's no windshield."

"What the hell does that have to do with you telling me to keep my mouth shut?" Milo snapped, then started hacking and coughing.

Birdie slowed the boat until Milo got his coughing under control. Then Milo spat into his handkerchief and wiped his mouth.

"You got a mouthful of bugs, didn't you?"

"Yeah," Milo said.

"I tried to warn you," Birdie said, accelerating.

"Shut your mouth, Birdie."

"Now, there's some good advice," he said, then cackled as he opened the throttle to full.

**Oscar, in** a full-on panic, was beginning to wonder if he'd peed his pants. But since so much water was splashing in over the sides of the boat, it was impossible to tell. Using his empty flask to bail with one hand, he steered with the other and stared out at the horizon that, for the moment, remained a distant, invisible dream.

As he drove, he wondered where he should put the five cases on the trip back. Storing all of them in the bow might lower the front of the small boat dangerously close to the waterline. But putting them in the stern might result in a torrent of water pouring in over the transom. Finally deciding that he would line all five cases in a row running the length of the twelve-foot boat and just take his chances, Oscar twisted the throttle open as hard as he could hoping to squeeze just a bit more power out of the laboring engine.

**Roland tied** his boat to the town dock in Rockport and climbed out. In the darkness, he pulled the pint bottle from his coat and took a long pull. Then he put the bottle back in his pocket and turned around to watch the silhouettes of the three other boats take up their position. Roland made his way carefully through the darkness doing his best not to stagger. At the end of the dock, he turned left and headed for the furniture store trying to look casual. The streets were empty, but he saw the police car parked out front and headed for it. A man climbed out, gently closed the door, and leaned against the car with his arms folded across his chest.

"Chief Adams?" Roland said, extending his hand.

"Yes. And you must be Mr. Doyle. I sure hope you know what you're doing. Clint has been a respected member of this community for a very long time."

"I assure you, Chief, that I definitely know what I'm doing," Roland said. "The man is at the center or a major smuggling ring operating right under your nose."

"Okay," Chief Adams said, shrugging. "Let's get this over with."

"We'll be going in the front. We'll start by asking a few questions, but as soon as we get into the back of the store where the booze is located, the others will be joining us. And if the man decides to run, feel free to shoot him in the leg. But don't kill him. I want him alive."

"I wouldn't worry too much about Clint trying to run," Chief Adams said, laughing.

"Why not?"

"Because he's close to seventy and has a hard enough time walking."

"Well, you can never be too careful," Roland said, climbing the steps and peering through a window. "Interesting. This late at night and there's a light on."

Roland knocked loudly on the front door and moments later a man opened the door with a confused look on his face.

"I'm sorry, but we're closed."

"Are you Clinton Farwell?" Roland said.

Chief Adams burst out laughing. Roland stared at him, then realized his mistake.

"Well, he could just look young for his age," Roland said, then turned back to the man.

"No, Clint's not here," the man said.

"I see," Roland said, peering through the opening in the door. "And who might you be?"

"I'm Tom Collins."

"Like the cocktail?"

"Yeah, like the cocktail," he said, then noticed the police chief standing next to Roland. "Hey, Chief. What the hell is going on?"

"Sorry to bother you, Tom," Chief Adams said, still grinning. "But we need to speak with Clint."

"Clint's gone," Tom said, shrugging. "He sold me the place a month or so ago and left town."

"I was wondering why I haven't seen him around," Chief Adams said. "Where did he go?"

"He said something about traveling for a while," Tom said. "Then he mentioned he might head up to Toronto to spend some time with a lady friend he's got up there."

"Oh, sure. Gladys. I met her a couple of times when she used to visit. Nice woman," Chief Adams said. "Okay, Mr. Doyle. Can we go now?"

"Absolutely not," Roland said, pushing past Tom into the store.

He glanced around, hands on hips, then looked at Tom.

"We're going to need to take a look around, Mr. Collins."

"Well, if you're looking for value, I just got a nice living room suite in you might like," Tom said.

"We're not here for furniture, Mr. Collins," Roland said, then cocked his head at Tom. "Do you always work this late into the night?"

"No, I try not to," Tom said. "But I'm way behind on taking inventory. What the hell are you doing here?"

"I'm looking for illegal booze," Roland said.

"Given those bloodshot eyes, I'm not surprised," Tom said, grinning. "Give me a sec. I think I have a bottle around somewhere."

"We're looking for a lot more than a bottle, Mr. Collins," Roland snapped. "I believe your place of business is a front for a major bootlegging operation."

"Do you now? Well, I do have a couch with a beer stain I'm having one hell of a time getting out if that helps."

Chief Adams laughed and got a glare from Roland.

"I'm going to have to take a look at the back of your store," Roland said.

"You got some sort of warrant to search my property?" Tom said, glancing at the local police chief.

"It's complicated, Tom," Chief Adams said. "Mr. Doyle has convinced his people on the other side that Clint was up to no good. And now he's got the Prohibition Unit, the Coast Guard and the Border Patrol involved."

"I see. How embarrassing for you, Mr. Doyle," Tom said.

"What?"

"By all means, follow me," Tom said, heading for the door that led to the warehouse.

Tom stepped inside and flipped the light switch. The warehouse was filled with a wide variety of household furnishings. Roland's mouth dropped as he looked around the crowded space.

"Oh, this is nice," Chief Adams said, running a hand along an upholstered couch. "Mary's been looking for something just like this."

"Take it," Tom said. "It's the least I can do since this guy has obviously dragged you out in the middle of the night for no reason."

"Gee, thanks, Tom. That's mighty kind of you," Chief Adams said, admiring the couch.

"I don't understand," Roland whispered.

"Sorry, but I can't help you, Mr. Doyle," Tom said, heading for the double doors that led to the dock. "But just so you don't think I'm hiding anything, why don't you take a look outside at the dock area?"

He pulled the doors open and noticed several men carrying guns striding down the dock toward him.

"It looks like your friends are here," Tom said, waving at them.

Moments later, they stepped inside the warehouse and looked around, puzzled.

"You want to try explaining this, Mr. Doyle?" Johnny Matters said.

"He must be trying to cover his tracks," Roland said, pointing at Tom. "After the shipment left earlier, he put all this furniture in here."

"Uh, Mr. Doyle," the Coast Guard guy said, glancing around the crowded warehouse. "Far be it for me to question your thinking, but you'd need a small army to move all this furniture in here."

"No, I did it all myself," Tom said.

"See?" Roland said. "What did I tell you?"

"It took me most of the week, but I saved a ton of money doing it alone."

"We're done here," the Coast Guard guy said, shaking his head. "Sir, on behalf of the U.S. Coast Guard, please accept my sincere apology for bothering you."

"Wait a minute," Roland said.

"Let's go, Mr. Doyle," the Coast Guard guy said. "Maybe you'll have better luck at our next stop. Although I seriously doubt it."

**Oscar pulled** into the dock outside the hunting camp, tied the boat off, then slowly climbed out of the boat and managed to get onto the dock without falling in. He glanced around through the darkness, then used his flashlight to locate the five cases that were tucked under the dock on the ground near shore. Grunting, he dropped to his knees and was about to lift the first case when he heard the sound of boats approaching and saw the beam of a searchlight scanning the shoreline. Oscar turned the flashlight off and hunkered down under the dock behind the whiskey cases.

A few minutes later, and dealing with leg cramps, Oscar heard a boat approach, then felt it bump the dock as it landed. The sound of footsteps on the dock followed, then Oscar caught a glimpse of flashlight beams searching the immediate area.

"We shouldn't be using the flashlights," a voice that Oscar recognized said. "We don't want to tip them off that we're here."

"Roland Doyle?" Oscar whispered as his mind starting racing.

"Yeah, we want to make sure we get the drop on them," a man said, laughing.

"If I don't use my flashlight," another man said. "I'm liable to fall off the dock. I can't see my hand in front of my face."

"Shhh," Roland Doyle said. "Follow me."

"I wonder if that's the getaway boat?" the laughing man said, pointing his flashlight at Oscar's boat. "Not exactly seaworthy, huh?"

"Yeah, that guy's budget must be worse off than ours."

Another burst of laughter ensued. Oscar had to concede the man's point and shrugged in silence under the dock.

"Shhh. C'mon, follow me."

"Yeah, okay. Lead the way, Mr. Doyle," the laughing man said.

Oscar listened to the footsteps until they reached the grass lawn. For the next several minutes, he sat listening to the sound of his own breathing until the footsteps and laughter returned.

"For this, I had to pass up dinner with my in-laws," the laughing man said. "So, I guess I should thank you, Mr. Doyle."

"What a friggin' waste of time," a very grumpy man said.

"Let's get the hell out of here."

"I don't understand," Roland Doyle said.


**Milo and** Birdie, sat inside their boat that was tucked in the cattails near shore about a hundred feet from the hunting camp and watched the boats depart one by one.

"Where's Roland?" Milo said.

"It looks like he's getting back in his boat," Birdie said. "But I can't see shit."

"That was the plan," Milo said.

"What do you want to do?"

"Well, I have a feeling that Roland is going to stick around and lick his wounds," Milo said.

"You mean, drown his sorrows, right?"

"Well put, Birdie. And if he does, I can't wait to see what he does if he sees Oscar."

"This is gonna be fun," Birdie said with a soft cackle.

"Hey, if business can't be fun once in a while, what's the point, right?"


**Roland pulled** a fresh bottle from under the seat then drank and drifted. Grateful that he was no longer forced to listen to the taunts and laughter of his supposed colleagues, he tried to relax but knew he'd have to do some serious damage control over the upcoming days.

He stretched out and wondered if Violet Hollman had gotten the day or locations wrong.

Or if the smugglers had been tipped off and changed their plans.

Or maybe the information provided to the phone operator had been a ruse to hide the actual location of where the shipment was taking place.

Then Roland wondered what the hell was making the putt-putt noise he heard off in the distance.


**Oscar loaded** the five cases. After deciding that trying to lower the whiskey from the dock down into the boat had disaster written all over it, he waded through the water and gently set each case down then climbed in. The boat rocked and came precariously close to taking on water, but it came to rest, and Oscar removed a bottle from one of the cases, started the motor and slowly made his way through the darkness.

A half-mile from the camp, and halfway through the fresh bottle, Oscar relaxed a bit as the boat maintained its speed and six-inch clearance above the waterline. The drone of the motor, along with the night air and whiskey, made him drowsy, and he was about to drift off when he heard the roar of a boat approaching.

The boat screamed past Oscar, only a few feet off his starboard side, and he jerked the motor handle hard. The boat rocked back and forth as it changed course and threatened to tip before eventually settling down. In the process, one of the cases fell overboard, and he considered turning around to retrieve it before quickly discarding that crazy notion. Oscar's nerves were frazzled as he drove blindly in the darkness, and he took several quick swallows as he scanned the blackness for any sign of the invisible boat.

Moments later, the bottom of the boat hit something, scraped along for a few seconds, then came to a gentle stop with the motor still running. Oscar frowned, turned the engine off, and glanced around wondering how the hell he'd managed to come to a complete stop in the middle of the River. He stood up in the boat and tried rocking it back and forth using his feet, but the boat had discovered a newfound stability. Oscar grabbed his flashlight and shined it down into the water and realized he was perched on a massive rock that sat only a few inches below the water.

"Huh," Oscar grunted, glancing around, flashlight in hand. "Now what?"

Oscar, terrified, climbed out of the boat and waded through the ankle-high water pointing the flashlight down as he explored the shoal he and his boat were stuck on.

**Milo and** Birdie, safely downwind, laughed until tears streamed down their face.

"I think he scratched his boat," Milo said.

"But still a perfect landing," Birdie said.

"In this light, it looks like he's actually walking on water."

"Praise the Lord," Birdie said.

"You sure do know the River, Birdie," Milo said, wiping his eyes. "I suppose it would be too much to ask for Doyle to find him there."

"Keep the faith, Milo."

**Roland heard** the roar of the boat, but it was impossible to see. But he continued to scan the horizon in vain. Then he caught a glimpse of a beam of light and climbed into the driver seat. He drove the boat slowly in the direction of the light. As he got closer, he drew his gun and turned on his flashlight. Roland squinted as he scanned the surface of the water, then spotted something floating nearby. He put his gun away and set the flashlight on the seat, then reached over and hoisted the case of whiskey into the boat.

He refocused on the beam of light that seemed to be slowly moving away and felt a rush of adrenaline as his crimefighting juices started to flow again. He pointed the bow at the light and pressed down on the throttle. The boat accelerated then planed, and Roland focused his flashlight on the rapidly approaching beam of light.

Seconds later, Roland's boat came to a sudden stop as he slammed into an immovable object. The flashlight disappeared into the night air, and he was launched over the bow into the darkness. Roland landed with a half-splash, half-thud, and was knocked unconscious. When he came to moments later, he opened his eyes and saw the flashlight beam pointing down at him. He blinked and waved the beam away. In the dim light, he looked up at the man standing over him holding the flashlight.

"Oscar?" Roland said, rolling over and sitting up on his knees in the shallow water.

"Roland Doyle? I thought that was your voice."

"What?"

"Nothing. What the hell are you doing out here?" Oscar said, frowning.

"At the moment, getting ready to arrest you," Roland said, fumbling for the gun in his holster.

"For that?" Oscar said, nodding at the remaining four cases in his boat. "Geez, you're bleeding."

"Give me that flashlight," Roland said, pointing his gun at Oscar.

Roland staggered to his feet, and Oscar glanced at the gun before reluctantly handing it over. Roland shined the light into Oscar's eyes, then at the boat.

"Okay, Oscar," Roland growled. "Where's the other nine hundred and ninety-five cases?"

**Birdie let** the boat drift until the flashlight beam was a distant speck. Then he started the engine and glanced at Milo.

"I was just wondering something, Milo."

"What's that?"

"How the hell are they going to get off that shoal?"

"I wouldn't worry about it, Birdie. I'm sure they'll think of something."

**Annabelle sat** up in bed, took a moment to catch her breath, then lit two cigarettes and handed one to Milo.

"Tell it again, Milo."

Milo took a moment to admire her naked back, then took a long drag on his cigarette. Then he exhaled smoke and nodded.

"Okay, but you gotta hear Birdie's version. He tells it much better."

"Your version will do just fine, for now, Milo," she said, stretching out and nestling against his chest.

Milo inched his way up in bed and used his hands to paint the picture.

"Imagine a long stretch of rock lurking right below the surface of the water that's just waiting to bite you in the ass."

**Melvin whistled** as he walked down the long hallway with a bounce in his step, then remembered at the last second to veer right. The handful of slobber flew through the air and landed harmlessly a few feet away. He looked at the drooling man with the multi-directional stare and beamed at him.

"How ya doin?"

# Season 2 of
# The Whiskey Run Chronicles
# is coming soon!

"Milk might build strong bones and bodies. But I've found that a milk can builds fortunes."

Milo Razner